Praise for David Gemmell

"I am truly amazed at David Gemmell's ability to focus his writer's eye. His images are crisp and complete, a history lesson woven within the detailed tapestry of the highest adventure. Gemmell's characters are no less complete, real men and women with qualities good and bad, placed in trying times and rising to heroism or falling victim to their own weaknesses."

—R. A. SALVATORE
Author of *Mortalis*

"Gemmell is very talented; his characters are vivid and very convincingly realistic."

—CHRISTOPHER STASHEFF
Author of the *Wi*

"Gemmell's great read
up; he's several rungs a
the fabulous!"

—ANNE M[...]FREY

By David Gemmell
Published by The Ballantine Publishing Group:

Books published by The Ballantine Publishing Group
are available at quantity discounts on bulk purchases
for premium, educational, fund-raising, and special
sales use. For details, please call 1-800-733-3000.

The Sword in the Storm

2479 2340

David Gemmell

Independence Public Library
Independence, Oregon 97351
Phone (503) 838-1811

A Del Rey® Book

BALLANTINE BOOKS • NEW YORK

If this book is coverless, it may have been reported to the publisher as "unsold or destroyed" and neither the author nor the publisher may have received payment for it.

A Del Rey® Book
Published by The Ballantine Publishing Group
Copyright © 2001 by David Gemmell

All rights reserved under International and Pan-American Copyright Conventions. Published in the United States by The Ballantine Publishing Group, a division of Random House, Inc., New York, and simultaneously in Canada by Random House of Canada Limited, Toronto.

Del Rey is a registered trademark and the Del Rey colophon is a trademark of Random House, Inc.

www.randomhouse.com/delrey/

Library of Congress Catalog Card Number: 00-107144

ISBN 0-345-43234-7

Manufactured in the United States of America

First Edition: February 2001

10 9 8 7 6 5 4 3 2

Prologue

I WAS A child when I saw him last, a scrawny straw-haired boy living in the highlands. It was the afternoon of my eleventh birthday. My sister had died in childbirth the day before, the babe with her. My widowed father was inconsolable, and I left the farm early, leaving him with his grief. I was sad, too, but as with most children, my sorrow was also tinged with self-pity. Ara had died and spoiled my birthday. I shiver with shame at the memory even now.

I wandered through the high woods for most of the morning, playing games. Warrior games. I was a hero, hunting for enemies. I was the deadliest swordsman of them all. I was Demonblade the King.

I had seen him once before when he and several of his companions had ridden to our lonely farm. They were merely passing through, and my father gave them water and a little bread. The king had dismounted and thanked Father, and they stood talking about the dry summer and the problems it was causing. I was around five, I think, and all I remember was his size and the fact that his eyes were strange. One was a tawny brown, the other green, like a jewel. My father told him how our one bull had died, struck by lightning. Three days later a rider came by leading a fine big-horned bull, which he gave to us. My father was a king's man after that.

I was just eleven when I saw him again. Tired of playing alone, I went to my cousin's house in the Rift Valley, some three miles from home. He gave me food and let me help while he chopped wood. I would roll the rounds to where he stood and place them on the low stump. He would swing his ax and split them. After he had finished chopping, we carried the wood to the log pile and stacked the split chunks against the north wall of the house.

I was tired and would have spent the night, except that I knew Father would be worried, so an hour before dusk I headed for home, climbing the Balg Hills and making for the high woods. My journey took me close to the old stone circle. Father told me giants had crafted it in a bygone age, but my aunt said that the stones themselves were once giants, cursed by Taranis. I don't know which story is true, but the circle is a splendid place. Eighteen huge stones there are, each over twenty feet high. Hard, golden stone, totally unlike the gray granite of the Druagh mountains.

I had no intention of going to the circle, for it was more than a little out of my way. But as I was making my way through the trees, I saw a pack of wolves. I stopped and picked up a stone. Wolves will rarely attack a man. They steer clear of us. I don't blame them. We hunt and kill them whenever we can. The leader of the pack stood very still, his golden eyes staring at me. I felt a chill and knew with great certainty that this wolf was unafraid.

For a moment I stood my ground. He darted forward. Dropping the stone, I turned and ran. I knew they were loping after me, and I sprinted hard, leaping fallen trees, and scrambling through the bracken. I was in a panic and fled without thinking. Then I reached the tree line no more than a few yards from the stone circle. To run farther would be to die. This realization allowed me to overcome my fear, and my mind began to clear.

There was a low branch just ahead. I leapt and swung myself up to it. The lead wolf was just behind me. He leapt, too, his teeth closing on my shoe, tearing it from my foot. I climbed a little higher, and the wolves gathered silently below the tree.

Safe now, I became angry both at myself and at the wolves. Breaking off a dry branch, I hurled it down on to the pack. They leapt aside and began to prowl around the tree.

It was then that I heard riders. The wolves scattered and loped back into the woods. I was about to call out to the new-comers, but something stopped me. I cannot say what it was. I don't think I was afraid, but perhaps I sensed some danger. Anyway, I crouched down on the thick branch and watched them ride into the stone circle. There were nine of them. All wore swords and daggers. Their clothes were very fine, and their horses tall, like those ridden by the king's Iron Wolves. As they dismounted, they led their horses out of the circle, tethering them close by.

"You think he'll come?" asked one of the men. I can still see him now, tall and broad-shouldered, his yellow hair braided under a helm of burnished iron.

"He'll come," said a second man. "He wants peace."

They rejoined their comrades, who were sitting in a circle within the circle. Having decided not to show myself, I lay there quietly. They were talking in low voices, and I could hear only a few words clearly.

The sun was going down, and I decided to risk the wolves and make my way home. That was when I saw the rider on the white stallion. I knew him instantly.

It was Demonblade the King.

I cannot tell you how excited I was. The man was close to myth even then. His beard was red gold in the dying sun-light. He was wearing a winged helm of bright silver, a breastplate embossed with the fawn in brambles crest of his house, and the famous patchwork cloak. At his side was the legendary Seidh sword with its hilt of gold. He rode into the circle and sat his stallion, staring at the men. They seemed to me to be tense, almost frightened by his presence. They rose as he dismounted.

I would have gone down then, just to be close to the legend. But he drew his sword and plunged it into the earth before him. The man with the braided yellow hair was the first to speak.

"Come and join us, Connavar. Let us talk of a new peace."

Demonblade stood silently for a moment, his strong hands resting on the pommel of his sword, his patchwork cloak billowing in the breeze. "You have not asked me here to talk," he said, his voice deep and powerful. "You have asked me here to die. Come then, traitors. I am here. And I am alone."

Slowly they drew their swords. I could feel their fear.

Then, as the sun fell in crimson fire, they attacked.

◇ **1** ◇

O N THE NIGHT of the great man's birth a fierce storm was
moving in from the far north, but the lowering black
clouds still were hidden behind the craggy, snow-capped
peaks of the Druagh mountains. The night air outside the
birthing hut was calm and still and heavy. The bright stars of
Caer Gwydion glittered in the sky, and the full moon was
shining like a lantern over the tribal lands of the Rigante.

All was quiet inside the lamp-lit hut as Varaconn, the soft-
eyed horse hunter, knelt at his wife's side, holding to her
hand. Meria, the pain subsiding for a moment, smiled up at
him. "You must not worry," she whispered. "Vorna says the
boy will be strong."

The blond-haired young man cast his gaze across the small,
round hut to where the witch woman was crouched by an iron
brazier. She was breaking the seals on three clay pots and
measuring out amounts of dark powder. Varaconn shivered.

"It is time for his soul-name," Vorna said without turning
from her task.

Varaconn reluctantly released his wife's hand. He did not
like the stick-thin witch, but then, no one did. It was difficult
to like that which one feared, and black-haired Vorna was a
fey creature with bright blue button eyes that never seemed to
blink. How was it, Varaconn wondered, that an aging spinster
with no personal knowledge of sex or childbirth could be so
adept at midwifery?

Vorna rose and turned, fixing him with a baleful glare. "This is not the time to consider questions born of stupidity," she said.

Varaconn jerked. Had he asked the question aloud? Surely not.

"The soul-name," said Vorna. "Go now."

Taking his wife's hand once more, he raised it to his lips. Meria smiled, then a fresh spasm of pain crossed her face. Varaconn backed away to the door.

"All will be well," Vorna told him.

Varaconn swirled his blue and green checkered cloak around his slender shoulders and stepped out into the night.

It was warm, the air cloying, and yet, for a moment at least, it was cooler than the hut and he filled his lungs with fresh air. The smell of mountain grass and pine was strong there, away from the settlement, and mixed with it he could detect the subtle scent of honeysuckle. As he grew accustomed to the warmth of the summer night, he removed his cloak and laid it over the bench seat set around the trunk of the old willow.

Time for the soul-name, Vorna had said.

In that moment, alone under the stars, Varaconn felt like an adult for the first time in his nineteen years. He was about to find the soul-name for his son.

His son!

Varaconn's heart swelled with the thought.

Following the old goat trail, he stepped out onto the green flanks of Caer Druagh, the Elder Mountain, and began to climb. As he journeyed high above the valley, his thoughts were many. He recalled his own father and wondered what he had been thinking as he had climbed this slope nineteen years before. What dreams had he nurtured for the infant about to be born? He had died from wounds taken in a fight with the Pannones when Varaconn was six. His mother had passed over the Dark Water a year later. Varaconn's last memories of her were of a skeletal woman, hollow-eyed, coughing up blood and phlegm.

The orphan Varaconn had been raised by an irascible uncle who had never married and loathed the company of people. A kind old man, he had tried hard to be a good father to the boy but had managed—among many good lessons—to pass on to his ward his own wariness of fellowship. As a result Varaconn never courted popularity and found intimacy difficult. He was neither popular nor unpopular with the other young men of the Rigante, and his life had been largely undistinguished except for two things: his friendship with Ruathain the First Warrior and his marriage to the beautiful Meria.

Varaconn paused in his climb and stared down at Three Streams settlement far below. Most of the houses were dark, for it was almost midnight and the Rigante were a farming community whose people rose before the dawn. But lamplight was flickering in some of the windows. Banouin the Foreigner would be checking his tallies and preparing his next journey to the sea, and Cassia Earth Maiden would be entertaining a guest, initiating some young blood in the night-blessed joys of union.

Varaconn walked on.

His marriage to Meria had surprised many, for her father had entertained a score of young men seeking her hand—even Ruathain. Meria had rejected them all. Varaconn had not been one of the suitors. A modest man, he had considered her far above him in every way.

Then one day, as he was gentling a mare in the high meadow paddock, she had come to see him. That day was bathed in glory in the hall of his fondest memories. Meria had leaned on the fence rail as Varaconn had moved around the paddock. At first he had not known she was there, so intent was he on the bond with the mare. He loved horses and spent much of his early life observing them. He had noticed that herd leaders were always female and that they disciplined errant colts by driving them away from the safety of the herd. Alone, the colt would become fearful, for predators would soon descend on a single pony. After a while the mare would allow the recalcitrant beast back into the fold. Thus chastened, it would then remain obedient. Varaconn used a similar technique in training ponies. He would isolate a wild horse in his circular paddock, then, with a snap of his rope, set it running around the inner perimeter of the fence. The instinct of a horse was always to run from danger and only when it was safe to look back to see what had caused its fear. Varaconn kept the pony running for a while; then, not knowing Meria was watching him, he dipped his shoulder and turned away from the mare. The pony dropped her head and moved in close to him. Varaconn continued to walk, slowly changing direction. The mare followed his every move. As he moved, he spoke to the mare in a soft voice and finally turned to face her, rubbing her brow and stroking her sleek neck.

"You talk to horses more easily than you talk to women," said Meria.

Varaconn blushed deep red. "I'm . . . not a talker," he said. Trying to ignore her, he continued to work with the pony and within an hour was riding it slowly around the paddock. Occasionally he would glance toward Meria. She had not moved. Finally he dismounted, took a deep breath, and walked to where she waited. Shy and insular, he did not look into her eyes. Even so, he saw enough to fill his heart with longing. She was wearing a long green dress and a wide belt edged with gold thread. Her long dark hair, except for a top braid, was hanging loose to her shoulders, and her feet were bare.

"You want to buy a pony?" he asked.

"Perhaps. Why did the mare suddenly start to obey you?" she asked.

"She was frightened. I made her run, but she didn't know what the danger was. Did you see her snapping her mouth as she ran?"

"Yes. She looked very angry."

"That was not anger. Foals do that. She was reverting to infant behavior. She was saying to me, 'I need help. Please be my leader.' So I dropped my shoulder and gently turned away. Then she came to me and joined my herd."

"So you are her stallion now?"

"In truth that would make me the lead mare. Stallions do the fighting, but a mare will command the herd."

"Ruathain says you are a great fighter and a good man."

This surprised him, and he glanced briefly at her face to see if she was mocking him. Her eyes were green. Large eyes. So beautiful. Not the green of grass or summer leaves but the bright, eternal green of precious stones. Yet they were not cold . . .

"Now you are staring at me," she chided.

Varaconn blinked and looked away guiltily. She spoke again. "Ruathain said you stood beside him against the Pannones and broke their charge."

"He is too kind. He knows I was too frightened to run," he admitted. "Ruathain was like a rock—the only safe place in a stormy sea. I've never known anyone quite like him. The battle was chaotic: screaming men, clashing swords. It was all so fast and furious. But Ruathain was calm. He was like a god. You could not imagine him being hurt."

She seemed annoyed, though he did not know why. "Yes, yes, yes," she said. "Everyone knows Ruathain is a hero. He wanted to marry me. I said no."

"Why would you say no? He is a wonderful man."

"Can you really be so foolish, Varaconn?" she said, then turned and strode away.

Totally confused, he carried the problem to Ruathain. The powerful blond-haired young warrior had been out with three of his herdsmen, building a rock wall across the mouth of a gully in the high north valley.

"Every damn winter," said Ruathain, heaving a large slab into place, "some of my cattle get trapped here. Not anymore."

Varaconn dismounted and helped the men for several hours. Then, during a rest break, Ruathain took him by the arm and led him to a nearby stream.

"You didn't come all the way up here to build a wall. What is on your mind, my friend?" Not waiting for an answer, he stripped off his shirt, leggings, and boots and clambered out into the middle of the stream. "By Taranis, it is cold," he said. The water was no more than a few inches deep, flowing over white, rounded pebbles. Ruathain lay down, allowing the water to rush over his body. "Man, this is refreshing," he shouted, rolling to his belly. Varaconn sat by the stream and watched his friend. Despite the awesome power of the man, his broad flat face, and his drooping blond mustache, there was something wonderfully childlike about Ruathain: a seemingly infinite capacity to draw the maximum joy from any activity. The warrior splashed water to his face, ran his wet fingers through his hair, then rose and strode to the water's edge. He grinned at Varaconn. "You should have joined me."

"I need your advice, Ru."

"Are you in trouble?"

"I do not believe so. I am merely confused." He told him about Meria's visit. As he spoke, he saw the young warrior's expression harden, only to be replaced by a look of sadness. Varaconn cursed himself for a fool. Ruathain had asked Meria to marry him. He obviously loved her, too! "I am sorry, Ru. I am an idiot," he said. "Forgive me for troubling you."

Ruathain forced a smile. "Yes, you are an idiot. But you are also my friend. She obviously doesn't want me, but I think she is in love with you. Go see her father."

"How could she love me?"

"Damned if I know," Ruathain said, sadly. "Women are a mystery to me. When we were all children, she always used to follow us around. You remember? We used to throw sticks at her and shout for her to go away."

"I never threw sticks," said Varaconn.

"Then maybe that's why she loves you. Now go and make yourself look handsome. Cefir will not tolerate a shabby suitor. Best cloak and leggings."

"I couldn't do that," said Varaconn.

But he had. The marriage took place three weeks later on the first day of summer, at the Feast of Beltine.

And so had followed the finest year of his life. Meria was a constant joy, and Varaconn could scarcely believe his good fortune. During the spring and the following summer Varaconn caught and gentled sixty-two ponies. Sixteen of them had been of high quality, and most of these had been sold as cavalry mounts to the nobles who followed the Long Laird. The profit had been high, and Varaconn was determined to buy an iron sword like the borrowed blade he now wore.

He patted the hilt, drawing strength from it. Even so a touch of fear returned.

The next day the Rigantes were to march in battle against the Sea Raiders, who were camped beyond the Seidh River. Varaconn hated violence and was not skilled with sword or lance. What he had told Meria was true. When the Pannones had charged, he had stood frozen beside the powerful Ruathain. Yes, he had fought, swinging his bronze blade with the fury of terror, and the Pannones had fled. Ruathain had wounded three and killed one.

Varaconn had prayed never again to be drawn into a battle. That fear had turned to terror five days before, when he had killed the raven. He was riding a wild pony, galloping over the hills. As he topped a rise, the raven flew up from the long grass. Startled, the pony reared, lashing out with its hooves. The raven fell dead to the ground. Varaconn had been horrified. His birth *geasa* had prophesied that he would die within a week of killing such a bird.

He had confided those fears to Ruathain. "The horse killed it," said Ruathain. "You have not broken your *geasa*. Do not concern yourself. Stay close by me, Cousin, and you will live through the battle."

But Varaconn was not comforted. "I was riding the pony. It was in my control."

So great was Varaconn's panic that in the end Ruathain drew his sword, which was of iron and cunningly crafted. "Take this," he said. "It is blessed with four great Druid spells. No one carrying it in battle will suffer death."

Varaconn knew he should have refused at once. The blade was priceless. Most warriors had bronze weapons, but Ruathain had journeyed to the coast with his cattle and had returned to the Rigantes with this sword two years earlier. The young men of the tribe would gather around him at the Feast of Samia and beg him to let them touch the gray blade. Varaconn felt the onset of shame, for he reached out and took the blade, perhaps condemning Ruathain to death in his place. He could not look his friend in the eye.

"Vorna says your child will be a son," said Ruathain.

"Aye, a son," Varaconn agreed, glad of the change of subject.

They sat in silence for a while, and the shame grew. Finally Varaconn hefted the sword and offered it back to the warrior. "I cannot take it," he said.

"Whisht, man, of course you can. I'll not die tomorrow. I have not broken my *geasa*. Hold the sword and return it to me after the battle."

"It is a great comfort to me," admitted Varaconn. They sat in silence for a moment, then the frightened young man spoke again. "I know you love Meria," he said, not looking at his friend. "I see it every time you look at her. And I have never known why she chose me over you. It makes no sense even now. But I ask you—as my dearest friend—to be a strength to her if I do . . . die."

Ruathain gripped Varaconn's shoulder. "Now you listen to

me. Let the words burn themselves into your soul. I will not let you die. Stay close to me, Cousin. I will guard your back when the battle begins. That is all you have to do. Stay close to me."

Alone on the mountainside, Varaconn curled his hand around the hilt of Ruathain's iron sword. The touch of the leather binding and the firmness of the grip eased his fears once more, and he sat upon a boulder and prayed to Samia for an omen so that he could give his son a good soul-name. The boy's Rigante name would be Connavar, Conn son of Var. This would be the name to earn honor among his people. But the soul-name would bond him to the land and carry with it the magic of the night.

Varaconn prayed to see an eagle. Eagle in the Moonlight would be a good soul-name, he thought. He glanced at the sky, but there was no eagle. He prayed again. A distant rumble of thunder sounded from the north, and he saw the advancing clouds snuffing out the stars. Lightning flashed almost overhead, lighting up the mountain. A fierce wind blew up. Varaconn rose from the boulder, ready to seek shelter. The sword brushed against his leg.

The iron sword!

Fearful that the lightning would strike him, Varaconn drew the blade and hurled it from him. The three-foot sword spun in the air, then lanced into the earth, where it stood quivering.

At that moment the lightning flashed again, striking the sword and shattering it.

Then the rain fell.

Varaconn sat slumped by the boulder, staring at the broken shards of blackened iron.

Then he rose and began the long walk back to the birthing hut.

As he came closer, he heard the thin, piping cries of his newborn son echoing above the storm winds.

The door of the hut opened, and Vorna, witch and midwife, stepped out to greet him.

"You have the name," she said. It was not a question. He nodded dumbly. "Speak it aloud," she ordered him.

"He will be Connavar, the Sword in the Storm."

◇ 2 ◇

RUATHAIN WAS RIDING back from the lands of the southern Rigante when he saw the boys playing on the hilltop above the smithy. He reined in the chestnut pony and dismounted, watching the youngsters from the edge of the trees. They were chasing each other, and he could hear the sounds of their laughter and joy. Ruathain smiled. It was a good sound. He was especially glad that the ten-year-old Connavar was among them. At least it meant he was not getting into trouble—which was, sadly, the boy's greatest talent.

Ruathain was anxious to be home, for it had been a long ride from the southern cattle market, with the last ten miles steadily uphill. His pony was tired and breathing hard. He patted its muzzle. "Take a breather, boy. When we get back, I'll see you fed the finest grain."

From there, far below where the boys were playing, he could see his house, which had been built at the junction of the three streams after which the settlement had been named. It was a good house, well constructed of seasoned timber and heavily thatched with straw. Cool in summer, with the wide windows open to the breeze, and warm in winter, with the shutters drawn and the central fire lit. Tiny figures were moving in the paddock behind the house. Ruathain smiled. Meria had saddled the dwarf pony and was leading him around the paddock while their youngest son clung to the saddle. Bran was only three, but already he was fearless and a great source of pride to the swordsman. Beside him his own pony snickered, pushing its head against his chest.

"All right, boy. We're going," said Ruathain. He was about to mount when he heard the start of a heated exchange among the boys on the hilltop below.

By the time Ruathain ran in among the boys the fight had become brutal. Govannan had blood streaming from his nose. Ruathain's nine-year-old son, Braefar, was lying on the grass, half-stunned, and his adopted son, Connavar, was laying into the other three boys like a whirlwind, fists swinging, head butting, feet lashing out in kicks. Another boy went down, having taken a terrible blow to the right ear. Connavar leapt on him, slamming his fist into the boy's nose.

Ruathain ran up behind him, grabbing Connavar by the collar of his green tunic and lifting him clear. The ten-year-old swung in his grip, his small fist cannoning into Ruathain's face. Ruathain dropped the boy and cuffed him hard, sending him spinning from his feet.

"That is quite enough!" he bellowed. Silence descended on the hilltop. "What in the name of Taranis is going on here?" None of the boys spoke, and none would look him in the eye.

"We were just playing," Govannan said, at last, blood dripping to his tunic. "I'm going home now." The youngster and his four bruised friends trooped off down the hill. Connavar was sitting on the grass, rubbing his head. Braefar tried to stand but fell down again. His father moved to him and knelt on the grass.

"Where are you hurt?" he asked the slender boy.

Braefar forced a smile, but his face was gray. "I'm not hurt, Father. Just dizzy. I fell just as Govannan's knee was coming up. Now I can see stars in the daytime."

"An interesting way of putting it," observed Ruathain, ruffling the boy's blond hair. "Lie there for a moment until the world stops spinning." Rising, he walked to where Connavar was sitting. "That was a good punch," he said, rubbing his jaw. "I can still feel it."

Making a joke of a problem usually worked with Conn. His angers were always short-lived. At the jest he would relax, an impish grin spreading across his features. Then the situation—whatever it was—could be resolved. But this time the boy did not smile. He looked up into Ruathain's face, and for the first time the powerful swordsman found himself disconcerted by the look in Conn's strange eyes. One was green, the other a tawny brown that turned to gold in the sunshine.

In that moment Ruathain knew that something momentous had occurred. He sat down on the hilltop and looked at the boy's strong, flat features. A bruise was beginning on his right cheek, and his lower lip was cut. "What was the fight about?" he asked.

Connavar was silent for a moment, then he pushed his hand through his red-gold hair. "He said my father was a coward. That he ran away." The strange eyes searched Ruathain's face, watching his expression intently.

Ruathain had lived with this fear for many years, and now that it was upon him, he felt a sinking of the heart. "Your father was my friend, Conn. He stood beside me in two battles. I was proud to have him for a friend. You understand that? I would not befriend a coward."

"Then he didn't run away?" The green-gold gaze locked to Ruathain's eyes.

Ruathain sighed. "He broke his *geasa*. He killed a raven. You had just been born, the night before the battle. Varracon was desperate to see you grow, to be there to guide you. The thought of death weighed him down. It sat on his shoulders like a mountain." He fell silent, his thoughts drifting back to that dreadful day ten years before, when the tribes had banded together to fight the raiders from the sea. Twelve thousand fierce-eyed reavers faced by eight thousand determined tribesmen. It was a day of blood and bravery, with neither side giving a yard of ground. At the height of the battle, a terrible storm broke overhead and lightning flashed down, hurling fighting men into the air, their flesh blackened.

Ruathain took a deep breath. "Listen to me, Conn, Varracon was my sword brother. He stood beside me all that day, protecting my back as I defended his. That is what counts."

"Did he run?" asked the boy. Everything in the child's face begged for the great, comforting lie.

And Ruathain could not give him that gift. Honor was everything to him. Yet he knew the young viewed the world with all the certainty born of inexperience. A man was either a hero or a coward. There were no shades of gray. He made one last attempt to still Connavar's concerns. "Listen to me. The raiders were beaten, but they launched a last charge. It was almost dusk. We had won. But they almost broke through. Four of them rushed at your father and me. He was killed there. Let that be an end to it. I lost a friend. You lost a father."

But Conn would not be shaken. "Where was his wound?" he asked.

"You are concentrating on the wrong things, Conn. He was a fine, brave, and noble man. For one moment only he . . . knew panic. Do not judge him harshly for that. When the battle was over, I sat with him. His last words were of you and your mother. He wanted so much to see you grow. And he would have been proud, for you are a strong boy."

"No enemy will ever see my back," said Connavar. "I will not run."

"Do not be stupid," snapped Ruathain. "I have run. A good warrior knows when to stand and fight and when to withdraw to fight another day. There is no shame in it."

"No shame," repeated Connavar. "Who was guarding *your* back when my father ran?"

Ruathain said nothing. Connavar pushed himself to his feet. "Where are you going?" asked the swordsman.

"To find Govannan. I must apologize to him."

"You have nothing to apologize for."

Connavar shook his head. "He was right. My father was a coward."

The boy stalked away. Ruathain swore softly.

Braefar came over to him. "Is he still angry?" he asked.

"Angry and hurt," agreed Ruathain.

"I think he might have beaten them all. He didn't need me at all."

"Aye, he's strong," said his father. "How are you feeling, Wing?" he continued, using the abbreviation of Braefar's soul-name, Wing over Water.

"Better. Govannan has hard knees." Braefar grinned. "It was worth the blow to see Conn knock him down. He is not afraid of anything or anyone."

Yes, he is, Ruathain thought sadly. He's afraid of being like his father.

He gazed up at the blue sky. "I told you to stay close to me," he said sadly.

"What did you say, Father?" asked the bemused Braefar.

"I was talking to an old friend. Come, let's go home."

Lifting Braefar, he settled him on the pony and then led the beast down the hillside. I could have lied to him, he thought, told him his father had not run. But more than twenty of the Three Streams men had seen it. At some time the story was bound to have surfaced. Meria would be furious, of course. She was fiercely protective of Conn and loved him more than either of her sons by Ruathain.

And certainly more than she loves me!

The thought had leapt unbidden to his mind like a poisoned arrow shot from ambush.

They had wed a mere four months after the battle. Not for love—he had known that—but because she believed that

Connavar would need a strong father to teach him the skills of the Rigante. Ruathain had been certain that she would come to love him if he treated her with kindness and compassion. At times he even thought that he could detect in her a genuine affection for him. The truth, however, was that no matter how hard he tried, there always remained a distance between them that he could not cross.

One night, at the Feast of Samain, when Conn was a year old, Ruathain had spoken to his mother, Pallae, about the problem. His father had been dead for two years, and Ruathain was sitting beneath the vast branches of Eldest Tree, Pallae beside him. All around them the people of the settlement were drinking, feasting, and dancing. Ruathain himself was a little drunk. He would not have raised the subject if he had been sober. His mother, a tall and dignified woman who despite her iron-gray hair retained an almost ethereal beauty, listened in silence. "Have you ever done anything to offend her?" Pallae asked him.

"Never!"

"Are you certain, Ru? You are a lusty man like your father. Have you sown your seeds in any other field but your own?"

"No. I promise you. I have been faithful always."

"Have you ever struck her?"

"No, or even raised my voice."

"Then I cannot help you, my son, except to say that she holds some grievance against you. You must hope that her anger fades. I expect that it will when she has borne your son."

"And if it does not?"

"Does she respect you?"

"Of course. She knows—everyone knows—I would do nothing base."

"And you love her?"

"More than I can say."

"Then build on that respect, Ru. It is all you can do."

They did not speak of it again until six years later, as Pallae lay on her deathbed. Sitting quietly beside her, holding her hand, Ruathain had hoped she would slip away quietly in her sleep. The cancer had stripped away her flesh, the pain of it causing her to writhe and cry out. Vorna's herbs had at first dulled the agony, but lately even the strongest of them had little effect. Despite the pain and her increasing frailty, Pallae clung to life. Often delirious in the last days, she would sometimes fail to recognize Ruathain, speaking to him as if he were his father. But on the night of her death she opened her eyes and gave him a wan smile.

"The pain has gone," she whispered. "It is a blessed relief." He patted her hand. "You look tired, my son," she said. "You should go home and rest."

"I will. Soon."

"How goes it with you and Meria?"

"The same. It is enough that I love her."

"That is never enough, Ru," she told him, her voice edged with sadness. "I wanted more for you than that." She lay silently for a moment, her breathing harsh. Then she smiled. "Is Connavar behaving himself?"

He shook his head. "The boy was born to mischief."

"He is only seven, Ru. And he has a good heart. Do not be too hard on him."

He chuckled. "Too hard? I have tried talking to him. He sits and listens, then rushes off and gets into trouble again. I tried beating him with my belt, but that had no effect. He took his punishment without complaint and a day or so later stole a cake from the baker in the morning and left a live frog under my bedcovers in the evening." He laughed suddenly. "Meria got into bed first. I swear she rose up toward the ceiling like a startled swan."

"You love him, though?"

"Aye, I do. Last week, when I was telling Meria about a lone wolf in the high woods, Conn was listening. He stole my best knife and went missing. Seven years old, and I eventually found him crouching in the woods, a tin pot on his head for a helm, waiting for the wolf. He has spirit. And when he grins, you could forgive him anything."

The lamp by the bedside guttered, and the bedroom fell into darkness. Ruathain cursed and walked back into the main living area, lifting a lantern from the far wall. He returned to her at once, but as the light fell upon her face, he saw that she had gone.

Meria lifted Bran from the dwarf pony and hugged him close. "Did you like that, my pet?" she asked him.

"More, Mama," he said, reaching out toward the little gray horse.

"Later," she promised. "Look, there is Caval," she said, pointing to the black war hound lying in the shade. Distracted, Bran struggled to get free. Meria lowered him to the ground, and the boy ran across to where the hound was resting. Bran threw his small arms around her neck and snuggled down alongside her. The hound licked his face. Bran giggled. A black shape glided across the sky, and a huge crow landed awkwardly on the thatched roof. The bird tilted its head, its eye of glittering jet staring down at the tall, slim green-clad young woman below.

Another woman stepped from the house. "Your husband is home," said Meria's cousin Pelain. Meria glanced up toward the hills and saw the tall figure of Ruathain leading his pony down the slope. Young Braefar was sitting in the saddle. For some reason that she could never later recall, Meria found herself growing angry.

"Aye, he's home," Meria said softly.

Pelain gave her a sharp look. "You do not know how lucky you are," she said. "He loves you."

Meria tried to ignore her, but it was difficult. Once Pelain got her teeth into a subject, she was harder to shake than a mastiff. "You'd know what I mean if you were married to Borga," Pelain continued with a wry smile. "He gets into bed from the left, rolls across me to the right. And somewhere between he grunts and asks, 'Was it also a wonder for you?' Happily he's usually asleep before I answer."

Meria grinned. "You shouldn't talk that way. Borga is a fine man."

"If he made his bread with the speed he makes love, we could feed the tribes all the way to the sea," said Pelain. She transferred her gaze to the walking warrior. "I'd wager my dowry that he doesn't brush across you like a summer breeze."

Meria reddened. "No, he doesn't," she admitted, immediately regretting the comment.

"Then you should value him more," observed Pelain. "I know I would."

The anger flared again. "Then you should have married him," snapped Meria.

"I would have—had he asked me," answered Pelain, no hint of offense in her voice. "Two strong sons and no dead babies. Strong seed in that one."

Pelain had lost four children in the last five years. Not one had survived beyond five days. For a moment only Meria's anger subsided, replaced by affection and sympathy. "You are still young," she told her cousin. "There is time."

Pelain shook her head. "Vorna says there will be no more."

Ruathain opened the paddock gate, leading his pony inside and lifting his son to the ground. Braefar took the reins and led the pony away. The warrior kissed Meria's cheek, then swung to Pelain. "If you are here making mischief for me," he said with a smile, "I shall throw you over my shoulder and carry you back to your husband's house."

"Please do so," she replied, "since he's not there and I have a wide bed just waiting to be filled by a real man."

For a moment Ruathain stood shocked. Then he laughed

aloud. "By heavens, you have become a wicked woman," he told her.

Even the normally outspoken Pelain seemed surprised by her own comment. "Wicked or not, I know when I am not needed," she replied lamely before heading back into the house.

Ruathain took his wife's hand and kissed it. Above him the crow suddenly cawed and danced along the rooftop. Ruathain glanced up. He had no love of carrion birds, but he knew they served a purpose and was normally content to leave them be. But this one caused the hackles to rise on his neck.

"Did you get a good price at market?" asked Meria.

"Fair. No more than that. The Norvii also brought their cattle. I was lucky to sell on the first day. By the third the price dropped considerably. Have the boys been well behaved?" The question caused her anger to flare again. Why should his absence bring a change in their behavior? Did he think her some weak-minded wench who could not control unruly children?

Ignoring the question, she told him: "There is a hot pie just baked. You must be hungry."

"Hungry for sight of you and the boys," he said. She gave a wan smile and moved away toward the doorway. He was about to follow when Connavar appeared from the far side of the house. Meria gave a broad smile, her mood seeming to lift momentarily, like the sun breaking through clouds.

"Where have you been, my bonny lad?" she asked him.

"Is the pie ready, Mam?" he countered.

She stepped in close, peering at the bruise on his cheek and the cut lip. "Why, what have you been doing? Not fighting again, Conn?"

"Just playing, Mam," he told her, squirming from her embrace. "Anyway, I've already told the Big Man all about it." He darted into the house.

Meria swung on Ruathain. "What did he mean? What has he told you?"

"He got into a fight with Govannan and some of the other boys. It is over now. It matters not."

"It matters to me, husband. Why were they fighting?"

Ruathain shrugged. "Boys fight. It is the nature of things. They make up soon enough." Young Braefar had walked in unnoticed from the stable.

"Govannan said Conn's father was a coward who ran away," said the boy. "But Conn broke his nose for it. You should have heard it, Mam. It broke with a mighty crack."

"Get inside!" roared Ruathain. Surprised, for his father rarely raised his voice, Braefar backed away, then ran into the house.

Meria stepped in close to her husband. "What did you tell him?" she whispered. Above them the crow sent out a series of screeching cries.

"I told him the truth. What else would you have me do?"

"Aye, that must have made you feel good," she hissed, her green eyes angry. "You'd like him to despise his father, wouldn't you?"

"Nothing could be farther from the truth, woman. It saddens me you should think it."

"Saddens you? Why would it sadden you? You're the man who let his father die. Just to win his bride." As soon as the words were spoken she regretted them. Never in their ten years together had she voiced them before. The sound of flapping wings broke the silence, and the crow flew off toward the northern woods.

Ruathain stood very still, his face expressionless, his pale gaze locked to her face. "That is what you believe?" he asked her, his voice terribly calm.

Pride made her stand her ground. "I do," she said.

The sudden coldness in his eyes frightened her, but when he spoke, his voice was heavy with sadness. "Twenty men saw him die. Not one of them would say that of me. It is simply not true. I protected him all day. Then he ran. That was the way of it." His voice hardened. "But any woman who would wed a man she believed had connived in the murder of her husband is no better than a pox-ridden whore. And I'll have no part of her. Not now. Not ever."

Then he walked past her into the house. That night, as the candles were snuffed and the lamps extinguished, Meria found herself alone in the large bed.

Ruathain took his blanket and slept in the barn.

The following morning he summoned workmen and carpenters, who began the construction of a new house at the far end of the long meadow. Three weeks later he moved his belongings into it.

The settlement of Three Streams was mystified by the separation. Was he not the most handsome of men, rich and brave? Was he not a good father and provider? Was she not lucky to have found a man to take on a young widow and her son? It was well known that he adored her and had raised her child as his own. Why, then, they wondered, should he have moved out?

Vorna the witch woman could have told them, for she had been picking herbs in the high meadow and had seen the great crow circle the house. But she said nothing. It was not wise for humans to meddle in the affairs of gods. Especially gods of death and mischief, like the Morrigu.

Drawing her cloak around her, she moved away into the Wishing Tree Woods, there to commune with the Seidh.

If the separation caused confusion in the community of Three Streams, its effect on Ruathain's children was devastating. For weeks nine-year-old Braefar was inconsolable, believing himself responsible for the rift. Connavar also felt a powerful sense of guilt, knowing that his fight with Govannan had led to the breakup. Three-year-old Bendegit Bran was also tearful, though he was too young to understand the enormous ramifications of the affair. All he knew was that he no longer saw his father as regularly and could not understand why.

Meria herself did not speak about it. She tried to give her children the same amount of love, attention, and care, but she was distracted often, and many times they would find her sitting by the window, staring out over the hills, her eyes moist with tears.

Connavar, as would always be his way, tried to tackle the problem head on. A month after the separation the ten-year-old walked across to the Big Man's house one evening and tapped on the door. Ruathain was sitting by a cold hearth, a single lamp casting a gloomy light over the main room. The Big Man was sharpening his skinning knife with a whetstone. "What are you doing here, boy?" he asked.

"I came to see you," Connavar answered.

"You saw me today in the high meadow. You helped me mark the cattle."

"I wanted to see you alone. Why are you here? Is it something I did? Or Wing? If so, I am sorry."

"It has nothing to do with you, Conn. It is just . . . the way of things."

"Was it what Mother said to you?"

Ruathain gently raised his hand, signaling an end to the questioning. "Conn, I shall not be talking about this matter. It is between your mother and me. However, no matter what passes between us, know this: She and I still love you—and Wing and Bran—and we always will. Now go home to bed."

"We are all unhappy," said Conn, making one last attempt.

Ruathain nodded. "Aye, all of us."

"Can we not be happy again?"

"You will be, Conn."

"What about you? I want you to be happy."

Ruathain rose from his chair and walked across to the boy, hoisting him high and kissing his cheek. "You make me happy, my son. Now go." Opening the door, Ruathain lowered Conn to the porch step. "I shall watch you run home in case the Seidh are out hunting small boys."

Connavar grinned. "They will not catch me," he said, and sped off across the field.

In the months that followed Ruathain and Meria rarely spoke except for those times when the Big Man came to visit Bran. Even then the conversation was coldly and punctiliously polite.

Connavar found it all impossible to understand, even though he had heard from the kitchen the last angry words between Ruathain and Meria. But they were just words, he thought. Words were merely noisy breaths. Surely they alone could not cause such damage.

A year after the separation he finally spoke to an outsider concerning the problem. Conn had become close to the foreigner Banouin. The dark-haired, olive-skinned merchant had arrived in Rigante lands twelve years before, bringing with him a baggage train of ponies bearing dyed cloths, embroidered shirts, spices, and salt. His goods were of high quality and rightly prized. He had spent three months among the Rigante, buying bronze and silver ornaments from the metalworker Gariapha and quality hides from the Long Laird's curious black and white cattle. Those hides, he said, would be highly desired back in his own distant land of Turgony. When he came for the second year he paid for a house to be built and spent the winter and spring among the people, a practice he continued ever since. In his third year he took to wearing the plaid leggings and long blue shirt tunic of the northern Rigante. No one took offense, for such was Banouin's charm that all knew he wore the attire as a mark of respect.

For his own part Banouin had also taken a liking to the fierce, strange-eyed Connavar. They had met one evening three years before, when Conn had climbed through the window of the small warehouse-stable where Banouin kept his goods. Unknown to the eight-year-old, the little merchant had seen him creeping through the long grass and had watched him scale the outside wall, easing himself through the window. This took some nerve, since, with the permission of the village council, Banouin always told the children he was a wizard who would turn any young thief into a toad. The tale was widely believed, and the youngsters of Three Streams generally steered clear of Banouin's house.

Intrigued, Banouin had moved silently into the warehouse, where he saw Conn delving into the saddle packs stacked against the far wall. Banouin waited in the shadows. At last Conn came to the pack containing ornate weapons and drew out a bronze dagger with a hilt of hand-worked silver crafted by Gariapha. Slashing the air, the boy began to move through a mock fight, twirling and leaping as if surrounded by enemies.

At last he stopped, then walked to the window and waved the blade in the air. This last move surprised Banouin, as did the next. Rather than climb out and make off with the dagger, the boy came back and returned the blade to the pack.

"Why did you not steal it?" asked Banouin, his voice echoing in the rafters.

The boy swung around, fists clenched. The merchant emerged from the shadows and sat down on a long wooden box. Conn darted back to the pack, drew out the blade, and stood ready.

"You intend to fight me?" inquired Banouin.

"You'll not turn me into a toad, foreigner," said the boy.

"I would have if you had tried to leave with my knife. However, since you did not come here to steal, why did you come?"

Conn shrugged. "It was a dare. Do they have dares where you come from?"

"Yes," said Banouin. "A friend once dared me to climb a rock face without a rope. Sixty feet high it was."

"Did you do it?"

"Almost. I fell and broke my leg. After that I avoided stupid dares."

At that moment a large rat scuttled from behind the packs. Banouion drew something from his sleeve. His right hand swept up, then down. A bright blade flashed across the room, and the boy saw the creature impaled against the far wall. Conn peered at the body and the small iron throwing knife jutting from it.

"Rats spread disease," said Banouin. "Now, what were we talking about?"

"Stupid dares," said the boy.

"Ah, yes. Put back my dagger, retrieve my knife, and come into the house. There we will talk—if you are still not frightened, that is."

"I'll be there," promised the boy.

Banouin doubted it and returned to his house. Moments later Conn appeared, carrying the throwing knife, cleaned of blood. They sat and talked for an hour. At first Conn was ill at ease, but soon he was all questions. Could he learn to throw a knife? Would Banouin teach him? Where had the foreigner come from? What were the lands like to the south? From that day they had struck up a friendship they both enjoyed.

Often, in the evenings, he and Conn would sit on the boardwalk outside Banouin's home and talk of events in the wider world, a world of mystery and adventure to the Rigante youngster. Banouin had journeyed far and often traveled on ships that crossed the great water to the lands beyond. Conn had never seen a ship and found the prospect of journeying on such a vessel dangerously exciting. Also, he had been amazed to learn, the people across the water spoke different languages. When Banouin had first told him, he had thought it to be a jest of some kind, and when the foreigner had spoken in his own tongue, it had sounded like gibberish and Conn had laughed aloud. Yet after a year he had learned many phrases in Banouin's language.

"You have a gift for learning and language," the foreigner said one day after a short conversation in Turgon. "Most tribesman have difficulty mastering the placement of our verbs."

"It is fun," Conn told him.

"Learning should be fun," said Banouin. "Indeed, so should life. The gods know it is short enough." His dark eyes fixed to Conn's gaze. "You don't laugh as much as you did," he said. "What is wrong?"

Connavar did not want to talk about the private grief in his household, but all the fears and anxieties caused by the separation suddenly flooded his emotions, and he found himself telling this outsider the whole terrible story. As he finished, he felt a wave of embarrassment. "I shouldn't have spoken of it," he said.

"That's not true, Conn," Banouin told him gently. "That is one of the great advantages of having friends. You can unburden your soul to them, and they will not judge you for it. Nor will they repeat what you have said."

Conn was relieved. "But can you understand why they remain apart? They love one another. It was just words. That's all."

"Words are stronger than iron," said Banouin. "Everything we do—everything we are—is born from words. A man's prejudices are passed on to him by the words of his father and mother or by older friends he worships. Religion and myth— though both may be the same—are kept alive by words more than deeds. Last year you broke Govannan's nose because of words. Are you friends yet?"

"No."

"There you are, then. Words."

"But Mother blames the Big Man for Varaconn's death. It is not true. Varaconn died because he was a coward, because he ran away. Not being true should make a difference, shouldn't it?"

"Perhaps it should, but it doesn't," Banouin told him. "I don't think it matters to Ruathain that she was wrong. It was that she *believed* the story. He is a man of great pride. And that pride is well founded, for he is a fair, brave, and honest man. It means much to him that others see he has these qualities, for they are rare and hard won. It is not easy to be honorable. The world is full of cunning, crafty men who have no understanding of honor or loyalty. They connive, they steal, and invariably, in the eyes of the world, they succeed. To be honest requires great effort and continuous courage. And as for fairness, that is hardest of all. Ruathain is a good man. That his wife should think him so base must have felt like a death blow."

Conn's heart sank. "Then you think they will never get back together?"

"I will not lie to you, Connavar. It would take a miracle. Your mother, too, has pride. And he likened her to a pox-ridden whore. She will not forgive that insult."

"He has taken no other wife," said Conn. "Nor has he put her aside in the council."

"Aye, that is a spark of hope," agreed Banouin. "But only a spark."

"I shall never lie to any person I love," Connavar said with feeling.

"Then you will be an unusual and foolish man," said the merchant.

"You think it is foolish to be truthful?"

"Your mother said what she truly believed was the truth. You think she was wise?"

"No," agreed the boy. "It was not wise. It is all so confusing."

"Life is often confusing when you are eleven years old." Banouin smiled. "It gets even more confusing as you grow older."

"Is there anything I can do to bring them together?"

Banouin shook his head. "Nothing at all, boy. It is a problem for them to solve."

◇ **3** ◇

DESPITE HIS ADMIRATION for the foreigner, Connavar could not accept that he was powerless to help his mother and the Big Man. The following evening he saw the witch Vorna on the high southern hillside, gathering flowers for her herbal medicines. Connavar left his chores, climbed the paddock fence, and ran out over the meadow and up the slope. She saw him coming and paused in her work.

"Can I speak with you?" he asked her.

Vorna laid down her herb sack and sat on a small boulder. "Are you not frightened I will turn you into a weasel?"

"Why would you do that?" he asked.

"Is that not what witches are famed for?" she countered.

He thought about her answer for a moment. "Can you do that? Is your magic so strong?"

"Perhaps," she told him. "If you annoy me, you will find out. Now, what do you want? I am busy."

"My father is Ruathain, my mother—"

"I know who your parents are," she snapped. "Get on with it."

He looked into her deep-set blue eyes. "I want a spell cast on them so that they will love one another again."

She blinked suddenly, and her hard face relaxed into a rare smile. "Well, well," she said, scratching at her tangled mop of black and gray hair. "So you want me to use my magic. No doubt you can give me a good reason."

"They are unhappy. We are all unhappy."

"And how will you pay me, young Connavar?"

"Pay?" he repeated, confused. "Are witches paid?"

"No, we work for love alone," she snapped, "and we dine on air, and we dress in wisps of cloud." Leaning forward, she fixed him with a piercing stare. "Of course witches are paid! Now let me think . . ." Resting her chin on her hand, she held to his gaze. "It would not be a big spell; therefore, I will not take your soul in payment. A leg, perhaps. Or an arm. Yes, an arm. Which should it be, your left or your right?"

"Why would you want my arm?" he asked, taking a step back from her.

"Perhaps I collect the arms of small boys."

"I am not small! And you are mocking me, witch. Go ahead, turn me into a weasel. And when you do, I'll run up your leg and bite your arse!"

Though Vorna did not show it, she was impressed by the child. Few Rigante youngsters would have dared to come this close to her, and not even the adults would have spoken to her in this manner. She was feared, and quite rightly. She knew the boy was frightened, but even so he had stood up to her.

"You are right; I am mocking you," she admitted. "So now let us speak plainly. My spells can kill, or they can heal. I can also prepare potions to make a man love a woman. That is not difficult. But Ruathain already loves Meria. And though she only realized it when he was gone, she loves Ruathain. The problem is pride, Connavar, and I will cast no spells to take that away from either of them." Dipping into the pouch at her side, she pulled forth a few dark seeds. "Do you know what these are?" she asked him.

"No."

"They are from the foxglove flower. A tiny amount of them can give a dying heart fresh life. Like a miracle. But just a pinch too much and they become the deadliest poison. Pride is like that. Too little and a man has no sense of self-worth. The world will wear him down to dust. Too much and he becomes arrogant, vain, and boastful. But just enough and he is a man to walk the mountains with. Ruathain is that man. To tinker with his pride would be to destroy all that he is. As for Meria, she is wise enough to know that she has lost him. I cannot help you, Connavar. I doubt even the Seidh could help you."

"But they might?" he asked.

His response worried her. "Do not even consider such an action," she warned him. "The Seidh are more dangerous than you could possibly imagine. Go home and leave your parents to solve their own problems." As he walked away, she called out. "And if I ever do turn you into a weasel, it will be a weasel with no teeth."

Swinging back, he gave a dazzling grin, then ran back to the paddock field.

That night, just before midnight, he crept from his bed and dressed quietly. In the bed alongside his own, Braefar stirred but did not wake. From her place under the western window the hound Caval raised her great black head and watched him. Connavar tugged on his shoes, then knelt beside the hound, patting her brow and scratching behind her ears. He thought of taking her with him. It would be good to have company on such a quest. Then he considered the dangers and decided against it. What right had he to risk Caval's life? Rising, he moved to the wall and eased his way past the curtain that separated his sleeping quarters from the main living area. The house was dark, and he moved with care toward the kitchen, from which he took an old long-bladed bronze knife, which he tucked into his belt. Lifting the latch bar on the kitchen door, he slipped out into the night, heading north toward the Wishing Tree Woods.

The moon was high, but its light did not seem to penetrate the darkness of the trees. Connavar's heart was beating fast as he climbed the slope. He had never seen a Seidh, but he knew many stories of them—spirit beings of great magic and dark prophecy. Some of their names were enshrined in Rigante legend, such as Bean-Nighe, the Washerwoman of the Ford. Warriors doomed to die would see her kneeling by a river washing bloodstained clothing. Connavar did not wish to see her or her sister Bean-Si, also known as the Haunting or the Yearning. One look at her stone-white face would fill a man with such sorrow that his heart would burst. The Seidh he was hoping to encounter was known as the Thagda, the old man of the forest. It was said that if one approached him and touched his cloak of moss, he would grant three wishes.

Connavar slowed in his climb. It also was said that if he took a dislike to a man, he would open his coat, and from his belly would come a mist that would eat away flesh of a human, leaving only dried bones.

The boy stopped at the tree line. His mouth was dry, his hands shaking. This is stupid, he told himself. He stared at the forbidding line of trees. They seemed now so sinister, and he imagined the horrors that might await him. Anger flared, drowning his fear. I am not like my father, he thought. I am not a coward. Taking a deep breath, he strode forward into the woods.

All was quiet within the trees, and through gaps in the leaves above, shafts of moonlight shone through, columns of bright silver illuminating a ground mist that drifted through the undergrowth. Connavar wiped his sweating palms on his leggings and was tempted to draw his knife. You are coming to ask a favor, he told himself sternly. How will it look if you approach the Thagda with a blade?

He walked on. The mist swirled around his ankles. A breeze blew up, rustling the leaves above him. "I am Connavar," he called. "I wish to speak to the Thagda." His voice sounded thin and frightened, which made his anger flare once more. I will not be fearful, he told himself. I am a warrior of the Rigante.

He waited, but no answer came to his call. He walked

deeper into the wood, scrambling down a steep slope. Ahead was a small clearing and a rock pool shimmering in the moonlight. He called out again, and this time he heard his own voice echoing around him. Nothing stirred, not a bat or a fox or a badger. All was still.

"Are you here, Thagda?" he shouted.

Thagda . . . Thagda . . . Thagda . . .

The sound faded away. Connavar was cold now, and the weariness of defeat sat upon him like a boulder. It is just a wood at night, he thought. There is no magic here.

Then came a sound from his left. At first he thought it to be a human voice, but almost immediately he realized it was an animal in pain. Moving to his left, he saw a patch of bramble. At its center was a pale fawn struggling to stand. Brambles had wrapped themselves around its hind legs, and small spots of blood could be seen on its gleaming flanks.

"Be still, little one," Connavar said, soothingly. "Be still and I will help you."

Warily he eased his way into the brambles. They tugged at his clothes and pricked at his flesh. Drawing his knife, he cut through an arching stem. A second stem, freed by the cut, slashed upward. Conn partly blocked it with his arm, but it whiplashed across his face, drawing blood. The brambles grew thicker as he struggled forward, their long thorns pricking and piercing. Panicked by his approach, the little fawn struggled harder. Conn spoke to her, keeping his voice gentle. By the time he reached her, she was exhausted and trembling with terror. Carefully Conn sliced through the brambles around her, sheathed his knife, then lifted her into his arms. The fawn was heavier than he expected. Holding her fast to his chest, he slowly turned and struggled out of the brambles. Every step brought new pricks of pain, and his leggings were shredded.

On open ground he lowered the fawn and ran his hands over her flanks. The cuts were not deep, and the wounds would heal swiftly. But where was the mother? Why had the fawn been left? Sitting down beside the small creature, he stroked her long neck. "You'll know to avoid brambles in future," he said. "Go away now. Find your mam."

The fawn stepped daintily away, then turned and stared at the boy. "Go on," he said, waving his arm. It took three running steps, then bounded away into the trees. Conn gazed down at his torn clothes. Meria would not be pleased with him. The leggings were new. Pushing himself to his feet, he struggled up the slope and walked away from the Wishing Tree Woods.

Just after dawn he awoke. Braefar was already dressed and was tugging on a calf-length pair of boots. Conn yawned and rolled over in the bed. "You slept a long time," said Braefar.

"I was out last night," said Conn. Sitting up, he told his brother of his adventure with the fawn in Wishing Tree Woods.

Braefar listened politely. "You were dreaming," he said, at last.

"I was not!"

"Then where are the cuts you spoke of?" Conn gazed down at his arms, then threw back the covers and checked the flesh of his thighs and calves. His skin was unmarked. Rolling from the bed, he picked up his discarded leggings. Not a nick or tear could be seen.

Braefar grinned at him. "Better get dressed, dreamer, or there'll be no breakfast left."

Alone and mystified, Conn pulled on his leggings and reached for his tunic shirt. As he lifted it from the floor, a knife fell clear, clattering to the wood.

But it was not the old wooden-hilted bronze knife he had taken to the woods. The weapon glinting in the dawn light had a blade of shining silver and a hilt carved from staghorn. The cross-guard was of gold, and set into the pommel was a round black stone etched with a silver rune. It was the most beautiful knife Conn had ever seen.

His fingers curled around the hilt. It fitted his hand perfectly. Wrapping it in an old cloth, he left the house and ran across to Banouin's home. The foreigner was asleep but awoke to see Conn sitting by his bed. He yawned and pushed back the covers.

"I am not a farmer," he said. "I do not usually rise this early."

"It is important," said the boy, handing the man a goblet of cold water.

Banouin sat up and drank. "Tell me," he said.

Conn talked of his trip to the Wishing Tree Woods, his rescue of the fawn, and his return. Then he told how he had found the knife.

Banouin listened in weary silence. His expression changed when Conn unwrapped the blade. Banouin lifted it reverently, then swung from the bed and carried it to the window to examine it in daylight. "It is magnificent," he whispered. "I do not know the nature of the metal. It is not silver, nor is it iron. And this stone in the hilt . . ."

"It is a Seidh weapon," said Conn. "It is a gift to me."

"I could sell this for a hundred, no, five hundred silvers."

"I do not want to sell it."

"Then why did you bring it to me?"

"I cannot tell anyone I went to the Wishing Tree Woods. It is forbidden. And I cannot lie to my mam. I thought you could advise me."

"It fits my hand to perfection," said Banouin. "As if it were made for me."

"Mine, too," said Conn.

"That cannot be, boy. My hand is much larger than yours." He passed the knife to Conn, who gripped the hilt.

"See," said Conn, raising the weapon. His fist covered the

hilt completely, the golden cross-guard resting under his thumb and the black pommel stone touching the heel of his palm.

Slowly Banouin transferred the knife to his own hand. The hilt seemed to swell in his grip. "It is a magical blade," said Banouin. "I have never seen the like."

"What should I do?" asked Conn.

"Do you trust me?" countered the foreigner.

"Of course. You are my friend."

"Then give the blade to me."

"Give . . . I don't understand. It is mine!"

"You asked for my help, Conn," said Banouin. "If you trust me, do as I ask."

The boy stood very still for a moment. "Very well," he said. "I give you the knife."

"It is now mine?" asked the foreigner.

"Yes. It is yours. But I still do not understand."

Banouin, still holding the knife, gestured for Conn to follow him and walked from the bedroom to the hearth. Taking a long stick, he stirred the ashes of the previous night's fire, blew some embers to life, and added kindling. When the fire was under way once more, he hung a copper kettle over it. "I have always liked to start the day with a tisane," he said. "Something warm and sweet. Dried elder flower and honey is a personal favorite. Would you like some?"

"Yes," said Conn. "Thank you." The boy was ill at ease and could not take his eyes from the knife. Banouin was his friend, but he was also a merchant who lived for profit. When the water was hot, Banouin prepared two cups of tisane and brought them to the table. Laying the knife on the polished wood, the foreigner sipped his drink.

"You have been very helpful to me, Connavar," he said gravely. "It is the custom of my people to reward those who assist us. I would therefore like to make you a gift. I would like you to have this knife. It is a very fine knife, and many people will wonder where you acquired it. You will tell them—and it will not be a lie—that it was presented to you by Banouin the Foreigner. Does that help you with your problem?"

Conn gave a wide smile. "Yes, it does. Thank you, Banouin."

"No, let me thank you for your trust. And let me caution you never to place so much trust in anyone ever again. Every man has a price, Conn. And damn my soul, this came awfully close to mine!"

Banouin the Foreigner led his train of sixteen ponies down the narrow trail to the ferry. The shallow wound in his upper arm was still seeping blood through the honey- and wine-soaked bandage, yet even so, his mood was good. In the distance he could see the craggy peaks of the Druagh mountains standing sentry over the lands of the Rigante.

Almost home.

He smiled. The home of his birth was Stone, the city of the Five Hills, in Turgony, eighteen hundred miles away, across the water. He had believed for most of his life that Stone was the home of his heart. Now he knew differently. Caer Druagh had adopted his soul. He loved those mountains with a passion he had not believed possible. Banouin had spent sixteen years moving among the many peoples of the Keltoi: the Rigante, the Norvii, the Gath and Ostro, the Pannones, the Perdii, and many more. He admired them and the shrewd simplicity of their lives. He thought of his own people, and it was as if a chilly wind blew across his skin. In that moment he knew that one day they would come to these mountains with their armies and their roads of stone. They would conquer these people and change their lives forever, just as they had in the lands across the water.

He thought of Connavar with both fondness and sadness. It was almost five years now since the boy had come to him with the Seidh blade. He was growing to manhood, secure in the mistaken belief that he was part of a culture that would endure. The boy was now—what?—fifteen, nearing sixteen. Almost a man and already tall and broad-shouldered, powerfully built.

Across the water Banouin had witnessed the aftermath of a great battle, the bodies of thousands of young Keltoi tribesmen—men like Ruathain and Connavar—being dragged to a great burial pit. Thousands more had been captured and sold into slavery, their leaders nailed by their hands and feet to sacrificial poles to die slow, agonizing deaths by the roadside as they watched their people march into oblivion.

Banouin had been asked if he would like to take part in the organization of the slave sale.

He had declined, even though the profits would have been huge.

How long will it be before they come here? he wondered. Five years? Ten? Certainly no longer.

Reaching the foot of the hill, Banouin and his pack ponies moved slowly to the ferry poles. There he dismounted. An old brass shield was hanging on a peg by the far post. Alongside it was a long wooden mallet. Banouin struck the shield twice, the sound echoing across the water. From a hut on the far side came two men. The first of them waved at the small trader. Banouin waved back.

Slowly the two men hauled the flat-bottomed ferry across the Seidh River. As the raft reached the shore, old Calasain unhooked the front gate, lowering it to the jetty. Leaping nimbly ashore, he gave a gap-toothed grin. "Still alive, eh, foreigner? You must have been born under the lucky moon."

"The gods look after a prayerful man," Banouin replied with a smile.

Calasain's son, Senacal, a short, burly man, also stepped ashore and moved down the line of ponies, untying the rope attached to the ninth beast. The ferry was small and would take only eight ponies per trip.

Banouin led the first half of his train aboard, drew up the gate, and helped Calasain with the hauling rope. He did not glance back, for he knew that Senacal would be helping himself to some small item from one of the packs. Calasain would find it, as he always did, and upon Banouin's next trip south the old man would shamefacedly return it to him.

As they docked on the north side, Calasain's wife, Sanepta, brought him a cup of herbal tisane sweetened with honey. Banouin thanked her. When young, he thought, she must have been a beautiful woman. But the weariness of age and a hard life had chiseled away her looks.

Within the hour, with all his ponies on the northern shore, Banouin walked with Calasain back to the jetty. There the two men sat, sipping tisane and watching the sunlight sparkle upon the water.

"Trouble on the trip?" asked Calasain, pointing to the wound on Banouin's arm.

"A little, but it lifted the monotony. What has been happening here these last eight months? Any raids?"

The old man shrugged. "There are always raids. The young need to test their skills. Only one man died, though. Made the mistake of tackling Ruathain. Not wise these days. Not wise any day, I guess. What are you carrying?"

"Colored cloth, pearls, bright beads, threads of silver and gold. The cloth will sell fast. It is invested with a new purple dye that does not run when wet. Plus a few spices and some ingots, iron, silver, and two of gold for Riamfada. It should all trade well."

Calasain sighed, and a blush darkened his leathered features. "I apologize for my son. Whatever he has taken I will find."

"I know. You are not responsible for him, Calasain. Some men just cannot resist stealing."

"It is a source of shame to me." For several minutes they

sat in companionable silence. Then Calasain spoke again. "How are things in the south?"

"There has been a sickness among the Norvii near the coast. Fever and discoloration of the skin. Swept through them like a grass fire. One in six died."

"We heard of that. Did you cross the water?"

"Yes. All the way to my homeland."

"They are still fighting?"

"Not at home. But their armies have moved west. They have conquered many of the adjoining lands."

"Why?" asked Calasain.

"They are building an empire."

"For what purpose?"

"To rule everyone, I suppose. To become rich on the labor of others. I do not know. I think that perhaps they like war."

"A stupid people, then," observed Calasain.

"Is Ruathain reunited with Meria?" asked Banouin, seeking to change the subject.

"No. Nearly six years now. Yet he does not put her aside. Strange man. There is no good humor in him anymore. He rarely smiles and never laughs. Men walk warily around him. He got into an argument with Nanncumal the Smith and punched him so hard that the smith's body broke a fence rail as it fell. What went wrong with his marriage? Why do you think they separated? Was she unfaithful to him?"

Banouin shrugged. "I don't know. Whatever the reason, it is sad for them both. I like them. They are good people."

"They are Rigante," Calasain said with a smile. "We are all good people. Welcome home, foreigner."

Four hours later, with the dying sun bathing the mountains in fire, Banouin crested the last rise and gazed down on the settlement of Three Streams. The heaviness lifted from his heart as he saw the scattered houses and farms, the bridges over the streams, the cattle and sheep feeding on the rich grass.

And there, at the center of the settlement, was the colossal oak known as Eldest Tree, its lower branches hung with lamps.

Home, thought Banouin, savoring the word. I am home.

Connavar liked to climb, and he sat now in the topmost branches of Eldest Tree, his mind wrestling with problems he could not, at fifteen, fully understand. He loved both Ruathain and his mother, and it hurt him that they should still be living apart. His mother had insulted the Big Man, unfairly accusing him. She knew she was wrong but was too proud to apologize and humble herself. He knew that she knew but would not make a single effort to bridge the gap. It seemed so foolish to the young man.

Sometimes, in the night, he would hear Meria weeping softly, trying to muffle the sound in the thick, embroidered pillow on the bed Ruathain had crafted. It was a mystery to Connavar. All his life he had watched Meria being cool toward her husband, apparently uncaring. Now she grieved as if a child had died. Yet with all that grief she could not bring herself to take a deep breath and acknowledge she was wrong.

And the Big Man had changed. He was surly now and quick to anger. Connavar shivered when he recalled the fight with Govannan's father, Nanncumal.

Connavar had been walking with Ruathain and Braefar when Nanncumal had stepped out from his smithy. There was no love lost between the men, for it had been Nanncumal who had caused the trouble in the first place, telling Govannan about the death of Conn's father. The smith was a large man, powerful in the shoulders, with massive biceps.

"You keep that boy of yours away from my smithy," he said, pointing to Connavar.

Ruathain looked at the man. "And why should I do that?"

"He's a thief, that's why. Stole some nails from my rack."

"That's a lie!" said Conn, outraged. Clenching his fists, he stepped toward the smith, but Ruathain drew him back.

Nanncumal sneered at him, then spoke again. "They were gone after you were here, sniffing around my daughter. That's good enough for me. Now, you keep the boy away," he said, swinging toward Ruathain. "If I catch him here again, I'll split his ears."

"You'll split his ears?" repeated Ruathain, his voice terribly calm. "You'd threaten my son while I stand before you? You are not a wise man, Nanncumal."

"He's not your son," snapped the smith. "He's the get of a coward!"

Ruathain took one step forward. Nanncumal threw up his left arm to defend himself, but the blow was too fast, a heavy clubbing right hand that took the smith on the left cheek, splitting the skin. Nanncumal was hurled from his feet to smash headfirst into the fence beside the smithy. The central rail snapped under the impact. The smith struggled to rise, then slumped to the hard-packed ground. Several men came running to watch the fight, but it was over. Ruathain stepped in close to the fallen man, turning him with his boot. The smith's eyes were open.

Ruathain spoke again, his voice still flat and cold. "Connavar's father rode with me to the battle and fought beside me all day. You, however, were not there, I recall. You had a bellyache or some such. In fact, smith, I have never seen you in battle. Do not be so swift to call others a coward. The next time you do, I will seek you out again."

Connavar shivered with both pleasure and pain at the memory. Nanncumal had deserved it. He knew Conn had stolen nothing. His real grievance was Conn's friendship with his daughter Arian. Conn's good humor faded. She had been avoiding him since the fight, and he missed her company, her quick smile, and the scent of her golden hair. Closing his eyes, he recalled the day of the chase, early in the spring.

Arian, her sister Gwydia, and several of the other settlement girls had been gathering flowers on the edge of the western wood. Connavar had been out walking and had come upon them. Arian, holding the hem of her yellow dress above her knees, was wading in a fast-moving shallow stream. Connavar called out a greeting. Leaning down, she sent a splash of water over him. Laughing, he waded after her, but she eluded him, crossing the stream and running into the woods. Conn followed, catching her around the waist. They fell together in the soft undergrowth.

"Why did you splash me?" he asked.

"To cool the fire in your eyes," she told him. His right arm was resting across her, his hand on her slim waist. He glanced down at her bare legs. Sunlight was dappling the fair skin. Suddenly his throat was tight, and he could feel his heart beating wildly. He looked into her blue eyes. The pupils were large, and he could see himself reflected there, as if he floated within her. He felt as if he were slowly falling through water, and before he could resist the impulse, he was kissing her. Arian's mouth was warm. Her tongue touched his lips. Connavar groaned. His hand slid down to her thigh. Suddenly she struggled free and rolled away from him. Sitting up, she pushed her hands through her long blond hair. "I see the water did not cool you enough," she said. Conn could scarcely speak. She giggled suddenly and put her hand over her mouth. Conn followed her gaze and, glancing down, saw the embarrassing bulge in his trews. Blushing, he rolled to his knees, then struggled to stand.

Arian ran to him, throwing her arms around his neck. "Do not be angry with me," she said, mistaking the blush of shame for a more violent emotion.

Conn drew her close. "I am not angry," he said. "I love you. Next year, at the Feast of Samain, I will speak with your father. We will be wed."

Pulling away from him, she smiled. "Perhaps I will agree," she said. "Perhaps I won't."

Conn did not know what to say, but his eyes narrowed. "Now you are getting angry," said Arian, gaily, stepping in close and stroking his face. He tried to grab her, but she spun away, then ran back to the other girls.

Sitting high in the tree, Conn recalled the heat from the skin of her thigh. Discomfort flared in him.

A movement to the south caught his eye. A line of ponies was moving down the far slope. Conn's heart leapt. Banouin was back!

Swiftly he scrambled down the tree, dropping to the ground and setting off toward Banouin's house. He heard the hooves of the pack ponies on the last wooden bridge and called out to the foreigner.

Banouin saw him and grinned. The foreigner seemed smaller, and his short-cropped dark hair was flecked with silver. He was old, Conn knew, close to fifty. But he was still fit and strong. The foreigner dismounted. The fifteen-year-old was now several inches taller than the man. "How goes it with you, Connavar?" he asked.

"Banias tol var," answered the boy.

Banouin clapped his hands. "That is good, Conn. You remembered."

"I do not forget anything," the young man answered seriously. "It is good to see you again. Let me help you unload the ponies. Then you can tell me about your travels."

Banouin moved to his warehouse and unlatched the door. Together he and Connavar removed the packs, carried them inside, then turned the ponies loose in the paddock field beyond.

Banouin's house was, like all Rigante dwellings, built entirely of wood. But he had laid a mosaic stone floor in the main living room, and there were three couches there and no chairs. The room was clean and free of dust.

"I see you have been looking after my home," said Banouin. "I thank you for that."

"I shall fetch some food," said Conn, rising and moving toward the door.

Banouin was about to protest, but the youngster was gone, running across the field back toward his own home a quarter mile distant. He returned with a canvas sack containing a large portion of meat pie, several ripe apples, a round of cheese wrapped in muslin, a loaf of fresh bread, and a pottery jar full of rich salted butter.

After they had eaten, Banouin lit two lamps and stretched out on the sofa. "What I really miss from my homeland," he said, "is a warm scented bath at the end of a journey. Every town this size would have a bathhouse, and many of the houses would boast their own bathrooms."

"Do your people bathe a lot?" asked Connavar.

"Every day."

"Why? Do they smell bad?"

"If they don't bathe, they smell foul."

"How unfortunate for them," said Connavar.

Banouin chuckled. "It is a strange thing. The more you bathe, the more you need to. I had a bath two months ago in Turgony. It was wonderful. Then I set off on the road home. Within three days I stank. After ten I could almost not bear my own company. Then the odor faded away." Banouin rose from the couch, removed his long coat, and threw it over a couch. Connavar saw the bloodied bandage on his upper arm.

"How did you get the wound?" he asked.

"Four days ago I was accosted by robbers. Three Norvii outcasts. One of them managed to scratch me with his knife. It is not a serious wound."

"Did you kill them?"

"No, you bloodthirsty young savage. I broke the knifeman's arm. Then they ran away."

"You should have killed them. They may lie in wait for you again next spring."

"If they do, I shall bear your advice in mind. Now tell me what's been happening in Three Streams."

"Braefar won the solstice race two weeks ago. There isn't a happier lad in the land now," said Conn. "He's been strutting around like a gamecock."

"What about you?"

"I came in second."

Banouin sat back. He could see the gleam of amusement in Conn's eyes and guessed there was more to the tale. "What about Govannan? I thought he was the fastest runner among you youngsters."

"So did he," Conn said with an impish grin. "Apparently the wind caught one of the race signposts and swung it. Govannan and those following ran into a swamp. He was game, though, and still finished third. Arian says he spent most of the evening prizing leeches from his buttocks. Perhaps he'll have better luck next year."

"Why is it that I don't believe the wind moved the sign?" asked Banouin.

Conn laughed aloud. "Because you have a suspicious mind, foreigner. Just like Govannan."

"Indeed I do," agreed Banouin. "You mentioned Arian. Are you still intent on marriage?"

"Yes, she is the most beautiful girl. I love her dearly."

"You will acquire Govannan as a brother-in-law," pointed out Banouin.

"Aye, he is most definitely one of the worms in the apple. Her father is another. But love will conquer all, foreigner. A Rigante woman has the right to choose her own husband. Will you dance at my wedding?"

"I am not a dancer, but I will attend—and happily. Now you should get off home. I am tired and in need of a good night's sleep in a soft bed."

"Can I come here tomorrow? Will you teach me more of the language of your people? Will you tell me of the cities of stone?"

"You are always welcome here, Conn. But do you not have labors to perform?"

"Only until midday."

"Then I will be pleased to see you after that. Give my best wishes to your mother. Tell her I have the green satin shirt I promised."

Connavar walked to the door. "Have your people won more wars?" he asked.

"I am afraid that they have, Conn."

"You must tell me all."

Arian was not sure which was worse, the fear or the cure, for the two were intertwined, dancing through her mind, twisting and turning. The panic would strike unannounced, coming upon her as she walked, or lay in her bed, or washed clothes in the shallow water of the stream. Her fingers would begin to tremble, and a great emptiness would assail her, a darkness that took the heat from the sun.

She remembered the terrible day when the fear was born. Her little five-year-old sister, Baria, who slept in her bed, was coughing and feverish. Mother had given her an herbal tisane sweetened with honey, and she had cuddled up to Arian. The older girl, close to thirteen, had pushed her away, for the child was hot and it was a summer night, muggy and close. Baria had rolled over, clutching her rag doll. She had coughed a little more, then fallen asleep. In the middle of the night Arian awoke, struggling to remember a dream. She felt Baria's chubby leg against her. The leg was cold.

"Come here, little one," she said. "I will warm you." Rolling over, she put her arms around the still figure, drawing her close. Baria was limp. For a while Arian cuddled her, but then she became alarmed at the lack of movement. It was pitch dark in the room, and she could not see her sister's face. Rising from the bed, she climbed down from the loft and went to the fire. It was almost out. Kneeling by the hearth, Arian added a little tinder, then blew on the fading embers. A flame licked up. Holding a candle wick to the flames, she waited for it to light, then climbed back to the loft. Moving to the bedside, she held the candle over Baria's face. Pale, dead eyes stared up at her. A drop of hot wax fell to the child's cheek. "I'm sorry," Arian said without thinking. There was no answer. There would never be an answer again. Arian began to shake. She sat for a while, hot wax dribbling over her fingers.

Then she woke her parents. Her mother wailed and wept, and even her father—the gruff and surly smith—shed tears by the bedside. Govannan came to Arian, putting his arm around her and drawing her close, running his thick fingers through her golden hair. He said nothing, for there was nothing to say. A sweet child had vanished into the night, never to return, and the family's grief was beyond words.

The following day, while walking in the high woods, the fear had come upon Arian. Her legs gave way beneath her, and she sank, sobbing, to the ground. "I don't want to die," she said. "Not ever. I don't want to be that cold."

The fear, once begun, continued to grow. She sat by the tree, terror feeding on her soul, gnawing at her. She heard the sound of a walking horse and, desperate for company, pushed herself to her feet and ran toward the sound. The rider was a middle-aged man with a round, kindly face. He was not Rigante, and she guessed him to be a merchant or an emissary heading for the hall of the Long Laird. Drawing on the reins, the rider stopped.

"What is wrong, young lady?" he asked, his accent and rounded vowels showing him to be from the south.

"Nothing," she said, wiping the tears from her face. "I was just . . . a little frightened."

"Is there an animal close by?"

"No." She felt foolish now and forced a smile. "I fell asleep and was dreaming."

"You are trembling," he said, dismounting. He was not tall—no more than an inch or two taller than she. Stepping in close, he put his arm around her. "There, there," he said soothingly. "Don't be frightened. It is a lovely, bright day, and there is nothing in these woods to harm you."

The fear began to subside, but she knew it was still there, hiding, waiting. She snuggled in close to the man, feeling him pat her back and stroke her hair. She began to feel a little calmer. Then his hand slid down over her buttocks. She tensed, but his voice was soothing. "I can make all your fears go away," he said. "I can bring you joy and make the sun shine brightly. Trust me." He kissed her cheek and then, gently placing his hand under her chin, tilted her head toward him. His lips brushed against hers. His right hand slipped over her hips and across her belly. She shivered. He was right. The fear had gone now. And the sun was shining brightly.

What she remembered most about that first time was the warmth of skin upon skin, the man above her, his flesh wet with sweat, her body responding, full of life. No fear now, no terrifying emptiness, no thoughts of the grave.

"Was it good for you?" he asked her as they lay together on the grass.

"Yes, it was good."

"How old are you?"

"Thirteen. Almost fourteen."

"Not an Earth Maiden, then?"

"No. My father is the smith at Three Streams."

"You are a fine girl," he said, rising and pulling on his leggings and shirt. Reaching into his pouch, he tossed her a silver coin. "Let us keep this little tryst to ourselves, eh? A private little moment of wonder and joy."

She nodded and said nothing more as he mounted his pony and rode away.

Two months later she was seeking the advice of Eriatha, the red-haired Earth Maiden, who informed her bluntly that she was pregnant. Arian was terrified and begged Eriatha to help her. The Earth Maiden supplied her with an herbal potion. The taste was sickening, and when it hit her stomach, the effect was hideous and painful. But the pregnancy was ended, and Arian gave Eriatha the merchant's silver coin.

Afterward they sat in the small, round hut where Eriatha entertained her clients. Eriatha gave Arian a clay cup of sweetened cider to take away the taste of the potion. "You are too young to play this game," said Eriatha. "Why did you do it?"

Arian haltingly told her of her sister's death and the terrible fear it had left behind, a cold fear that the merchant's hot, sweating, heaving body had taken away. Eriatha listened patiently, and when she spoke, it was without criticism. "We all deal with fears the best way we can," she said. "But—and I want you to believe me—rutting with strangers carries too many dangers. I know. When I was thirteen—which seems a hundred years ago now, though it is only ten—I, too, discovered the heady joys of the game. It was with a married man, a friend of my father. When we were found out, my family disowned me, my tribe cast me out. Now I rut for money, and I live alone. I am suited to this life, Arian. You are not. And think on this: In trying to overcome *your* fear of death, you have caused the death of a child inside you. That is no small matter, girl."

"It wasn't a child," insisted Arian. "It was only blood. I would never harm a child."

Eriatha sighed. "Find another way to deal with the fear."

"Oh, the fear is gone now," said Arian. "I will not be so stupid again."

But it had not gone, and three times more that year she passed silver coins to Eriatha, coins given to her by men on the road. And now a second fear had been born to torment her. What if one of the merchants should ride into Three

Streams and recognize her? What if Father should find that she had been living as an Earth Maiden? Like Eriatha, she, too, would be cast out.

Arian pushed such thoughts from her mind. Soon both fears would be ended for good. The Feast of Samain was coming, and Connavar had promised to marry her. Then there would be no need to sit, as she was doing now, by the roadside. Conn would be with her to take away the fear, to hold her close, as she should have held Baria close.

Death could not come for her while Connavar was near. He was strong and brave and warm with life.

As Arian sat on the grass thinking of Conn, two men came walking, leading a laden wagon.

Her hands were trembling, and she felt the need upon her. Rising, she tossed back her golden hair and stepped out to meet them.

Eriatha the Earth Maiden opened the door to her hut and beckoned the young man inside. Conn ducked under the low door and entered the dwelling. The hut was small and round. There were no windows and no upper rooms, just a central fire within a circle of stones, the smoke drifting up through a hole in the cone-shaped roof. By the western wall was a wide bed and a coverlet stuffed with goose down. There were two high-backed chairs and two old rugs by them on the hard-packed dirt floor. This was not where Eriatha lived, Conn knew, merely where she plied her trade.

Ruathain had told him she was from the Pannone tribe, and the Big Man had supplied the coin for Conn to give her. "Treat her with respect, Conn," Ruathain said. "She is a good woman and pays her tithe to the settlement. Last year, when the floods were upon us, she was out from dawn till dusk shoring up the river defenses. She did not stint in her work."

"I do not need a whore," said Conn.

"All skills have to be learned, boy. Any man—like any

dog—can rut without instruction. But if you love your wife, you will want to bring her pleasure, too. Eriatha can teach you how. Then you won't have to blunder around your own bedchamber on your wedding night."

"You could teach me," said Conn.

Ruathain's laughter rang out. "No, Conn, I could *tell* you. Eriatha will *teach* you."

Now he was there and trying not to look at the bed. "I thank you for your welcome," he said formally as she invited him to sit. Eriatha gave a practiced smile and a bow. She was a small woman, slender but not thin, her red hair hanging loose to her pale, freckled shoulders. Her dress was of soft wool dyed blue and boasted no adornments, no embroidered wire, no brooches. She sat opposite him, so close that their knees were almost touching. Conn looked into her face. She was older than he had thought at first, perhaps as old as twenty-five. From a distance she looked much younger. They sat in silence for a few moments. She seemed at ease, but Conn was growing more uncomfortable. His hand moved toward his money pouch.

"Not yet," she said. "First tell me why you have come to me." Her voice was deep for a woman, the sound husky.

"I am to be married," said Conn. "The Big Man . . . my father . . ." His voice trailed away. He found his embarrassment rising.

Eriatha leaned forward and took his hand. "Your father," she said, "wants you to be a good husband and to be able to satisfy your wife on your wedding night."

"I will be able to do that," Conn said defensively.

"Of course you will, lover," she told him. "Tell me, are you skilled with the sword?"

Conn relaxed. This line of conversation was much more to his liking. "Yes, I am. I am fast and strong, and Banouin tells me my balance is good."

"And were you skilled the first time you picked up a blade?"

"Of course not. But I am a fast learner."

"Making love is no different, Connavar. There is an art to it. Two lovers are like two dancers, moving in unison to a music only the soul can hear. All men can rut, Connavar. There is no skill in that. But to make love . . . now therein lies a greater joy."

Smoothly she rose from her seat and slid her dress over her shoulders, allowing it to fall to the rug. Then she knelt and removed his boots. Rising, she took Conn's hand. He stood before her, tense and wishing he had never come there. Lifting his hand, she pressed it to her breast. The nipple was hard under his palm. He could smell perfume in her hair. Eriatha moved in closer, her arm circling his neck.

"I think I should go," he said. "This was a mistake."

"Are you afraid?"

The question was asked in a whisper, but it sounded in his ears like a voice of thunder. Instead of making him tense, it somehow relaxed him. He grinned. "Yes, I suppose that I am. Do you think me foolish?"

"No," she said, her fingers unlacing the front of his shirt, her hands sliding up over his chest. Dipping his head, he kissed her. Her mouth was warm, the taste of her tongue sweet. She undid his belt, and he felt her warm hands on his hips, the heat of the fire on the bare skin of his legs. She dropped to her knees before him, pushing her cheek against his swollen penis. Taking it in her hand, she kissed the glans, running her tongue over the tip. He groaned and heard her give a throaty chuckle.

"Are you still afraid, Connavar?" she asked.

"No." Stooping, he took her by the arms and lifted her to her feet.

Eriatha led him to the bed, and they lay down side by side. Conn moved above her. Her legs swung expertly over his hips, and he entered her. The warmth alone was joyful, but it was as nothing compared to the sense of harmony that engulfed him. This was perfection of a kind he had never experienced or even dreamed of. Skin on skin, her lips upon his, their bodies moving together. Lost in ecstasy, he began to move faster and faster, his entire being focused on the movement, the warmth, and the wetness.

There was no sense of time or place now. The universe was the hut, the world this bed. Nothing mattered save the desperate need within him to thrust harder and harder. His body was soaked in sweat. Rearing up on his elbows, he gave one final thrust. He cried out as he came, then sank to the bed, breathing heavily.

They lay in silence for several minutes. Then Eriatha began to stroke his chest and belly. Arousal came swiftly, and he made to mount her again.

She pushed him away. "No, lover. Now is the time for your education to begin. You have already shown me you can rut. And you do it wonderfully well. Now let us see how you swift a learner you really are."

"What must I learn?" he asked her.

"To treat your lover's body as if it were your own. To bring the same pleasure to her that she brings to you, with hand and mouth and body. And to learn patience, Connavar, and control. Will you be able to do what I tell you?"

He smiled. "Let us see," he said.

"Then we will lie here for a while and merely touch," she said. "And I will show you the secrets of the game."

Throughout the evening and into the night she taught him. He would never know that she feigned her first orgasm, nor would he ever learn how surprised she was that the second and third were entirely natural.

At the last they sat quietly on the bed, sipping cider. "I wish there was more I could teach you, Connavar," she said. "But you are—as you promised—a fast learner. And you will bring your wife great joy. Who is the lucky girl?"

"Arian—she is the blacksmith's daughter. You must have seen her. She has golden hair and the face of a goddess."

"Yes, I have seen her. She is very pretty," said Eriatha, climbing from the bed and putting on her faded blue dress.

Conn sensed the change in her mood. "What is wrong?"

"Nothing is wrong," she answered. "But it is late and time for you to go."

"Was it something I said?" he asked, rising and moving to his clothes.

"Foolish boy," she said, gently stroking his face. "You have said and done nothing to offend me. Quite the reverse, in fact. Go home and leave me to get some rest. You have tired me out, and I need my sleep."

Conn dressed and stepped to the door. Taking her hand, he kissed it. "I will never forget this night," he said.

"Nor I. Go home."

Only when he had left and was walking home through light rain did he remember that he had not given her the coin. Slowly he trudged back to the hut and was about to knock on the door when he heard the sound of weeping coming from within the darkened hut. The sound was plaintive and, more than that, infinitely private. Silently he took three silver coins from his pouch and left them by the door.

Then, lifting his hood into place, he walked home.

As summer waned and the corn was cut, threshed, and stored, the young men of the settlement took to the high woodlands with their elders to replenish the winter fuel stores. Younger boys, carrying long canvas sacks slung over their shoulders, gathered branches for kindling, then hauled them down the hill. Several work teams of adults selected trees for cutting, then set to with ax and saw. There were many dead trees, and they were felled first, and then stripped of branches so

that the older boys could saw the trunks into rounds that
could be rolled downhill.

On either side of a fallen trunk Connavar and Braefar
dragged and pushed a four-foot double-handed saw. Stripped
to the waist, sweat streaking their tanned skin, they worked the
serrated blade deep into the wood. Braefar had an old cloth
wrapped around his blistered right hand. Blood had stained
the cloth. Younger than Conn by a year, he was a head shorter
and twenty pounds lighter than his half brother. It was as if nature had played a cruel trick on the swordsman Ruathain. The
son of the slender Varaconn looked more like Ruathain every
day, tall and powerful, already showing prodigious energy and
strength, while the swordsman's own son was sparrow-boned
and puny.

It was a source of some shame to Braefar, who, though he
could outrun the fastest Rigante tribesman and shoot a bow
as well as most men, could not yet wield a bronze longsword
or wrestle a bull calf to the ground. His skin was soft, and no
matter how hard he worked, he could build no calluses. Every
time he was called on to use the copper saw, his hands bled.

The two young men had worked all morning, and as the
sun neared noon, they laid aside the two-man saw and sat in
the shade of a spreading oak to eat. Scattered clouds drifted
across the blue sky, dappling the green valleys with shadow,
and darker clouds hovered around the Druagh peaks, threatening rain in the late afternoon.

The brothers shared a meal of bread and honey washed
down with cool water from a cold spring that trickled down
the nearby rock face.

"You have been very quiet today," said Conn, tipping a cup
of water over his sweat-soaked red-gold hair.

For a moment Braefar was silent, and when he did speak,
he did not look Conn in the eyes. "I think you like the foreigner more than you like me," he said.

The comment surprised Conn. His half brother was never

one to complain and disliked emotional confrontations. Conn understood now why Braefar had seemed so distant these past weeks. "I'm sorry, Wing," he said. "You are my brother, and I love you dearly. But Banouin knows much of the world. And I am eager to learn."

"What is there that he can teach?" Braefar answered sourly. "We learn how to farm, how to ride, how to shoot, how to fight. We learn the great songs of the Rigante. What more will we need?"

Conn finished the last of his bread, then licked the honey from his fingers. "Do you know what a 'soldier' is?" he asked.

"A soldier? No."

"It is a man who fights all year round."

"Such a man is an idiot," said Braefar. "Who works his farm while he fights? Who gathers his crops or feeds his animals?"

"He has no farm. He is paid in gold to fight wars. And because he has no farm, he does not have to return home in late summer to gather his crops. Banouin's people have armies of soldiers."

Braefar laughed. "They must be very bored in winter, when all their enemies have gone home."

Conn shook his head. "Their enemies have no homes. For the soldiers follow them and kill them and take over their lands."

"That is stupid," said Braefar. "What can you do with land that is far away from yours?"

"Banouin says you force the surviving people to pay tributes to the conqueror. Gold, or corn, or timber, or cattle."

"It still makes no sense," insisted Braefar. "You can eat only so much bread. And cattle need wide grazing lands. If someone offered Father a thousand more cattle, he would refuse. There would not be enough grass for them."

Conn chuckled. "It is complicated, and I do not fully understand it myself. But these armies of soldiers march into a land and conquer it. The plunder they take is sent back to the cities of stone where their rulers live. With this plunder they create more armies of soldiers and conquer more lands. There they build more cities with great stone roads joining them."

"Stone roads? You are making fun of me."

"No," said Conn. "Banouin says there is now a stone road in the land across the water that stretches for a hundred miles. And there are stone bridges built across rivers."

"I don't believe any of it," scoffed Braefar. "Who would be crazy enough to build a stone road? And why?"

"So that wagons and armies can move faster."

"I think he has fooled you, Conn," said Braefar, rising. "Now let's get back to work."

"How is your hand?"

"It hurts, but it will hurt less when we have finished."

Conn moved across to his brother and threw his arm around Braefar's slender shoulder. "You are my brother and my best friend, Wing. And I will never let anything come between us."

Braefar forced a smile. Banouin had left for his yearly trip south, and only now did Conn return to him. A cloud drifted across the sun, and the clearing was bathed in shadow. Braefar eased away from Conn's embrace and returned to the saw. As they worked, he found his melancholy hard to shift. The last few years had been painful for him as he watched his father grow more bitter, his mother more distant. Now Conn had become attached to the foreigner, and Braefar felt bereft of friends. Especially after winning the solstice race: Govannan and his friends were not speaking to him.

The brothers labored for another two hours, then Braefar's strength gave out. His arms felt as if they had been beaten with wooden sticks, and the joints of his shoulders burned. None of the other youngsters had stopped working, and Braefar had struggled on long after he should have stopped.

The saw moved ever more slowly. Finally he let go and stood shamefaced. Conn wiped sweat from his brow and clambered over the thick trunk.

"Sit down. I will massage your muscles."

"I feel like a fool," whispered Braefar.

"Nonsense. Most of the boys your size are gathering kindling. You have done a man's work, and you have done it well." Conn's hands settled on his shoulders. Braefar tensed, but the touch was gentle, as was the slow kneading that followed.

A spattering of rain fell on the clearing, and the workers around them took a break. Braefar felt his irritation rise. If he had been able to last for a few more heartbeats, no one would have seen him fail.

On the hillside below he saw the village girls climbing toward them, carrying wicker baskets of food and jugs of apple juice. Conn's fingers slowed still further, the kneading becoming distracted. Braefar glanced up. His brother was staring down at the girls. Braefar's eyesight was not strong, and he could make out no individual faces. "Is she there?" he asked.

"Aye, she's there," whispered Conn, sitting down alongside him. As the girls approached, Braefar saw her. Arian was talking to her dark-haired sister, Gwydia, and both girls were laughing. The rain ceased, the sun breaking through the clouds. Arian's yellow hair shone suddenly gold in the sunlight. It was like magic.

"She is so beautiful," said Conn. Some of the girls moved to their brothers, others to sweethearts. The remainder gathered at the center of the clearing, laying down their baskets. Arian glanced coolly around the clearing, her gaze drifting over the two boys. Conn cursed. "She is still ignoring me."

"Why would she do that?"

"I was supposed to meet her three days ago, but the Big Man heard there was wolf sign in the high pasture, and we rode out to check. I was only an hour late, but she was not where we agreed to meet. Since then she has avoided me."

"Shall we get some food?" asked Braefar, anxious to change the subject.

"No. I am not hungry." Conn rose and wandered to the spring. As soon as he had gone, Arian and the dark-haired Gwydia strolled over.

"Your hand is bleeding," said Gwydia, sitting down on the fallen trunk.

"It will heal," Braefar told her. A swift shadow swept across the clearing. Braefar glanced up to see a crow swooping overhead. Opening its wings, the bird slowed its flight, settling on a high branch at the edge of the trees.

"It is waiting for any discarded crumbs," said Arian. Lifting the linen cover from the basket, she took out a slice of apple cake and handed it to Braefar.

"That should be mine," said Govannan, striding across the clearing. "Why are you giving away my food?" He was a tall, wide-shouldered, square-jawed young man with deep-set dark eyes that always looked angry.

"Gwydia has your food," said Arian. "Meria asked me to carry this basket for Connavar and Wing."

"Then my food should have been brought first," said Govannan, snatching the basket from Gwydia. "Men should be fed before children. Is that not so, little Wing?"

Braefar tried a conciliatory smile. Govannan was two years older and considerably larger. He was also notoriously quick-tempered.

"Leave him alone," said Gwydia, making Braefar's heart sink. Why did girls never understand? Govannan *would* have left him alone, but now a female had intervened and he was obliged to continue.

"What have I said?" asked Govannan. "Was it anything but the truth? Look at him. He looks like a girl, and his poor little hand is bleeding."

"Which shows how hard he has worked," said Arian, her pale blue eyes growing angry.

Please be quiet, thought Braefar. You're making everything worse!

"Perhaps I have wronged him," said Govannan. "Perhaps he really is a little girl."

Grabbing Braefar, he hauled him upright. His hands grabbed the waistband of Braefar's leggings and dragged them down. Govannan laughed cruelly. "No, he is not a girl, but he has no man's hair, either." At that moment Govannan was spun around. Conn's fist smashed into his cheekbone. Blood exploded from a cut on the cheekbone. Govannan was hurled from his feet. He rolled on the grass and pushed himself upright, fists clenched.

Then he charged. Conn sidestepped and sent a powerful left cross into his chin. Govannan went down again. He rose more slowly and advanced cautiously. Braefar, full of shame, hauled up his leggings and walked away. Gwydia ran alongside him.

"I apologize for my brother," she said. "He really is an idiot sometimes."

"You caused this, you fool!" stormed Braefar. "Now leave me alone."

Back in the clearing Govannan had been knocked down four times, but still he came back. One eye was swollen almost shut, and his lips were bleeding. So far he had not landed a single blow. Conn hit him again, a straight left that jarred him to his boot heels. He swayed but did not fall. As suddenly as it had come, Conn's anger evaporated. He stepped in, throwing his arms around his opponent. "This is enough, Van," he said. "Give it up."

Govannan butted Conn above the eye. Blood spurted, and he fell back. Govannan hit him with a right, then a left. Conn staggered, then whipped a ferocious uppercut into Govannan's face, followed by a right cross that sent him sprawling again to the grass. His strength all but gone, Govannan forced his arms beneath him and slowly came to his knees. Rising on trembling legs, he tottered forward and tried to throw a punch. As he did so, he fell. Conn caught him and lowered him to the ground. Arian and Gwydia knelt beside him, dabbing at his wounds with linen. Arian flashed an angry look at Conn. "You are a vicious bully," she said.

Anger flared in Conn, but he did not respond. Instead he rose and stalked off into the woods.

Above him glided the black crow.

◇ **4** ◇

CONNAVAR'S MOOD WAS murderous as he walked, pushing aside dangling branches and forcing his way through the undergrowth. It was all Arian's fault! She should not have ignored him. It was discourteous at the very least. That alone had caused his temper to spark. Then, when Govannan had shamed Wing, the spark had hit dry tinder and flared.

Emerging onto a narrow deer trail, Conn strode up the hillside, cutting right by a wall of rock and heading toward the Riguan Falls. A swim, he decided, would cool his temper. Blood dripped into his eye, and he pressed his fingers to the cut on his brow, applying pressure until the bleeding stopped.

Movement caught his eye at the edge of the trees, and he saw a black crow bank and drop toward the ground as if struck by an arrow. Intrigued, he swung to his left and pushed his way through the thinning undergrowth.

An old woman wrapped in an ancient green shawl was sitting in a gray wicker chair. Over her knees was a small fishing net, which she was repairing. Conn looked around for any sign of a house or cabin, but there was nothing. Perhaps she lived in one of the caves, he thought. It was surprising that he had not seen her before.

"Daan's greetings," he said.

She did not look up from her work. "May Taranis never smile upon you," she replied, her voice dry and harsh. It was

67

an odd response, but Conn shared the sentiment. Who would want the god of death to smile upon him?

"May I fetch you water, old one?"

Her head came up, and he found himself looking into the darkest eyes he had ever seen, pupils and iris blending perfectly, her orbs like polished black pebbles. "I need no water, Connavar. But it was kind of you to ask."

"How is it you know me?"

"I know many things. What is it you wish for?"

"I don't understand you."

"Of course you do," she chided him, laying aside the net. "Every man has a secret wish. What is yours?"

He shrugged. "To be happy, perhaps. To have many strong sons and a handful of beautiful daughters. To live to be old and see my sons grow, and their sons."

She laughed scornfully, the sound rasping like a saw through dead wood. "You have picked your wishes from the public barrel. These are not what your heart desires, Sword in the Storm."

"Why have I never seen you before? Where do you live?"

"Close by. And I have seen you, swimming in the lake, leaping from the falls, running through the woods with your half brother. You are full of life, Connavar, and destiny is calling you. How will you respond?"

He stood silently for a moment. "Are you a witch?"

"Not a witch," she said. "*That* I promise you. Tell me what you wish for."

A movement came from behind him, and Conn spun. Standing behind him was the Rigante witch Vorna. Her hands were held before her, crossed as if to ward off a blow. But she was not looking at him. She stood staring at the old woman. "Move back with me, Conn," she said. "Come away from this place. Do not answer her questions."

"Are you frightened to voice your wish, *boy*?" asked the crone, ignoring Vorna.

Conn was indeed frightened, though he did not know why. But when fear touched him, it was always swamped by anger. "I fear nothing," he said.

"Conn! Do not speak," warned Vorna.

"Then tell me!" shrieked the old woman.

"I wish for glory!" he shouted back at her.

A cool wind whispered across the clearing, and a bright light flashed before his eyes. He fell back, blinking.

"And you shall have it," whispered a voice in his mind.

"You should not have spoken," Vorna said sadly.

Conn rubbed at his eyes and looked into the pale face of the witch. Her long white-streaked hair was matted, her cloak stained by mud and frayed by the years. She looked soul-weary. Conn flicked his gaze back to the crone. But she was gone.

There was no wicker chair, only an old decaying tree stump, and no fishing net. But joining the stump to a nearby bush was a huge spider's web, the dew upon it glittering in the sunshine.

Fear of the supernatural brushed over his bones like the breath of winter. "Who was she?" he whispered, backing away from the small clearing.

"It is best we do not speak her name. Come with me, Connavar. We will talk in a place of safety."

Vorna lived in a cave a mile from the falls. It was wide and spacious, with thick rugs on the floor and well-crafted shelves lining the western wall. There was a small cot bed covered with a blanket of sheepskin and two simple chairs fashioned from elm. A spring flowed from the back wall, trickling down into a deep pool, and sunlight shone through three natural windows in the rock, shafts of light piercing the gloom above their heads like rafters made of gold.

Conn was nervous as he followed the witch inside. To his knowledge no Rigante male had ever been inside the home of Vorna the witch. As his eyes grew accustomed to the gloom, he saw that some of the shelves were filled with pots and jars, while others held clothing, carefully folded. The cave was neat and surprisingly free of dust. Against one wall stood a broom, and by the rock pool were two buckets and a mop. Conn looked around him.

Vorna moved to a chair and sat down. "What did you expect?" she asked. "Dried human heads? Bones?"

"I don't know what I expected, save that this is not it," he admitted.

"Sit down, Connavar. We must talk. Are you hungry?"

"No," he said swiftly, unwilling to contemplate what a witch might keep in her food store. He sat down opposite her.

"The woman you saw was a spirit—a Seidh goddess, if you will. Listen to me carefully, and when you guess her identity, do not say it aloud. The name alone is unlucky. As you know, there are three goddesses of death. She was one. Sometimes she is observed as an old woman; at other times a crow is seen close by. In terms of the soul-world and its magic she is the least powerful of the Elder Spirits, but when it comes to the earth-world and the affairs of men, she is the most malignant of beings. I first knew of her interest in you when I saw the crow fly over the home of your father, Varaconn, on the night of your birth. She summoned the storm that night, the storm that destroyed the blade that would have saved Varaconn's life. I saw her again on the day your mother spoke those awful words to Ruathain. You see, Connavar, she is a mischief maker, a breaker of hearts. When she is close, dark deeds are born where before there was only light and laughter. You know her name?"

Conn nodded. All Rigante children were taught of the Morrigu, the bringer of nightmares.

"How can you be sure it was her?" he asked.

She sighed and leaned back in her chair. "I am a witch. It is my talent to know these things. You should not have spoken of your deepest desire to her. She has the power to grant it."

"Why would that be so terrible?"

"A long time ago a woman prayed to her, asking to be loved by the most handsome man in the world—a rich man, kind and loving. The wish was granted. He loved her. But he was already wed, and the bride's brothers rode to her cabin and cut her into pieces, the man with her. Now do you understand?"

"I asked for glory. There is no price I would not pay for it."

Anger showed briefly in Vorna's thin face. "Can you be so stupid, Connavar? Of what worth is glory? Does it feed a family? Does it bring peace of mind? Fame is fleeting. It is a harlot who moves from one young man to the next. Tell me of Calavanus."

"He was a great hero in my grandfather's day," said Conn. "A mighty swordsman. He led the Rigante against the Sea Wolves. He killed their king in single combat. He had a sword that blazed like fire. He knew glory."

"Yes, he did," she snapped. "Then he got old and frail. He sold his sword to a merchant in order to buy food. His wife left him; his sons deserted him. When last I saw him, he was weeping in his cabin and still talking of the days of glory."

Conn shook his head. "I will not be like him *or* like Varaconn. My enemies will not see my back, and men will not spit on my name. Banouin has promised me a sword of iron. I will carry it into battle. It is my destiny."

"I know something of your destiny, Connavar. Only a little, but enough to warn you. You must seek a higher purpose than mere glory. If not, you will merely be another swordsman like Calavanus."

"Perhaps that will be enough for me," he said stubbornly.

"It will not be enough for your people."

"My people?" he asked, confused now.

She fell silent for a while, rising from her chair and moving to a stone hearth. The light from the windows was fading, and she laid a fire but did not light it. "Last year," she said, "a starving pack of wolves attacked a lioness with five cubs. She fought them with great ferocity, leading them away from her young. She was willing to die to save her cubs. But she did not die, though she was sorely wounded. She killed seven of the wolves. But four others had moved around behind her. When she limped back to her cave, her cubs were dead and devoured. It could be argued that she earned great glory. But what was it worth? Her injuries meant there would be no more cubs. She was the last of her line, a line that stretched back to the first dawn. You think she cared that she had killed seven wolves, that her courage shone like a beacon?"

Vorna gestured with her right hand. The fire burst into life, causing dancing shadows to flicker across the far wall. With a sigh she pushed herself to her feet and walked to the western wall. Taking a small box from the first shelf, she opened it and lifted clear a slender chain of gold from which hung a small red opal. "Come close to me," she ordered him. Conn did so. He could smell wood smoke in her faded clothing, mixed with the sweet scents of lavender and lemon mint. In that moment his fear of her drifted away, and he felt with sudden certainty that Vorna was not merely the witch everyone feared. She was also a lonely, aging woman, unfulfilled and far from happy.

He looked into her bright blue eyes. "I thank you for helping me," he said.

She nodded and stared into his face. "I do not need your pity, child," she said softly, "but I welcome the kindness from which it sprang." She fastened the golden chain around his neck. "This talisman will protect you from her. But nothing I can do will prevent her manipulation of those around you. Show me the knife, Connavar."

He winced inwardly. She had not said "your" knife, but "the" knife. Did she know?

Slowly he drew the silver blade from the sheath he had made. She took it in her thin fingers. "You were born with luck," she said. "Had you not rescued that fawn, you would have died in those woods, your blood drawn from your veins. Did you guess that the creature was a Seidh?"

"No."

"No," she echoed. "They would have known. Your thoughts would have been loud to them, like the music of the pipes. They are a fey people. They kill without mercy, sometimes with terrible tortures. Yet they can allow a stupid child to live because he saves a fawn. And even reward him." With a sigh she returned his knife. "Go home, Connavar, and think on what I have said."

Everyone said that Riamfada was a happy youth, always smiling despite his disability. Women prized the brooches and bangles he created, and men marveled at the sword hilts and belt buckles cast from bronze or sometimes silver. His father, Gariapha the Metal Worker, was proud of the boy and praised him constantly. That said much for Gariapha, for not many men, seeing their sons outshine them, would have been so generous of spirit.

When Riamfada was seventeen years of age, his talents had made his family almost wealthy. Banouin the Foreigner had taken his work and sold it across the water for what seemed to Riamfada fabulous prices. It was those profits which enabled him now to begin working in small amounts of gold.

The boy had been born in the Year of the Crippling, when two in three Rigante babes had entered the world paralyzed or stillborn. As was the custom, the disabled babes were laid on a hillside to die in the night. Alone among the deformed and crippled Riamfada had not died.

His mother, Wiocca, had gone to him at dawn, cuddled him close, and held him to her breast, allowing him to suckle. Everyone thought she had lost her mind. She ignored them. The full council debated her actions and called on Gariapha to give evidence. The balding, round-shouldered metal crafter stood before them and defended his wife's right to nurse her son. "He was placed in the hands of the gods," he said. "They did not take his life. Now his life is hers."

"How can he ever contribute to the Rigante?" asked the Long Laird.

"In the same way that I do," said Gariapha. "I do not need the use of legs to create brooches."

At the request of the council the Long Laird sought out Vorna and asked for a prophecy. She refused to give one. "You may call upon me only when the people are threatened," she said. "This babe threatens no one."

The council debated long into the night. Never before had such a seriously crippled child been allowed to survive, and there was no precedent to call upon. Finally, as Riamfada's second dawn approached, they made their judgment—by a vote of eleven to ten—in favor of Wiocca's right to raise her son.

By the age of six Riamfada had shown great skills in the crafting of wax and the preparation of casting shells. He had a good eye, nimble fingers, and a creative talent his father could only envy. By the time he was ten he was designing complicated patterns and knots, creating brooches of exquisite beauty. Every day Gariapha would carry him to his workshop and set him down in a high-backed chair. A woolen blanket would be placed over his stunted, useless legs, and a long belt would be wrapped around his frail, emaciated body, holding him in place. Then he would lean forward and begin his work.

And as everyone observed, Riamfada was always happy.

It was not true, of course. He seldom knew real joy, not even when he created delicate pieces that brought gasps of admiration from those who saw them. Riamfada was never truly content with any of his designs; that in part was the source of his genius.

But had people asked him what was his first great moment

of joy, he would have told them of the day, one year earlier, when he had run in the hills and learned to swim in the pond below the Riguan Falls.

He had been working at his bench when a shadow had fallen across him. He had turned to the window to see a wide-shouldered boy with strange eyes, one green and one gold.

"I am Connavar," he said. Riamfada knew who he was. On warm days Gariapha would carry him out onto the open ground beyond the workshop, and there father and son would eat their meals in the sunshine. Often Riamfada would see the village boys running and playing. None ever approached him.

"I am Riamfada. What do you want?"

"I was curious to see you," said Connavar. "Everyone talks about you."

"Well, you have seen me," said Riamfada, returning to his work by dipping his brush into the mixture and applying it to the crafted wax.

"What are you doing?"

"I am painting a mixture of cow dung and clay on the wax."

"Why?"

"So I can gradually build up a shell around the wax. When it is thick enough, I shall fire it. Then the wax will melt away, and I will have a mold into which I can pour bronze or silver."

"I see. It must take a long time."

"I have the time."

Connavar stood silently for a moment. "I am going to the waterfall," he said. "To swim."

"Good. I hope you enjoy yourself."

"Would you like to come?"

Riamfada forced a bright smile. "That would be pleasant. You go ahead. I will finish this and then run along and join you."

"You cannot run," said Connavar, ignoring the sarcasm. "But why should you not swim? It is only a matter of floating and moving your arms. And I am strong. I could carry you to the falls."

"Why? Why would you do this for me?"

"Why should I not?" countered Connavar.

"You do not know me. We are not friends."

"That is true, but how does one get to know anyone save by talking to them? Come with me. Learn to swim."

"I don't think so."

"It is very beautiful there, the sunshine sparkling on the water, the silver-backed fish, the willows. Are you afraid?"

"Yes," admitted Riamfada.

"What of?"

"I am afraid that I will enjoy it. That I will happy there."

"Afraid of being happy?" said Connavar, surprised.

"Go away. Leave me alone," said Riamfada.

But Connavar did not leave. He stood silently for a moment. "I understand," he said. "You think I might tire of your company and never carry you there again."

Now it was Riamfada who was surprised. "That is very perceptive."

Gariapha, who had been listening in the background, came forward. "You should say yes, my son. He is right. It is very beautiful there."

Riamfada said nothing and returned to his painting. Gariapha moved to his son's side, putting his hand on the youth's shoulder. "Listen to me, lad. I was already getting old when you were born. I never had the strength to carry you into the hills, though I wish I had tried. Go with him. For me."

The anguished boy stared at Connavar. "How old are you?" he asked suddenly.

"Almost sixteen," answered Connavar.

"Then why now? Where have you been these last sixteen years? Did you not know I was here?"

"I knew. But to be honest, I never really thought about you. I am sorry for that. Then, last week, I went to the falls with my brother Braefar. We were talking, and he mentioned you. He said it was a great pity that you could not walk and wondered if you might be able to swim. I have been thinking about it for the last few days. It might be worth trying."

"If your brother thought of it, then why is he not here?"

Connavar grinned. "My brother is the thinker in the family. Lots of good ideas. Easier ways to clean the house or catch rabbits or gentle horses. However, his ideas are always for other people to implement. He's usually too busy thinking up new ideas. Now, do you want to come?"

"Yes," said Riamfada. "I do. But there are . . . things you need to know. Firstly, I have no control over my bowels or bladder. I wear cloth padding, but it leaks sometimes." He knew he was blushing as he spoke, but better, he thought, to say it now than to have the shame later.

"Do not concern yourself," said Connavar. "I promise you it does not concern me. Now, I have food and drink in my sack, and I am strong as an ox. We should go now. The sun is high and hot, the water cool."

He had not lied when he had said he was strong as an ox. He carried Riamfada on his shoulders for two miles before cresting the last hill before the falls. Then, on a stretch of flat ground, he began to run. It was exhilarating for the young metal crafter to be moving at speed for the first time in his life, to be high, taller than the tallest man.

Connavar slowed as they reached the downward slope, then carefully picked his way down toward the falls pool. It was the most beautiful sight Riamfada had ever seen, hundreds of feet of clear blue water, foaming white beneath the waterfall. On the far side willows hung their branches into the pool, and brightly colored birds were flying overhead. Connavar lifted him down, sitting him on the grass with his back to a tree trunk. Then the younger boy stripped off his shirt and boots and leggings. Riamfada saw that the back of his green shirt was drenched with urine. "Don't worry," Connavar said with a grin. "We'll wash it in the pool. Now let's get those clothes off you."

For the next two hours Riamfada knew the flowering of an immense joy. At first he was terrified the water would close over him, but Connavar held him, telling him to breathe deeply. "The air in your lungs will keep you afloat," he promised. "When you need to breathe out, do it slowly and evenly, then breathe in swiftly."

At the end of the two hours Riamfada was exhausted but almost deliriously happy. He had for five strokes moved himself through the water. Under his own power he had propelled himself forward, Connavar swimming alongside.

His new friend carried him from the pool, and the two youngsters sat in the fading sunshine, allowing the warm air to dry their skin.

"This has been the greatest day of my life," said Riamfada. "And I was wrong. Even if I never come here again, I will always treasure it."

"You will come again," promised Connavar. "Not tomorrow, for I have many chores. But the day after, if the weather is fine, I shall call for you."

"I do not care about the weather," said Riamfada.

"Very well, then, whatever the weather."

They arrived at Riamfada's house just before dusk. Both Gariapha and Wiocca were waiting in the doorway, their expressions full of worry. But they smiled when they saw the happiness on their son's face.

"I swam," he told his father. "Truly. Didn't I, Conn?"

"You certainly did," agreed his friend.

Through the weeks that followed Riamfada's swimming grew stronger and stronger. Once carried into the water, he would roll to his back and power himself out into the center of the pond. The tight and aching muscles of his upper back were eased by the exercise, and as his strength grew, so, too, did his appetite, and he began to put on weight.

"It's like carrying a small horse," Connavar said one day as they neared the last crest.

Riamfada was about to reply when he looked down and saw that other youngsters were already in the pool. His heart sank. "Take me back!" he said.

"Why?"

"I don't want anyone else to see me."

Connavar lifted him to the grass, then sat beside him. "You are my friend, and you are as brave as anyone I know. If you want to go home, I shall take you. But think on it for a moment."

"You cannot know what it is like," said Riamfada, "to be less than a man. The shame of it."

"You are right, my friend, I do not know. But I know that we both like to swim, and there is plenty of room in the pool."

Riamfada sighed. "You think me cowardly?"

"I think it is up to you," Conn said, with a smile. "I make no judgment."

Riamfada looked into his friend's face. Conn was not telling the truth. He would be disappointed if forced to go all the way back. Riamfada sighed. What was one more embarrassment in a life of shame? "Let us go down and swim," he said.

Connavar lifted him. He did not place him on his shoulders but carried him in his arms. As they neared the pool, one of the young men there climbed from the water and strode out to meet them. He was tall, with deep-set dark eyes.

Riamfada felt Conn tense at his approach. "Who is he?" he whispered.

"Govannan, the smith's son."

The other youths also moved from the pool. Govannan halted before the pair.

"You must be Riamfada," he said. "I am Govannan. My friends call me Van." He held out his hand. Riamfada shook it. One by one the smith's son introduced the others. Then he shivered. "It is cold once you are out of the water. We'll talk again in the pool." Turning, Govannan ran down to the water's edge and dived in. His friends followed him, and they swam to the falls, clambering out to run up the rocky path and jump back into the pool from a jutting boulder.

"They made me welcome," said Riamfada.

"Why would they not?"

"I noticed he did not speak to you."

"We are not friends. Now come, let us swim. I do not have too long today. I am meeting Wing for a hunt. Mother says she will need meat for at least six game pies in time for Samain."

"I do not eat meat," Riamfada said, as Conn set him down.

Conn stared at him. "Meat makes you strong—especially beef."

"Perhaps. But a creature must die first, frightened and in pain."

Conn laughed, but it was not a scornful sound. "You are a strange one, my friend. You should have been a Druid. They, too, eat only vegetables, I'm told. It's why they are all so scrawny."

Braefar was growing irritated. The light would soon be gone, and he hated to hunt alone, fearing that wolves or lions would spring from the undergrowth at him. Then he saw Conn running up from the settlement.

"What took you so long?" he asked.

Conn grinned at him. "Eager for the kill, little Wing?"

"Mother says she wants at least a dozen pigeons and as many rabbits as we can find."

Conn crouched down and patted the black hound Caval. She lifted her muzzle into his hand, then licked his face. "You want the bow or the sling?" Conn asked Braefar.

"I have no preference. I'm better than you with both."

"You are getting cocky, my brother. It is good to see. I'll take the bow. Caval and I will scare up some rabbits."

By the time the light had faded and they were heading

home, the two boys had killed three rabbits and five wood pigeons. It was not as many as Braefar had hoped, but Meria would be pleased.

On their way back across the first of the bridges they heard a peal of laughter coming from behind a barn. Braefar tensed. The sound was infectious, and he knew the source. It was Arian, and Braefar understood her well enough to know that she was not alone. Worse, she was with a man. That throaty laugh was reserved for would-be suitors. "We should be getting back," he said. Conn handed him the rabbits and strode toward the barn. Braefar followed glumly.

The moon was out, and by her light Braefar saw the youth Casta standing with Arian. He was leaning against the barn, his hand resting on the wood just above Arian's shoulder. They were talking in low tones.

"What are you doing with my woman?" asked Conn.

Surprised, Casta jumped. Two years older than Conn, he was a powerfully built young man. "What do you mean, 'your woman'?" he countered. "Arian is not pledged to anyone."

"She knows I am to ask for her hand at Samain," said Conn.

"I didn't say I'd give it to you," said Arian, her voice more shrill than she intended.

"There you have it," put in Casta. "So why don't you leave us alone."

Braefar winced. Then he cast a glance at Arian. Her eyes were bright, and in that moment he knew she was excited by the thought of two men fighting for her. It sickened the youngster. "Don't fight him, Conn," he said softly.

"What?"

"It's what she wants. Look at her."

"Stay out of this, Wing. It is none of your business." Conn advanced on the older youth.

"You have me at a disadvantage," Casta said smoothly. "I work for your father, and if I give you the thrashing your boorish behavior calls for, he'll send me away."

"Even if that unlikely event were to take place," said Conn, "he won't know of it."

"Glad to hear it," said Casta, sending a thunderous left straight into Conn's face. Conn staggered. Casta followed up with a right cross that slashed through the air as Conn ducked. The younger man hammered an uppercut into Casta's belly, then a left hook that exploded against his jaw. Casta fell back, then charged. Conn dropped to his knees, then surged upright, hurling Casta from his feet. The older man landed hard but rolled to his knees. Conn stepped in and caught him with a right as he was rising. Casta went down again. He rose slowly, lost his footing, and fell back into the wall of the barn. Arian spun on her heel and walked away. Conn followed her.

Hampered by the game he was carrying, Braefar struggled to help Casta to his feet.

"I was just talking to her," mumbled Casta. "She invited me back here. Now I've a sore head, and I've made an enemy of the lord's son."

"You've made no enemy," Braefar assured him. "Conn doesn't know how to hold a grudge. Anyway, you got the best of it."

Casta gave a rueful smile. "I'll take some convincing of that."

"He ended up with Arian. Believe me, she's trouble."

"Aye, but she's worth it," said Casta. "I'd risk far more than a beating for one kiss."

"I think the blows have addled your wits," Braefar told him. "No man who weds her will ever be sure he is the father of her children." But he could see he was making no impression on Casta.

It was after midnight when Conn made his silent way to their bedroom. Braefar awoke as a bed board creaked. "I take it all is now well between the two of you?" he asked the darkness.

"All is well, little brother," came Conn's voice.

"You still intend to wed her?"

"Of course. Why would I not?"

"She is a flirt. Why can't you see that? And I don't believe she cares for you."

Braefar read the anger in the silence and decided to say no more.

Conn lay awake, his mind in turmoil. The events of the evening had more than unsettled him. Not so much the fight, which, truth to tell, he had enjoyed, but rather the strange, fey mood that had come upon Arian as they had walked into the woods. At first she maintained an angry silence, but then, as they came to the stream she began to tremble. He asked her if she was cold and put his arm around her. Her reaction astonished and delighted him. Throwing her arms around his neck, she kissed him with such passion that it took his breath away.

Conn had dreamed of this moment, especially since the night with Eriatha, but he had been more than willing to wait for the Feast of Samain and the marriage walk around Eldest Tree. What they were about to do was against the law of the Rigante and risked the severest punishment, at worst flogging and banishment for both. Even knowing this, Conn could not restrain himself, and within moments both were naked, lying on a blanket of their clothes. He tried to use the skills Eriatha had taught him, but Arian pulled at him, drawing him over her, into her. Her movements were fast and frantic. Conn gazed down into her face. Her eyes were wide and unfocused, her teeth bared as she powered her body against his. Her nails raked his back, and she was moaning softly.

With Eriatha the lovemaking had been very good and wonderfully satisfying, but here, with the great love of his young life, Conn felt himself reaching new heights of ecstasy. She shuddered beneath him and cried out again and again. As he had been taught, Conn held back, his movements slow and rhythmic. Her blue eyes were focused now, the pupils huge. Conn kissed her gently, then slowly increased the pace of his movements. Within minutes she shuddered and cried out again, her body arcing up against him. Conn did not stop but finally allowed himself to finish. It seemed to him that his soul rushed into her with his seed, merging with her spirit. In that moment she whispered in his ear: "I love you." It was the sweetest sound he had ever heard. His heart swelled, and his vision misted. Unable to speak, he kissed her again, then rolled to his side, drawing her into his embrace. Her golden head lay on his shoulder, and he stroked the skin of her hip.

"I am yours," he said, "now and always."

"I will never be frightened again," she told him. The words jarred, and he did not understand them, though he heard the relief in her voice and did not question her further.

Now, as he lay in his bed, he could not tear his mind from Braefar's words.

"She is a flirt. Why can't you see that?"

Of course he could see it and could remember vividly the sound of her laughter as she stood in the dark with Casta. That alone would not have been enough to trouble him, but there was also the unfocused passion. He had not sensed it at the time, his blood roaring and his senses aroused, but looking back, he felt that Arian had not even known who he was before her first orgasm. Only afterward had she responded.

Pushing away his doubts, he concentrated on the one great truth of the night. She had told him she loved him.

And within a few days she would be his wife, the mother of his children, the one eternal love of his heart.

The following morning was bright, clear, and cold. On the high hill to the north of the settlement Ruathain drew on the reins and stared gloomily down over the meadows where his herds were grazing. Six hundred long-haired, sharp-horned highland cattle were gathered there. A cold wind blew down from the north. Ruathain shivered, for he had left his cloak at home and wore only a blue tunic shirt and thin leggings. He glanced at the northern sky. It was gray and forbidding, heralding what he feared would be a hard, bitter winter.

The Feast of Samain was twelve days away. Touching heels to his pony, he rode slowly through the herd, occasionally leaning over to smear blue ocher on the backs of selected cows and bullocks. The eight-day feast was always a time of great joy for the peoples of the Rigante. This year it was to be held in Three Streams, and tribesmen would travel from all over the land to the settlement. Hundreds of tents would be pitched, and by the last day more than nine thousand tribesmen would be gathered there.

But Ruathain's thoughts were not of feasting and dancing. He was a cattle breeder, and the winter was a time not only of danger, hardship, and struggle but also of loss. Only the hardiest of the breeding stock would survive. Vicious cold would kill some; falls and snapped legs would destroy others. Added to this the wolves would come, and the great cats, and even—occasionally—bears roused from their hibernation.

Choosing which stock should be given the chance to survive was always hard, as was slaughtering the less fortunate to feed the feasters. Dipping his hand into the bucket slung from his saddle horn, he rode alongside Bannioa. He had hand reared her as a calf when her mother had been killed by a lioness, and she had proved a good breeder. But she was eight years old now and had been barren for two years. Leaning over, he smeared the ocher on her broad back.

Beyond her was the old bull Mentha. Would he survive the coming cold, the wolves, and the lions? And if he did, would he still be able to subdue the younger bulls come spring and sire fine sons from his herd?

Ruathain's chief herdsman, Arbonacast, rode alongside him. He said nothing, sitting silently alongside his lord. "Well?" Ruathain asked, as the silence grew.

Arbonacast saw that his lord was staring at Mentha. The herdsman shrugged. "I'd give him the chance."

"Give him the chance? Is that sentiment?" asked Ruathain.

"Partly. But he is a fine bull. And insatiable." On the hillside below, as if sensing they were talking about him, old Mentha's massive head came up. His long horns, wickedly curved at the tips and stretching for almost seven feet, glinted in the sunlight.

Ruathain sighed. "He can't last forever, Arbon."

"Nothing does," said the herdsman.

Ruathain glanced at the man. Arbonacast was short and slightly built with black hair peppered with silver and bristling black brows over deep-set gray eyes. His face was a sea of fine lines, a map charting fifty years of hardship and struggle. It was a strong face, hard and lean, and Ruathain trusted him as he did no other man.

"One more winter, then. But if he survives and still loses his herd to a younger bull, it is the feasting pit for him."

"Bad winter coming, I think," said Arbon, swinging his horse and riding out over the hillside.

Ruathain turned for home. Of course it would be a bad winter. Just as it had been a bad spring, summer, and autumn. There were no good times without Meria. He still saw her daily, watched her walking to the stream or sitting in the sunshine. But he had not had a conversation with her in three years. Ruathain ensured that food was delivered to his old home, and coin when he had it. And he spoke often with his sons. Yet most nights he would dream of her. They were together again, and he was lying beside her in a sunlit meadow, stroking her hair and gazing into her green eyes. Then he would wake and groan as reality struck home like a cold knife to his heart.

He spoke to no one of his anguish and tried to conduct his life as he always had.

Without the joy it was not possible, and almost everyone in Three Streams became aware very swiftly that Ruathain was not the man he had been. Gone was the bluff good humor and the easygoing charm. In the old Ruathain's place was a restless man, short-tempered and hostile.

In the spring he and five other men had ridden out to intercept some Norvii cattle raiders. In the short fight that had followed Ruathain had killed two. It was unusual for men to die in such raids. Prisoners were often taken and held for small ransoms, but on those rare occasions when men died it was usually accidental, a clumsy fall from a horse or a rider caught in a stampede. On this day Ruathain had charged in among the Norvii, his iron sword singing out. Two men had gone down instantly, the others throwing down their weapons.

Ruathain had ridden toward the prisoners, his eyes bright with battle fury. Arbonacast had cut his pony across his lord's path. "It is over now, I think," he had said. For a moment the Rigante riders had thought he would strike his own man, but Ruathain had dragged on his reins and ridden back to Three Streams.

Although he did not speak of it, he thought of the two dead men often. Both had been young and on their first raid. An initiation into manhood. Neither had expected to die. Ruathain felt great guilt over the slayings. He could have—should have—unhorsed them with the flat of his blade. He was thinking of them now as he rode down to his house. Unsaddling the pony, he turned it out into the paddock.

As he did so, he heard the sound of hoofbeats and swung to see a rider galloping across the eastern bridge. It was another of his herdsmen, Arbon's son, Casta, who should have been gathering stock in the southern hills. The young man dragged on his reins.

"What is it, boy?" asked Ruathain.

"Rogue bear, lord. It attacked three children outside a Norvii settlement. Killed two, made off with the third. They hunted it and claim to have wounded it. But it was last seen heading west through the woods."

"They drove it into our lands and didn't have the guts to follow it."

"It seems so, lord. They say it is big—the largest bear they have ever seen."

"Where did they corner it?"

"Six miles east of the Riguan Falls."

Fear touched Ruathain. His boys had gone swimming at the falls.

"Gather the men," he told Casta. "Bring lances and ropes." Running into the house, he buckled on his iron sword and lifted his hunting lance.

◇ 5 ◇

DESPITE THE COLD, Riamfada had no wish to leave the water. He knew this was the last day he would swim that year, for winter was approaching fast and there had already been flurries of snow in the hills. He floated on his back, then rolled and watched the late-afternoon sunlight sparkling on the waterfall. A rainbow flared into life to the right of the falls. Riamfada stared at it, lost in wonder. Then a wispy cloud drifted past the sun, and the rainbow faded. If only I could work with such colors, he thought. High above him he heard Govannan call out. Glancing up, he saw the smith's son leap from the ledge and spin into a dive. Govannan surfaced, flicked the water from his long hair, and swam over to him.

"Had enough, little fish?" he asked.

"Just a little more," said Riamfada.

"Your lips are turning blue. I think it's time you got dry." Treading water, Govannan glanced at the bank, where Connavar and Braefar had lit a small fire. Three other youngsters were sitting huddled around the flames. Riamfada had been disappointed to find Galanis and his brothers at the falls. They always stared at him, and invariably the conversation would turn to his crippled legs. They were recent arrivals at the settlement, their father having come up from the south to work for Ruathain.

Reluctantly Riamfada struck for the shore, Govannan swimming alongside him. When they reached the bank, the smith's son lifted Riamfada clear, carrying him to the fire. Conn dried his legs, then wrapped a warm cloak around him. "Going to be a cold winter," he said.

"It will be a long one," Riamfada said sadly.

Govannan toweled himself down then dressed and walked to the shoreline, where he began skimming stones across the water. Connavar wandered down and also hefted a handful of stones. Immediately a contest began to see who could skim the farthest.

Braefar sat alongside Riamfada. "They are at it again," he said. "Everything is a competition with those two." Riamfada shivered. Braefar helped him into his clothes and added more fuel to the fire.

"Perhaps a spell was cast on you," said Galanis. He was a tall, rangy, red-haired youth with a pockmarked sallow face.

"A spell? What do you mean?" replied Riamfada, his heart sinking.

"My brothers and I were wondering if the Seidh put a curse on your legs."

The other two young men, Baris and Gethenan, were also staring at him now.

"I don't think anyone cursed me," he said. "The year I was born there were many children afflicted. They all died. Vorna says it was a sickness that attacked the mothers."

"I'd sooner be dead than a cripple," said Baris.

"Oh, shut up, Baris," snapped Braefar. "What a stupid thing to say."

"Well, it's true," said Baris, reddening.

"It is probably true for you," said Riamfada. "But then, you have enjoyed a life of walking and running. For you the loss of your legs would be terrible. But I have never had the use of my legs, so I have grown accustomed to my condition."

"What is the surprise you promised us?" asked Braefar, anxious to change the subject. Riamfada smiled, and called out to Conn and Govannan. The two young men wandered back from their skimming contest.

"I had a seven," said Van. "Beat him by two."

"You found the best stone," grumbled Connavar.

Once they were seated, Riamfada untied his belt pouch and laid it in his lap. "I have some presents for the three of you," he said. "You have been very kind to me, and I wanted to repay you. I hope you won't be offended." Unfastening the string loop, he pulled open the pouch. From it he drew a cloak brooch of gleaming bronze, which he passed to Govannan. It was in the shape of a leaping deer and engraved with swirls of silver. "It is a wondrous piece," said Van. "I have never seen anything so beautiful." From the pouch Riamfada took a second brooch. It was a copy of a wicker shield, cunningly crafted from intertwined wires of silver. Braefar turned it over in his hands. Lastly Riamfada handed Conn a brooch: a bronze fawn trapped in silver brambles, encased in a band of bright gold.

"I do not know what to say," said Conn.

"Then let me speak for you, Brother," said Braefar. "We thank you, little fish. These are very fine gifts."

"Nothing for us then?" put in Galanis. "I didn't realize carrying cripples reaped such fine rewards."

"Watch your mouth!" stormed Govannan, "or you'll be wearing your teeth as a necklace."

"Where we come from blunt speech is considered a virtue," replied Galanis.

"There is a difference between blunt speech and rudeness," said Braefar. "You had best learn that if you wish to be accepted among us. For example, I do not recall any of us pointing out that you are the ugliest trio we have ever seen. Your face, Galanis, looks like a woodpecker tried to nest in it. Still, I expect that back where you came from that would be considered blunt speaking."

The three brothers rose from the fire and stalked off toward the settlement. An awkward silence followed. Riamfada looked downcast. Conn leaned forward and placed his hand on the young man's shoulder. "I thank you, Riamfada," he said softly. "But there was no need to reward us. You are our friend, and we enjoy your company."

"It was not a reward," objected Riamfada. "I just wanted to find a way to show how much I appreciated your friendship. All of you. You have given me great joy. More than you can ever know. You like my gifts?"

"No one ever gave me a finer present," said Govannan. "I will treasure it, little fish."

They sat together for a while longer, but as the sun began to fall, Govannan put out the fire and Connavar lifted Riamfada to his shoulders for the long walk home.

As they walked, they heard a distant scream. "What was that?" whispered Braefar. The sound hung in the air. They walked up the hillside, emerging from the trees onto open ground. A body lay on the grass, its belly ripped open, its face gone. Patches of blood stained the grass like a stand of poppies. Connavar laid Riamfada on the grass and drew his silver knife. From the clothes the corpse wore, they knew it was Galanis.

"Bear," whispered Govannan. "And a big one." He, too, unsheathed his blade. Braefar, who had no weapon, stood petrified, staring at the mutilated corpse. "The others must have run off. Climbed a tree or something," continued Govannan.

Riamfada sat on the grass, scanning the tree line. Another scream sounded from deep in the trees. It was cut off abruptly. A breeze was blowing from the woods. "It will not be able to scent us," whispered Connavar. "Let's move!" Sheathing his knife, he lifted Riamfada, and the three young men set off across the hills. The land was open there, with no ground cover and no trees in which to hide. Held in Connavar's arms, Riamfada stared back at the tree line, praying that the bear would not emerge.

He heard Govannan swear. "The wind is changing," he said.

Almost as soon as Govannan spoke, Riamfada saw a huge form burst from the trees a hundred paces behind them. Time froze in that moment. The beast moved to the body of Galanis. Its great jaws opened, closing on the corpse. Then, with a flick of its head, it tossed the body high into the air. The bear reared up, catching the corpse as it fell and ripping at it with its talons. "Please do not let it see us," Riamfada prayed softly.

The great head swung. Dropping the body, the beast turned toward the fleeing youths. "It's coming," screamed Riamfada. Conn glanced back then began to run. Riamfada soon realized that there was no way, burdened as he was, Conn could outrun the beast. "Put me down!" he shouted. "Save yourself!"

Conn ran on, then glanced back once more. The bear was no more than thirty paces behind them. Slowing to a halt, he laid Riamfada on the grass, drew his knife, and swung to face the charging beast. "Oh, please run!" Riamfada begged him.

"I'll cut its bastard heart out," hissed Conn.

The bear came on and reared up in front of the defiant youth. Riamfada could not tear his eyes from the beast. Over eight feet high, its black muzzle and chest fur drenched in blood, it spread its paws and lumbered forward. Conn did not wait for it but hurled himself at the colossus, plunging his blade deep into the bear's chest. Talons ripped across his back, sending a spray of blood that splashed across Riamfada's face. Connavar was hurled clear of the beast, but it turned on him again. A shadow fell across Riamfada as Govannan ran in, leaping to the bear's back and slamming his knife into the creature's neck. The bear reared and twisted. Govannan was thrown to the ground, his knife still embedded in the bear's flesh. Bleeding badly, Conn pushed himself to his feet and attacked again. Talons tore into his shoulder, but the silver knife swept up, then down, slicing through fur and bone and flesh. The bear dropped to all fours, pinning Conn beneath it. Govannan, hefting a large rock, ran at the bear, smashing the stone down upon its head. The creature swung, its snapping jaws just missing the youth. It reared high, talons slashing out. Beneath it the blood-covered Connavar surged to his knees and drove his knife two-handed into the bear's belly. A huge paw thundered against his shoulder, and Riamfada heard the sound of splintering bones. Connavar was hurled across the grass, limp and boneless as a rag doll.

Then came the sound of galloping horses. A pony leapt over Riamfada, the rider leaning down to ram a long lance through the bear's chest. The bear lashed out, talons ripping through the pony's neck. The rider was thrown clear. Rolling to his feet, he drew a longsword of iron. The beast turned toward him. A rope sailed over the bear's head, drawing tight and dragging it back. The swordsman ran in, plunging his blade deep into the bear's stomach. More horsemen galloped in. Some threw rope loops over the beast, and others stabbed lances into the wounded creature. And all the while the swordsman hacked at it with his iron blade. It seemed to Riamfada that the bear would never die. It killed a second pony but then became completely entangled in the ropes. The swordsman delivered three terrible blows to the back of its neck, and it collapsed to the ground. The riders dismounted, plunging their lances again and again into the massive form.

"Look to Conn!" shouted Riamfada. "Please help him!"

The swordsman dropped his blade and ran to the fallen youngster. Riamfada tried to crawl over to him. Govannan lifted him, holding him close. "You don't want to see him," he said sadly. "He's dead."

"No. No, he can't be."

"If not, he will be soon. No one could lose that much blood and live."

Govannan set Riamfada down on the grass, then ran over to where the men had gathered around the still form of Connavar. Riamfada could see them battling to staunch the wounds. A little way to the right Riamfada caught sight of Braefar. The boy was kneeling on the grass and sobbing. He wanted to call out to him, to comfort him, but he felt powerless to make a noise within that grim tableau. A few feet away the colossal bear, still entangled in ropes, lay dead alongside the two ponies he had killed. Several of the men moved to their mounts and rode back up the hillside. Riamfada wondered where they were going. Then he remembered the dead Galanis and his missing brothers. He began to tremble.

A woman with white-streaked black hair came walking from the woods. She was carrying a long staff. The remaining men backed away from her, and Riamfada saw her kneel beside Connavar. Her skinny arm came up, and it was obvious she was directing the men. Three of them lifted the wounded youngster. The woman strode back into the woods, the men following. Govannan walked back to where Riamfada sat.

"He is alive. Barely," said the smith's son.

"Who was the woman?"

"Vorna the witch. He is being carried to her cave."

"You should speak to Braefar," said Riamfada.

Govannan took a deep breath. "What would I say?" he countered. They sat together for more than an hour. It was growing dark and cold as the men returned from Vorna's cave. The other riders had found the bodies of Galanis and his brothers, and, wrapped in cloaks, they were taken back to the settlement.

Ruathain emerged from the woods and walked across to where the two youngsters waited. Govannan rose and stood silently as Ruathain approached.

"What happened here?" asked the swordsman.

"It was my fault," said Riamfada.

The swordsman knelt before the crippled youth. "How so?" he asked.

"Conn could not outrun the beast while carrying me, and

he refused to leave me. He stood with his knife and then attacked the bear. Govannan helped him." Tears fell to his
cheeks. "I urged him to leave me and run. He is my friend,
and I didn't want him hurt."

"He is my son," said Ruathain, his voice choked with emotion. "He would not leave a friend in peril. Govannan helped
him, you say?"

"Yes, sir. Conn faced it, then Govannan leapt to its back
and stabbed it."

The swordsman rose and turned to the smith's son. "There
was no great affection between you two," he said. "And yet
you risked your life for him. I will not forget that. I have had
trouble with your father, but you have my friendship for as
long as I live."

"My father is a good man, sir," said Govannan. "But like
me, his mouth sometimes hits the gallop before his brain is in
the saddle. How is Conn?"

"He is dying," said Ruathain, struggling to control his
emotions. "His shoulder and left arm are smashed beyond repair, and his lung is punctured. The witch says she will use all
her power to save him. But we had to leave him with her. She
refused my request to stay at his side. Said my presence
would disturb the spells she must cast."

"I am truly sorry, sir," said Govannan.

The swordsman nodded. When he spoke, his voice was
close to breaking. "You should feel proud, boy. Today you
stood beside my son and faced a terrible enemy. Believe me,
that will have changed you. You are no longer merely the
smith's eldest son. You are a man in your own right. And more
than that, you are a hero." He took a deep breath, then
dropped to one knee in front of Riamfada. "Do not blame
yourself. Even without you these lads could not have outrun
the bear. Heroes come in many forms. Not all of them are
fighters. When you asked Conn to leave you and save himself, you were prepared to sacrifice your life for his. You

understand? You, too, should feel proud. Now I must get you home."

Vorna was close to exhaustion when she heard the ponies approaching the cave. She had known they would come. One did not need the powers of a witch to realize that a mother would not be parted from her son when his life hung in the balance. And as for the man, Vorna had seen the anguish on his face earlier that day. He could not stay away. Rising from Conn's bedside, she took up her staff and walked out into the night. Ruathain and Meria had dismounted and were approaching the entrance.

What a fine pair they make, she thought, the tall broad-shouldered warrior and the proud woman beside him. She looked into their faces and saw the determination there. Meria's green eyes showed anger and the readiness of defiance. Vorna raised her hand. "The man cannot enter," she said wearily. "If he does, he will shatter the web of spells and the boy will die. The mother can follow me, but know this, she puts her son in peril by doing so."

"How can a mother's love imperil her son?" demanded Meria.

"Can you think of a single reason why I would lie to you?" countered Vorna. "I have cast spells, delicate, fragile spells. The sound of your footfalls could disturb them. And they—and my powers—are all that hold Connavar to the land of the living."

"Then I shall move silently. But I must see him."

Vorna had known that would be her answer. Moving in close, she whispered: "You must not speak within the cave or sigh or cry out. You must not, under any circumstances, touch Connavar. Do you understand this?"

"Will he live?" asked Meria.

"I do not know. But tell me you understand what I have

said. It is vital that you obey me. Not one word. Not one sound must you utter. If you cannot do this, then stay away."

"I will do as you say," said Meria.

"He hovers on the edge of the abyss of death," said Vorna. "His wounds are terrible to behold. Prepare yourself now and be strong." Taking Meria by the arm, she led her into the lamp-lit cave. Connavar was lying facedown on a pallet bed. The hair had been shaved from his left temple, and a long jagged cut had been stitched from his scalp to his chin. His back was a blood-covered mass of stitches, his left arm held in wooden splints. He looked so pale. Meria stood very still, Vorna's hand clamped to her arm. The witch drew her back. "No sound," she whispered. "Not until we are once more under the stars."

Hand held over her mouth, Meria backed away from her son, then turned and ran from the cave. Vorna followed her.

Ruathain stepped forward as they emerged. "How is he?" he asked.

"He should be dead," Vorna told him, "but I have cast all the healing spells I know."

"Is he conscious?"

"No. You must go now, for I have much to do."

"Ask anything of me," said Ruathain. "I will do it if you save my son."

Vorna was too tired to be angry. "I am doing all I can, Ruathain. You could promise me all the stars on a necklace and I could do no more. But you can bring food every day and a little wine. Honey is good for strength and healing." With that she trudged back into the cave, drew up her chair, and sat beside the dying youth.

Lightly touching his throat, she felt for a pulse. It was weak and fluttering. "Be strong, Connavar," she whispered. "My spirit to your spirit, draw on my strength." Heat flared through her fingertips, and she felt the power move within her, flowing into his flesh. Only when she grew dizzy and weak did she withdraw her hand. He did not move, and his breathing was so shallow that she was forced to hold a brass mirror by his mouth to see if he still lived. "Where have you gone to, Connavar?" she asked. "Where does your spirit fly?"

She sat with him for an hour longer, then slept for a little while. She awoke with a start and checked his breathing once more. He was barely clinging to life. The bear had ripped his back to shreds, and he had lost a great deal of blood. Vorna had inserted more than 140 stitches in his wounds. He ought to be dead, she knew. There was much here that she did not understand. Why was the Morrigu so interested in this boy? Why had the Seidh not killed him when he had entered Wishing Tree Wood? Why was he still alive?

Vorna knew the power of her spells was great, but not all of them together should have kept Connavar breathing. The wounds were too deep for that.

Why, then, did he live?

Rising from the chair, she crossed the cave to the rock pool and drank several cups of water. On the edge of the pool she had placed the two items Connavar had had with him when he had been carried here: the gift knife and a cloak brooch in the shape of a fawn trapped in brambles. It was a pretty piece and reminded her once more of the mystery of Wishing Tree Woods. The Seidh had no love for humans, and their law was iron. Any human venturing there risked death. Yet they had not killed him. Instead they had given him a test. But what was the purpose of it? Why a fawn? And why reward him with a knife? She had, of course, asked them. But they had not answered her.

Vorna prepared herself a breakfast of dried fruit and cheese, then returned to the bedside.

Even if he lived, he would be changed by his ordeal. What fifteen-year-old would not?

True, he had shown enormous courage in facing the beast. However, youth could be like that, she knew, charged with all the confidence of perceived immortality. The young always believed they would live forever. Connavar, if he survived, would now know different. He would have learned that some foes could not be overcome and that the world was an infinitely dangerous place. Would he still be as courageous? As caring?

Vorna hoped so. "But first you have to live," she told the comatose youth.

Ruathain rode a little distance ahead, and Meria found herself staring at his huge hunched shoulders. The night was cold, the wind blowing hard. Her pony was trudging on, head down against the wind, and Meria drew her shawl more tightly around her shoulders. Stars were shining brightly, and moonlight bathed the flanks of Caer Druagh. Meria felt numb—but not with the cold. Her mind was filled with thoughts of the past, dancing across the barren halls of her memory: the night of Conn's birth, when Varaconn had returned from the mountain, his eyes bright with the fear of impending death. He had taken her hand then, and he had cried for all that he would miss.

"Don't go," she pleaded. "Stay and watch him grow. Ruathain will understand."

"Aye, he would. But what kind of man would I be if I left my sword brother to fight alone?"

"He won't be alone. There are hundreds of warriors to stand with him."

But he had gone. And he had died.

She had tried so hard not to blame Ruathain for his death, but the bitter seed, once planted, had grown in the empty place of her heart.

Then, three months after the angry words that had driven Ruathain away, the witch Vorna had come to her as she was picking mushrooms in the yew glade. "You are wrong about your husband," said Vorna. "I think you know it."

"Go away and leave me be," Meria told her. "You do not understand."

"I understand you are nursing a lie to your heart. It sits like a black rat, chewing on all that is good."

"He promised to keep my Varaconn alive," shouted Meria, her eyes filling with tears.

"Aye, it is the nature of men to make large promises. Come, walk with me." Vorna took Meria's arm. A mist grew up around them, seeping up from the damp earth. It was cold and dank and soon became as thick as a winter fog. Meria could hardly see Vorna's face. Holding fast to Meria's arm, the witch kept walking.

"Where are we?" asked Meria.

"Nowhere," answered Vorna.

In the distance Meria heard the sound of war trumpets and the clash of blade upon blade. The sound was strangely muted. "Is there a battle?" she whispered.

"There *was* a battle," said Vorna. "Keep walking."

Slowly the mist cleared, and the two women found themselves walking across a ghostly battlefield. All around them were fighting men, their shapes pale and insubstantial, their cries thin and wavering. The women moved on. The fighters were oblivious to them. Meria stared around her, stunned by the chaotic ferocity of the battle. Many of the warriors wore horned helms and mail shirts, and she realized they had to be Sea Wolves, the raiders from over the water. Vorna tugged her, and she stumbled on. Now she saw the Rigante charging. Her heart thudded in her chest.

There. There was her love, Varaconn, swinging his bronze blade two-handed as he fought alongside Ruathain. Meria sighed and wiped tears from her eyes. He seemed so frail alongside the blond giant. A man with a spear ran at Varaconn. Ruathain saw him and leapt to intercept, smashing the man from his feet. Twice more, when Varaconn was in danger, Ruathain hurled himself forward to thwart the peril.

And then it was over, or so she thought. The raiders fell back. She saw Varaconn raise his sword and shout with delight. She heard his voice cry out. "I am alive!"

Suddenly a small group of raiders burst through the chasing line and ran at him. Ruathain leapt to meet them. At that moment Varaconn dropped his sword and tried to flee. Ruathain cut down the first two raiders, but the other three had caught Varaconn. One plunged his sword into the fleeing man's back. Ruathain gave a great shout. "No!"

The raiders ran on, hacking and slashing at Rigante warriors until they were cut down. Ruathain dropped to his knees alongside his friend, pulling the body into his arms and hugging it close. Meria saw Varaconn's hand reach up to grip Ruathain's arm, and she saw his mouth move. But she could not hear the words. She struggled to get closer, but Vorna held her back. Varaconn's head sagged against Ruathain's chest.

"Time to go," said the witch. The mist swelled around them. For a moment Meria stood, eyes straining to catch a last glimpse of her dying lover. Then he was gone. She stumbled back with Vorna, and when the mist cleared again, they were standing in the yew glade.

"Why did you show me that?" asked Meria, her voice breaking.

"Why do you think?" Vorna walked away.

Meria called after her. "What am I to do?"

But the witch did not answer.

For days the vision she had seen haunted Meria. And the awful truth of Ru's words sank into her like the claws of a cat. *"Any woman who would wed a man she believed had connived in the murder of her husband is no better than a pox-ridden whore. And I'll have no part of her. Not now. Not ever."*

Not ever.

A bat flew past her pony's head, causing it to rear. Meria was jerked back to the present. She had watched her husband die. Now her firstborn son was dying. She rode on down the hillside. Below she could see the lights of Three Streams, lanterns hung in porches, candlelight glinting through shutters, moonlight upon the water. The wind whipped at her, tearing her shawl from her shoulders. She did not notice. Ruathain glanced back, saw the garment fly away, and swung his pony. Retrieving the shawl, he rode alongside Meria. She was sitting staring ahead. Gently he laid the shawl over her shoulders, but she did not move her hands to hold it in place, and the wind lifted it again. Ruathain caught it, then led her pony down the hill, over the first of the bridges, and on into the paddock behind the house. Meria did not dismount. She sat, staring ahead, her mind lost in memories.

Ruathain lifted her clear and carried her into the house. Braefar was sitting at the table. Nine-year-old Bendegit Bran was crouched by the fire, making toast. Ruathain moved by them into the back bedroom. Braefar ran in.

"Is Mam hurt?"

"No," said Ruathain. "Pull back the covers and we'll put her to bed."

Braefar did so. Bran brought in some buttered toast. "For Mam," he said.

"She'll eat it in a while, boy. Leave us now."

The boys wandered back into the hearth room. Ruathain laid Meria on the bed and pulled the covers over her. Then he sat beside her and stroked the dark hair from her brow. "Sleep now," he said. "Get some rest."

She blinked and looked up into his broad face. Tears spilled from her eyes, and she turned her head away.

"The boy is a fighter," he said, misunderstanding the cause of her tears. "You rest. We'll go out again tomorrow."

She lay for a while, lost in thought. Then she spoke. "I am so sorry, Ru," she said. "For everything. Can you forgive me?"

There was no answer. Sitting up, she gazed around. Ruathain had gone.

* * *

For three days there was no change for the better in his condition, and on the morning of the fourth Vorna's concern increased. She was outside the cave when Meria rode up, carrying provisions. Vorna gave a wan smile to offset the fear in Meria's eyes, a smile that said: "Your son still lives." The relief was immediate. Drawing rein, Meria slid from the pony, tied its reins to a bush, and carried the small sack of provisions to where Vorna sat.

"Is he awake yet?" asked the mother.

"No. And I have not yet found his spirit."

"But he is healing?"

Meria's desperation brought a fresh wave of weariness to the witch. Taking the provisions, she opened the sack and removed a chunk of freshly baked bread and a wax-sealed jar of honey. Meria sat silently beside her, waiting patiently as Vorna broke the seal and began to eat, tearing off small pieces of bread and dipping them into the honey. When she had finished, she faced Meria. "Given time, the lung will heal itself," she said. "The flesh on his back, however, was badly ripped, and the wounds are turning sour. But even that is not my main concern. If his fever worsens, which I think it will, lack of water will kill him."

"Then we must wake him, force him to drink," said Meria.

"You think I have not tried? I told you his spirit has fled."

"Yes, but you could Merge," insisted Meria. "You did it for Pelain when she passed out in childbirth. You took over her body. You have done that for many women. You could do it for Connavar. Then you could make the body drink."

"You do not understand what you are asking me to risk," Vorna told her. "He is on the verge of death. If my spirit enters his body and the body dies, I die with it. Then there is the pain. A Merging would mean I become Connavar. His pain was so great, it sent his spirit fleeing from the agony. But I would have to endure it. And lastly, and most important, there is the fact that he is male. My power is born of the Great

Mother. It was never intended for men. They have their Druids and their blood magic."

"If you are too frightened, then teach me!" stormed Meria.

Anger touched the witch, but she fought to hold it back. There was no energy to waste at this time. "You could not learn it, Meria, for you have been touched by man. I have not. That was the price I paid to receive the power. No warm penetration for Vorna, no children to watch playing under the sun. Yes, I have used the Merging and borne the pain of childbirth for other women. But never for Vorna." Despite her attempt to control it, the anger seeped through. "Vorna lives alone and will die alone, unloved and unmourned. Too frightened? Aye, I am frightened. I am thirty-seven years old. I surrendered my youth and my dreams to help my people. Now you say, Give it all up, Vorna. Lose your power that my son may take a drink of water before he dies."

"Is he doomed, then?" asked Meria, her voice breaking.

"I do not know. That is the simple truth of it. And the struggle to keep him alive is all but killing me."

Meria sighed, then reached out and took Vorna's thin hand in her own. Vorna was unused to the touch of others, and the simple warmth of the contact caused her to tremble. Meria instantly withdrew her hand. "I am sorry, Vorna. Forgive me. I do not wish to seem ungrateful. But tell me, is there a way I can help him? I would give my life for his."

"I know," Vorna replied wearily. "You are his mother, and you love him dearly. I wish I could tell you that there was a role for you. I know it would ease your pain. But there is not, Meria, save in prayer. Go home now, for I must return to his side."

As Vorna struggled to her feet, Meria put her arms around her, kissing her cheek. Vorna felt the warmth of tears touching her skin. "Whatever happens, I will always be grateful to you," she said. Vorna patted Meria's back, then pulled away and walked back to the cave.

For several hours she rested, then she moved to Connavar's side. The fever was building, and his heartbeat was wildly erratic. The tortured flesh of his back was an angry color, and pus was seeping through the stitches. From a shelf on the western wall Vorna took a large pottery jar, resting it on a slab of rock. Then she rubbed dried lavender onto a linen scarf and wrapped it around her face, covering her mouth and nose. Vorna drew in several deep breaths, then returned to the jar and loosened the wooden lid. A stench filled the cave. Even the lavender mask could not overcome the hideous smell, and Vorna felt her stomach heave. Reaching into the jar, she removed what had once been a slab of bacon but was now covered in a slimy blue-green mold, writhing with maggots. This mold she gently smeared over Connavar's back.

Moving from the cave, she washed her hands in the stream, then removed the linen scarf. Daylight was fading when she returned to the boy's side. The stench had gone, and the maggots were feeding on his infected flesh.

Sitting beside him, she placed her hand on his red-gold hair. He would not last the night. "Where are you, Connavar?" she whispered. "Where does your spirit walk?"

There was no movement from the boy, only the writhing of fat maggots on his back.

Meria's face came to Vorna's mind. She saw again the sad green eyes, the pride, and the willingness to die for her son. If I had a son, would I be willing to die for him? Vorna wondered. "You will never know," she said aloud.

Her right hand still on his head, she gestured with the left toward the far wall. It shimmered and seemed to dissolve. Blue sky shone over hills of rich green grass. Three youths were running, one of them carrying the boy Riamfada. Vorna watched as the bear burst from the undergrowth, moving after them. She gestured again. Now she could see Connavar's face clearly. He was sweating under his burden. He glanced back, then stopped and set Riamfada on the grass. Vorna leaned forward, staring at Connavar, reading his expression, feeling his rising fear. She watched him leap at the giant beast, plunging his knife into its chest—and winced as the bear's claws tore into him.

With a flick of her fingers the scene faded, and the bare gray wall of the cave shimmered back into view. Vorna sighed. "You knew you were going to die, Connavar. Yet you did not run. I think that if you were my son, I would give my life for you." She stroked his hair and felt a tear drip to the dry skin of her cheek. Lifting her hand, she brushed it away.

"Such sweet sentiment," came a voice from the cave mouth. Vorna turned. The Old Woman stood there, the black crow perched on her shoulder.

"What do you want?" asked Vorna.

"I come to guide his soul to the Dark River."

"He is not dead yet."

"Soon, Vorna. Soon."

"You sent the bear to kill him."

The Old Woman shrugged and spread her arms. The movement made the crow flutter its great wings. "He wanted glory, Vorna. Now he has it. The story of his courage has spread to the Norvii, the Pannones, and beyond—across the water. He is the boy who fought the beast. Is that not what he desired? To be famous?"

The Morrigu advanced into the cave, pausing before the fire. She gazed around her at the stark gray walls. "I give people what they ask for. You know that. Your mother was a whore, and you yearned for respect, for power. Did I not grant you all that you sought? You will live ten times longer than any of your tribe, and you have their respect."

"They fear me."

"Respect, fear—it is all the same."

"I hate you," hissed Vorna.

The Old Woman gave a harsh, dry laugh. "Everyone hates the Morrigu. I find that charming. Still, as you say, he is not yet dead. I shall return with the dawn." Her jet-black eyes grew large, and she loomed over the witch. "You could, of course, save him. His mother was right. The Merging *might* bring him back. You, however, might not survive the winter without your powers. You could die here in this cold, lonely place. Unloved and unmourned. Isn't that what you said?" The Morrigu smiled. "I will leave you with your thoughts."

The Old Woman walked out into the night. The cave was growing cold now, and Vorna lit a fire. Once it was blazing brightly, she made a broth from the meat and vegetables Meria had brought earlier. To this she added herbs and spices, stirring the mixture until it was ready. Pouring some of the broth into a wooden bowl, she carried it to the bedside and waited for it to cool. When it had done so, she filled a large cup with clear water and placed it alongside the broth.

Moving her chair to the head of the bed, she laid her hands on either side of Connavar's face. For an hour she sat, honing her concentration, freeing her mind.

Then she Merged . . .

. . . and screamed as the pain tore into her. For a moment she almost passed out. Marshaling her power, she sought to blanket the raw, boiling agony searing through the tortured frame. The boy's body was weak, and it took all her strength to force it to turn to its side. Then she pushed the right arm beneath the body and came up on one elbow. Tears seeped from the eyes, and Vorna felt herself dying within the torn and bleeding shell that had once been Connavar. Do not give in to despair, she warned herself. Hold back the pain and make him sit! The left arm was broken and useless. With a cry of agony she forced the body to a sitting position, then, with a trembling hand, reached for the broth, lifting it to the lips. Opening the mouth, she forced the body to swallow. Nausea flowed over her, but she held it down. Then she drank the water, feeling the cold liquid seeping into fever-dried tissue.

Dropping the cup, she laid the body down and retreated to the security of her own exhausted frame.

The memory of the pain was almost as strong as the pain itself, and she passed out, falling from the chair to the cold stone floor of the cave.

It was night when she awoke. The fire was almost dead. With fear in her heart she pointed at the hearth and whispered a single word of power. She knew, even as she spoke, that the magic had gone from her. She was a witch no longer.

Rising, she checked Connavar's pulse. It was stronger now, his breathing deeper. She lit three lamps and by their light examined the boy's back. The combination of mold and maggots had cleaned the wounds. With a needle she carefully pricked each one, lifting the maggots one at a time from his flesh and flicking them into the fire. When at last his back was free of them, she poured a cold herbal tisane over some linen and laid it on his tortured flesh.

Wrapping herself in a warm cloak she walked out into the night. The stars were bright over Caer Druagh, the breeze chilly.

And in the breeze, as it rustled through the winter-naked branches above her, she thought she heard the wicked, mocking laughter of the Morrigu.

Connavar clung to the rock face. High above him the summit beckoned, far below a river of fire flowed over black rocks. Birds of prey hovered around him, pecking at the flesh of his back. One landed on his shoulder, the curved beak ripping into his face. He struck it hard and forced himself on. Arian was waiting. He would not die . . .

He was crawling across a desert. Huge ants emerged from the sand, clinging to his flesh with their mandibles, tearing at him. Ahead was an oasis. Everything in him screamed to close his eyes and float away on the bliss of sleep. Yet he did not. For in his mind was the face of a goddess. His goddess. His love. His flesh burning, he crawled on . . .

He was lying naked in a bramble patch, the spiked branches growing around him, through him, biting into his back, eating into the flesh of his face. The pain was terrible, and now he could not move. He lay there knowing at last that he was dying. A movement to his right caught his eye. A fawn was moving daintily through the brambles. Reaching his side, the creature gazed into his eyes. It made no sound, but Connavar knew it was asking him to reach out, to drape his arm over the slender neck. He tried, but pain seared through him. The fawn waited. Twice more the youth tried to move. Each time the pain was greater. Anger touched him, renewing his strength. He screamed as he wrenched his arm clear of the brambles and curled it over the neck of the fawn. The little creature settled down beside him and began to grow. As it did so, Connavar was pulled clear of the brambles and found himself sitting on the back of a powerful stag with great antlers. The stag swung and bounded from the thicket, coming to a halt beside a rock pool. Connavar slid from the beast's back and drank deeply.

Then he woke . . .

His left arm was heavily strapped and throbbing painfully. His back felt as if a fire had been laid on his flesh. Opening his eyes, he found he was lying facedown on a pallet bed. For a moment he could not identify his surroundings. Then he saw Vorna, lit by the light of a flickering fire, standing with her back to him. He heard a voice and remembered it as the old woman in the woods, the Morrigu!

"Who would have thought you could be so stupid, Vorna? Two hundred years of life surrendered for an arrogant boy. How does it feel to be without your powers? Are you afraid? Will the wolves eat your flesh, Vorna? Will the lions come down from their mountain lairs and tear you with their fangs?"

"He lives," replied Vorna, and Connavar could hear the weariness in her voice.

"Yes, he lives," hissed the Morrigu. "His body torn, poison seeping into his tissues, running in his blood. A whisper from death. For this you threw away the power I gifted you? You humans are so sentimental."

"You are neither wanted nor needed here," said Vorna. "Go and torment someone else."

Connavar heard the fluttering of wings, then saw Vorna walk to the fire. Pushing his right arm beneath him, he forced himself up. The stitches on his back pulled tight. He grunted. Vorna was immediately at his side. Dizzy, he fell against her. "Lie down, child. You are too weak to sit."

"No," he whispered. Drawing in several deep breaths, he waited for the dizziness to pass. "I am better now," he told her. "Could . . . I have . . . some water?" She fetched him a cup, but he was too weak to hold it and she lifted it to his lips. He drank greedily. Sweat bathed his face, burning against the vivid wound on his cheek. Reaching up, he ran his fingers across it, feeling the stitches. Then he remembered the bear: the slavering jaws and the terrible fangs. He had a fleeting vision of Govannan running to his aid and the stricken Riamfada lying on the grass. For a moment he hesitated, almost too frightened to ask the question. "What happened to the others?" he said at last.

"You were the only one hurt," she told him. "Your father and other men from the settlement rode up and killed the bear. Rest now. We will talk tomorrow."

Sleep came swiftly. And there were no dreams.

For another ten days Connavar drifted in and out of delirium, but on the morning of the eleventh he awoke clearheaded. The pain from his back had faded, but his shoulder still throbbed. Awkwardly he climbed from the bed. The cave was empty, but a bright fire was blazing in the hearth. He could not feel its heat, for a cold breeze was flowing from the cave mouth and Conn could see snow drifting in the opening. Fresh clothes were lying folded on the wooden table. Conn took a pair of green woolen leggings and struggled into them. It was not easy using only one arm. By the time he had them on he was bathed in sweat and feeling nauseous. Never had he felt this weak. With the heavy splint on his left arm there was no way to pull on his tunic. Draping it over his shoulders, he moved to the fireside.

His memories were hazy. How long he had been in the cave? He seemed to recall his mother sitting beside him, first in a green dress, then in a blue one, and finally in a heavy coat with a collar of sheepskin. It was all so confusing.

Vorna entered the cave. She was wearing a black hooded cloak, and a thick red scarf was wrapped around her neck. Snow had settled on her shoulders and also on the bundle of wood she carried. Dropping the fuel to the hearth, she swung toward him. "How are you feeling?"

"I have felt better," he admitted.

"The poison is gone from your body. Soon you will be able to go home. Perhaps tomorrow."

Conn sat down on the rug in front of the fire. Vorna removed her cloak, brushed the snow from it, and hung it on a peg. Drawing up a chair, she sat and held her hands out to the blaze. The skin of her fingers was blue with cold.

"Was the . . . Old Woman here?" he asked. "Or did I dream it?"

"She was here."

He shivered as a freezing draft whispered over him, touching the fire and causing the flames to dance. Vorna rose immediately and fetched a blanket, which she laid around his shoulders. Conn looked up at her. "She said you gave up your power to save me."

"That is no concern of yours," she snapped.

Conn was not deterred. "What will you do without your power?"

Vorna placed a fresh log upon the fire. She looked at the youth and smiled. "I will survive," she said. "I have not lost my skill with herbs and potions. Only the magic is gone."

"Will it return?"

She shrugged. "It will or it won't. I'll waste no sleep over it. So tell me, Connavar. Why did you fight the bear?"

He shivered at the memory, seeing again the immensity of the beast, the horror of its blood-smeared jaws. "I had no choice."

"Nonsense. Life is full of choices. You could have dropped your burden and run."

"Had I been carrying a *burden*, I would have done just that," Conn said softly. "But is that what you think I should have done?"

"It matters not what I think," said Vorna, lifting a copper kettle to hang above the blaze. "You did what you did. Nothing can change it now." Her dark eyes glinted in the firelight. "Would you do it again, Connavar?"

He thought about the question. "I don't know," he said at last. "I have never known pain like it. Nor fear." He sighed. "But I hope I would."

"Why?"

"Because a true man does not desert his friends. He does not run from evil."

Steam hissed from the kettle. Wrapping her hand in a cloth, Vorna lifted it clear of the flames, setting it down on the hearthstone. Silently she prepared two herbal tisanes sweetened with honey.

The cave was warm now, and Connavar felt sleepy once more. When the pottery cups had cooled, Vorna handed one to him. "Drink," she said. "It will help your body repair itself. Tomorrow I will remove the splints. The bones of your arm have already knitted. Happily, I accomplished this before my power was gone."

"I will find a way to return it to you. To repay you," he promised.

She smiled and, in a rare gesture of affection, pushed her fingers through his red-gold hair. "It was not a loan, Connavar. It was a gift, freely given. And it cheapens a gift to talk of repayment."

"I am sorry, Vorna. I did not mean to offend you."

"No offense was taken. You have much to learn, Connavar. There are some things even a hero cannot achieve. Have you not understood that yet? You cannot give Riamfada the power to walk. You cannot bring Ruathain and Meria together. You cannot kill a raging bear with a knife, even a blade cast by the Seidh. And you certainly cannot bring back my magic. But what you have done is far more important."

"What is it that I have done?" he asked.

"You have lifted the hearts of all who have heard the tale of the boy and the bear. During that time you made men feel proud to be Rigante, for they shared in your courage. One of *them* stood against the beast. One of *them* faced death with true courage. You are now and always will be a part of Rigante legends. And when you are long dead, the story will still be told. It will inspire other young men to be courageous. Now let me get you back to bed. Ruathain is coming to see you tomorrow. If you are well enough, I will allow him to take you home."

"What will you do?" he asked sleepily.

"Survive," she said.

Ever since he could climb, Braefar had spent much of his free time sitting on the thatched roof of his house, high above the cares of the world. From there he could see the whole of Three Streams, the wooden houses, the thatched round huts of the itinerant workers, the forges, the bakeries, and the high barns for winter storage. He would often sit in the early morning and watch as people moved through the settlement, women heading down to the lower stream to wash clothing, men saddling their ponies to ride out and work their cattle or patrol the borders. He would wait for Nanncumal the Smith to light his fire, then listen for the sound of his hammer on the anvil.

On the roof Braefar was a king, gazing down on his people. There he was secure, unafraid, and content.

But not today.

For Braefar the homecoming of the hero was proving a painful affair. He sat watching as the two riders made their slow way down the snow-covered hillside. At first only a few people came out to meet them, but as word spread, more and more Rigante ran from their homes, forming two lines and clapping their hands as the riders approached.

Nanncumal was there with his son Govannan and his daughters, and the bread maker, Borga, with his wife, Pelain. Then the metal crafter Gariapha and his wife, Wiocca, came running to join the crowd. Scores of men, women, and children lined the way.

A cold wind was blowing, but Braefar could scarcely feel it through his anger. Look at them, he thought. Fools every one! Could they not see that what Connavar had shown was not courage but stupidity? Only an idiot would face a bear with a knife. Never had Braefar known such resentment. He had adjusted to being small and slight, to knowing he would never be as strong as Connavar, and though he had envied his brother's skill and strength, he had never been jealous. Until now.

It was all so terribly unfair.

Ever since that dread day people seemed to talk of nothing but the fight with the beast and how Conn had leapt at it. They praised the bravery of Govannan, who had run to his aid, first with a knife and then by striking the beast with a rock.

"And what did you do, Braefar?" they asked him.

"I had no weapon," he replied.

"Ah," they said. Such a little sound, such a wealth of meaning.

Braefar knew what they were thinking. He was a coward. The other two boys had fought, while he had merely stood, petrified.

The ponies were closer now. He saw Govannan run alongside Connavar and reach up to shake his hand. Men cheered loudly as he did so. The two heroes together again!

Braefar felt sick.

Ruathain had come to him on that first, terrible night as Connavar had lain close to death. He had asked him to describe the fight. Braefar had done so.

"I couldn't help them, Father. I had no weapon," he had said.

His father had patted his shoulder. "There was nothing you could have done, Wing. I am just glad you are alive."

But Braefar had seen the disappointment in Ruathain's eyes. It had cut him like a knife.

Since then he had played out the fight with the bear many times in his mind. If he had run in, even to throw a stone, all would be different. Now, as he watched the hero's ride home, he pictured himself sitting in the saddle, listening to the cheers of his people. If Banouin had given me such a knife, he thought, I, too, could have shared the applause.

The riders halted before the house. Ruathain helped Conn to the ground, then half carried him inside. The crowd drifted away.

Braefar climbed from the roof, in through the loft, and down the wooden ladder to the ground floor. Conn was sitting at the long table, Meria fussing over him. His skin looked gray, his eyes red-rimmed and tired. A horrible red scar disfigured his face, and his left arm was heavily bandaged. Ruathain was standing silently by the doorway.

"Welcome home," Braefar said lamely.

Conn looked up and gave a tired smile. "Good to see you, Wing," he said.

"You need rest," said Meria. "Come, let me help you to your bed." Conn did not resist. Pushing himself to his feet, he allowed his mother to support him. Slowly they moved past Braefar.

Later, as Braefar climbed into his own bed alongside Conn's, he saw that his brother was awake.

"I would have helped if I'd had a weapon," he said.

"I know that, Wing."

There was kindness in the voice, and understanding.

Braefar hated him for it. And he said the one thing he knew would cause the most pain. "I suppose you haven't heard about Arian. She married Casta at the Feast of Samain."

His brother groaned in the darkness. Instantly Braefar felt shame. "I'm sorry, Conn. I tried to tell you that she didn't care for you."

◇ **6** ◇

THE WINTER WAS one of the fiercest in Rigante memory, with freezing blizzards and temperatures so low at times that trees shattered as their sap froze. So much snow fell that huge drifts blocked the high passes, and the weight of fallen snow caved in the roof of Nanncumal's forge. Ponies could not carry the feed to cattle trapped in the high valleys, and men wearing snowshoes struggled through the drifts, bales of hay on their shoulders.

Ruathain and Arbonacast almost died trying to reach Bear Valley, where many of the herd had taken refuge. Caught in a blizzard, they had dug under the snow-buried branches of a tall pine and crouched there huddled together throughout the deadly night. In the morning they had crawled clear, hefted their bales, and located the herd. Two of the younger bulls had died. But old Mentha, indomitable and powerful as ever, had, with eight of his cows, found shelter in the lee of a cliff face.

Back in the settlement Connavar's weakness lasted throughout the bitter winter. He lost weight and succumbed to three fevers, none of them life-threatening. He developed a hacking cough, his shoulder ached continuously, and his injured lung did not seem to be repairing itself, leaving him constantly out of breath. Meria worried over him constantly and could not understand his loss of spirit.

Braefar knew that he was sick at heart over losing Arian, and his envy of his brother faded. He tried to cheer him, encouraging him to exercise and build his strength. But Connavar seemed to have little energy and even less desire. He slept in the afternoons, lying by the hearth, wrapped in a blanket.

Even when he did try to exercise, the freezing sleet and bitter winds would drive him back inside. One day, when the sky was the dull gray of a sword blade, he walked as far as the second bridge and paused by the frozen stream.

Arian, wrapped in a heavy green shawl, came out to stand beside him. "You look stronger," she said. Conn ignored her and made to walk on. She took hold of his arm. He winced as pain flared into his shoulder. "Don't hate me," she said. "They told me you were dying."

He swung his head and looked into her eyes. She fell back a step when she saw the fury there. "Aye," he said, "I do understand. Had I been told you were dying, I, too, would have rushed off to a feast and shagged the first woman I saw. Get away from me, whore. You are nothing to me now. Less than nothing." It was a lie, a terrible lie, yet the hurt on her face as he spoke lifted him.

Slowly he trudged away through the snow. And as he walked, he realized that Arian had supplied him with one last gift. His anger had returned, and with it the desire to be strong again.

Every day after that he would stand in the cold for up to an hour, splitting logs with the long-handled ax. It was painfully slow. He would stop every few minutes, trying to regain his breath, sweat coursing down his face. When weariness came upon him, he would think of Arian and allow the anger to fuel his muscles.

Gradually, as the first warm breezes of spring drifted across the mountains, his strength improved. He began to take longer walks, pushing himself to the point of exhaustion, a point that arrived with remarkable swiftness.

His left shoulder continued to trouble him, especially on

cold or rainy days. Ruathain set him several exercises to strengthen and stretch the muscles. There was a young oak some thirty paces from Ruathain's house with a thick branch that jutted out eight feet above the ground. Every day Connavar would stand beneath it, jump, and curl his hands around the wood. Then he would haul himself up until his chin touched the branch, lower himself, and repeat the move. The first time was incredibly awkward. He could not raise his left arm without pain and was forced to jump, hold on with his right, then maneuver the left over the branch. Once in place, with Ruathain watching, he hung for several heartbeats and managed one lift.

He cursed aloud as he fell to the ground. Ruathain moved to his side. "You must think of your strength as a deer you are hunting," he said.

"I don't understand," Conn answered, rubbing his throbbing shoulder.

"You do not take a bow and rush out into the woods. You search until you know all the deer's habits, then you find a place to wait. Even when you see him, you do not shoot too soon, and you never loose a shaft at a deer on the run. His blood will be up, and that makes the meat tough and hard to chew. The hunter needs patience. Endless, quiet, calm patience. Your strength is the deer. You must seek it calmly, methodically. Plan your strategy. Look for small gains. Come here every morning. Do not try too many lifts. You will disappoint yourself and damage your wounded muscles. Today you almost made one. Tomorrow look for two."

"I am sick of being weak," said Conn.

"You are *weak* because you have been *sick*. As I said, look for a small improvement every day. When you walk, mark the spot where you feel that you cannot go on. The following day seek to go ten paces past it."

Conn felt calmer as they spoke. "Have you ever been wounded?" he asked.

"Once, when I was a year older than you. Not as badly. I took a spear in the right shoulder. I thought my strength would never return. But it did. Trust me, Connavar. You will be stronger than you were before. Now let us walk for a while."

It was a bright clear day, but in the distance rain clouds were hovering over Caer Druagh. Ruathain led the youth up a short hill, stopping several times to allow him to catch his breath. At the top the two of them sat down and stared out over the valley. Ruathain's herds were grazing, and Conn could see Arbonacast sitting his pony on the far slope.

"I do not see Mentha," said Conn. "I thought he survived the winter."

"He did," said Ruathain. "And a young bull challenged him for mastery of the herd. He and Mentha fought for several hours." Ruathain gave a sad smile. "Mentha finally beat him. It was his last moment of triumph. We found him the following morning. His heart had given out in the night."

"That is sad," said Conn. "He was a bonny bull."

"Aye, he was. But he died as a king, undefeated and unbowed."

"Do you think it mattered to him?"

Ruathain shrugged. "I like to think so. How are you feeling?"

"I'm having trouble getting my breath."

"The lung worries me. Tomorrow, when I take her provisions, you will ride with me to see Vorna."

Conn glanced at the Big Man. Every two days throughout the winter Ruathain had traveled to Vorna's cave, carrying provisions. At first he had ridden out, but when the winter was at its coldest he had trudged in snowshoes through the drifts. Once there, he had gathered wood for her and made sure she was safe. "You have been good to her," said Conn. "I thank you for it."

"A man stands by his friends," said Ruathain. "No matter

what. You understand this better than most." He smiled suddenly. "Have I told you how proud you made me?"

Conn laughed aloud. "Only every day."

"It cannot be said often enough. Now let us walk back. Take your time."

As they made their slow way across the fields, Conn saw a thin plume of smoke rising from the chimney of Banouin's house. The merchant had not returned for the winter, and this had depressed Conn, for he feared that the Norvii robbers had indeed lain in wait for him and that he lay dead in some forest thicket.

Ruathain saw him staring at the smoke. "The foreigner arrived back last night," he said, "with twenty-five heavily laden ponies. Only the gods know how he brought them through the storm."

For the first time that winter Conn forgot his weakness. "I feared he was dead."

Ruathain shook his head. "He'd be a hard man to kill," he said, his expression suddenly grim. "He is far tougher than he looks. I hope all his people are not like him."

"Do you not like him?" asked Conn, surprised at the Big Man's mood change.

"He is a foreigner, and his people make war on all their neighbors. Before you can go to war in a strange land, you must first send out scouts to study the terrain. If his people ever cross the water and attack our land, who do you think will have supplied them with maps?"

Conn was no fool, and the Big Man's words struck home. Even so, he did not want to consider them. Banouin was a friend, and until he was proved to be a spy, Conn was willing to put aside any doubts about his actions. Yet the seed had been planted, and in Banouin's company he found himself listening with even more care as the foreigner told the stories of his travels.

"Did you know," said Banouin as they sat before his hearth drinking watered wine, "that the story of your fight with the bear has reached the southern coast?"

"It was not a fight," Conn said, with a shy grin. "I stabbed it twice, and it ripped me apart."

"According to the tale being sung there, you fought it for a long time and it was almost dead when the other men arrived. Oh, yes, and you were protecting not a crippled boy but a beautiful young maiden out gathering flowers."

Conn laughed aloud. "A princess, no doubt."

"Indeed so. And you, it seems, have noble blood. Born from a line of Rigante heroes."

"People are stupid to believe these things. What is happening beyond the water?"

Banouin's smile faded. "My people are at war with one another again. Great battles are being fought. Thousands have already been slain. But Jasaray will emerge triumphant. Of that I have no doubt."

"He is a great fighter, then," said Conn.

"I don't believe he knows how to use a sword," answered Banouin. "But he knows how to use an army." They sat in silence for a while. Banouin added fuel to the fire and refilled their goblets. "There is something I want to show you," said the foreigner, moving into the back room. When he returned, he was carrying a short sword of burnished iron. "I brought this back," he said, offering the carved wooden hilt to the young man.

Conn took the weapon and hefted it. "It has good balance, but the blade is very short. It is not much longer than a good hunting knife."

"This sword is changing the world," said Banouin.

"Are you jesting?" asked Conn. The blade was no longer than his forearm, the wooden grip protected by short quillons of bronze. Rising, he swung the sword. It felt clumsy, lacking the grace of the more familiar longsword.

"It is not a hacking weapon," said Banouin. "It is designed to thrust."

"If I came against a man carrying this and I was wielding Ruathain's longsword, I know who would win," Conn told him.

"Probably true if, as you say, it is one on one. But you are missing the point. When a Keltoi army clashes with a Stone army, the Keltoi are always outnumbered three to one."

"How so? You told me that in most of Jasaray's battles he was facing huge numbers of tribesmen."

Moving to the shelf by the wall, Banouin lifted down a small chest. From it he took several handfuls of small silver coins, which he scattered on the thick, red rug at his feet. "If thirty Rigante warriors were to charge an enemy on foot, how far apart would each warrior need to be?"

Conn thought about it. In battle, with each man swinging a longsword with a three-foot blade, they would be at least five feet apart. Any closer and there was the risk of being injured by a friend's sword. He said this to Banouin. Kneeling on the rug, the foreigner separated thirty coins, spreading them out. Then he looked up at Conn. "The attacking Rigante would look like this?" he asked.

Conn looked down at the shining silver pieces and pictured them as charging Rigante. "Yes," he said at last. "Not too far apart but not too close."

Banouin took a further ten coins, setting them close together in two tight lines of five. "These are men standing shoulder to shoulder. Each of them has a rectangular shield on the left arm. The shields can be brought together, forming a wall, then pushed outward to allow the short swords to thrust." Gently he eased the wide spread coins forward until they almost touched the two lines of five. "Picture this as two groups of warriors, and you will see that every Rigante, to reach the line, will face three shields and three swords. A short thrusting sword enables the soldiers to stand close together, fighting as a unit. It also means that no matter how great the enemy force, they will be at a huge disadvantage, for as each warrior reaches the battle line, he will face three opponents. Either that or the attacking force will become so closely packed that they will be unable to use their swords."

"I am sure any Rigante would be a match for three Stone soldiers," Conn said, loyally.

Banouin smiled. "You have seen only the sword. I did not bring the bronze shield, the iron breastplate, the plumed iron helm. Or the greaves to protect the shins, the baked leather wrist and forearm protectors, or the chain-mail tunic. Most deaths in battle among the Rigante follow neck wounds or body-piercing cuts to the heart, belly, and groin. Sometimes warriors bleed to death slowly. At other times they succumb to infection and gangrene. Like all the tribal people I have met here and beyond the water, you fight largely without armor. You fall upon the enemy in great numbers, and each battle breaks down into a thousand skirmishes between heroes. You will need to learn to fight a different way if you wish to retain your independence."

"You speak as if war with your people was inevitable," Conn said, quietly.

"I fear it is. Not this year or next. First Jasaray must subdue his own enemies from within the empire. Then he will tackle the Perdii, or the Ostro, or the Gath. That will take several years. But if he survives, he will come here, Conn."

"Will you have supplied him with maps?" asked Conn.

Banouin shook his head. "No. I carry no maps anymore. It is all in my head. And I will not fight again. I have seen war. I have witnessed the desolation and the torment. No. When the war comes, I will hire a ship and sail to the west. It is said there are fabulous lands there, rich and fertile. Perhaps the people there have no use for war."

"A weak, soft people they will be," muttered Conn. "A strong man will always have enemies, and those who live on good land will need to defend it against those who dwell on poorer soil. That is the way of the world, Banouin. I may be young, but I know this to be true. The strong will always rule, the weak suffer. This is the way the gods planned it. Why else would it always be so?"

"Do not bring religion into this debate!" warned Banouin. "I have no patience for it. Let me turn this argument around. If my people come here and destroy your armies, does this mean you deserve to lose your lands? Would that be fair?"

Conn laughed. "Only the defeated, the luckless, and the weak talk of fairness and unfairness and what is deserved or undeserved. All I know is that I will fight for my people and kill any enemy who comes to Caer Druagh."

"As you killed the bear?" Banouin asked, softly.

Conn blushed. "That was different. I did not have the weapons to kill the bear."

"No difference, Conn. The Rigante do not have the weapons to stop my people." His words hung in the air.

Conn thought about them, rolling them over in his mind. "When do you head south again?" he asked finally.

"In three months. High summer is a good time to travel."

"I will travel with you. I will see these armies and this Jasaray."

Once the thaw was under way, Vorna left the sanctuary of her cave and made the long trek down to the settlement. It was not that she was particularly anxious for company. People had never liked Vorna, even as a child. There was something fey about her, they said. Other children avoided her. Once her powers developed, she was even more isolated, and the coldness in the eyes of others became fear. Even when she arrived at the homes of the sick and healed them, she could sense their relief as she moved toward the door to leave.

No, it was not exactly company she sought. But after a winter trapped in a cold, gray cave, she yearned for movement and sound: the rhythmic thudding of the forge hammer, the laughter of children, the sound of hoofbeats on the firm ground, the lowing of cattle, the chatter of people as they greeted the arrival of the new sun. And taste! Freshly baked bread, hot honey tarts, sour milk porridge.

She was thinking of those delights as she crossed the bridge. The first person she saw was a crofter named Eanor, whose wife she had healed ten days before the bear had attacked Connavar. He looked up from his work, digging over the earth of his vegetable patch, and smiled warmly at her. "Daan's blessing, lady," he called. "Is it not a fine day?" The greeting shook her. No one spoke when Vorna passed by. Surprised, she merely nodded and walked on. Eanor was right: The day was fine, the sun warm, the sky clear and blue.

Farther on she saw the baker's wife, Pelain, spreading seed for her chickens in the outer yard of the bakery, the birds clucking around her feet. Seeing Vorna, she smiled and moved across to intercept her. "Welcome home," said Pelain. Vorna felt as if she were in a dream and did not know how to respond. Pelain shook the last of the seeds from the fold in her dress and took Vorna's arm. "Come inside and eat," she said. "Borga made cheese bread this morning. It melts in the mouth."

Meekly Vorna allowed herself to be led into the house. Borga was sitting at the pine table, dipping bread into a bowl of rich stew. "We have a guest," said Pelain.

Borga's fat face eased into a warm smile. "You are welcome, lady," he said. "Sit yourself." Pelain took Vorna's heavy hooded cloak and hung it on a hook by the door. Vorna sat down at the table. Borga poured water into a goblet and handed it to her. She nodded her thanks but could think of nothing to say. Pelain cut three thick slices from a warm loaf and smeared them with butter. Vorna ate quietly.

"The boy is doing well now," said Borga. "Yesterday I saw him running over the hills. It was a fine thing that you did.

Very fine." He rose and moved through to the back of the house and into the bakery.

Pelain sat opposite Vorna. "The bread is good, isn't it?"

"Yes. Tasty." Vorna was recovering some of her composure now, but she was unused to small talk and felt uncomfortable.

Pelain leaned in, her voice low. "He may be useless in bed, but he makes a loaf the gods would die for." The baker's wife chatted on for a while, then noticed the silence from her guest. "I am sorry, Vorna," she said. "I do tend to talk too much."

"Why are you being . . . so nice to me?" asked the former witch.

Pelain shrugged and gave a shy smile. "Because you are one of us now. You gave up your powers to save Connavar. Meria told me. She said you risked death to bring him back from the Shadowlands. Everyone feels the same, Vorna. You don't mind, do you? I know you like to keep to yourself, but . . ." Her voice tailed away, and she rose from the table to cut herself some bread.

"I do not mind," said Vorna. "And I thank you for the breakfast."

Pelain turned and grinned at her. "Isn't it nice to see the sun shine again?"

"Yes," agreed Vorna. Moving from the table, she took her cloak and draped it over her arm. As she reached the door, Pelain called out.

"You are welcome whenever you choose to call."

"I will remember that."

Vorna stepped out into the sunshine and walked into the settlement. As she made her way toward Meria's house, people waved to her or called out a greeting. By the time she reached Meria's door, she was trembling and her eyes were filled with tears.

When Meria saw her distress, she put her arms around Vorna and drew her close. The warmth of the contact was too much for the witch, and she buried her head on Meria's shoulder and began to weep.

As with all the Keltoi race, the Rigante were a passionate and volatile people, and there were often fights among them. Sometimes the fights ended badly, and tribesmen died of their wounds. But such tragedies were rare. Rarer still were the crimes of rape and murder.

Thus, on the spring morning when the first body was discovered, a feeling of disbelief and shock swept through the settlement of Three Streams.

The corpse of a middle-aged man had been found early that morning. A Rigante out with his bow and his hound, hunting rabbits, had stumbled across the first body. It had been dragged away from the main trail and hastily hidden in a thicket. Within two hours a twenty-strong hunting party led by Ruathain had assembled some fifty meters away from the murder site. Arbonacast, Ruathain, and Banouin moved carefully away from the other riders, examining the tracks around the scene.

Arbon knelt by the side of the trail. "Four horses," he said. "All of them shod." He moved farther down the trail, stepping lightly around the tracks. "The old man was pulling a handcart when the riders came up." Leaping lightly across the trail toward the undergrowth, he paused again. Then he swore softly.

"What have you found?" called out Ruathain.

"The old man was not alone. A young woman or a child was with him. Small feet." Arbon gestured for them to cross the trail and enter the woods beyond. Within minutes they had discovered the second body, that of a naked girl no more than fourteen years old. That she had been raped was obvious. Then her throat had been cut. Ruathain closed the dead eyes. Banouin stood by impassively. He alone felt no shock. On his travels through other lands he had long since learned that such crimes were common. But not here in Rigante territory. He surveyed the scene and waited for Arbon to study the spoor. The herdsman, his face pale with anger, rose at last and walked back to the first body. The dead man, dressed in a long pale blue tunic hemmed with red, had been stabbed through the throat, the blade breaking his neck. His cart lay on its side, the contents strewn around the bushes. There were two broken chests that had mostly been full of clothes and three small sacks of provisions.

Arbon approached Ruathain. "The man and the girl were walking. Then the riders came alongside them. One of the riders drew a blade. The old man threw up his arm—hence the cut on his wrist. It did not stop the blow, and the blade crushed his neck. In panic the girl ran into the woods. The riders dismounted and chased and caught her. When they had finished with her, they ransacked the cart, dragged the old man's body into the bushes, and rode off toward the north."

"What can you tell of the men?" asked Ruathain.

"One was very tall, more than six feet. Another was short and heavy. One of them is riding a mare. One or more of them carry the marks of a struggle. There is blood under the girl's nails. There is little else I can tell save that they were killed no earlier than yesterday, probably late in the afternoon."

"They are foreigners," said Banouin.

"We all know that," Ruathain said, coldly. "No Rigante would commit such a crime."

Banouin shook his head. "I meant they came from over the water. The sword used to kill the old man was a gladius. They are not common here. Also, the killing of the girl was likely part of a ritual—a sacrifice to Gianis the Blood God. He is worshiped by the Gath and many other tribes across the water."

"I have heard the name," said Ruathain.

"It is also possible," continued Banouin, "that the riders knew the old man. His clothes show him to be from the Ostro tribe. Their land borders the Gath homeland. They may even have traveled over on the same ship."

"We'll know when we find them," said Ruathain, striding back toward the horsemen.

Banouin remained where he was, staring down at the dead child. Connavar walked up to stand beside him. His face was ghostly white, his eyes filled with cold fury. "You do not need to see this, Conn," said Banouin.

"Yes, I do," whispered Conn.

Leaving four men to bury the dead, the Rigante rode off in pursuit of the killers.

By late afternoon they had lost the trail, and the party split up into teams of two to search for sign.

Connavar and Banouin rode together, heading northeast and deep into the Langevin Woods. They pushed on until dusk, then Banouin suggested riding home. Conn shook his head. "I will rest my pony here for a while, then push on," he said.

"The others may already have found them," Banouin pointed out.

"Perhaps, but I do not think so," said the young man, dismounting.

"What makes you say that?" Banouin asked, intrigued.

"If they are, as you say, foreigners, then they must have a purpose here. They are seeking trade treaties with the Rigante or the Pannones. If it is with us, then they will be traveling to Old Oaks to seek an audience with the Long Laird, or they will be making for the Cavellin Pass. Either way they will have taken this route."

"They could be intending to cut to the west for the wool route," Banouin pointed out. "Anyway, we are supposed to be seeking *sign* of them. You sound as if you want to catch them yourself."

"I do. And I will."

Banouin swore. "That would not be wise. There are four of them. How will it benefit the dead for you to die also?"

"I do not intend to die."

"No warrior *intends* to die, but what makes you believe you can subdue all four?"

"Did you not say I was the best pupil you have ever had?"

"You are the *only* pupil I have ever had. And yes, you are swift and wonderfully adroit in practice. But this is not practice, Conn. This is harsh, deadly reality." Banouin sighed. "I am going back for Ruathain and the others. Will you come with me?"

"No."

"Will you at least wait here until I return?"

"Of course."

Banouin swung his pony. "Please, Conn, do nothing stupid."

"I am not a stupid man," said Conn.

As Banouin rode away into the darkness, Conn remounted and steered his pony deeper into the woods.

For an hour he rode, then he spotted the twinkling light of a distant campfire. Moving in close, he tethered his pony and began to make his way silently through the undergrowth. The fire had been built in a small hollow beside the road. Three men were sitting around it, finishing off a meal. The smell of meat broth hung in the air. Circling the camp, Conn saw that three ponies were tethered close by.

Where was the missing fourth man?

Doubt touched him. Perhaps they were not the men he was hunting.

Edging closer, he saw that two of the men were wearing short swords. Conn was close enough to hear their conversation. So strong was the dialect that it was hard to make complete sense of it. Beside them were some copper plates and pots, and they seemed to be discussing who should clean them. Finally a short, fat man gathered them and walked to a stream. The other two laughed at him, and he sent back a curse.

One of the two rose and stretched. He was tall, over six feet.

Crouched in the shadow of the trees, Conn thought back to Arbon's description of the men. One tall. One shorter and heavier. Foreigners. These men matched the description, and if there had been four of them, he would have been convinced. But they could be innocent travelers.

How could he be sure?

The fat man returned to the fire, packed away the plates in a saddlebag, and sat down. One of the others threw fresh wood to the flames. As the fire brightened, Conn saw that the left side of the fat man's face bore three vivid weals. Arbon had said that the dead girl had blood under her fingernails.

Conn took a deep breath as cold anger flowed through him.

These were the men—or at least three of them.

Banouin had urged him to do nothing stupid. Conn knew that walking in on three killers could not be considered wise, yet he felt he had little choice. It was not about revenging the dead, he knew, though perhaps it should have been. It was more selfish than that. Since the fight with the bear Connavar had been subject to many bad dreams, full of anxiety and pain. Usually he was running from something frightful, his mind in a panic, and he would wake bathed in sweat, his heart pounding. All his life Conn had dreaded being a coward like his father. Yet since the day of the bear he had been plagued by terrible fears.

And fear, like all enemies, had to be overcome.

Drawing the Seidh knife and the short sword Banouin had given him, he rose from the bushes and stepped into the campsite. The fat man was the first to see him. Rolling to his right, he dragged out his sword and surged to his feet, almost tripping on the hem of his black cloak. The others leapt back, one running to where his blanket lay and gathering up his sword.

"What do you want here?" asked the tall man, scanning the night-shrouded trees for sign of more men.

"You killed an old man and a girl today," said Conn. "I am here to send your souls screaming into darkness." They were brave words, but his voice was shaking as he spoke them, robbing them of real threat.

"And you will do this alone?" inquired the fat man with a wide grin. The others were smiling, too.

"Why would I need help against gutless scum?" countered Conn, his voice stronger, his anger overwhelming his fear.

"You are an arrogant pup," the tall man said, scornfully. "Kill him, Tudri," he told the fat man.

Screaming a battle cry, Tudri rushed forward. A surge of fighting fury swept through Conn. Tudri's iron sword flashed at Conn's chest. Stepping in to the charge, the young Rigante parried the lunge, then sent the Seidh blade scything up and across.

Tudri stumbled on for several paces, blood bubbling from his severed jugular and drenching his shirt. Then he pitched forward to the grass, his body twitching.

The other two advanced more warily now. Conn waited motionless, watching them. The tall man was graceful, and Conn guessed he would be fast. The other man was more nervous, licking his lips and blinking rapidly. The two men spread out. Then the tall man leapt forward. Conn parried the thrust and tried a riposte that missed. At that moment the second man rushed in. Conn barely had time to swivel and block the lunge. The Seidh blade licked out, slashing open the man's shoulder. He cried out and dropped his sword. Conn spun on his heel and hammered his right foot into the man's belly, hurling him from his feet.

The tall man threw a knife. It hit Conn hilt first, high in the face, under his right eye. The blow hurt, but if the throw had not been clumsy, the fight would have been over there and then, six inches of iron buried in Conn's eye socket. The tall man attacked again. He was, as Conn had guessed, fast, and twice Conn had to leap back from disemboweling thrusts. The second man had regained his sword and was waiting for an opening. Conn lunged at the tall man, but he sidestepped and smashed his fist into Conn's unprotected face. Conn staggered but did not fall. The tall man slashed his sword at Conn's throat. Conn parried, then stabbed up and across with the Seidh blade. The blow had been aimed at the neck, but it entered the tall man's face just below the cheekbone and punched through the mouth and out the other cheek. The sudden pain made the tall man jerk backward. Conn lost hold of the knife but rammed his short sword through his opponent's belly, driving it deep.

As he did so, the last man rushed in. Conn dragged back on the sword, but it was trapped in the tall man's body. Releasing the hilt, he parried a lunge with his left forearm. The iron blade sliced through his shirt, nicking the skin of his forearm. Conn sent a right cross into the man's chin, spinning him around. Leaping high, Conn kicked the man in the temple. He fell awkwardly. The tall man was on his knees, his hands gripping the hilt of the blade that had gone through his belly. Conn grabbed the Seidh knife, ripping it clear of the man's face. The last fighter was back on his feet, but he saw the knife in Conn's hands and panicked, swiveling to run for his pony. Conn gave chase, leaping on the man's back and bearing him to the ground. Conn grabbed his hair, hauling back his head.

"Here is another gift for your blood god," hissed Conn, slicing the knife across his exposed throat.

Rising from the corpse, he walked back to where the tall man knelt. Blood had drenched his leggings, and his face was ashen.

"Where is the fourth man?" asked Conn.

"I hope . . . you . . . rot and . . . die," whispered the man.

"It is you who is doing the dying," said Conn. "But it can

be more painful yet." Reaching out, he took hold of the sword hilt, twisting it. The man screamed.

"Where is the fourth?" Conn asked again. The man toppled to his right. A rattling breath came from his mouth. Then there was silence. Pushing the corpse to its back, Conn retrieved his sword and cleaned it on the man's black cloak.

Moving to the fire, he sat down. His hands were trembling again after the shock of the fight, but this time he was not ashamed.

The bear had not robbed him of his courage, as he had feared.

He was alive. And he had conquered.

The euphoria did not last long. Conn sat at the fire and thought of the dead men lying behind him. He shivered and glanced back nervously. There they lay, terribly still. The tall man's eyes were open and seemed to be staring at him. Conn stood and walked to where the men lay. One by one he pulled off their black cloaks and covered them. The cloaks were well made and embroidered at the center with five interlocking silver circles. They made expensive shrouds.

With the excitement and the fear gone, Conn found himself slipping toward melancholy. The mood surprised him. Had he not killed three warriors? Did this not prove he was a man? Adding fuel to the fire, he wrapped himself in his cloak. An owl swooped over the hollow, then veered away. To the right a fox pushed its head from the undergrowth and stared at the man by the fire. It can smell the blood, thought Conn. They are not people anymore. They are meat.

As one day you will be meat.

The thought was an unpleasant one.

"A man should never be alone in victory," said the Morrigu. Conn jerked. She was sitting on the other side of the fire, a gray shawl over her skinny shoulders. A gaunt black crow glided down from the branches above, flapping its wings as it landed on the ground beside her. Conn reached inside his shirt, curling his fingers around the red opal Vorna had given him. The Morrigu laughed. "I did not come here to harm you, Sword in the Storm."

"Then why did you come?"

"You interest me. Tell me, why did you kill those men?"

"They murdered an old man and a child."

"Ah. A simple matter, then. A crime followed by a just sentence. Suppose I were to tell you that the old man was a necromancer who had killed many and that the child was his familiar, a dark and demonic creature who devoured the souls of children? And that the men sent to apprehend him were heroes of the Gath? What then?"

"They were not heroes," said Conn, though her words unsettled him.

"How can you be sure?"

"Heroes would not have raped the girl, and if the man was a necromancer, why did he not use his powers against them?"

"Perhaps they wore talismans like yours, and as for the rape, you know better than any that a woman blessed with earth magic must never merge with a male. Perhaps they abused her to rob her of her magic."

"I do not believe it."

"I did not say it was true," the Morrigu pointed out. "But it could have been."

"What is it you want from me?"

"I want for nothing, human. As I said, you interest me. I asked you once what you desired. You told me glory. You have tasted it. Was it to your liking?"

"I think that you are evil," he told her. "I want no more to do with you."

The Morrigu smiled. "I am beyond evil, child. Evil is a small creature, short-lived and petty. Evil is like a plague. It comes, it hurts, and it leaves. I am the Morrigu. I am always here. I am a giver. People come to me and ask me for presents. I give them what they ask for."

"You sent the bear to kill me."

"You wanted glory, Connavar. Your name is now known throughout Keltoi lands. You are a hero. Perhaps you should thank me. Ask me for something else. See how generous I am. Would you like to be a king?"

"I want nothing more from you," he told her. "The bear was gift enough."

"Have your dreams become so small, Sword in the Storm? Where is the boy who yearned for fame?"

"He grew up," snapped Conn. "Tell me, why did you rob Vorna of her powers?"

The crow flew up, the beating of its wings causing sparks to fly from the fire. Several hot cinders landed in Conn's lap. He brushed them away. Then he blinked, for he was now sitting alone, staring at the grass beyond the fire. He had not seen the Morrigu disappear, just as he had not witnessed her arrival. It was like waking from a dream, and for a moment he wondered if he had imagined her presence. But there, on the other side of the fire, lay a single black feather. Conn shivered. Moving around the blaze, he flicked it to the flames, watching it shrivel and burn.

What would he have asked for? He thought about it, and the answer was simple. Nothing would have given him greater pleasure than to see Arian step from the shadows of the trees and sit beside him by the fire. He pictured the tilt of her head, the music of her laughter, the sway of her hips. He had lied when he had told her she meant nothing to him. She was constantly in his thoughts. Even her marriage could not change that.

Conn tried to sleep, but he dreamed of corpses rising up with bright knives in their hands and awoke sweating and afraid. A movement behind him sent a wave of panic through him, and he rolled to his knees, scrabbling for his knife. A fox was pulling at the arm of one of the corpses. Relieved, Conn threw a stone at it. It yelped and ran into the undergrowth. Fully awake now, he added the last of the wood to the dying fire. He knew instinctively that the Morrigu's tale of necromancers and demons had been a lie, but even so . . . What if there had been more to the tale? What if it had not been merely a case of casual rape and murder? Then I would have slain three men unjustly, he thought.

He became aware of a thudding pain beneath his eye and reached up to find the skin swollen and tender where the knife hilt had struck him. Better not tell either the Big Man or Banouin about that part of the fight, he thought. If the knife had been better thrown, the fox would now be tearing at his dead flesh.

He wondered how Ruathain would react to his stupidity. Would he be angry? Probably. But he was a warrior himself, and his anger would be muted by his pride in Conn's achievement. Or so Conn hoped.

Just before dawn he heard horses moving through the woods. "Over here!" he yelled.

The first riders he saw were Banouin and Ruathain, then Arbon, Govannan, and a score of others. Ruathain slid from his pony and advanced to the dying fire. "What happened here?" he asked.

"I found three of them," said Conn. "There is no sign of the fourth."

"I think we have him," said Ruathain, pointing back to one of the riders, a slim man with a drooping blond mustache who sat his horse silently, his hands tied behind him. "We found him at the Blue Valley settlement buying supplies. He is a foreigner." Ruathain moved to the corpses, pulling clear the blankets.

Arbon dismounted and examined the bodies. "These are they," he told the riders. "See, the fat man bears scratches upon his face. You did well, Conn."

Conn accepted the praise without comment but glanced up

at Banouin. The foreigner looked angry and said nothing. And Ruathain's expression was unreadable.

"What will you do with the fourth man?" Conn asked Ruathain.

"He claims to have been traveling alone. I will take him to the Long Laird for judgment. You can ride with me. You will need the laird's permission to leave the land and travel with Banouin."

Some of the men dismounted and searched the camp and the bodies. They found three small pouches full of silver coin, and this was distributed among the riders. Ruathain and Banouin took nothing. Following their lead, neither did Conn. Then they buried the three dead men and rode away, leaving the youngster with Ruathain and the prisoner. Only then did the Big Man allow his anger to show.

"What were you thinking of, boy? Three grown men! They could have been skilled warriors."

"Maybe they were," Conn said, defensively.

Ruathain shook his head. "I am not as accomplished as Arbon, but I can read spoor. The fat man rushed at you like an idiot. The smaller man was running away when you bore him to the ground and cut his throat. Only the tall one had any skill, and he marked your face. What would I have said to your mother had you died here?"

"You would have told her I did not run," said Conn, his anger rising.

Ruathain closed his eyes and took a deep breath. "Your courage is not in question. For that matter, neither was your father's. But we are not talking of courage; we are talking of stupidity. What you did here was reckless. The fact that you won does not lessen it. I have known a lot of brave men, Conn. Many of them are dead now. Courage is meaningless unless it is allied to a keen mind." Stepping forward, he laid his hand on the youngster's shoulder. "I love you, Conn, and I am proud of you. But learn from this."

"I had to do it," Conn said softly. "It was the bear. I couldn't stand the fear anymore."

"Ah, I understand. Are you clear of it now?"

"Yes."

Ruathain put his arms around Conn and hugged him. "Then let us not mention this idiocy again," he said, kissing Conn's cheek.

The prisoner kneed his pony forward. "Would you mind freeing my hands?" he asked. "I can no longer feel my fingers."

Ruathain released Conn and gave the man a cold look. "Why should I care?" he asked.

"Listen to me," said the prisoner, "I appreciate that you think me guilty of murder, but I am an innocent traveler, as I am sure will be decided at the court you speak of. Or is it your habit to accost and bind every foreigner who has the misfortune to ride through your lands?"

Ruathain moved to the man, checking the bindings. They were indeed too tight, and he loosened them. The man winced as blood flowed through to his fingers. "Now let us ride," said Ruathain.

Brother Solstice was a Druid, though those who saw him for the first time did not believe it. Druids were in the main older men, solemn and deadly serious, ascetic and disdainful of the world and its pleasures. There were, of course, younger Druids, but since to the average observer they were men desperately trying before their time to become old, solemn, and deadly serious, they were viewed in exactly the same way as their seniors. Brother Solstice was altogether different: tall, wide-shouldered, barrel-chested, a man given to booming laughter and occasional practical jokes. He was also, unlike his brother priests, hugely popular. Curiously, this popularity even extended among the ranks of his brothers. It was rare to see a Druid laugh, but when such an event occurred, the black-bearded Brother Solstice would be at the center.

But today, Brother Solstice knew, there would be no laughter. He sat quietly in the hall of the Long Laird as the prisoner was brought in. The many trestle tables upon which the nobles usually dined had been pushed back to the walls, and the hall thronged with people waiting to see the murder trial. Before it could commence defendants in other cases were brought forward, men accused of small crimes against their neighbors, fights and scuffles mostly. A woman charged with assault caught the imagination of the crowd, and they hooted and jeered as she was brought in. She had, according to witnesses, hit her husband in the face with a lump of wood, breaking his nose and loosening his teeth. According to three witnesses, the husband had been seen in the company of an Earth Maiden earlier on the evening of the assault. The woman was acquitted, the assault deemed righteous. She was followed by a horse hunter said to have sold a lung-blown mount and a tinker accused of robbing a widow. The horse hunter was fined twenty silver pieces and ordered to return the pony price to the buyer, and the tinker was sentenced to a public flogging. Those cases would not alone have brought so many to witness the proceedings. Certainly the services of Brother Solstice would not have been requested. No, the populace of Old Oaks had come to see Brother Solstice question the man accused of rape and murder.

The prisoner was tall, his clothes, though travel-stained, expensive: a tunic shirt of fine blue wool edged with silver thread over leggings of soft black leather. Brother Solstice stared at the man's face. His eyes were pale blue, his hair blond, his mouth full under a drooping mustache. It was a good face, the kind of face one would trust, square-jawed and fine-boned.

Brother Solstice glanced at the Long Laird seated on the dais above him. The laird raised a heavy hand to quell the rising, angry murmurs from the crowd that had accompanied the arrival of the prisoner. "We'll have silence, if you please," said the Long Laird, his voice rumbling like distant thunder. Obedience was instantaneous. Brother Solstice smiled. The Long Laird had a manner most princes would have given a limb for. Past sixty now, his left arm arthritic and useless, his back bent, the Long Laird remained a commanding figure. The laird stroked his silver beard, then leaned forward to squint at the prisoner, who stood between two guards, back straight, arms bound behind him. The Long Laird waved the guards back, and the prisoner stood on his own at the center of the hall, the crowd pressing in around him like a human horseshoe.

The Long Laird leaned back in his chair and called Ruathain forward. Brother Solstice watched the man closely. He had met Ruathain on a number of occasions and liked him. There would be no need to waste his power seeking to ascertain whether the Three Streams man spoke the truth. Ruathain always spoke the truth. A butterfly wing of doubt touched him. Do not be complacent, Brother Solstice warned himself. A man's life is at stake here. Closing his eyes, he reached within himself, opening the hidden door to his power. Warmth flowed through him, and he opened his eyes.

The scene before him was the same except that the colors were infinitely brighter. Ruathain's green tunic shirt shone with the glory of spring, and around his exposed face and hands was an aura of pale golden light. Everything about the man was revealed to Brother Solstice: his pride, his courage, his need for honesty, his fears—even his dreams. And under the light Brother Solstice could see the darkness that touched every soul but in this man was held in check with chains stronger than iron.

I like you, Ruathain, he thought.

Under the questioning of the Long Laird, Ruathain told of the discovery of the murdered man and the girl, the chase, and the eventual discovery of the defendant purchasing supplies. He also added that the other three men had been killed in combat by his son, Connavar.

The Long Laird called the young man from the crowd. Brother Solstice leaned forward. Here, too, was the same golden light, but beneath it the darkness roiled like a caged lion, seeking a way to break free. The Druid gazed at Connavar, at the jagged red scar that ran from his temple to his jaw, and recalled the story of the boy and the bear. Then he saw the knife at the boy's belt. A shiver went through him.

A Seidh blade!

The Druid's eyes narrowed, and he felt his skin tingle. What are you, boy? he wondered.

The Long Laird questioned the youngster, who told of his fight with the three hunted men. The story was outlined without embellishment and became the more dramatic for it. At the conclusion the audience clapped their hands and cheered. Connavar reddened.

"How old are you, lad?" asked the Long Laird.

"Two months from sixteen, lord," answered Connavar.

"We have heard of you and your battle with the beast. You are a fine Rigante and a youngster we can be proud of. As your laird I name you a man before your time. From this moment forward you have a man's rights in council and in life. You may ask a gift from me and I shall grant it."

Connavar stood silently for a moment. "I need no gift, lord, but I did come here to seek your permission to travel with Banouin the Foreigner to his home across the southern sea."

The Long Laird was surprised, the Druid knew. Most men would have asked for a tract of land or a string of ponies. The boy asked for nothing, for even without his heroics, it was unlikely his request for travel would have been denied. The old man smiled. "You seek too little from me, tribesman. I grant your wish to travel south, and more than that I shall supply a fine horse and a sword. Come to my house after the trials are concluded." Connavar bowed and returned to the crowd.

The Long Laird levered himself painfully to his feet. He was a tall man and had once been the most powerful warrior in the north. Even now he was a formidable figure. Tucking his useless arm into his wide belt, he approached the prisoner. "You are accused of a crime most dreadful, the penalty for which is death by drowning. There is no physical evidence with which to convict you, which is why Brother Solstice is here. He is, as you can see from his white robes, a Druid. Of his many skills, the one which should concern you most is his ability to detect lies. He will question you. I urge that you speak the truth."

"I will speak the truth, lord," said the man, "for I have nothing to fear."

"Tell us your name and your tribe," said the Long Laird.

"I am Lexac of the Ostro tribe. My father is a merchant and sent me here to acquire exclusive rights to ship and sell the oiled woolen coats crafted in the isles."

The Long Laird turned to Brother Solstice. The Druid rose and walked forward to stand before the prisoner. Dipping his hand into the pocket of his robe, Brother Solstice produced a small black rat, which he held high, gently stroking the fur of its back.

"Let us be clear, Lexac of the Ostro, about what is to take place here. I shall ask you questions, and you will answer them. If you speak the truth, no harm will befall you in this place. If you lie, great will be your pain. Do you understand what I have said?"

"Yes," said Lexac, his eyes watching the rat.

"Good. This is my little helper. He is the truth seeker." Brother Solstice raised his arm high above his head. The sleeve of his robe slid down, revealing the powerful muscles of his forearm and biceps. The black rat sat up in his hand, then vanished. The prisoner blinked. "The truth seeker has gone," he said. "But he will return. Now, you say you were sent here to buy rights to the oiled wool."

"Yes," answered Lexac.

"Think carefully before you answer the next question. Three killers met their deaths two days ago. Did you know them?"

"Yes, I did."

"How so?"

"I saw them on the ship and spoke to them. Two of them were known to me before that."

"Did you ride with them after you landed?"

"Yes, for a time."

"But you were not with them when they came across the victim and his daughter?"

"No, I—" The prisoner suddenly convulsed, his back arching. Blood sprayed from his mouth. The crowd gasped as something black pushed itself from inside the prisoner's mouth. The black rat scrabbled clear of the man's lips and leapt to the waiting hand of Brother Solstice. Lexac fell to his knees and vomited. Two guards came forward, hauling the prisoner to his feet. He was trembling uncontrollably, his eyes wide and staring at the small creature in the Druid's outstretched hand. Once more Brother Solstice raised his arm. Once more the rat disappeared. The prisoner screamed.

"Be calm!" ordered the Druid. "Speak the truth and you will not suffer. But lie once more and the truth seeker will appear deep in your belly. Then with fang and claw he will tear himself a way to freedom. Do you understand?"

Lexac nodded dumbly, blood dribbling from his torn lips.

"You were with them when the deed was done?"

"Yes."

"You took part in it?"

"Yes."

"Was the dead man known to you?"

"Yes. He was a rival of my father's."

"Also seeking the rights to the oiled wool?"

"Yes."

"So the murder was done for greed? The rape was merely an afterthought?"

"Yes. I am sorry. I am so sorry."

Brother Solstice held up his hand. The rat appeared there, and the Druid turned away from the prisoner.

The Long Laird stepped forward. "Tonight Brother Solstice will come to you. He will write your account of the deed. This account will be sent to your father, as will mine of how you met your death." Two guards moved in and took hold of the prisoner's arms. Lexac began to weep piteously. The crowd, still stunned by the Druid's magic, was silent as the prisoner was led away.

Brother Solstice strode from the hall into the bright sunlight beyond. The rat in his hand began to shrink until it was no more than it had always been, a piece of black fur two inches square. The blood had come when Lexac in his panic had bitten his own lips. Only the Long Laird knew the secret, and even he could not quite comprehend at first why Brother Solstice used such magic.

"We all know your skills, Brother," the Long Laird had said. "If you just tell us a man is guilty, we will execute him."

"That is not safe, my friend. You are right. I always tell the truth in these matters. But evil can strike anywhere: in a peasant, in a laird, in a Druid. In days to come, when I am long dead, another Druid might come, a liar and a cheat. It would be dangerous to establish a precedent that says his word alone can bring about the death of an accused man. As it is, my little truth seeker ensures that the guilty man himself confesses his sin."

In the bright sunshine outside the hall Brother Solstice drew in a deep, cleansing breath and let the power pass from him. His heart was heavy, for the condemned man had not been wholly evil. Indeed, there was much good in him. Now the good as well as the evil would be confined to the murky waters of the peat marsh.

Brother Solstice was not anticipating with any pleasure the evening he would spend with the prisoner.

Connavar left the hall and wandered toward the high palisade. Wooden walls crafted from sharpened tree trunks circled the hill fortress, creating the image of a crown high above Old Oaks. Climbing a set of wooden steps, Connavar reached the battlements and stared out over the settlement far below. Hundreds of small round houses stretched south for over a mile to the river, with larger homes decorating the eastern hills. The fortress of the Long Laird was an impressive structure that three times during the last fifty years had withstood sieges from Sea Raiders. The hill on which it was set was steep, and attackers, with no cover, were prey to a hail of missiles raining down on them from the defenders.

Connavar strode along the battlements, gazing across to the woodlands far to the south. Thoughts of Arian filled his mind. How could she wed another? Especially after that night of passion by the stream. It had been the most perfect time of his young life, and he felt that their spirits had bonded together in a manner so wonderful as to be unique. No one in the world, he believed, could have ever known such magic, such harmony. And yet she had betrayed him.

Now that passion and those anguished moans were for Casta. He felt the anger building within him and pictured his blade plunging into Casta's belly, ripping free his soul. Guilt followed instantly. Casta was not to blame. He had not forced her to wed him. She had done so willingly as Conn lay close to death. It was all so confusing. She had said she loved him. And it had been a terrible lie. Why, then, had she said it? What was there to gain?

Hearing the rampart steps creak behind him, Conn turned to see Brother Solstice climbing to the battlements. The man was powerfully built, looking every inch a fighter, which to Conn made nonsense of the ankle-length white Druid robe he wore. He had never seen anyone look less like a priest. As he came closer, Conn saw a scar similar to his own showing beneath the Druid's black beard.

"I fought in three battles," said Brother Solstice, touching the scar. "But that was before I heard the call."

"You read minds," said Conn, feeling suddenly uncomfortable.

"Yes, but that would be discourteous. I merely noticed you staring." Brother Solstice wandered to the wall and gazed out over the land. "It is beautiful from here, high above the sorry troubles of the world. Look at the homes. Do they not seem tranquil and uniform? Yet each of them houses a host of emotions: love, lust, anger, greed, envy, and hatred. And, to a sadly lesser degree kindness, compassion, caring, selflessness. The view may be beautiful, but it is unreal."

"Where is your rat?" asked Conn.

"I see you are not interested in my philosophy," Brother Solstice said, with a rueful smile. "What does interest you, Connavar?"

Conn shrugged. He did not want to talk to this man of magic, and he cared nothing for the emotions raging within the little round houses below. But the Druid stood quietly waiting for an answer. "The people of Stone," said Conn at last. "They interest me."

"They are the enemy to come," said Brother Solstice.

Conn was surprised. "You have had a vision?"

"I don't need a vision, Connavar. When the leaves fall from the trees, I know winter is approaching. Across the water many Druids have been murdered by them. They are a hungry people, and their ambition is limitless. Is that why you asked for permission to cross the water? To study these war bringers?"

"Yes."

"And what exactly will you study?"

The answer seemed all too obvious. "Their armies and how they fight."

"That would be a beginning. But to defeat them you will also need to learn *why* they fight."

Conn's irritation was growing now. "What does that matter?" he snapped. Brother Solstice fell silent. He closed his eyes, and for a moment only Conn felt a cool breeze touch his face. A sense of calm flowed through him, submerging the anger he felt at Arian's betrayal.

"Can we talk now?" asked Brother Solstice.

"You cast a spell on me?" replied Conn.

"Not *on* you. *Around* you. It will prove fleeting. I would ask what is troubling you, but I fear such a question would bring back your anger. You are a strong young man, Connavar, but you need to offer your mind the same dedication you give your body. However, I do not wish to lecture you." He smiled. "But I would be interested to know how you acquired a Seidh blade."

Normally Conn would have said, as he usually did, that it was a gift from Banouin, but embarrassed by his earlier rudeness and appreciating that he was in the presence of a man who could detect lies, he told the truth, about his determination to seek help in the matter of his parents' continuing separation and the fawn he had found in the brambles.

Brother Solstice listened intently. When Conn had finished, the Druid looked perplexed. "So, apart from the fawn, you did not see a Seidh or speak to one?"

"No."

"How strange they are. But know this, young man: They had a purpose of their own. They saw in you something that would benefit them. Gifts from the Seidh are not without a price."

"What are they?" asked Conn.

Now it was Brother Solstice who shrugged. "I could not

begin to explain their origins. Some believe they are the souls of great heroes living forever in a world like our own; others see them as demons or gods. I do not have all the answers. What I do know is that they are vital to the land."

"In what way?"

Brother Solstice smiled. "You would have to become a Druid and accept all our vows in order to learn *that* secret. But it should be enough for you to know they are a fey race and often malevolent. And they are old, older than the moon and the oceans."

"Have you ever met one?" asked Conn.

"Only one, and we do not speak her name," said the Druid.

"Ah," said Conn. "I, too, have met her. She it was who sent the bear to kill me. And when I fought the killers, she came to me and offered me a gift. I did not take it."

"You were wise to refuse."

"If I were truly wise, I would have refused the first time, and then the bear would not have ripped away my flesh and cost me my love."

"Your love?" inquired the Druid.

Conn was surprised at himself, for the words had slipped out before he could stop them. And in that moment he realized that he needed to speak of Arian. Slowly he told Brother Solstice the whole story. The Druid listened in silence, and when Conn had finished, he stood lost in thought. Finally he turned to the young man and spoke, his voice sorrowful. "Her betrayal must have cut worse than the talons of the bear," he said.

"Aye, it did. Why did she do it?"

"I do not know her, Connavar, so I can only guess at her reasons. You have learned a savage lesson. Just because we feel great love does not necessarily mean it is reciprocated. For you it was a wondrous—almost spiritual—moment. For her it was—perhaps—merely pleasure. Or need. Ruathain told me last year that you carried the crippled boy to the falls and taught him to swim. For Riamfada the gift you gave him was greater than a mountain of gold. For him swimming was freedom and a joy he had never before experienced. For you swimming is a refreshing and pleasant diversion. You see what I am saying? To an outsider there are just two boys enjoying themselves. The reality is wholly different."

Conn took a deep breath, then sighed. "You are saying that with Arian I am like Riamfada."

"More than you probably realize even now," said Brother Solstice. "Now let us speak of it no more. She is wed to another and gone from your life."

"I doubt she will ever be gone from my life," Conn said sadly.

"I hope that you are wrong."

Below them, the hall doors opened and the crowd streamed out, heading for the gates and the winding path to the settlement below. "You should go back now," said Brother Solstice. "It would be discourteous to keep the laird waiting."

Conn thrust out his hand. "Thank you, sir. And I apologize for my earlier behavior."

Brother Solstice grinned and grasped the offered hand. "You do not need to apologize. Go now and choose your sword and your pony."

The death of winter and the promise of a new season was a time of celebration for the Rigante, and the Feast of Beltine was always a joyous occasion. The maidens of Three Streams and the surrounding settlements dressed in their finest clothes and decorated their hair with green leaves and fresh flowers. The young men, stripped to the waist, daubed blue ocher on their faces and upper bodies and took part in fire dancing, footraces, and wrestling bouts. At dusk the people assembled at the center of the settlement and, linking arms, danced around Eldest Tree before forming a torch-lit procession that wound past all the homes, across the Three Streams, and back to the feasting pits.

Banouin watched the scene with both affection and envy. The closeness of the Rigante, their easy tactility, and their obvious enjoyment in each other's company were good to see, yet it was a joy he could not share. Not just because he was a foreigner, though that was a part of it, but more because he was a solitary man not given to any form of tribalism. He understood the need for a community spirit. These people depended on each other. The success or failure of any individual would have repercussions on the community as a whole. But Banouin was different. He liked people well enough as individuals, but a gathering such as this left him feeling isolated and alone.

Across the feasting area he saw Connavar drinking and laughing with his friends, among them the crippled Riamfada. Even from here Banouin could see the terrible scars on Connavar's upper body. He shuddered. To call his survival a miracle would be to understate the matter. To the right Ruathain was talking to the widow Pelain. Her husband, the fat baker, had collapsed and died six days before. Vorna said his heart had given out. Pelain did not seem to be wholly grief-stricken, and Banouin was amused to see her making obvious efforts to impress Ruathain. Constantly she ran her fingers through her dark hair, her gaze fixed to his face, her body turned fully toward him. Banouin looked to the left, where Meria was talking with Vorna and the black-bearded Druid Brother Solstice. Every few heartbeats Meria would glance toward Ruathain, her face expressionless. Banouin thought he could see the anger in her eyes.

Toward midnight, as Banouin sat quietly beneath Eldest Tree, nursing his sixth mug of strong ale and watching the young dancers twirling in the firelight, the former witch Vorna came and sat beside him. She had put on weight in the last few weeks, which had the effect of giving her a more

youthful appearance. Banouin was surprised that he found
her attractive. He gazed into his ale. Could it be that powerful? he wondered.

"You do not dance, you do not sing," she said. "You merely
sit and watch."

"There is joy in that for me," he told her. "I love the Rigante: the people, their customs. Everything."

"I, too." The music faded as the pipers moved away to re-
fresh themselves.

"I notice that you do not dance, Vorna. Nor have I heard
you sing."

She smiled, leaned back against the huge tree, and gazed
up through its branches to the crescent moon above. "I dance
in my mind, I sing in my heart."

"You sound happy."

"Merry," she said. "I have drunk too much wine. But yes, I
am happy, too. The spring is here, and my people have survived the winter."

"There is more to it than that," he said, raising his voice
slightly as the music of the dance started up again.

She smiled at him. "Yes, there is more. I feel alive for the
first time. My heart is open. There is great strength in magic
and enormous knowledge to be gained. Even so the magic
separated me from my people. In some ways it separated me
from me. I feel whole. Complete. Can you understand that?"

"No, but I am happy for you."

"Will you dance with me, foreigner?"

"I think that I will," he said, carefully placing his mug on
the ground and pushing himself to his feet. For a moment the
ground swayed under him, then he took her arm and joined
the other dancers under the moonlight.

He was not as drunk as he had feared and found himself
moving in perfect time to the music, twirling and leaping,
drawn deeper into the heart of the joy that filled the Rigante.

It was a heady and powerful experience, and he lost all sense of time. At last Vorna took his arm and led him away.

Banouin found himself at his own front door. There was no lock, only a latch, which he lifted, pushing the door open. Stepping aside, he gestured Vorna to enter. She stood hesitantly in the doorway.

"Perhaps I should not come in," she said.

"Then again, perhaps you should," he said with a gentle smile. "It has been a long time since a woman graced my home."

"Since your wife died," she said. The pain of memory made him wince.

Vorna moved in close to him. "I am sorry, foreigner. When I had the power, I knew many things."

He took her hand and kissed it. "Do not be sorry. She was a fine and wonderful woman. I should think of her more often. But it is always so painful."

They stood in silence for a while, enjoying the closeness. "I have never been with a man," said Vorna.

He looked into her dark eyes and saw the fear and the loneliness. "It is merely another kind of dance," he said softly. "Will you dance with me, Vorna?"

"I think that I will," she said.

Back at the feast Riamfada was growing sleepy. He could not drink wine. It burned in his chest like a small fire, and he dared not drink ale for fear of wetting himself. He had sat quietly through the feast, watching his friends enjoy themselves and taking great pleasure from it. He leaned back into the V-shaped board that had been hammered in the grass for him to prevent him from falling and lifted his heavy blanket over his shoulder. It had been a joyous night. Govannan had been dancing with a young maiden from a settlement some thirty miles to the south. He had tripped over his own feet several times, but she had affected not to notice. Connavar had not danced, and Riamfada saw him watching Arian on the far side of the bonfire. She had danced with several men, much to the chagrin of her new husband, Casta, who sat glumly nearby. Farther to the right Riamfada saw Braefar. The boy was nursing a slight burn to his leg he had incurred when he had tried to leap the feasting pit with taller, stronger boys. He had fallen back, and hot coals had pressed against his knee. He was sitting now beside his younger brother, the eight-year-old Bendegit Bran, who was asleep, curled up against the grizzled, white-muzzled old hound Caval.

Riamfada yawned and looked around for his father. Gariapha was sitting at a bench with the Long Laird. Both men were drinking and laughing. Riamfada pulled his cloak around his thin shoulders. A spasm of pain shot through his chest, and he grunted. He should not have added Banouin's spices to the beef.

Connavar wandered over and sat down beside him. "How are you faring, little fish?" he asked.

"I am enjoying myself. But I am getting very tired."

"I'll carry you home."

"No, not yet," said Riamfada. "It is a wonderful night. I have been watching people dancing in the torchlight. Everyone is so happy."

"And you, are you happy, my friend?" asked Conn.

"The swimming starts next week," Riamfada said with a smile. "I have been looking forward to it all winter." He coughed suddenly, and his emaciated body shuddered. Conn leaned in, taking Riamfada's weight and lightly tapping his back. The coughing subsided. "I will be strong again once we are back at the falls," he said.

"I will be with you only for a while," said Conn. "I am traveling south with Banouin. But Govanann will be taking you at least twice a week."

"I heard you were leaving." Riamfada glanced across to the long dining table. Conn's new sword was leaning there, its bronze hilt flickering in the firelight. "Will you show me the Long Laird's gift?" he asked. Conn strode across to the table, retrieved the weapon, and brought it back, laying it in Riamfada's lap. With difficulty Riamfada hefted it by blade and grip, bringing it close to his face. Then he let it drop. "I cannot tell if it is good iron," he said. "Not in this light. But the hilt is clumsily crafted, so I would guess not. One day I will make for you a special sword with a hilt designed for your hand alone. It will be a creation of beauty."

"I am sure that it will," said Conn. At that moment Gòvannan called out, urging Conn to join in the new dance. Conn looked to Riamfada. "Shall I carry you home?"

"In a little while. Go. Dance. I shall rest here."

Conn grinned and ran to the fire, where he was soon twirling and leaping the flames to the music of the pipes. The sword lay heavily on Riamfada, and he struggled to put it to one side. As he did so, another piercing pain sliced through his chest. He grunted and fell back against the V-shaped board. He tried to watch the dancers, but the images were fading, blurring. He could no longer make out individual figures, and the music seemed to be growing more distant, as if the pipers were dancing away from him. I must be more tired than I thought, he reasoned.

Glowing lights caught his eye. They were drifting through the air toward him. Three of them. How pretty, he thought. They were mostly golden in color, but there were flashes of blue and crimson within them. They flickered before him and settled down upon the grass around him. Riamfada tried to reach out to them but found he was unable to move his hand. Strangely, this did not concern him. He was at peace. The lights flowed over him, and he heard a voice whispering in his mind.

"Come with us. Know joy."

In that instant he had a vision of a workplace where every kind of metal could be fashioned by hand alone, without need of heat or hammer. He saw objects of incredible beauty, among them a rose crafted of gold and silver that was so perfect that its golden petals blossomed and opened like a true plant. "I wish I could work there," he said.

"That is what we offer you, child of man. Come with us!"

"I do not want to leave my friends," said Riamfada, though the longing was strong within him.

"You already have."

And he knew that it was true, for there was now no feeling in his body, no heartbeat weak and stuttering in his emaciated chest.

"Rise, Riamfada. Walk with us." A hand with a touch as light as a butterfly wing touched his own, drawing him upright, and he stood. There was no pain. Slowly Riamfada, surrounded by golden light, moved unseen through the dancers. There was Conn, arm in arm with Gwydia, and Govannan clapping his hands to the music. And there was Riamfada's father, Gariapha, holding his wife close and kissing her cheek. Riamfada looked back and saw the small, frail body wedged in death against the boards. Then he looked again at his friends, enjoying their happiness one last time.

"I love them," he said.

"We know."

Taking him by the hand, they led him toward the Wishing Tree Woods.

"Can I run?" asked Riamfada.

They released his hands. He suddenly felt the grass beneath his naked feet, the night breeze upon his chest.

And Riamfada ran toward the distant trees.

In the house of Banouin Vorna's eyes flared open. Slipping quietly from the bed, she moved to the window and saw the lights flowing toward the Wishing Tree Woods. Despite the loss of her power she could still commune with the Seidh and recognize their magic. And she could discern the difference between Seidh spirit and human souls. Transferring her gaze to the distant lights, she tried to make out who the Seidh had taken, but she could not. What she did know, however, was that the human was full of joy.

"What are you looking at?" Banouin asked sleepily.

"A small miracle," she told him, returning to the bed and sliding under the covers. He took her in his arms, and she settled her head upon his shoulder.

"I hope you have no regrets," he whispered. "For I have none."

"How old are you, foreigner?"

"Forty-nine."

"I regret not doing this twenty years ago."

His fingers stroked through her black and silver hair. "I fear that sex is not always as good as this," he said.

"Prove it," she said, sliding her thigh over his legs.

They made love until the dawn and then slept for several hours. Banouin awoke first, rekindled the fire in the main room, and cooked a breakfast of hot oats sweetened with honey and a hot tisane of dried elder flower petals. He carried the tisane to Vorna and woke her gently. Then he left her to dress.

She joined him in the main room, and they ate in companionable silence. "How long will you be gone?" she asked him.

"Four, five months. Will you miss me?"

"I think that I will," she admitted.

"That is good," he told her with a smile.

She fell silent and sipped her tisane. "What are you thinking?" he asked.

Vorna glanced up. "I was thinking of you and your *geasa*."

Banouin smiled. "A wonderful people are the Rigante, but they do suffer some odd customs. Why is it that every tribesman is forced to carry such a curse? It seems nonsense to me."

"The *geasa* is not a curse," she said. "It is a protective

prophecy. The village witch, or holy woman, or sometimes the Druid lays hands on a newborn and seeks a vision. What they are looking for is a pivotal moment in the child's future. Mostly *geasas* do not foretell death. They will point to areas of success or happiness. Eighteen years ago I placed a *geasa* on a baby girl. It was that if she ever saw a three-legged fox, she should follow it. Last year she saw a fox that had three legs, and she followed her *geasa*. She found a young man sitting by a stream. He was a Pannone, traveling with his uncle. He fell in love with her in that moment, and they were wed at the Feast of Samain."

"Well, you are far too young to have been at my birth, lady. And I am far too old to concern myself with superstitious fears." Suddenly he grinned. "But tell me my *geasa* anyway— if you know it."

"I know it, Banouin. I sensed it on the first day I saw you. Drink no wine when you see the lion with eyes of blood."

He laughed. "I would have thought that to see such a beast I would already have to have drunk far too much wine."

"You will know when the moment comes, Banouin. Be vigilant. I do not want to lose you now. Promise me you will remember my words."

"I will remember, and you will not lose me," he said. "What is Connavar's *geasa*?"

"He will die on the day he kills the hound that bites him."

"Then I shall see that he steers clear of dogs," said Banouin. "But let me understand this. If a man does not break his *geasa*, does he live forever?"

"No."

"Very well, another question, then: Nothing can kill me until I have seen a lion with eyes of blood?"

"No," she answered with a smile. "Sometimes—though not often—a man will die ahead of his time. A chance arrow, a fall from a horse, a plague or a sickness. All that is certain is that if you break your *geasa*, you will die on that day."

"I see. So with a *geasa* and ten silver coins I could buy a pony."

"It is always best to avoid mocking what we do not understand," she told him sternly.

Banouin was instantly contrite. "I am sorry if it sounded like mockery. I am feeling lighthearted and full of warmth. But I promise you I would never sneer at Rigante customs. I love your people and their culture. But I was talking to Ruathain about *geasas*, and he told me his: 'Be not the king's shield.' He was laughing about it, since the Rigante have no kings."

"Ruathain is not my concern at this time," she told him. "I did not make his prophecy. Do you promise me you will remember the lion?"

Banouin placed his hand on his heart. "I promise you," he said. Reaching out, he took her hand. "Now, will you stay here with me until I leave next week?"

"That would cause much talk in the settlement."

"We could walk the tree together," he said softly, still holding to her hand. The words hung in the air.

"Marriage is not a commitment to be made lightheartedly," she said.

"No, it is not."

"Tell me why I should," she whispered.

"Does it need words?" he asked, moving in close, his fingers stroking her face.

"It *always* needs words, foreigner."

His kissed her cheek, then lightly brushed his lips across her ear. "I love you," he told her.

"And I you," she replied. "We will walk around the tree."

◇ 7 ◇

THE WIND WAS picking up, the waves choppy beneath the small ship, causing it to rear and shudder. Connavar gripped the bow rail and stared back longingly at the chalk cliffs. Gulls wheeled and banked above the ship, filling the air with their screeching cries. Conn glanced up, his thoughts venomous. He found the noise wearing on his nerves. The deck lurched beneath his feet. Conn's fingers tightened on the rail. His stomach heaved. A sailor ambled past him and grinned. Conn felt like burying his fist in the man's face, but to do so would have meant letting go of the rail.

Banouin appeared alongside him. The little merchant was wearing a heavy coat of sheepskin and carrying a baked loaf of cheese bread. Ripping off a chunk, he offered it to Conn. The youngster shook his head.

"Best to eat. Otherwise you'll be spilling your guts over the side," said Banouin. Reluctantly Conn grabbed the bread and took a bite. It tasted of ash and bile. Slowly he chewed and swallowed. The white cliffs were smaller now, the gulls wheeling away to return to the land. Conn wished he had wings so that he could join them. "Keep eating," ordered Banouin. Conn finished the bread and was surprised to find that his stomach was settling. He glanced at the sky. It was the color of iron, and in the distance he could see storm clouds.

"How long before we reach Goriasa?" he asked.

"Four, five hours."

Conn shivered. Banouin walked across the flat deck to where the twenty pack ponies and two mounts were tethered and pulled Conn's pale blue cloak clear of the ties at the back of his saddle. Returning to the youngster, he lifted it over his shoulders. Conn smiled his thanks and clipped it in place with the fawn in brambles brooch Riamfada had made for him. Behind them Conn's steeldust gelding whinnied in fear as the ship lurched once more. Releasing the rail, Conn staggered over to where the pony was tied and stroked its long nose. "You are just like me," whispered Conn. "Neither of us has been on a ship before, and neither of us likes it." Feeling the confident touch of its rider, the gelding calmed down. Conn patted its neck and moved back to where Banouin was sitting on the deck, out of the wind. Crouching down, Conn joined him.

"Will the Stone army be at Goriasa?" he asked.

"No. They have not yet advanced into the lands of the Ostro or the Gath. The last war was against the Aiddui, about eighty miles to the east. The general Jasaray won two great victories on the coast there. He will now be solidifying his gains. I would not expect a war against the Gath for at least another two years, maybe three. No, I think the Perdii will be the next tribe to face the Stone Panthers. Jasaray was probably planning the Perdii war even before he marched against the Aiddui."

"What kind of plans?" asked Conn.

Banouin smiled. "War for the Rigante is like a lightning storm: fast, furious, and swiftly completed. Not so for the people of Stone. They seek to conquer and hold the territories they win. What is the most important consideration for a general?"

"Courageous fighters," Conn answered instantly.

"No," said Banouin, "it is food and forage. It does not matter how courageous your soldiers are if they are starving. An army of twenty thousand men needs an immense amount of grain, dried fruit, meat. Every day. Five thousand horses need hundreds of acres of grazing. Every day. When Jasaray advances into enemy lands, he will need to be supplied. Therefore, he will now be wooing various tribal chieftains—the Gath among them—who are hostile to the Perdii. These chieftains will supply his army when he marches."

A light rain began to fall. Moving once more to the ponies, Banouin untied a canvas sheet, which he carried back to the bow rail. Stretching it out, he lifted it over his head. Conn took the other end, and together they sat under the sheet as the rain began to increase. The constant pattering against the canvas made conversation impossible, and both men sat silently, each lost in his own thoughts.

Connavar was thinking of Riamfada and wondering, not for the first time, whether the crippled youth would still have been alive if he had carried him home when he first had complained of tiredness. There was no way he would ever know, and the guilt hung over him like a dark mantle. They had buried Riamfada on the edge of the Wishing Tree Woods, which was highly unusual, but Vorna had insisted that the burial site was fitting. She had sat quietly with Gariapha and Wiocca, out of earshot of the other mourners, discussing it. When they came out, Riamfada's parents seemed comforted by Vorna's words. Riamfada, his frail body wrapped in blankets, had been carried on a two-wheeled cart to the edge of the woods. There Gariapha, Connavar, and Govannan had dug a deep grave. Vorna had given a short oration commending Riamfada's spirit to the gods, then the mourners had poured wine over the grave, re-covered it with turf, and moved back down to the settlement.

As they walked back, Govannan had come alongside Conn. "Do you regret saving him?" he had asked.

Conn had found the question astonishing. "What do you mean?"

"Look at what you suffered. And it only brought him a few weeks of life. Was it worth it?"

"What do you think?"

Govannan shrugged. "Do not misunderstand me, Conn. I miss him already. And I feel heart-struck by his death. It is just . . . I don't know. It all seems so pointless. He lived in constant pain, couldn't walk, couldn't even control his bladder and his bowels. Now he's dead at seventeen. It feels . . . unfair."

Vorna, who was walking behind them, stepped forward. "You cannot judge the quality of Riamfada's human life. You did not live it. He died happy. Not many do. Believe me."

"Why do you say 'human' life?" asked Conn.

"I saw him run across the grass," answered Vorna, but when Conn made to question her further, she merely smiled and touched her finger to her lips. "All things in their own season," she said. "We will talk of this again." She moved away to where Banouin was waiting at the foot of the hill.

"Can you believe it?" whispered Govannan. "Vorna. Married!"

"I am pleased for her," said Conn. "And for Banouin. He has been lonely for too long."

On the day they left Vorna embraced Banouin publicly and gave him a cloak brooch of bronze inset with a blue opal. "This brooch carries a charm," she said softly. "It will always find a way to return to me. Keep it with you always."

"I shall," he said, tucking the brooch into his saddlebag.

The journey south to the sea took two months, crossing many tribal lands and visiting scores of settlements. Banouin traded at many of them, buying cloth, jewelry, ornately carved weapons, daggers, and hunting knives. By the time they reached the coast, the original eleven pack ponies were heavily burdened and Banouin had leased nine more. As they rode, Banouin pointed out landmarks during the day and on several occasions urged Conn to study their backtrail. "You'll be surprised how different the land will look on the return journey, when autumn strips the trees or the rivers swell. Always look back and fix in your mind the changing landscapes." He taught Conn about the different tribes: their beliefs and their codes. But rarely did he speak of Vorna. Conn began to wonder if the merchant was regretting his decision to wed.

On the last night, as they camped in a small wood overlooking the chalk cliffs, he broached the subject. Banouin smiled. "Regrets? No, I have none, Conn. I have lived too long alone."

"Your decision to wed was rather sudden," Conn pointed out.

"Aye, it was. I am a careful man. Too cautious, perhaps. But on the night of the feast she released in me a need for joy that I had forgotten. This will be my last journey, Conn. I have decided to settle down and live the rest of my days among the Rigante."

"What will you do?"

"Do? I will teach, and I will learn. Oh, I will still trade, but no more long journeys. I will walk the mountains with Vorna. She can teach me about herbs and Rigante lore."

"Will you not miss the traveling?"

"I would—if the world had remained as it was when I began. But it is changing, Conn. And not, I fear, for the better."

The following morning they led the ponies down to the harbor. Conn's heart sank when he saw the little ship with its flat, open deck and its two sails. It seemed to him to be flimsy, and when he gazed out at the gray, forbidding sea, he was filled with a sense of foreboding.

He felt it now even more strongly as he sat beneath the canvas sheet, the rain hissing down, the wind howling about him. The storm continued steadily for three long hours, then began to ease away as a bright shaft of sunlight bathed the rear deck. Banouin pushed back the canvas and stood. Conn rose beside him, shaking the surplus water from the sheet. "I do not like ships," he said.

"If you can think of a better way to cross the sea, I'd like to hear it," said Banouin, stretching his back. He groaned. "I am getting too old to sit under canvas. Tonight we will rest in a wonderful tavern where the food is glorious, the entertainment divine, and the beds soft. It will be a great experience for you." Reaching into the pouch at his side, Banouin produced four silver coins, which he passed to Conn.

"What are these for?"

"You may find use for them," Banouin said with a wide smile. "Pleasure in Goriasa is never free."

Goriasa proved an unpleasant surprise to Conn. Banouin had told him it was a large settlement, and Conn had pictured a village perhaps twice the size of Three Streams. The reality was vastly different. Goriasa was a city that flowed in a huge, ugly crescent around a sheltered bay. Thousands of wooden houses, storage buildings, stables, and paddocks were crushed together, separated only by narrow strips of muddy, foul-smelling earth. The few areas of open ground were covered by market stalls and thronged with crowds.

Banouin and Conn threaded their mounts through the mass, coming at last to a tall storehouse. A grizzled old man with only one ear stepped out to meet them. He and Banouin spoke, then the man led the ponies into the building. On foot now, Banouin and Conn moved out into the crowd. Conn was uncomfortable. His experience of large numbers of people was limited to feast days, when everyone was happy or drunk and there was dancing and joy. Here there was no joy. The people all seemed in a hurry, their faces strained. People did not greet one another or make eye contact.

Banouin cut to the left into a narrow alley, picking his way across wooden boards laid down over the mud. Conn followed him, and they emerged onto a wider, less crowded path. "It is not always this busy," said Banouin. "It is the start of the trading season, and thousands of merchants descend on Goriasa."

"Where are we going?"

"To travelers hall. I need to speak to Garshon. He is the senior councillor in Goriasa and will take—or so I hope— two-thirds of all my trade goods. We will travel on with only six ponies."

The travelers hall was an impressive structure some two hundred feet long and sixty feet wide built on the northern edge of Goriasa. It was a wooden building, two stories high, with no windows but more than a dozen doors on each side. It was the largest building Conn had ever seen. It seemed to him to be both magnificent and supremely ugly. Inside it was split into many areas. At the far end, to the left, there were bench tables where men sat eating and drinking. In the center was a large sand circle surrounded by tiered seats. These were full, and Conn could see a tall horse being led around the sand. The auctioneer was taking bids for the beast. Conn paused. The horse was a chestnut stallion at least sixteen hands high. It would dwarf the ponies of the Rigante. He listened to the bidding. The horse went for 110 silver pieces. A fabulous sum!

Banouin tapped his arm, and Conn followed him around the circle to another dining area with tables set around a raised dais. Most of the tables were full, but Banouin found a clear area by the western wall and sat down.

"We will eat here," he said. "The food is beyond compare." Conn looked around but could see no cook fires. Several women were moving among the diners, collecting plates. Then others came in from outside, bearing trays carrying plates laden with meats and vegetables and pottery jugs filled with ale. Banouin raised his arm and caught the eye of one of the girls. Blond and slender, she moved through the throng to halt beside the table. Banouin asked her what dishes were available. Conn sat quietly as she listed the meals: roasted duck, breast of pheasant, tender loin of beef, spiced swan, cold ham, pigeon pie, ox tongue, brain of sheep, larks' tongues. The food on offer seemed to be endless. Banouin ordered for them both, and the girl moved away. Conn's gaze followed her.

"Very pretty," said Banouin.

Conn blushed. "Did you see the horse?" he asked, determined to change the subject.

"Yes. Thassilian. Good mounts, fast and strong. Good for racing, bad for war."

"Why bad?" asked Conn. "Are they high-spirited?"

"I told you that food is the most important aspect in a campaign. Think of the horses. They need to survive on forage alone, and sometimes not much of that. They will be ridden hard every day, sometimes for weeks. Thassilian horses need grain feeding to remain at their best. Also, they have delicate constitutions and are prone to lung blight and worm."

"I have much to learn," said Conn. "But I will."

Banouin smiled. "Aye, you will. You have a quick mind."

The ale arrived first, and with it a loaf of brown bread dusted with poppy seeds. It was good bread, Conn decided, though not as fine as that produced by the late Borga. But the meat dish was a delight: roasted lamb with a sauce of shredded mint and wine vinegar. Conn devoured it with relish. They finished the meal with a pie filled with red fruit. Conn leaned back in his chair. "That was excellent," he said. "Just as you promised."

"There are many delights in Goriasa," said Banouin. "Do not judge the city merely by the ugliness of its exterior. Now, I must find Garshon. You wander the hall. There are many chambers and much to see and enjoy. I will meet you by the sand circle in a couple of hours." Summoning the serving girl, Banouin paid her, then rose and left the table.

The girl lingered. "Are you new here?" she asked Conn.

"Yes. We arrived this afternoon. By ship."

Reaching forward, she stroked his face. "How did you come by the scar?" she asked him. Her touch made him feel awkward.

"A bear's claw," he said.

"You have other scars?" She was leaning in really close now.

"Yes."

"I would like to see them."

"You like to see scars?" he replied, astonished.

"I would like to see yours. I will be finished here in an hour. You could come to my room. It will be the best silver piece you have ever spent." At the mention of coin Conn relaxed, remembering Eriatha.

"I will be here," said Conn.

Her smile widened, and she walked away. Conn rose and stretched, then made his way across to the sand circle, where he watched the horse trading for a while. The Thassilian horses were magnificent, bred for power and speed. Conn wondered idly about cross-breeding a Thassilian stallion with Rigante mares.

The auction concluded, and Conn wandered out into the night air and sat on a fence rail, looking down on the city by the sea. In the moonlight Goriasa was no longer ugly. Lantern lights glowed in hundreds of windows, and the paths and roads were lit by torches. The city gleamed and glittered like a jewel-encrusted necklace hung around the neck of the bay.

Conn climbed down from the fence and was about to return to the building when a movement to the left caught his eye. A man was walking up the hill toward the hall. He was tall and broad-shouldered, his hair closely cropped and shining like silver in the moonlight. Conn watched him, wondering what it was that had caught his eye. The man's movements were sure, his walk confident, his manner alert. Conn smiled. The man moved like Ruathain: the same easy grace and arrogant style. Suddenly dark shapes sprang from a side road. Conn saw moonlight glint on a blade. The walking man saw the danger and swung around, striking out at the first attacker. His assailant fell back, but a second, armed with a cudgel, lashed out. The cudgel struck the man's face, and he toppled to the ground. Conn drew his knife, shouted at the top of his lungs, and ran at the group.

Two of them rushed him. One held a knife, the other a long club. The knifeman was in the lead as they closed in. Conn twisted and kicked the knifeman in the knee. There was a loud crack followed by a piercing scream as the knifeman fell. Leaping over him, Conn threw up his left arm, blocking a blow from the club and slamming the Seidh blade deep into the attacker's shoulder. The man grunted, fell back, then turned and ran from sight. Two other men rose from beside the fallen man and fled back down the alley. Conn did not give chase but crouched down beside the victim. Despite his white hair the man was not old. Conn guessed him to be in his middle twenties. Blood was oozing from a cut on his swollen temple. The man pushed himself to his knees. Then he swore. Conn helped him to his feet.

"Come, I'll take you to the hall," said Conn.

"I can walk, my friend," said the tall man. "I've suffered worse wounds than this." He peered at Conn's scarred face. "As indeed you have. What was it, lion?"

"Bear."

"You are lucky to be alive."

Conn chuckled. "So are you. Do you know who your enemies were?"

"Let's find out," said the man, moving to where the knifeman lay groaning. The man's leg had been snapped below the knee, the lower part of the limb bent to an impossible angle.

The tall man knelt by him. "Who sent you?" he asked.

The knifeman swore and spit at his face. "I'll tell you nothing, Stone man."

"That's probably true," the tall man replied, casually picking up the assassin's fallen knife.

Connavar saw the deadly intent in the man's cold eyes. "Do not kill him," he said softly.

For a moment only the man remained very still, then his shoulders relaxed. "You risked your life for me. How, then, could I refuse your request? Very well, he shall live." He glanced down at the wounded knifeman. "If we leave you here, will your friends come back for you?"

"Yes," grunted the man.

"Good. Then I shall bid you farewell." Tossing the knife into the man's lap, he walked away. Conn followed him.

"He called you Stone man. Are you from that city?"

"Yes. My name is Valanus. What is your interest in Stone?"

"My friend and I are traveling there. I am eager to learn about it."

"It is a great city, boy. The center of the world. Now, I think I had better get this cut seen to." He paused. "So tell me, to whom do I owe my life?"

"I am Connavar."

"Gath? Ostro? What?"

"Rigante."

"Ah yes, the tribes across the water. I have heard of them. A proud people, it is said. You worship trees or some such."

"We do not worship trees," Conn told him as they walked toward the hall. "We worship the gods of air and water and the spirits of the land."

"There is only one god, Connavar. And he is in Stone." Valanus paused at the doorway to the hall. "So tell me, Connavar, why did you save my life?"

"Why would I not?" countered Conn.

Valanus gave a weary smile. "My head hurts too much to debate the point. I am in your debt, Rigante."

With that he turned away from Conn and moved into the hall.

* * *

Garshon was a short, slope-shouldered man close to sixty years of age. Bald and one-eyed, he wore a strip of red cloth over his blinded left eye. Gold bands adorned his muscular upper arms, and gaudy rings shone on every finger. His single eye was a pale, merciless blue, and it either stared or glared. There were no halfway measures with Garshon. There never had been. Not from that terrible day in the Doca Forest forty-four years earlier when they had burned out his right eye.

He had been hunting rabbits when the lord and his lady had ridden by. The young Garshon had been stunned by the beauty of the lord's wife and had failed to dip his head. Instead he had gazed upon her. She said later, as the retainers tied him down and prepared a fire, that he had winked at her.

Garshon had suffered on that day and for several months afterward. The pain had been awful. But it had released in him a terrible ambition that burned just as bright as the heated dagger blade that had destroyed his eye.

Revenge took him six years, four months, and eight days. Gathering together a small gang of outlaws, he raided through Doca lands, gathering wealth and amassing power and hiring more mercenaries and killers until at last he had besieged the lord's town. When it fell, he had the lord dragged naked into the town square. There Garshon castrated him, then hanged him. The lady he flung from a high cliff, and he watched with relish as her body was crushed against the rocks below. Her children he sold into slavery.

The other lords formed an alliance that all but destroyed his army. Garshon escaped and fled to the west with three ponies and a chest of gold, coming at last to the then-small port of Goriasa.

Thirty-eight years later he controlled the city and its trade routes, his power absolute, his influence extraordinary. Tribal kings and princes looked to him for advice and patronage, and a word from Garshon could influence events six hundred miles away. And yet he was not satisfied.

Truth to tell, he had never been satisfied. On the day he had killed the lord he had dragged his lady to the cliff top. "Why are you doing this?" she had cried.

"Look at my eye, you cow. How can you ask?"

She had stared at him blankly, totally noncomprehendingly. He knew in that moment that she had no recollection of ruining his life. As she fell screaming to her death, Garshon felt only emptiness. There was no joy in the revenge.

There had been no real joy since. He should have kept her alive, forced her to remember, to know that her punishment was a matter of justice and not merely vengeance. Then, perhaps, he would have tasted the sweetness of her death.

"You seem lost in thought," said Banouin.

Garshon took a deep breath and returned his concentration to the little merchant. He actually liked the man, which was rare. "I was thinking of old times."

"Not good ones," observed Banouin.

Garshon grinned. "You are nearly as sharp as me." Forcing himself to think of business, he haggled with Banouin for a while, finally making an offer on the merchant's ponies. As they shook hands, Garshon realized the price was too high and cursed himself for allowing the past to distract him. "You want the money in gold?" he asked.

"Hold it for me," said Banouin. "I will be back in the autumn."

"You are a very trusting man, Banouin," said Garshon. "What if you do not make it back?"

"Then give it to Connavar, who is traveling with me. And before you ask, if we both fail to return, send it to my wife in Three Streams."

"You are wed? My congratulations, Banouin. It will be as you say. And I thank you for your faith in my honesty."

Banouin gave a broad smile. "I would trust your word with more than my gold, Garshon."

The one-eyed merchant was both touched and embarrassed. He rose, bade farewell to Banouin, and moved from the small office out into a narrow corridor and up the stairs to his inner quarters on the upper floor of the travelers hall. His guest was sitting on a wide couch, his legs stretched out on the soft fabric. Garshon noticed he had removed his boots, which was more than he would have expected.

"I understand you were attacked," said Garshon, snapping his fingers. A young maidservant ran forward, pouring red wine into a goblet of blue glass. Garshon sipped it.

"I thought I had lost them," said Valanus. "They surprised me."

"And I thought you Stone warriors were invincible."

"No man is invincible," said Valanus, swinging his legs to the floor and sitting up. He winced as a sharp pain seared behind his eye.

"You have a lump the size of a goose egg. Perhaps your skull is cracked." Garshon grinned as he said it, then pulled up a chair and sat down opposite Valanus. He peered at the swelling. "Who was your savior?"

"A young Rigante not old enough to know better."

Garshon stared hard at his guest. At the mention of the word "savior" Valanus' expression had changed momentarily. The change had been fleeting, but Garshon had caught it. What had it signified? Irritation? Possibly. But something more. "Did you gain information from the survivor?" asked the merchant.

"No."

"Ah, you killed him, then?"

"No, I did not. Connavar asked me to spare him."

Garshon leaned back and smiled. "Asked you? The blow to the head must have put you in a very good mood. It is not like you, Valanus, to spare your enemies."

"I have come here to talk about other matters," said Valanus, casting a look at the servant girl.

"Ah, yes. Other matters." Turning to the girl, Garshon waved his hand. She bowed and walked from the room. Garshon sat quietly for a moment, and when he spoke it was in the language of Stone. "The general Jasaray is very generous. My man in Escelium sends word that three thousand gold pieces have been left with him for safekeeping."

"Only five hundred is for you," Valanus reminded him. "The rest is to be used for our allies."

"Allies? You have no allies. You have only servants. What is it you require of my . . . friends among the Gath?"

"Large amounts of grain, beef, spare horses, and two thousand auxiliary cavalry. We will pay ten silver pieces for every warrior. But they must supply their own mounts."

"How much grain?"

"I will send you full details when the general has decided on his line of march."

Garshon poured more wine. "What would you do, Stone man, if you could not find traitors?"

"We would still win, Garshon, but it would be more slowly. And I do not think of our allies as traitors. They help us defeat their own enemies. Nothing treacherous in that." Valanus rose. "I think I will go to my bed. My head hurts like the hammers of Hades are pounding in it."

"You will not require a woman tonight, then?"

"Not tonight."

The tall silver-haired warrior strode from the room. Garshon watched him go. The Stone soldier was a tough man, apparently fearless. And yet . . .

Garshon walked from the room, down a long corridor, and into a small side room. Three men were there. One had a heavily bandaged shoulder, and the second had three splints on his broken leg.

"What happened?" asked Garshon.

The uninjured man, a thin, balding fellow with a pock-marked face, spoke up. "We had him, but then this youngster ran in. He broke Varik's leg and stabbed Jain. He was very fast, Garshon. And we didn't know if he was alone. So we ran."

Garshon said nothing. They had known the boy was alone, but he had frightened them. He turned to Varik. "How is the leg?"

"The break is clean, just below the knee. It will be weeks, though, before I can walk."

"Why did Valanus let you live?"

"The boy told him not to kill me. I tell you, Garshon, my heart almost gave out."

"He asked him, you mean?"

"No. He just said: 'Don't kill him.' For a heartbeat I thought he was going to do it anyway. But he didn't, thank Taranis!"

"What do you think the boy would have done had Valanus stabbed you?"

Varik shrugged. "I don't know."

"Was he carrying a blade?"

"Yes. A shining knife."

"Describe the scene. Exactly." Varik did so. Garshon listened, made him repeat it, then turned away from the trio. As he went to leave the room, the pockmarked man spoke again.

"Why don't you just have the bastard killed in his bed?"

"I might have *you* killed in your bed," said Garshon. "You think I want Jasaray as an enemy? There is no way I can kill Valanus in my own home. However, I had thought that four of you would be enough. How foolish of me. But then, I could not know that you would be surprised by a boy."

Leaving them, he wandered out along the corridor and down into the hall. Women were dancing on the raised dais, and he scanned the crowd of watchers, locating Banouin and the lad. For some time he stood and stared at the young man. Then he summoned a serving maid and sent her to Banouin.

Returning to his rooms, he laid out two more goblets and another jug of wine. Moments later Banouin entered, followed by the Rigante youngster. The boy moved well, perfectly balanced, like a fighter. Garshon gestured his guests to be seated, then poured them wine. "Your young friend has done me a great service, Banouin," he said. The Stone merchant seemed surprised and glanced at his companion. "He rescued a guest of mine from robbers. I am in his debt." He smiled at the youngster.

"It was nothing," said the youth, his voice deep and resonant. A voice that would one day hold power, thought Garshon. He rolled the name around in his mind. Connavar. He had heard it before. His single eye noted the jagged scar on the youngster's cheek and the green and gold eyes. "Ah," he said, "you are the boy who fought the bear and saved the princess."

"There was no princess," said Connavar. "Though there was a bear."

Garshon pointed to the knife at his belt. "Is that the blade that struck the beast?"

"Yes."

"May I see it?"

Connavar rose, drew the knife, reversed it, and handed it to the merchant hilt first. "It is very beautiful," said Garshon. "If you ever consider selling it . . ."

"I will not," said the youngster.

"I do not blame you." Handing the knife back, he turned to the astonished Banouin. "I take it your young friend has not mentioned his heroics."

"Not as yet," said Banouin, seeking to mask his irritation.

"He tackled four robbers. Broke one man's leg, stabbed another in the shoulder. The others ran. He was very compassionate. My guest would have killed one of them, but Connavar stopped him." The pale blue gaze moved to Connavar. "Why was that? Surely the world would be a better place with less robbers."

"I have killed men who deserved to die," said Connavar. "But I did so in combat. The robber was defenseless." He shrugged. "I have no regrets."

"Something only the young can say," observed Garshon. Moving to a chest, he opened the lid and lifted clear a pouch, which he tossed to Connavar. "There are twenty silver pieces there. Please accept them as a mark of my gratitude."

He saw the lad glance at Banouin, who gave an almost imperceptible nod. Connavar tied the pouch to his belt but made no show of thanks. "I am keeping you from the pleasures of the hall," said Garshon. "You will stay here tonight as my guests, and any services you require will be free: wine, women, food, and lodging."

"Thank you, Garshon," said Banouin, rising. "That is most gracious."

"Not at all." He turned to Connavar. "If ever you have need of my services, you have only to ask."

Connavar nodded but did not reply.

Garshon walked them to the door, then returned to his couch.

How interesting, he thought. The fearless Valanus had been afraid of the boy. And now Garshon knew why. There was something very dangerous there, lurking beneath the surface.

Something deadly.

Conn was glad to leave the turbulent city of Goriasa. The air there seemed dense, full of harsh scents and foul aromas. And the Earth Maiden had been a huge disappointment. She had lacked the skills of Eriatha, and her breath had stunk of stale wine. On the open plain he felt himself relax. Here he could smell the grass and feel the whispering breeze, cool from the sea.

For almost a hundred miles the land was flat with barely a hill to break the visual monotony. Rarely did they see travelers, and when they did, Conn was impressed by the knowledge Banouin had of them, identifying tribes from the various colors of the cloaks, shirts, or adornments worn by the riders. Banouin was greeted everywhere with warmth and recognition. The merchant had removed his Rigante clothing and wore a red knee-length tunic, leather leggings and boots, and a conical blue hat. The hat was old, the fabric worn away, exposing the wooden rim beneath. Banouin claimed it was a lucky hat. Conn's clothes excited great interest in the travelers they met, for the design of his Rigante cloak of checkered blue and green was not well known among the Gath, and he was asked many questions about his homeland.

In the main people were friendly, and only once in the early part of their travels did Conn feel under threat. They came upon five riders wearing black cloaks. There were no smiles from the newcomers, who blocked the road and waited, grim-faced.

"Stay calm, Conn," said Banouin, keeping his voice low. Lifting his right hand in greeting, Banouin edged his pony forward. Conn touched heels to his own mount and rode alongside. The five men wore curved cavalry sabers and carried short hunting bows. Conn glanced at their faces, assessing them. They seemed tough, and their manner showed they were tensed for action. Conn well knew that Banouin could fight without weapons, for he had spent many an afternoon with the foreigner sparring, but five armed men were not to be taken lightly. "A fine morning," said Banouin. "May Daan smile upon the riders of the Gath and, more importantly, on those from the village of Gudri."

"I know you, Blue Hat," said the lead rider, a young man

with a drooping blond mustache and braided hair. "You are the merchant who brought honey sweets in the fell winter."

"And you are the boy who was in the tree," said Banouin. "Osta? Was that it?"

The man laughed aloud. "Ostaran, but Osta is what my friends call me. Are you carrying honey sweets?"

"Not this trip, my friend. You are a long way from your village. Is all well there?"

The two men chatted for some time. Conn saw the tension easing from the riders, and when at last they rode away, he saw Banouin breathe a sigh of relief. "That was close," said the foreigner.

"They were planning to rob us?"

"Indeed they were."

"How did you know they were from Gudri?"

"The cloak brooches. All in the shape of an oak branch."

"So lives were saved by your knowledge of brooches," said Conn.

"All knowledge is useful, my friend. But they would have killed us only if we had put up a fight. They are not generally wanton slayers."

Conn smiled. "Have you considered carrying a weapon? Perhaps there will come a day when you cannot identify a brooch."

"I know all the brooches. But tell me, Conn. What would you have done had they tried to rob us?"

"I would have stabbed the man to the left of the leader," Conn answered swiftly.

"Why him?"

"Because you would have charged your pony into the leader's mount, causing it to swerve to the right, blocking the others. The only man free to draw his weapon and attack you would have been the rider on the left."

Banouin took a deep breath. "A good assessment, Conn. You are learning fast. Now let us move on."

◇ 8 ◇

F OR THE FIRST five nights the travelers camped on open
ground, but on the sixth they stayed at a small settlement
known to Banouin. Some eighty people had built their homes
on the banks of a wide river, earning their living by fishing
the waters or towing barges down to Goriasa. The people
were swarthy, and Banouin told Conn they had originally—
many hundreds of years before—journeyed from the eastern
mountains, where they had been a nomadic people. They
were friendly and invited Conn and Banouin to join them for
their communal meal, taken in a long wooden hall thatched
with dried grass. At the end of the meal—black bread dipped
in fish stew—several musical instruments were brought out
and a lean fisherman sang ballads in a deep baritone. When
the songs were finished, the people stamped their feet in
praise, then went off to their homes. Banouin and Conn remained in the company of the village leader, a powerfully
built black-bearded man named Camoe. His two young wives
cleared away the plates, and Camoe offered his visitors jugs of
beer. The drink was stale and flat, and Conn barely sipped it.

"How far are you traveling?" Camoe asked Banouin.

"All the way to Stone."

"Dangerous country you will be passing through," said
Camoe. "Stone army is advancing on the people of the Perdii
River. Big battles coming, I think."

"I am well known to the Perdii," said Banouin. "Their king, Alea, is an old friend of mine."

"Alea is dead," said Camoe. "Drowned, they say."

"I am sorry to hear that. He was a good man. Who is king now?"

Camoe shrugged. "I have not heard. But it is said they have a hundred thousand fighting men waiting to rip the hearts from the Stone men. I think they won't do it. I think this Jasaray is a devil in human form."

"He is not a devil," said Banouin, "but he is a wily general."

"How long before they come here, you think?"

Banouin spread his hands. "Two years maybe. But they won't trouble you, Camoe. They will buy your fish."

"They will trouble all of us, foreigner. I am Gath. I will fight when called." His gaze flickered to the small pack at Banouin's side. "This beer turns the stomach. I remember when we had a fine harvest of red fish and bought several jugs of amber fire. Good days."

"It so happens," said Banouin, "that I remembered your fondness for it." Digging into the pack, he produced two jugs of Uisge that had been wrapped in straw and tossed one to Camoe. The village leader broke the wax seal and hefted the jug to his lips. He took several swallows.

"Oh, but that is good," he said. "It burns wonderfully all the way down. How much do I owe you?"

"Not a copper coin, my friend. It was good to see you again. There is a second jug in the pack for you to enjoy when we are gone."

Camoe leaned forward and thumped Banouin's shoulder. "You are too good to be a Stone man. Are you sure you weren't adopted?"

The travelers slept that night in the hall and then continued their journey east. The farther they traveled, the more they heard of the advancing army of Stone. Jasaray was said to be assembling an army of fifteen thousand men. It would be vastly outnumbered by the Perdii.

"Perhaps they will be crushed," said Conn, "their threat ended."

"I doubt it," said Banouin, drawing on the reins and dismounting to give the pony a breather.

Conn joined him. "How will the battle be planned?"

Banouin thought about it. "Fifteen thousand men means four panthers and a wing of cavalry. Each panther is made up of three thousand fighting foot soldiers. The cavalry will be auxiliaries, tribesmen who are enemies of the Perdii. Jasaray will march into Perdii territory and try to coax the enemy into a mass charge. They will break upon his battle lines like water upon rock."

"What if they do not attack him in that way?"

"Then he will raze their villages and settlements, taking their women and children into slavery. He will destroy their crops and cripple their economy. They will have to fight him."

Banouin also took the time on the journey to continue teaching Conn more of the Turgon tongue and the language and history of Stone. Defeated in a distant war four hundred years before, the survivors had fled across the sea to found a new city. They had seen a blazing sign in the sky, a huge rock streaking from the clouds, trailing fire. It had struck a wooded hilltop, leveling all the trees. On this newly flattened land they had built a temple and around it a stockaded town. As the years had passed, they had subdued surrounding tribesmen and extended their authority. Gradually the wooden town became a stone city with great walls and aqueducts, temples, and places of learning.

Conn listened intently, but his attention grew more avid only when Banouin talked of wars and strategies and of the peoples conquered during the last twenty years. Great had been the suffering, said Banouin, and the destruction.

"I hate them," said Conn. "What they are doing is evil."

"In what way evil?" asked Banouin as they led the six pack ponies slowly along the crest of a series of wooded hills.

Conn pointed down to a small settlement along the banks of a river. "Those people have their own lives," he said, "each dependent on the skills of his neighbor. They are a community. They live and thrive. It is a good life. I know this, for it is the same among the Rigante. They care for one another. The Stone people will take away what they have by conquest. Surely that is evil."

"The question is much wider than that," said Banouin, reining in his pony. "Come," he said, swinging his mount. "We will take a detour to the high country."

"Why?"

Banouin smiled. "There are sights there you should see."

They rode through the morning and into the afternoon, ever higher. Both riders unfurled their cloaks, for the wind was colder there. By dusk they had reached a thinly wooded ridge of land, and Banouin dismounted, leading the ponies into a shallow cave, where he built a fire and prepared a meal of rich stew. In the firelight Conn saw that the walls of the cave were covered with paintings of deer and bison, lion and bear. Here and there were handprints in faded red, large hands with long thumbs.

"Who made these?" he asked Banouin.

"The Old Ones. There are still some of them living in the high country, hiding from the world. Very few now. Perhaps a hundred or so. They are like us and yet not like us. They are heavy-browed and have huge jaws."

"Ah, yes," said Conn, with a smile, "the Ugly Folk. They used to dwell near the Seidh Woods. Our legends tell how they stole babies and ate them. They were destroyed by Ela-gareth hundreds of years ago."

Banouin shook his head. "They ate no babies, Conn. They were—and are—a primitive folk with tools of flint. Leaf eaters, root grubbers. Occasionally they would hunt down a deer and devour its meat raw. But they were not cannibals. I have visited their few remaining settlements. They are a gentle people with no understanding of the savage violence we carry in our hearts."

"So you brought me here to see these paintings?"

"Not just the paintings. I wanted you to think about the people who roamed these lands for thousands of years, living free, without war. Then, one day, a new race came with bright swords of bronze and bows that could send death over a distance. They slaughtered the people, driving them high into the cold country. Even now, if one of the people is seen, hunting parties will gather to give chase and do murder. These murderous newcomers took the lands of the people and settled them, building farms and settlements. You understand?"

Conn nodded. "And now a new race has come with swords of iron."

"Exactly. And in a few hundred years some other powerful tribe—or groups of tribes—will descend upon the gentle peace-loving people of Stone. Then a young man just like you will rail against the evil of it."

"As he should," said Conn. "A man should be ready to fight for his land, his people, and his culture. What are we if we don't? When the wolf attacks our herds, we kill the wolf. We fight to defend what is ours. That is what makes us men."

"Indeed it is," agreed Banouin. "But before there were men, it was the wolf who kept the herds strong. By killing the weak and the old, by controlling the numbers so that the herds did not grow so large that they ate all the grass. Nature in balance, Connavar."

Conn laughed aloud. "If I take what you suggest to its logical conclusion, then when a robber comes to my home, I allow him to take all that is mine. I do nothing. I let him rape my wife, slay my children, and steal my belongings. This is not a philosophy I can embrace."

"Nor I," said Banouin. "But now we come to the crux of

the question. I am not saying do not fight. I am saying do not
hate. It is not war that leads to murderous excesses, but hate.
Whole villages, cities, peoples wiped out. Hatred is like a
plague. It is all-consuming, and it springs from man to man.
Our enemies become demons, their wives the mothers of
demons, their children infant demons. You understand? We
tell stories of our enemies eating babes—as was done with
the Old Ones. Our hearts turn dark, and, in turn we visit a terrible retribution upon those we now hate. But hatred never
dies, Conn. We plant the seeds of it in every action inspired
by it. Kill a man, and his son will grow to hate you and seek
revenge. When he obtains that revenge, your son will learn to
hate him. Can you see what I am saying?"

"No," admitted Conn. "It is necessary to hate one's enemies. If we don't hate them, how can we kill them?"

Banouin sighed, and Conn could see he was disappointed.
They sat in silence for a while and ate the stew. Banouin
cleaned the dishes and returned them to the pack. Conn
spread his blankets and lay down by the fire.

The little merchant sat beside the blaze for a while. "There
are only three ways to deal with an enemy," he said. "Destroy
him, run away from him, or befriend him. The man who has
come to hate you will never befriend you."

Then he, too, lay down and pulled his blanket over him.

Conn rolled over and looked at the wall paintings in the
flickering light of the fire.

The one abiding truth he did know was that the strong
would always conquer the weak.

When the Stone army comes, he thought, the Rigante will
be strong.

Eight days later the travelers reached the outer borders of
Gath land. To the northwest were the high settlements of the
Ostro. "We will visit them on our return," said Banouin. "It
will be good experience for you. The Ostro are born to trade

and like nothing better than to haggle for hours for the finest prices." The smile faded from his face, and he drew in a deep breath. "But for now we must endure the lands of the Perdii."

Ahead of them lay the wide expanse of the Perdii River, and beyond it a range of high wooded hills. It was midafternoon as the riders rode their weary ponies down to a settlement on the riverbank. Across the fast-flowing water, moored to the far bank, was a flat-bottomed ferry. There was no sign of a ferryman. Conn transferred his gaze to the settlement. The eleven homes at the riverside were crudely and carelessly constructed, some from green timbers that had warped as they dried, leaving great gaps that had been plugged by clay. Beyond them was a more solid log-built structure with a sod roof. Here there was a paddock. Banouin rode to it, slid open the rail bar, and led the ponies inside. As Conn dismounted, Banouin moved in close. "The men here are not to be trusted," he said. "There are robbers and thieves among them. Tempers are always short. Follow my lead and be careful what you say and do."

"Perhaps we should have camped in the hills," said Conn.

"We were spotted yesterday. Nowhere here is completely safe, but I did not want to be surprised in open country." He forced a smile. "Do not be too concerned, my friend. I have passed this way before without incident. I am only saying we should be wary."

Conn said nothing. He could see the tension in the little merchant. Banouin was a tough man, not given to groundless fears. Conn scanned the buildings. Young children were playing in the mud by the riverbank, and a woman was sitting on a rock close by, sewing a patch onto a threadbare cloak. She was wearing a simple dress that had once been blue but was now a washed-out gray. Her hair was long and filthy, her skin dry. Everything about her spoke of loss and defeat. Conn looked away.

Banouin gestured to Conn, and the two men strolled to the

log dwelling. There was no door, merely a long, threadbare cowhide hanging over a pole. Pushing it aside, they entered the single room. Four men were sitting at a table, gambling with painted knucklebone dice. One glanced up as the newcomers entered. His head was huge and totally bald, his eyes small and dark. "You'll be wanting the ferry," he said. "Dovis and his brother took some cattle to market. They won't be back until tomorrow."

"Thank you," Banouin said, with a friendly smile.

"You want to play?"

"Perhaps later. We need to tend to our ponies."

"I saw them," said the man, rising from his chair and stretching his back. He was big, several inches over six feet, and his bearskin jerkin served to make him look even more formidable. "Heavily laden. You're the merchant Banouin."

"Yes. Have we met?"

"No. I recognized you from the blue hat. You should join us. It would be friendly. Don't you want to be friendly?"

"I am always friendly," said Banouin. "But I am a terrible gambler. Luck never favors my throws." Turning away, he walked back to the door.

"Perhaps your lady friend would like to play? A long time since we had such pretty company," said the man. The others laughed.

"Indeed I would," Conn said with a smile. "Knucklebones is a great favorite among my people." He walked across to stand before the big man, and when he spoke, it was with easy familiarity. "Before we play we first need to understand one another. I am a stranger here and unused to your customs. But I am a fast learner. Now, we have not met before and yet you insult me. Back home I would have killed you." Conn smiled and tapped the big man's chest. "I would have cut out your heart. But what I must consider is that I am in a different land. Here it is obviously customary to engage in banter with strangers. Am I right, you fat, ugly mound of cow shit?"

The big man's jaw dropped, and his eyes narrowed. With a foul curse he lunged at the Rigante. Conn did not move back. Instead he whipped a straight left into the man's face, following it with a right cross that sent him spinning across the table, which upended, spilling knucklebones and copper coins to the dirt. The big man came up fast, but Conn had moved in and thundered a right into his face that split the skin under his eye. He grabbed Conn's tunic and tried to haul him into a rib-snapping bear hug. Conn head butted him in the nose. The man cried out and fell back. Conn hit him with two straight lefts followed by a right uppercut to the belly. Air whooshed from the man's lungs, and he bent double—straight into Conn's rising knee.

The big man slumped to the floor unconscious.

The first of the other men surged to his feet and froze as Conn's knife touched his throat, pricking the skin and causing blood to ooze onto his filthy shirt. "Where I come from," Conn said, conversationally, "it is considered wise to know the nature of a man before making him an enemy. Here, in this stinking cesspit, you obviously have other ideas. The question is, Do I cut your throat and kill your friends or do I wander out and see to my ponies? Do you have any thoughts, scum breath?" The knife blade pricked deeper.

"See . . . to the . . . ponies?" ventured the man.

Conn smiled and turned his attention to the other two, who were sitting very quietly watching him. "What about you? Do you disagree?" The men shook their heads. "Excellent! Then we all understand one another." Conn sheathed his blade, turned his back, and strode to where Banouin waited.

As they stepped outside, Conn glanced at his companion. "I am sorry, foreigner. I do not have your diplomatic skills."

"You have nothing to apologize for. Diplomacy must always be backed by strength. You handled that situation well. There was no other way. They were spoiling for a fight. Now, perhaps, they will think again. However, if you will permit a

criticism, the first right cross was a little clumsy. You hit him off your back foot. It robbed the blow of real power. I thought I taught you better than that."

Conn laughed. "What would I do without you, teacher?"

"Fairly well from what I've seen," replied Banouin.

Removing saddles and packs from the eight ponies, they groomed them, forked hay into the paddock, and fetched water from the river. Then Banouin made a camp beneath a spreading oak, preparing a small fire. The night was clear, the stars bright.

Soon after sunset a young woman approached them. She was scrawny, her clothes ragged. For a share of their meal she promised to pleasure both of them.

"That is very kind," said Banouin. "But you are welcome to join us anyway. It would be nice to entertain a guest."

The girl stood for a moment. "I have a child," she said.

"Bring the child also," said Banouin.

The girl moved away to a nearby hovel and returned carrying a toddler. Banouin prepared a broth, seasoned it with spices, then produced two flat loaves they had bought the previous day in a settlement to the west. The girl said nothing throughout the meal, and Conn noticed that she fed the toddler before devouring her own broth and bread.

"Have you been here long?" Banouin asked her.

"Two years, I think."

"Where is the boy's father?"

"He went away," she answered. "Left one night. Never came back."

"Where are you from?"

"Long Branch. It is a Perdii settlement."

"I know it," said Banouin. "It is less than three days walk from here. Why do you not go home?"

She did not reply. The toddler, his belly full, was asleep in her arms. She looked immensely weary. "I am ready to pay you now," she said.

"There is no need of payment, child. Take your son to bed. And if you wish to travel with us tomorrow, I will take you to Long Branch."

"There is nothing for me there," she said. "There is nothing for me anywhere. Except for my little one." Kissing the toddler's head, she pushed herself to her feet and walked away.

"She is no older than me," said Conn.

"Old enough to know sorrow," observed Banouin. "I am going to get some sleep. Wake me in four hours, then I will stand watch. Wake me earlier if they come. Do not try to tackle them all alone."

"They won't come for us," said Conn. "I read the fear in their eyes."

"Confidence is to be applauded, arrogance avoided," quoted Banouin, settling down under his blanket.

The lands of the Perdii were heavily wooded and increasingly mountainous, which pleased Conn, for it was more like home, and in truth, his spirit was restless for the sight of Caer Druagh and the home fires of the Rigante. Yet Banouin grew more tense once they had crossed the Perdii River and, as he rode, constantly scanned the countryside.

"What are you looking for?" asked Conn.

"Trouble," the Foreigner answered tersely. He seemed in no mood for conversation, and the two riders journeyed on in silence for most of the morning.

By dusk Conn was casting around for a place to rest the ponies and enjoy a midday meal. They had made a brief stop at noon, finishing the last of the bread. As the sun was sinking, Conn saw a stand of oak trees that dipped down into a valley. From where they rode Conn could see the distant, glittering ribbon of a stream shining gold in the dying light. Moving alongside Banouin, he pointed down to the valley. "A good place to camp?" he asked.

The foreigner shook his head. "Talis Woods," he said.

"That is what the Perdii call the Seidh. No one goes there. They have a legend here that tells of a warrior who entered the Talis Woods one morning and emerged in the afternoon an old man. We will move on. There is a farm close by. I know the farmer well. He will put us up for the night."

They arrived at the wooden farmhouse within the hour to find it cold and deserted, the door hanging on its leather hinges. Banouin dismounted and moved inside, pushing open the shutters. Finding several stubs of candles, he lit one, holding it high and examining the main room. It had been stripped of furniture, the shelves cleared. Slowly he walked through the other three rooms. All had been emptied of any items that could be carried away with ease. There was a broken chair in the main room, and several chipped pots and pans were scattered in the wide kitchen area.

Conn joined him. "Robbed, do you think?" asked the younger man.

Banouin shook his head. "No. He was always fearful of war coming to this part of the land. I think he just moved away. Sad, for he loved this parcel of land."

There was a stone hearth against the northern wall, and Banouin built a fire while Conn tended to the ponies. Later, after they had eaten, they sat on the dirt floor in front of the small blaze.

"Now will you tell me what is troubling you?" asked Conn.

Banouin removed his blue hat, running his fingers around the wooden rim. "The Perdii are a difficult people: volatile, violent, and terribly arrogant. They have dominated this section of the continent for hundreds of years. The Ostro and the Gath pay tribute, and that is why there are few raids now. I made a friend of Alea, the king, some years ago. But I am not popular with his family, especially his brother, Carac. He bought some goods from me five years ago, then sent men to steal the price money back. They failed. After that he claimed

I cheated him. He would have had me killed, but he knew Alea would punish him for it."

"And now Alea is dead," said Conn. "Did he have sons to rule after him?"

"One son, a nice boy. He should be around seventeen now."

"Should be?"

"I rather doubt he had the strength or the skill to defeat Carac. He's probably dead. Ritually strangled. It is the Perdii way."

"He would strangle his own nephew? What kind of a man is this Carac?"

"The lives of princes are not like those of ordinary men, Conn. Perdii history is littered with tales of infanticide, patricide, incest, and murder. Carac even married his sister, since it would give him a double claim to the throne."

"I take it we will not be trading at his capital."

"No, we will not trade. However, I will have to go in, for I have business to conclude. A merchant there holds capital for me, and I will need that for my new life with Vorna. I shall go in at dusk and leave with the dawn. It is a large town, almost the size of Goriasa. I should pass unnoticed."

"Not wearing that blue hat," observed Conn.

Banouin chuckled. "I will leave it with you."

"How soon will we reach the town?"

"Late tomorrow. Then it is a further four days ride east to the border and the first roads of stone. We will travel more swiftly then."

The following morning a storm blew in from the north, and heavy rain prevented their departure. They stayed in the farmhouse and talked of the journey ahead. Banouin was anxious for Conn to see the wonders of Stone and better understand the threat posed by the people of that city. In the afternoon Conn wandered out onto the porch. There was a roughly cut bench there, protected by an overhanging slanted roof, and he sat watching the rain and listening to the howling wind. He felt a strange sense of unease he could not pin down. He found himself thinking of Riamfada and their days together before the coming of the bear. It seemed to him that the period had been golden, though he had not appreciated it at the time. On the day of the last swim Riamfada had had but weeks to live, though no one knew it. Would the swim, he wondered, have been more or less joyous if they had known?

The rain began to ease, and in the west the sun shone through a break in the clouds. The sudden light was magical. The dull, matte green and brown of the distant rain-swept forest shone now with vibrant color, the murky grassland becoming a glittering emerald sea. And, as the clouds parted further, the golden light swept across the farmhouse, and Conn saw for the first time a host of bright blue flowers at the edge of the trees. Banouin joined him. The little merchant took a deep breath. "Doesn't the air smell good?" he said. "I love the aftermath of a storm." Perching his old blue hat upon his head, he clapped Conn on the shoulder. "Time to be moving," he said.

Two days later Conn sat by a small fire in the darkness of a sheltered hollow, waiting for Banouin's return from the town of Alin. It was close to dawn, and the young warrior was growing increasingly anxious. He had urged his friend to allow him to travel with him, but Banouin had been adamant. "If I am to be in danger, my young friend, I can best deal with it alone. Believe me. Anyway, who would look after the ponies? If we left them here alone, any stray thief could find them. Or indeed wolves could kill them. No. You wait here and learn patience."

"Who is it that you are going to see?"

"A merchant named Diatka. He holds more than two hundred gold pieces for me."

"And you trust this man?"

"We merchants need to trust one another, Conn. We cannot

travel the world with bulging chests of coin. Wait here for me. I will see you as the first light of the sun clears the peaks."

The hours had passed by with an agonizing lack of speed. Conn held his hands out to the blaze and glanced to the east. The sky was lightening with the promise of dawn. Rising, he climbed to the edge of the trees and looked down on the walled town a half mile below. The gates were closed. Two sentries were walking the wooden ramparts.

He stood for some time, then returned to the fire. Hungry, he ate the last of the dried meat. The sun rose, the snow-capped peaks to the east turning to coral. Still there was no sign of Banouin. Conn could feel his heart hammering in his chest. In some strange way he knew Banouin would not come. That is fear talking, he told himself. Another hour passed.

Conn walked to a trickling stream and washed his face, then shaved with the Seidh blade. For two more hours he waited, unsure of what action to take. If Banouin had been merely delayed, it would do more harm than good to ride down into the town. Yet what if he had not? What if he had been captured?

Conn decided to wait until noon. Covering the fire with earth, he walked up to the tree line and sat down on a fallen log. From there he could see over the wooden ramparts. There were hundreds of buildings, all clustered together. People were moving now, crowds gathering in the open square of land at the center of town.

The gates opened, and several wagons moved out. Conn shielded his eyes from the sun and sought out Banouin. He was not there.

The wait became interminable. *"Learn patience,"* Banouin had told him with a smile.

He might just as well have asked him to learn to fly like a bird.

A half hour before noon Conn saddled his pony and,

leading Banouin's mount and the six pack ponies, rode down toward Alin.

A burly guard at the gate, armed with sword and spear, stepped out to meet him. "I don't recognize your colors," he said, pointing to Conn's blue and green checkered cloak.

"Rigante, from across the water," said Conn.

"You are a long way from home, boy."

"Aye, it feels like it. I am seeking the merchant Diatka. I have goods for him."

The man stepped forward, looking closely at Conn's scarred face. "You've been through the wars, looks like."

"An argument with a bear," Conn told him, forcing a smile. "And one I didn't win."

"You survived; that is victory enough," said the sentry. Swinging around, he pointed down the main street. "Take that road until you come to Merin's forge. You can't miss it. He has an old ox skull hanging from the gate. Bear left until you see a row of storehouses ahead of you, then turn right. You will see a small orchard of apple trees and a long building with a store-house attached. The building carries Diatka's sign, a circle of gold surrounding an oak leaf."

"Thank you," said Conn. As he urged his mount forward, the sentry spoke again. "It may take you some time. The crowds will be coming back from the execution."

Conn's stomach turned. "Who was killed?" he asked.

"A Stone spy by all accounts. Didn't see it myself. Been on watch since dawn."

Conn rode on. He did not turn left at the forge but headed toward the town square, where he had seen the crowds gather. People were streaming past him as he rode, but he ignored them, coming at last to a gibbet erected on a wooden platform.

Banouin's body was hanging from a bronze hook that had been plunged between his shoulders. The face had been savagely beaten, and one eye had been put out. Blood had drenched the little merchant's clothes, and incongruously,

Conn saw that one of his shoes was missing. A rock flew past Conn's shoulder, striking Banouin's dead face. Conn turned to see several small boys giggling and laughing.

Fighting for control, Conn turned away from the corpse and rode back down the main street, swinging right at the forge and seeking out the house of Diatka. He had at that moment no plan, no thought of action.

As he rode, he glanced at the people. In the main they were a tall race, fair-haired and handsome. Some of the men were wearing Perdii cloaks of sky blue stained with a red stripe down the center. A woman ran across the path of his pony and into a side street. She was lean, her dark hair streaked with silver. The image of Vorna came into his mind. Conn sighed as he thought of riding back to Three Streams and telling her of her new husband's death. She had come to him on the night before the journey, tapping at his door and walking with him out into the meadow.

"My powers are gone now," she had said. "But I remember, when first I saw the foreigner, seeing his *geasa*. Watch out, Connavar, for a lion with eyes of blood. It may be a crest or a statue. It may even be real."

"I will watch out for him," he had promised. Now he had broken that promise, and it meant nothing that Banouin had insisted that he remain behind. Guilt fell like rain on his soul.

Coming to the orchard, he located the sign of gold and oak and dismounted. Tying the ponies to a rail, he approached the house and rapped on the door. It was opened by a middle-aged man, stoop-shouldered and bald, wearing a long robe of blue wool.

"What is it?" he asked, peering shortsightedly at Conn's face.

"You are the merchant Diatka?"

"I am," snapped the man. "What do you want?"

"I have been sent with goods to trade," said Conn.

"Who sent you?" asked Diatka, his voice becoming more friendly.

"Garshon of Goriasa," Conn said instantly.

Diatka stepped out into the sunlight. "And what are you carrying?"

"Hides from the black and white cattle of the Rigante, brooches cast by Riamfada the Crafter, and twenty jugs of Uisge."

Diatka said nothing for a moment, then smiled and invited Conn inside the house. The floor was covered with fine rugs, and the main room was filled with boxes and chests piled one on top of the other. Diatka threaded his way through them, coming at last to a small space near the fire in which were two chairs with a small table between them. Offering Conn a seat, he said: "As you can see, I am having difficulty moving the goods I already have. It is the coming war. The eastern trade routes are largely closed to me. My storehouse is overflowing with merchandise. I am sorry I cannot help you. However, let me offer you a goblet of wine."

Moving back through the boxes, he disappeared for several minutes. Conn stared around the room. The walls were covered with ornaments, paintings, rugs, and weapons. But his eyes were drawn to a round shield of bronze emblazoned with the head of a lion. Conn clenched his fists and fought for calm. When Diatka returned, he was carrying two silver goblets. One of them he passed to Conn, and the other he placed on the table before him. Then he sat down and leaned back in his chair. "These are not good days for merchants," he said. "So how is Garshon?"

The youngster put his goblet on the table. "He was well when last I saw him." Conn was amazed that his voice remained soft and friendly.

"You are very young to be trusted by Garshon."

"I did him a service." Conn glanced again at the wall behind Diatka. "You have some very unusual ornaments. Where does that come from?" he asked, pointing to the bronze shield. Diatka turned.

"The lion shield? It is a nice piece. It came from a burial mound in the east. I had thought to sell it in Stone. The eyes of the lion are rubies. Very valuable gems." He turned back. "You are not drinking your wine. Is it not to your taste."

"I was taught to wait for my elders to drink," said Conn.

"Ah, a good upbringing. These days so few people seem to care about such courtesies." Diatka lifted his goblet and drank deeply. Conn followed him. The wine was rich and red, full of flavor.

"It is very good," said Conn. "Perhaps the best I have tasted."

"It is from the south," said Diatka. "So tell me, young man, why are you telling me lies?"

"Lies?"

"Rigante hides are always sold by Banouin, as indeed are the trinkets made by Riamfada. You were not sent by Garshon."

"No, I was not," admitted Conn. "I traveled here with my friend. He came to see you last night. Now he is dead. How did that happen? How did they catch him so quickly?"

"I drugged his wine," said Diatka. "Then, while he was sleeping, I sent a servant to Carac. It saddened me to treat poor Banouin in that fashion, but as I said, trade has been difficult and I had been forced to use most of his gold to remain in business. In short, I could not pay him."

"You had him killed for *money*," said Conn. "What kind of a man are you?"

"I am a merchant. I deal in trade. And I made a trade with Carac. Needs must, young man, when poverty beckons."

"I shall avenge him," said Conn. "I will kill you very slowly and with great pain. As you are dying, perhaps the thought of the money you made will bring you relief."

Diatka chuckled. "I do not think so, young man. I am long in the tooth and knew instantly you posed a danger to me. Your wine was also drugged. Try to move your legs. You will find you cannot. The legs are the first affected, then the hands.

Lastly you will fall unconscious. Unlike Banouin, you will not wake up, for I gave you a very large dose. There will be no pain."

Conn took a deep breath, then rose from his chair. Diatka was startled. His eyes widened, and he also tried to rise. His hands gripped the arms of the chair, but he did not move. "I switched the goblets," said Conn, "when you were telling me about the shield. A lion with eyes of blood. Did you know that a witch told Banouin not to accept wine if he saw such a beast?"

"No, no, no," whimpered Diatka. "I cannot die!"

Conn moved to a shelf, pulling clear a long, linen scarf. Approaching Diatka, he slapped down the man's flailing arms and swiftly gagged him. Then he moved to the fire, lifting a poker and thrusting it deep into the flames. "Oh, you will die," he said, his voice cold. "I saw my friend hanging from a hook. They had put out one of his eyes. With a hot iron, I think. Soon you will know how he felt." From outside came the sound of children's laughter and the patter of feet as the group ran by. Conn turned the poker in the flames. "You hear that sound, merchant? I promise you that the days of laughter for the Perdii are close to an end. I will do all in my power to wipe your tribe from the face of the earth. I will hunt them and kill them as if they were vermin. Know this as you die!"

Pulling the red-hot poker from the coals, he advanced on the stricken man.

Ruathain was close to death when Arbon and two other herdsmen found him. He was sitting propped against a tree on the edge of the woods at the high pasture, unconscious, a bloody knife in his hand. Four dead Pannone warriors lay nearby. Arbon ran to his lord and knelt by his side. Ruathain's green tunic was drenched with blood. Ripping it open, Arbon found four stab wounds: two high in the left shoulder, a third under the right collarbone, and the fourth low down above the left hip. Ruathain's eyes flickered open. His face was gray and drawn, his eyes fever-bright.

"Blood raid," he whispered.

"Do not speak," said Arbon. The blood flow from the three wounds in his upper chest was easing. But the fourth wound, low on the left side, was still streaming. Arbon's gray eyes narrowed as he watched the flow. It was even, which was a relief, for if an artery had been pierced, the blood would be pumping rhythmically. Even so the situation was critical. They were some five miles from Three Streams, and Arbon knew that even if Ruathain could ride, which was doubtful, he would be dead before they reached the settlement. Swinging to the other riders, he ordered one of them to race back to Three Streams and fetch Vorna. Removing his cloak, Arbon cut a long strip from it with his dagger. Laying Ruathain on his back, Arbon folded the strip, then laid it over the wound. Crossing his hands over the padding, he applied firm pressure. Ruathain had passed out again, and his breathing was shallow.

For some minutes Arbon applied pressure, resisting the urge to lift the pad and see if the bleeding had stopped. He cursed himself silently for not carrying needle and thread. When Ruathain's pony had galloped into the settlement, Arbon had guessed his lord was in trouble and in his haste to reach him had forgotten his medicine sack. Arbon's son, Casta, knelt on the other side of the wounded man. "What can I do, Father?" he asked.

"Make a pillow of your cloak and lift his head." Casta did so. "Now look for his heartbeat. Count it aloud for me."

Casta gently pressed his fingers under Ruathain's jaw. "One . . . two . . . threefourfive . . . six . . . seven. It is very erratic, Father."

"As long as it's bloody beating," muttered Arbon. "Gods, I am an idiot. I've had that medicine sack for twenty-six years. And when I need it, it's five miles away."

"You couldn't have known he'd been attacked." Casta glanced at the four bodies. "All of them had swords. The lord had only his dagger."

"Aye, he's a hard and deadly man. And he'll need to be to survive this. Take the pressure for me. My arms are weakening." Casta placed his big hands over the pad and pressed down as Arbon pulled away. The older man stood and stretched his aching back, then cast an expert eye over the area. "They came at him in a rush. Got in each other's way, thank Taranis!" He wandered to the bodies. They were all young men, not one of them past twenty.

"Why would they try to kill him?" asked Casta.

"Blood feud. Some time ago Ruathain killed two Pannone cattle raiders. These were probably relatives."

"He's starting to shiver," said Casta.

Arbon covered Ruathain's chest with his ruined cloak, then moved off to gather dry wood for a fire. He had it blazing well when he heard riders thundering up the slope. Twisting, he saw Vorna riding a painted pony. The former witch slid from the saddle, lifted clear a saddle sack, and ran to Ruathain's side. Other riders came up, Meria among them.

Vorna lifted the padding clear of the wound. A little blood was still seeping, but the flow had stopped. "You did well," she told Casta. Then she set to with needle and thread.

Ruathain's eyes opened. Meria took his hand and kissed it. He gave a weak smile, then lapsed into unconsciousness once more.

"Will he live?" asked Meria.

Vorna felt his pulse. "I believe that he will," she said. "Now let me finish these stitches." Swinging to Arbon, she called out. "Cut two long poles and make a stretcher. He'll not be able to ride."

It took almost four hours to bring Ruathain down from the mountain. Meria ordered that he be laid in her bed, then sent the men on their way. She and Vorna sat silently at the bedside. Ten-year-old Bendegit Bran waited with them. "Should I fetch Wing?" he asked.

"Where is he?" said Meria.

"Swimming at the Riguan Falls with Gwydia."

"No, don't worry. Your father will be fine." Meria's hand reached out, pushing a lock of hair back from Ruathain's brow. As she touched the skin, his eyes opened.

"Where am I?" he asked.

"Home," she said. "You are home." Her green eyes filled with tears.

"Whisht, woman! No point in tears. I'm not dying."

"You fool," she said softly, wiping away the tears with the back of her hand. "That's not why I'm crying."

For a moment they sat in silence. Then he lifted his arm and drew her to him. "I love you, lass," he said.

"And I you, foolish man."

Vorna rose and, taking Bendegit Bran by the arm, led him from the room, pulling shut the door behind them.

"Is my father going to be well?" asked the golden-haired child.

"Oh, yes," she said. "They'll both be well."

The sun was slipping behind the western peaks as Vorna made her way to Banouin's house. She still did not think of it as home. Somehow, without Banouin's vibrant presence and despite the abundance of furniture, rugs, and ornaments, it seemed strangely empty.

Vorna took a deep breath and paused in her walk as nausea struck her again. During the last month she had, despite the chamomile tea, been lucky to hold down one meal in three. She leaned against the fence rail of Nanncumal's paddock and closed her eyes. A cool breeze blew through her long black and silver hair. It was most refreshing.

As a witch Vorna had often experienced childbirth through

the Merging but thankfully had never had to suffer such sickness. For most women, she knew, nausea was commonplace early in the morning. It usually passed swiftly and was gone without too much discomfort. Others—and it seemed she was one—carried it like a curse. Vorna straightened. The ride out to Ruathain had unsettled her stomach and brought on a dull ache in her lower back. She stretched and carried on walking.

The house was cool, and she lit the fire in the main hearth. Suddenly she shivered and looked around. There was no one there. This surprised her, for in that moment she had felt certain she was not alone. Rising, she moved across the room, pushing open the bedroom door. Moonlight was shining through the wide window, illuminating the broad bed with its patchwork quilt. But the room was empty. Again she shivered. "Who is here?" she whispered. There was no answer.

Moving back to the hearth, she sat down in Banouin's favorite chair and closed her eyes. The powers the Morrigu had given her were gone now, but as a child she had enjoyed power of her own, a sensitivity to mood and atmosphere far beyond the norm. It was this that had allowed her to see Riamfada's spirit moving among the Seidh. She sought that talent now.

Something was close. Demon or spirit? Sitting quietly, she analyzed her feelings. No, she was not frightened; therefore, it was unlikely to be anything malevolent. A whisper of cold air brushed her brow. Then it was gone, and with it the emptiness returned to the room. Vorna opened her eyes. Just a passing spirit of the night, she thought, journeying to who knew where.

Vorna prepared a meal of boiled oats and milk and then sat down once more, waiting for the bowl to cool. She thought of Banouin, wondering where he was at that moment.

She pictured him wearing the bronze brooch with the blue

opal. "It will bring you back to me safely," she said aloud. "It is the strongest charm I possess."

Taking up the porridge bowl, she began to eat. Almost immediately the nausea came, and she put down the bowl and leaned back in her chair. A fluttering of wings made her start. A huge crow settled on the back of a couch and began to preen its feathers. Anger flared in Vorna's breast, swamping her nausea.

The Morrigu was standing in the doorway, her ragged shawl about her shoulders.

"What do you want?" hissed Vorna.

The Morrigu advanced into the room and sat down opposite Vorna, reaching out her ancient hands to the fire. "Perhaps I just wanted company," she said with a sigh. Resting her head on the back of the chair, the Morrigu closed her eyes. "Eat your porridge," she said. "I have taken away your sickness."

"I am not hungry."

"Do not be selfish. You are eating for two. Your son needs sustenance, Vorna. You will not want a sickly child or a cripple like Riamfada."

Fear sprang up like a blizzard in the heart. "Are you threatening me?"

"It is not a threat. The child is nothing to me. Be calm, Vorna. Eat your porridge."

Vorna once more took up the bowl. When she had finished the meal, she added another log to the fire and sat staring into the flames. She had no idea what the Morrigu really wanted, but she knew the Seidh would tell her in her own time. The room was silent except for the crackling flames and the occasional ruffle of feathers from the crow. Vorna glanced at the Morrigu. The Old Woman seemed to be asleep. After a while Vorna could stand the suspense no longer.

"Why did you really come?" she asked.

"I doubt you would believe me, Vorna," said the Morrigu.

"But I thought you would want someone here when the visitor raps at your door."

"What visitor?"

"A ferryman from the south. He will be here shortly. Go to the door. You will see him crossing the first bridge."

Vorna pushed herself upright and crossed the room. As she swung open the door, she could see a man walking in the moonlight. He was trudging head down as if weighed down by a pack. He paused at the third bridge, then saw Vorna framed in the doorway. Slowly he walked toward her. Vorna stepped out to meet him.

"My name is Calasain," he said.

"I know who you are, ferryman. I helped your wife with the birth of your son."

"So you did, yes. Yes." The old man licked his lips nervously. He did not—could not—look Vorna in the eye. "Your man . . . Banouin . . . crossed the river some three months back. My son . . ." He fell silent for a moment, then took a deep breath. "My son is a thief," he said suddenly, the words coming in a rush. "He stole from Banouin. I only found out a few days ago. I didn't know what to do. I thought I would wait for the foreigner to come back. Then . . ." He fell silent again.

"It is late, and I am tired," said Vorna. "Say what you have to say."

Calasain opened the pouch at his side and pulled clear a brooch. The blue opal glittered in the moonlight. "Senecal took this from the foreigner's saddlebag. I was going to wait, but it kept gnawing at me. I couldn't sleep. I just had to bring it here." Reaching out, he handed the cloak brooch to Vorna.

The former witch leaned against the door frame, her face ashen. Calasain stepped forward just as she fell. Catching her, the old man helped her to the chair by the fire. Vorna's eyes opened, and tears fell to her cheeks. Calasain knelt beside her. "Are you ill?" he asked.

"Your son . . . has killed my husband," she said.

"No, no. I swear he only stole the brooch. Banouin rode off with Connavar. I promise you."

"Go away. Get away from me," sobbed Vorna, turning her head.

Calasain climbed to his feet. He thought he heard a bird flap its wings and swung around. The room was empty. "I am sorry, lady," he said.

He stood for a moment, waiting for a response. When none came, he trudged out into the night, pulling the door shut behind him.

"I am sorry, too, Vorna," said the Morrigu.

"Get out and leave me in peace," said Vorna.

The Morrigu sighed. "I have a gift for you. Your powers will return as soon as I have gone. But they will vanish with the dawn."

Vorna surged upright. "I don't want—" she began. But the chair opposite was empty.

Lost and alone, Vorna sank back to the chair and began to cry.

Once more a soft breeze brushed through her hair, and this time she sensed the source. Settling back in the chair, she released her spirit and rose from her body. There, by her chair, stood the glowing figure of Banouin.

"I came back," he said.

◊ 9 ◊

VALANUS LEANED BACK in the hot perfumed water and stared across the new bathhouse with its marble columns and elegant wooden benches set in ornately carved recesses. It was a picture of elegance and style and a sight he had sorely missed during his missions among the barbarians. Easing himself deeper into the water, he felt his muscles relax. Splashing his face, he ran his fingers through his short-cropped white hair, then, closing his eyes, imagined himself back in the city with its theaters and gardens.

His contentment was sundered by a sudden commotion. Valanus sat up and glanced toward the marble-paneled doorway. Three Keltoi chieftains stood clustered there. The Stone officer suppressed a smile as a servant tried to encourage the chieftains to step inside and remove their clothing. One might as well teach a monkey to play the flute, thought Valanus, as teach these barbarians the essentials of civilized living. Dunking his head under the warm water, he rolled over and swam across the marble-tiled bath, emerging at the far end, just below where the three Keltoi were standing.

"It was only an invitation, Ostaran," Valanus said, with a forced smile, "not a command. You don't *have* to bathe. Some of your people, I understand, fear warm water."

Ostaran gave a cold smile, then stripped off his shirt, leggings, and boots and handed them to the servant. The man held the items at arm's length, as if fearing the garments would stab him, then carried them to a shelf nearby. Ostaran sat on the side of the bath, dipping his feet into the water. His two companions watched him, their expressions grim. Ostaran breathed in deeply. "It smells of lavender," he told them, then eased himself over the side. Once in the water, he splashed his face, rubbing his slender hands over his drooping blond mustache. Untying the two braids, he shook his hair loose and ducked under the surface.

"Not as bad as you thought?" asked Valanus as Ostaran surfaced. Looking up at the other men, he grinned. "Where a Gath can go, surely Ostro warriors can follow."

"Not always," said the first man, a powerfully built tribesman with a forked red beard. "I heard of a Gath who once stuck his head up a cow's arse on a bet. Turned his hair green. I never heard of an Ostro who would follow that." So saying, he gestured to his companion and they left the bathhouse. Valanus turned to see Ostaran smiling.

"You always smile when you are insulted?"

"He wasn't insulting me. He was mocking you."

Valanus called out for soap. A servant brought him a glass vial. The Stone officer poured the contents into his hands, then rubbed lather into his hair. Ducking down, he rinsed it, then rose again. "What do you think of the bathhouse?" he asked Ostaran. The Gath leader gazed around the building, scanning the four huge baths surrounded by stone columns, the high windows, and the elaborately carved benches and shelves. When he spoke, there was a mischievous twinkle in his eyes.

"Seems a waste of stone and labor," he said. "A man can wash in a stream if he has a mind to. However, it is pleasant. I'll grant that."

Moving to the side, Valanus sat on a ledge close to the inlet pipe carrying hot water. It was warmer there. Ostaran joined him. "What have your scouts heard about Connavar?" he asked.

"There is no sign of him. The Perdii thought they had him trapped in the hills. They captured his ponies, but he killed two of their warriors and escaped on foot."

"Two more? How many does that make?"

"Six—seven if you include the merchant he tortured to death in Alin. Apparently he captured one of their scouts. He left him tied to a tree with a message for Carac. He said to tell the king that he would be back to cut his throat, that nothing on earth would save him."

"A somewhat angry lad," Valanus observed, dryly. "But I must admit I would not want him for an enemy. You met him, didn't you?"

Ostaran nodded. "He was with the honey man. We didn't speak."

Valanus chuckled. "You are a fighter, Ostaran. As am I. Be honest. He unsettled you, did he not?"

"Any man who would tackle a bear with a knife unsettles me," admitted Ostaran. Lifting his hands from the water, he stared at his fingers. "My skin is wrinkling," he said, obviously disconcerted. "I shall leave now."

"Not before a massage, surely. We have highly trained slave boys who will rub warm oil into your muscles. Trust me, it is not to be missed."

"You have no trained women for this task?"

"Young men are better," said Valanus. "It avoids the complication of arousal. Or not, depending on your appetites. Come, try it. Then you can tell me all you have learned about Carac's army."

The two men stepped out of the bath. Immediately servants ran forward with warm towels. Once they were dry, Valanus led Ostaran through into a long room with seven flat couches. Two young men were waiting there. Valanus stretched himself out, belly down, on a couch. Ostaran sat down on the couch beside him, then rolled to his stomach. The two servants began their work. Valanus relaxed as the youth's nimble fingers stroked the muscles, easing out the last of his tension. He sighed and closed his eyes, wishing he was back in Stone, where he could have dressed and taken a carriage to the amphitheater and watched the latest play before dining at the River Room.

The servant worked on the muscles of his lower back and hips, then along his hamstrings and down over his calves. Valanus rolled to his back, allowing the youth to complete his work on his quadriceps and finally his chest and neck. When the massage was over, the servant, using a rounded ivory knife, scraped the excess oil from Valanus' lean body and offered him a white robe. As he donned it, Valanus saw that Ostaran had fallen asleep on the couch. The servant tending him glanced at Valanus for guidance. The Stone officer waved him away, then gently nudged the Keltoi. Ostaran opened his eyes and yawned.

"Good?" asked Valanus.

"Most excellent." Ostaran sat up and stretched his shoulders. Valanus saw an old scar extending from his collarbone and up over his shoulder blade.

"Looks like a spear thrust," he said.

Ostaran nodded. "A raiding party from the Perdii. It was months before it finally healed, and it still pains me in cold weather." He rolled his shoulder. "Your boy has loosened it wonderfully. I thank you, Valanus, for talking me into this."

"Think nothing of it, my friend. Now, tell me what you have learned."

"You were right about Garshon. He is supplying iron ore for swords, spearheads, and armor to the Perdii in return for Carac's silver. However, he has, on our behalf, reached an agreement with the Ostro, and they will supply Jasaray for the campaign."

"How many men can you guarantee from the Gath?"

"Two thousand cavalry, as you asked for. Each with his own mount. When do we ride?"

"Only Jasaray can say. We will see him this evening."

"I am looking forward to it," said Ostaran.

"He does not speak your tongue, but I will translate for you. How is your instruction coming? When last we spoke, you could say 'hello' in Stone. You will need to do better than that as a wing leader."

"I can say 'good-bye,' 'how are you,' and 'watch where you're going, you shit-eating barbarian pig.' " Will that do for now?"

"It is no joking matter, my friend. When the battle starts and the orders are issued, you will need to understand them. If you cannot, then Jasaray will not allow you to be leader."

"I will learn," said Ostaran.

"I am sure you will. Tell me, do you think Connavar will escape from Perdii land?"

"I do not see how he can. Carac has riders scouring the hills."

"I think you may be wrong. Shall we have a wager on it? I'll bet my horse against that gold necklet you wear."

Ostaran laughed aloud. "My torque is worth fifty of your mounts. We barbarians are not as stupid as you think, Valanus."

The skills of Parax the Tracker were known far beyond the lands of the Perdii. His talent was almost mystical. There was no animal track he could not read, no trail he could not follow. He had grown rich on the bounty offered for catching criminals and outlaws and even at fifty-one had an eye that could spot a broken blade of grass from the back of his piebald pony. Parax was whip-lean with dark, deep-set eyes and silver-shot dark hair that receded from his temples, giving him a sharp widow's peak. He had a hard face leathered by wind and sun, and there were few laughter lines around his eyes.

"What are you thinking?" asked Bek, the lean warrior who led the four warriors in the hunting group.

Parax did not answer. Heeling his mount forward, he rode away from the group. He did not like Bek and abhorred his king, Carac. When the previous king, Alea, had died while hunting, Parax had ridden to the scene and scouted alone. It was said by Bek and the others that Alea had fallen from his horse in midriver and drowned. Parax knew they lied. He had found the spot where they had pulled Alea from his horse and dragged him to the river's edge, pushing his head below the water. His right heel had gouged earth from the bank as they had pinned him there.

But it was not for the likes of Parax to oppose the methods of princes, and he had kept his findings to himself.

He had not been in Alin when the merchant had been murdered, but at his sheep farm twenty miles to the north. Carac had sent for him, and he had arrived a day later. It took a further morning to locate the tracks of the youngster, and then they had found him soon enough.

That was when the fun had started.

Parax had enjoyed it enormously. Bek had led his men in a breakneck gallop, and the boy had cut to the southwest, escaping into a thick stretch of woods. The riders had hurtled after him. Two had caught him. Both had died.

A week had passed since, and four others had followed them on the Swan's Path. Bek was coldly furious, and this pleased Parax.

"I asked what you were thinking," said Bek, riding alongside. "Ignore me again, you old bastard, and I'll cut your balls off."

Parax grinned at him. "That would take a man, sonny. And a better one than you."

Bek reached for his sword. Parax swung his pony in close. His hand flashed up, and the point of a skinning knife touched Bek's throat. "See what I mean?" The older man sheathed the blade. Bek lifted his finger to his throat. It came away with a spot of blood. "Now," said Parax, "what were we talking about? Oh, yes, the youngster. He's canny for his age, no doubt about that. Left a false trail going east—and a good one—then cut back toward the west. He's a thinker."

"He's on foot. We should have caught up to him by now."

"Maybe," agreed Parax. "But he's moving over rough ground and choosing his route with great care."

"What of his magic?"

Parax laughed, the sound full of scorn. After the last killings one of the survivors had talked about the boy having the ability to change his form. Three of them had walked into a clearing. Suddenly a bush had risen up before them, becoming a man. He had stabbed two of the hunters. The third claimed to have fought him off, and the boy had run away into the hills. Parax let his laughter trail away. "Surely you do not believe it, Bek. You think someone who knows magic would allow himself to be chased from tree stump to hollow all over these hills? All the boy did was remove his cloak, soak it in mud, make cuts in it, and thread branches and leaves through the cuts. Then he crouched in the undergrowth and waited for your men. When they came, he sprang upon them. The survivor did not fight him off; he turned and fled. I read the sign."

Bek swore and cast an angry look at one of the men riding behind. "The Rigante must be found and returned to face justice," insisted Bek. "Those are my instructions from the king."

Parax said nothing. He had listened to the men talking and had pieced together the story. Diatka had betrayed the boy's friend to a ghastly death. The boy had avenged him. This pursuit was not about justice. It was about fear. Carac's fear. The king had ridden out with the first hunting party and had heard for himself the message from the Rigante.

"Nothing on earth will prevent me killing you."

Carac's fat face had blushed deep crimson. "Bring me his head," he had told Bek. Then he had ridden back to Alin with twenty men for a guard. A real warrior would have stayed with the pursuers, Parax believed.

The old hunter dismounted and examined the ground. It was bare and rocky, and no track could be seen. To the left, by a jutting rock, lay an oak leaf. It had obviously fallen from the boy's cloak disguise. Parax ran his fingers through his hair. Hunting was like a courtship, a union of mind and heart. Slowly the hunter came to know his prey and, in knowing him, either liked or loathed him. Parax was beginning to like the boy. There was no panic in him, with his movements well planned and his route carefully considered. The previous day he had killed a rabbit with a thrown rock, skinned it, and eaten the flesh raw. He had also taken time to find edible roots and berries. And he did not run blindly. He doubled back occasionally to watch the hunters, judge them, and, when the time was right, pick them off.

Parax rode warily to the crest of a hill and shaded his eyes to scan the surrounding countryside. To the northwest were the Talis Woods. Did the boy know enough not to go there? Parax thought about it. He had traveled with the foreigner, and Banouin knew these parts well. He surely would have mentioned the dangers that lay in the dark heart of those woodlands. Where, then, would the boy head? The border with Ostro lands? It was likely. That was the direction he had come from, after all. Parax grinned. Sliding from the saddle, he sat down on the hilltop.

The boy was canny and tough. He would know what they were expecting. Parax flicked his gaze toward the northwest. Was he rash enough to chance those woods?

Hoofbeats sounded from the south, and the five riders galloped up the hill. Parax swore under his breath. What was the point of tiring out the ponies in such a way? The riders were all young men from Bek's clan. Parax watched them, studying their faces. They were frightened now. Death had come to six of their friends. None of them relished the thought of being next.

Bek spoke to the riders and then moved his mount alongside the older man and dismounted. "Did he come this way?"

"Yes. About two hours ago. He sat just below this rim," said Parax, pointing to a spot some ten feet away. "Just there, where his head would be hidden by yon bush. He watched us for a while and thought about where he could hide."

"And where is that?"

Parax swept his arm out in a wide circle. "You choose, Bek. There are folds and hollows all around, jumbles of boulders, stands of trees. Wherever he is, he is watching us now, wondering if we are clever enough to outguess him."

"And are we, old man?"

"No, *we* are not. But I am. I know exactly where he is. I reckon I could even pick out the tree he is watching us from."

"Then we have him," Bek said, triumphantly.

"*You* can have him. I want no part of him. But five young men ought to be enough."

"It will be. Tell me where he is."

"I will, but first do your best not to look in the direction I indicate."

"I am not a fool, Parax."

No, you are a murdering regicide, thought Parax, but he kept the thought to himself. "He is on the edge of the Talis Woods. It is his last chance. He will know of the legends, and he will know that we know. He is risking his life against what he hopes is your lack of courage."

Parax saw the color drain from Bek's face. "The Talis Woods? You are sure?"

"As sure as I can be."

"Then he is dead already."

"Perhaps. Perhaps not. As I said, he is at the very edge. Perhaps the Talis will not see him. Perhaps they are elsewhere. Are you afraid to follow him, Bek?"

"Yes, I am afraid," admitted the warrior. "Would you ride into those woods?"

"No," said Parax. "But then, I am paid only to track."

"Where exactly is he?"

Parax did not look toward the woods. "Take your men and ride east for a little way. Then turn back and move along the edge of the wood. Keep watching me. When you reach the point where I believe him to be hiding, I will stand up and mount my pony."

Bek took a deep breath, then vaulted to the saddle. Parax watched in silence as Bek rode to his men and told them the grim news. A heated debate began. None of the four had any desire to risk the Talis Woods. Bek asked which of them would be prepared to stand before Carac and tell him they had been too afraid to follow his orders. They fell silent at this, for Carac was not a forgiving man. "Look," said Bek, "we will ride in close, and when I get the signal, charge in and kill the Rigante. Then we will ride out. It should take no more than a few heartbeats."

They were not convinced, but Parax knew they would follow the warrior. Fear of Carac's rage was strong in them.

Bek led them slowly down the hillside.

Conn was bone-weary. He had not slept—except for a few snatched moments—in three days, and his diet of roots, berries, and raw rabbit meat had soured his belly, causing cramps and nausea. His head was pounding, with pain searing his temples. He crouched behind a thick screen of bushes, watching the riders on the hilltop.

He had hoped they would ride farther to the west, allowing him to slip behind them. But they had not. Whoever was tracking him was even more skillful than Arbonacast.

Conn glanced around, uneasy and troubled. Towering oaks filled his vision, and there was no sound of bird or beast, not even the buzzing of an insect. Yet despite the absence of animal sounds, the wood seemed vibrant with life. The giant trees stood motionless, no breeze stirring the branches. It felt to Conn that they were staring at him, waiting. He felt like an intruder. His belly cramped, and he doubled over and retched. His empty stomach had nothing left, and he tasted the foulness of bile in his mouth. Falling back exhausted, he looked back at the hilltop. All but one of the riders had gone. The last man was merely sitting on the crest of the hill, his pony cropping grass alongside him.

Sweat dripped into Conn's eyes. He wiped it away with the sleeve of his filthy shirt. As he lifted his arm, the wound on his shoulder opened again, and he felt blood trickling over his chest. A thousand miles from home, wounded and alone, he knew that his chances for survival were slim indeed.

Yet there was no fear, only a burning anger and a desire for revenge.

I will not die here, he thought. I will find a way to survive and kill Carac.

He tried to stand, but his right leg caved in beneath him and he sprawled to the dirt, where he lay unconscious for a while. When he opened his eyes, he heard the ponies. Struggling to his knees, he scanned the tree line. Five riders were skirting the woods. One of them kept glancing up at the lone man on the hilltop. Conn's mouth was dry, his mind hazy. His heart sank as he realized they were preparing to enter the wood. Had Banouin been wrong? Was this not an enchanted place?

He looked up at the lone man again. The riders were waiting for his signal. Has he spotted me? Conn wondered.

Easing himself farther back, he staggered to the thick bole of a tall oak, then drew his dagger. His sword had been lost two days before, wedged in the body of a Perdii warrior. He felt something brush against his face and rubbed his hand over the skin.

He shivered and began to notice a prickling sensation, unpleasant and invasive, first on the skin of his neck and face and then on his back and arms. The sensation increased, becoming painful, as if bees were stinging him. Then it was more powerful than bees, like hot needles piercing his flesh. He groaned and fell to the grass. The branches of the trees around him began to rustle and move, the sound whispering and malevolent. The pain swelled until it was almost unbearable, flowing across his chest and down his arms. Then it reached his right hand, which was curled around the hilt of the Seidh blade. Bright light flared from the knife.

And all the pain vanished.

"You are the fawn child," whispered a voice in his ear.

At that moment the riders came thundering into the wood. Conn tried to gather his strength to face them. The first of the Perdii, lance leveled, leapt his horse over a fallen log, the other warriors close behind him.

Conn raised his knife.

But the leaping horse never landed. It froze in the air, statue-still in midleap. All the riders were suddenly utterly motionless. The air in the wood was cold now and growing colder. Conn began to shake, but he could not tear his gaze from the men who had come to kill him. As he watched, they began to change, hair and beards growing, fingernails sprouting like talons, their clothes rotting, their hair turning white, their flesh melting away, the skin blackening and then peeling back from the bone beneath. Within seconds they had crumbled from their mounts and lay broken on the grass. The bones continued to writhe, calcifying and then turning to dust, which the breeze picked up and blew across the ground. The ponies were untouched, and as the last vestige of their riders blew away, they came to life and stood quietly. A wind blew up, and four of the ponies ran from the wood. The fourth, a chestnut gelding, remained, standing motionless.

Conn had fallen to his knees when the voice spoke again. *"Touch the tree, fawn child,"* it said. Conn turned and crawled to the oak, reaching out, his fingers holding to the bark. His stomach settled, and the intense cold melted away. He sighed. Sunlight flowed through a break in the clouds, bathing the area in golden light. The tree bark began to move, forming a face of wood. It was a young face, handsome yet stern. As it grew clearer, Conn realized it was a representation of his own features.

"You are sick, fawn child. Lie down. We will tend you," said the tree face.

With the last of his strength ebbing away, Conn lay down, his face touching the cold ground. It felt better than any pillow, and as his consciousness fled, it seemed to the young warrior that the grass grew up around him, drawing him down into the dark, safe sanctuary of the earth.

His mind awoke from blissful darkness into painful light, a brilliance so piercing that tears filled his eyes. Holding his hands over his face, he tried to shut out the glare, but it shone through his skin, causing blinding pain.

"Hold firm, Connavar," said the another voice. *"I will try to create a more comfortable environment."*

Immediately the light faded. Conn moved his hands away from his face and opened his eyes. At first he could see nothing. Then, as his vision cleared, he saw that he was sitting in a wood, beside a rippling stream that glittered in the afternoon sun. The sky was cloudless, and the trees boasted leaves of every color, from blood red to sunset gold, emerald green to faded yellow. The air was full of fragrance: lavender, rose, and honeysuckle. It was the most beautiful spot Connavar had ever seen, yet something was wrong with the scene. The trees were of every variety—oak, elm, pine, maple—all growing together in the same soil yet at different stages of season. Some were just showing new spring growth; others had leaves of dark autumnal gold. And there were no shadows anywhere. Conn stretched out his naked arm. The sunlight was strong on his skin, but the grass below him showed no silhouette.

Slowly he rose and stretched. He felt calmer now than at any time in his memory. Turning, he gazed around the meadow.

And saw the bear.

It stood—as had the riders—utterly motionless, glittering chains draping its massive shoulders and curling around its powerful paws. Its mouth was open, showing terrible fangs. Conn felt no fear and approached the beast. It was bigger than the creature that had torn his flesh and somehow more awe-inspiring. Conn walked around the bear, marveling at its size and strength. He saw that it was scarred from many fights, and some of the wounds were recent. Reaching out, he tried to touch it, but his hand passed through the bear as if through smoke.

"A frightening beast," said the voice. A glowing figure materialized alongside him.

Conn was not startled, though he felt he should have been. "Frightening but sad," he told his new companion.

"Why sad?"

"It is chained," said Conn. "No creature that proud should be chained."

The glowing figure moved in closer, taking his arm and leading him back to the stream. Conn tried to see the face, but the features seemed to shift and flow, ever changing under the light that glowed around it. A beard, then beardless, long hair, then no hair, as if his face were being reshaped moment by moment. The effort to focus made Conn's head swim, and he looked away. "Which of the Seidh are you?" he asked.

"I am not Seidh, Connavar. I am a man long dead whose soul was rescued and brought to the wood."

"Why can I not see you clearly? Your features shift and change."

"It is a very long time since I last assumed human form. Give me a moment." The figure sat motionless. Slowly the flickering lights around him faded away, and Conn found himself sitting beside a young man with dark hair and gentle brown eyes. "Is that better?"

"Yes. Is this how you looked in life?"

"When I was young. I was almost a hundred years old when I died."

"Why did the Seidh keep your soul alive?"

"They had their reasons. Now tell me why you saved the fawn."

Conn shrugged. "It was trapped in the brambles. I could not leave it there to die."

"As you could not leave Riamfada?"

Conn shook his head. "That was different. He was my friend. A man does not desert his friends."

"How do you feel?"

Conn smiled. "Tranquil. It is very pleasant here, but I know it is a dream place and my body remains in your wood, cold and wet and bleeding."

"Not so," he said. "It is being healed while you sit here. And fresh clothes will be there for you. And a gift from a friend."

"My friends are all dead," he said sadly, remembering Banouin. He found he could picture the corpse on the gibbet now without any hatred for the people who had killed him. He sighed. "What is it that you have taken from me?" he asked.

"We have taken nothing. We have merely . . . separated you from your more . . . human instincts. Had we not done so, you could not have come here."

"My human instincts?"

"Your anger, your violence, your hatred, your lust for revenge. None of these has a place here."

"But I am human," said Conn, "so which part of me is here?"

"The best part," answered the figure. "The spirit, free of the darkness of the flesh."

Conn sat in the sunshine, realizing that he felt more at peace than he had at any time in his life. He looked back at the chained bear. "Why is the bear here?" he asked. "And why the chains? It is already motionless."

"We did not put the chains on the bear, Connavar. They are *your* chains."

"Mine? I don't understand."

"The bear is the part of you that cannot exist here. The chains are self-imposed: duty, responsibility, honor. Without them the bear would be merely a savage and selfish killer. Are you ready to return now?"

He thought about the question. Here everything was peaceful, the air alive with harmony. "Could I stay among the Seidh, like you, if I wished to?"

"No," the figure answered sadly. "One day, perhaps."

Conn was not anxious to return to the world, and he sat quietly for a moment, savoring the tranquillity. "If the Seidh are truly a race without hatred or anger," he asked "why do they allow the Morrigu to walk among us, bringing such evil?"

"An interesting question, Connavar. In response, let me say this: You wanted glory, and the Morrigu gave it to you. Vorna wanted to be loved and accepted. Now she is. In what way does that make the actions of the Morrigu evil? All our actions, Seidh and human, result in consequences—consequences we do not always welcome. The Morrigu offers gifts. If a man—or woman—chooses to accept one, then surely he must also accept the possible consequences. You asked for glory. What if you had asked for true love, or the healing of Riamfada, or peace and harmony for your people? Think on that, Connavar. Those who seek the gifts of the Morrigu always ask for something for themselves: personal gain, fame, skill with a sword, beautiful women to grace their beds, or handsome men to woo and love them. Always selfish. Beware judging what you do not understand."

The voice faded away. And the world spun.

* * *

He awoke in the forest, opening his eyes to see a chestnut pony standing quietly, reins trailing to the ground. For a moment he retained the sense of harmony he had known in the dream world of the Seidh. Then it was gone. He remembered the hunters and the long days of the chase, the fighting and the killing. More than that he remembered why, and this time, when he thought of Banouin, the warm fires of rage flared within him.

Pushing himself to his feet, he saw that fresh clothes had indeed been left for him, folded and laid on a flat rock. There was a shirt of thin dark leather so soft that it felt like satin, a pair of black leather leggings with an integral belt of mottled snakeskin, and a pair of dark riding boots reinforced at the sides with a strip of silver. Stripping off his ruined shirt and leggings, he pulled on the Seidh garments. As he expected, they fitted him well. Then he moved to the pony. It eyed him warily, and he spoke softly to it, slowly raising his hand and stroking its muzzle.

It was then that he saw the sword resting against a tree. It was a rider's sword, the blade heavy and slightly curved. It was of the same shining silver metal as his knife, but it was the hilt that caught his eye. It was a mixture of gold, silver, and ebony, the black quillons shaped like oak leaves, the golden fist guard embossed with the head of a bear, and the silver pommel bearing a carving of a fawn trapped in brambles. Conn hefted the weapon. It was lighter than he expected and beautifully balanced.

A gift from a friend, the figure had said.

It was good to know he had such friends. He thought then of poor Riamfada. He would have made Conn a sword if he had lived. It would have been almost as beautiful. "I miss you, little fish," he said.

The scabbard lay beside the tree. It was of hardened black leather and sported its own dark baldric, which he looped over his shoulder. Then he gathered up the pony's reins and vaulted to the saddle.

Slowly he rode from the trees. He was surprised to see the lone hunter still sitting his mount at the top of the hill. The ponies of the dead men were cropping grass nearby. Conn rode toward the hunter. The man made no effort to flee but dismounted and sat on the grass waiting for him. Despite his dark hair, he was old, Conn saw, his face lined and his eyes knowing.

Hatred was strong in the young Rigante's heart, and he intended to kill the hunter. However, the man made no hostile move, and the youngster was intrigued.

"Are they all dead?" asked the man.

"Aye. Killed by the Seidh—the Talis, as you call them."

The older man sighed. "I am Parax the Tracker. I am glad you survived. I have always been fascinated by the Talis. I would dearly like to know why they let you live."

Conn shrugged. "I have no answers. Draw your sword and let us get this over with."

"I don't think so," said Parax. "Never was much of a swordsman. I'll do my best to stop you killing me, though, if that is your intention. Though I hope you will think better of it."

Conn scanned the countryside. There was no sign of other riders. He was confused now. He had expected his enemy to fight. Instead the man was sitting, relaxed, on a hilltop, conversing as if they were old friends. Conn had no experience of such a situation, but in spite of his hate, he felt it would be wholly wrong merely to cut the old man down. Parax pushed his hand through his hair and chuckled. "I have come to know you, Connavar. I have followed your trail and read your heart. You are a fighter, not a murderer. I think that I like you. I wouldn't say that of most men."

"I care nothing for your likes or dislikes," snapped Conn.

"When you saw me emerge from the wood, why did you wait here? You knew I would come to fight."

"There's the question of pride, young man. I am a hunter, and though I say it with all due modesty, I am the best hunter of men this land has ever seen. I was told to find you. Now I have done that. No one can say that Parax failed. That means a lot to me."

"Your people murdered my friend," said Conn, seeking now to rekindle his anger.

"I know," said Parax. "It was a foul deed committed by foul men. His killing was not the first. The Perdii had a good king, you know. Life was fine. He cared. Cared about his people, felt their sorrows, shared their joys. Carac had him murdered—dragged to a river and held under water. That was his reward for eighteen years of good rule. His wife was strangled, his son butchered. And all for a crown that will be torn from his grasp by Jasaray and his Stone army."

"You say 'the Perdii' had a good king. Are you not from that tribe?"

"No. I am of the Rodessi. But I have lived among the Perdii for twenty years." Parax rose smoothly and walked to his pony, dipping his hand into a sack hanging from the saddle. "You want something to eat?" he asked. "I have a little meat pie flavored with onion. It is good," said Parax.

Conn was becoming lost in this exchange, and he knew it. Parax pulled the pie clear, carefully broke the crust, and handed a section to the young warrior.

"Thank you," Conn said automatically.

"My pleasure," Parax answered with a grin. Then he sat down again and ate. Conn tasted the pie. Parax had understated its virtues. It was more than good. It was food for the gods! Forcing himself to eat slowly, he devoured the pie, then licked the gravy from his fingers.

"Better than raw rabbit, eh?" said Parax.

"I never tasted better," agreed Conn.

"I bought it from a crofter's wife yesterday. You should have tasted it hot. There's nothing like beef and onion to satisfy an appetite." Parax swallowed the last mouthful and wiped his hand across his mouth. "You know," he said, "I had the feeling you would survive the Talis Wood. I see that not only did you survive, you also emerged with gifts. New clothes, a sword. They are a fey people, but they seem to like you. Tell me, what do they look like?"

"I saw a face form in the bark of a tree, and I dreamed I was with a man whose features I could not at first see clearly even though he sat beside me in bright sunlight." He took a deep breath. "I have decided not to kill you, hunter."

"I knew that," said Parax, climbing to his feet. "As I said, you are not a murderer, young Rigante. Do you want me to carry a message to Carac?"

Conn's expression hardened. "I have already sent a message. One is enough."

"I heard it. So did he," said Parax. Turning his back on Conn, he walked to his pony and swung into the saddle. "There are riders to the west and to the north. Were I you, I would head due east. The border is less than a day away. There is a town there. The Stone army is camped nearby. You will be safe there, I think."

Swinging his mount, the hunter rode down the hill.

Conn watched him go. Then he mounted his pony and headed for the border. Parax was right. He was no murderer. But that was not why he had allowed the old man to live. Conn's hatred was for the Perdii only, for the people who had murdered his friend.

And the blood price for that crime would be high.

◇ **10** ◇

THE STONE GENERAL Jasaray moved slowly along the inner perimeter of the marching camp, his hooded, deep-set eyes scanning the activity around him. Eight thousand soldiers were working in highly skilled teams at preordained tasks, creating a fortress in a few hours that should have taken days. As Jasaray passed, all the soldiers felt the presence of the general and believed they could feel his pale blue gaze whisper across them like a winter breeze, judging their labors, the speed of their work, the precision of their actions. Not one of them risked a glance in his direction.

He walked with arms clasped behind his back, the sun glinting from his polished iron breastplate. There was little that was imposing about his physique. Several inches under six feet, the general was a slim figure, his face thin and ascetic, his short-cropped hair thinning at the temples and crown. Without the armor he looked like the teacher he had been before discovering his true vocation.

All his soldiers knew the story of the Scholar. At twenty-eight, during the first civil war, the mathematician and lecturer Jasaray had been hastily commissioned into the Third Army of the Republic, serving under the general Sobius. His role had been that of quartermaster, where, it was thought, his logistic skills could best be used in estimating quantities of supplies, numbers of wagons, and the provision and supply of equipment. Despite his lack of military training, Jasaray had asked for and been given the rank of second general. This, he maintained, was necessary when dealing with other officers. Without that rank his authority as quartermaster would be undermined. He had proved himself more than able in this role, and the Third Army was the best supplied and armed in the republic.

Unfortunately for the army, it was not the best led.

Sobius had been outthought, outflanked, and outclassed. The army had been crushed, fourteen thousand men slaughtered and a mere four thousand escaping. With most of the senior officers slain, the inexperienced Jasaray was forced to take command. Organizing a fighting rear guard, he staved off the rebel force for seventeen days until reinforcements arrived. With the leaders of the republic in disarray and ready to surrender, Jasaray led a counterattack on the rebel army, routing it and capturing two of its leaders. Three thousand rebel soldiers were crucified, the leaders beheaded. At twenty-nine Jasaray was the undisputed hero of the republic.

At forty-two he was the greatest general the people of Stone had ever known, respected and feared throughout what was still known, despite republican supremacy, as the empire. One campaign after another had been won with clinical efficiency as the empire expanded. Jasaray became ever more powerful within the republic.

To his soldiers the Scholar was a godlike figure to be obeyed instantly and to be feared. He was also a general who always made sure that there was hot food for his men and that their wages arrived on time. Added to this, he was a careful planner, never putting his men in unnecessary danger. These were qualities common soldiers valued above all others. That his discipline was harsh—floggings and hangings were commonplace—did not concern them unduly. Almost all of the disciplinary actions were related to carelessness, and carelessness could cost the lives of soldiers. The men understood this. And they liked the fact that the Scholar never wore embossed armor or carried jewel-encrusted weapons. His breastplate was iron, his sword standard-issue, his helmet—when he bothered to wear it—a battered bronze without plume or crest. The only sign of his rank was the purple cloak he wore and the fact that a mosaic stone floor was set out in his tent every night, the numbered stones carried in six huge chests on the lead wagon of the baggage train.

Jasaray watched the construction of the fortress, his gaze roving over the entire area, noting the work rate and the positioning of the colored flags that signified where tents would be pitched and baggage animals picketed. Behind him walked four junior officers and six runners, each hoping that nothing would cause the general any irritation.

They had all been on the march for six days and in that time had constructed six marching camps just like this one, the longest sides twelve hundred feet and the shorter nine hundred, an area of more than a million square feet. There would be two gates, one in the east and the other in the west, constructed from felled trees, their trunks expertly split. Even now horsemen were hauling the timbers from the woods to the south.

Stone armies had long known of the value of fortified camps, but it had taken the genius of Jasaray to refine the process until it was almost an art form.

Each day, three hours before dusk, while marching in enemy territory, the two lead panthers, six thousand hard-eyed veterans, would fan out in a protective screen around the area the officers of the flag party had decreed should be the marching camp. The officers would then measure out the defense perimeter line, marking it with green flags. Inside this vast rectangle of up to eighty acres they would flag the dimensions of the general's headquarters tent, the tents of other officers and men, the area of picket lines for mounts, and the section set aside for the baggage train.

As the next panther regiment arrived, its soldiers would remove their armor, form into work teams, take up their short, hinge-handled shovels, and begin to dig the rectangular defensive trench. Within an hour and a half the trench would be complete, with a rampart wall thrown up along its length.

By the time the baggage train arrived, the stockade would be almost complete and every unit would know where to go and what to do. Once the digging work was finished, the soldiers would put on their armor and retire into the fortification, along with the two panthers of the defensive screen. Last to arrive would be the cavalry units patrolling the outlying land for sign of the enemy.

Within the space of three hours a huge fortification would have been constructed in the heart of enemy territory. By nightfall the full army and all its wagons and equipment would be camped in relative safety.

Jasaray walked on as the soldiers carved out the great trench, hurling up turf to create the defense perimeter of the marching camp. Elsewhere officers were measuring out the area for Jasaray's tent headquarters, while his six personal servants stood waiting to lay the general's mosaic floor. Jasaray's gaze flicked to the north and the distant line of hills beyond which the enemy was gathering. He could see his scouts patrolling and wished once more that his military budget could have extended to more Stone cavalry. It did not sit well that he had to rely on Keltoi tribesmen. He had no doubt that the Gath Ostaran was a fighter, but he was, like most of his race, hotheaded and volatile, lacking any understanding of broad strategy.

Even as the thought occurred to him, he saw a tribesman walking toward the fortification. He was leading an injured pony. Something about the man created a flicker of interest in the general. But at that moment he saw the first wagon of the baggage train cresting a small hill. His eyes narrowed. More wagons appeared, with patrolling foot soldiers moving alongside them. The men were too close to the train. If the enemy attacked, they would be driven back into the line of the wagons, unable to form a fighting square. Jasaray flicked his fingers. A young runner appeared alongside him.

The general pointed to the protective line of soldiers. "Find the officer and tell him to open the regulation distance between his troops and the baggage train. Also tell him to report to my tent as soon as his men are inside the stockade."

Irritated now, the general began to pace up and down. The four aides and five remaining runners stood tensely by. Each of them was silently cursing the recalcitrant patrol officer, for Jasaray's anger could be assuaged only by victims. The general swung to the youngest of the aides, a seventeen-year-old on his first campaign. "Quote me the words of Getius concerning marching camps," he said.

The young man licked his lips. "I . . . do not know . . . precisely . . . sir," he said. "But the main cut of his theory—"

"I did not ask for the 'main cut.' " Jasaray was silent for a moment, his pale eyes fixed to the youth's face. "Go away," he said softly. "I shall ask you another question tomorrow. If you do not know the answer 'precisely, sir,' I shall send you home in shame." The young man started to turn, then remembered to salute. Jasaray waved him away contemptuously and turned his attention to the others. "I take it one of you knows the answer? What about you, Barus?"

The young man stepped forward. He was tall and slim, his hair closely cropped and raven black. "It is a difficult quote to remember, for all of Getius' work is wordy and grammatically indigestible. However, I believe he wrote: 'The importance of fortifying night camps appears not only from the danger to which troops are exposed who camp without such precautions but also from the distressful situation of an army which, after receiving a check in the field, finds itself without a retreat and consequently at the mercy of the enemy.' "

"Almost perfect," said Jasaray. "The correct quote is, 'to

which troops are *perpetually* exposed.' Perpetually. That is the nature of war. Now you can go and find the idiot I just sent away. You can spend the night teaching him. If he fails my test tomorrow, I shall consider sending you home also."

"Yes, sir," answered the youngster, giving a crisp salute.

"And Barus, pay particular attention to the topography required for marching camps."

"I will, sir," said Barus. As he walked away, the two remaining junior officers relaxed. Surely, they thought, two victims would be enough. Jasaray allowed them a few moments as he scanned the defensive ditch and the new rampart wall. The native scout he had seen before came walking into the compound, leading his pony. Jasaray gazed at the man, noting the way he moved, perfectly in balance. The man glanced at him, and Jasaray saw he had oddly colored eyes. One was green, the other tawny brown, and his handsome face was badly scarred on the left side.

"Do you speak any Turgon?" asked the general.

"A little," answered the warrior.

"What happened to your pony?"

"Stepped in a rabbit hole. He's lucky not to have broken his leg."

Swinging away from the tribesman, Jasaray returned his attention to the two junior officers. "How wide should the ditch be?" he snapped.

"Eight feet," they answered in unison. "And three feet deep," added the first, earning a withering glance from his companion. Jasaray smiled at their discomfort. His good humor was returning now.

"And what is the one priceless commodity a general can never replace?"

Both officers stood mystified, their minds racing. Jasaray noticed that the young tribesman was still standing close by, a smile on his face. "You find their predicament amusing?" he asked the man.

"No," answered the warrior, "but if I were you, I'd find their ignorance worrying." Taking the pony's reins, he started to walk away.

"Perhaps you would like to answer the question for them," said Jasaray.

"Time," said the young man. "And, if I quote you correctly, General, *'You can replace men and horses, swords and arrows. But never lost time.'*"

"You have read my work?" The question was asked in a flat, bored voice, but the general's eyes had narrowed and he was watching the tribesman closely.

"No, General, I do not read. I had a friend who taught me your words. If you will excuse me, I must tend to my pony."

Jasaray watched him go, then turned to his officers. "Find out who he is and have him attend my tent tonight following the briefing."

"I can tell you who he is, sir," said the first of the officers. "His name is Connavar, and he was recruited by Valanus. He is not of the Ostro or the Gath but a tribesman from across the water. According to rumor, he saved the life of Valanus back in Goriasa."

"And he has pledged to kill Carac," said the second man, not to be outdone. "He was the warrior who fought his way across the land after the murder of his friend, the merchant Banouin."

"Which tribe is he from?"

"I believe it is the Rigante, sir," the first officer told him. "Do you still wish him to attend your tent?"

"Have I said otherwise?"

Jasaray moved away to inspect the ramparts. The sun was falling behind the western hills, and storm clouds were moving in from the sea.

"If the Scholar has asked to see you, it means you will be either flogged or promoted," Valanus said cheerfully. Conn tugged his cloak tighter about him as the rain dripped through the canvas wall of the tent. The candle stub guttered, but before it could die completely, Valanus held a second candle over it. For a few moments only two flames lit the damp interior, making it seem marginally more homey. The tent was six feet long, four feet wide, and five feet high at the center. It was supported by a thin wooden frame. Attached to the frame were hooks from which hung two sacks containing clothing. There were four folding canvas-topped stools that could be linked together to form a narrow bed. One of them was burdened by a breastplate, helm, wrist guards, and greaves, balanced precariously above the wet ground.

"I thought you were a favorite of his," grumbled the tribesman. "Why, then, do you have a leaky tent?"

"Just bad luck," said Valanus, ignoring the steady drips that spattered him. "I am a soldier out of necessity. I do not come from a wealthy family. Therefore, I receive only standard issue. Most of the tents are dry. I'll try to find a better one tomorrow." His smile widened. "It should amuse Jasaray when you walk in like a drowned rat."

"Why do you think I risk a flogging?"

Valanus shrugged. "There are only two reasons the Scholar sends for tribesmen: to reward or punish them. You have done nothing to deserve punishment, so I expect you impressed him."

"Perhaps," Conn said doubtfully. "But then, none of us have done anything impressive so far, save to march and ride and build enormous fortresses that we leave deserted the next day. When will the Perdii fight?"

"When they are ready, I expect," said Valanus. "And when they do, we shall defeat them and you will have more revenge. Ostaran tells me you are a terror. Three skirmishes, five dead Perdii to add to your tally. You know what the Gath call you? Demonblade."

"I don't care what they call me. As you said, they were skirmishes. And my revenge will not be complete until I draw my dagger across Carac's throat."

The smile left the officer's face, and when he spoke, there was an echo of sadness in his voice. "And when he is dead, you think the hurt and pain will go away?"

"It will or it won't," said Conn, watching the white-haired young man closely.

Valanus seemed lost in thought for a moment. "I had a friend once," he said. "More than a friend. He was captured in the Tribante campaign. They put out his eyes, then cut off his hands and feet, then his balls. When we found him, he was still alive. They had cauterized his stumps, you see, with boiling tar." The candle flickered as a drop of water splashed close to its flame. Valanus shivered, then gathered himself and forced a smile. "I have made no friends since. Nor will I among soldiers and warriors."

From outside the tent came the tolling of a bell. It rang four times. "Well, my friend," said Valanus, "it is time for you to attend the general. If it is a reward he offers you, perhaps you could think about a new tent for me. Or a servant."

"You have a servant. I saw him put up this tent."

"I share him with eight other poor officers. And I cannot afford to slip him extra money. Hence . . ." He waved his arm and pointed to the rivulets running down the canvas walls.

Conn said nothing but rose smoothly, ducking under the tent flap and stepping out into the storm. Lightning flashed to the west, followed by a rolling clap of thunder. There were still three hours before midnight. On a clear day at this time of the year it would still be light, but the storm covered the land like a dark shroud. Conn trudged across the campsite, passed the lines of horses picketed nose to nose and the baggage wagons, then threaded his way through the ranks of round tents that housed the common soldiers.

Jasaray's tent was forty feet long and at least fifteen feet wide. Its walls glowed gold from the many lanterns within.

Two spear-carrying soldiers stood outside, shielded from most of the rain by a six-foot jutting flap supported by two poles. As Conn approached, they crossed their spears against him.

"What ... you ... want?" the guard on the left asked, in fractured Keltoi.

"I have been invited to see the general," Conn told him in Turgon.

The guard looked surprised. "Wait here," he said, handing his spear to his comrade and stepping inside the tent. He was gone only a few seconds. When he returned, he told Conn to wait, and the tribesman stood in the rain, his mood darkening. He could hear voices from within the tent but with the rain hissing down around him could not make out the nature of the conversation. After some minutes officers began to emerge from the tent and hurry away through the storm. Even then he was not invited inside. His anger mounting, he was on the verge of striding away when he heard a voice call out from inside.

"You can go in now," said the guard. "There is a brush mat inside. Wipe the mud from your boots. The general doesn't like mud on his floor. And you can leave your sword and dagger here. No weapons are allowed." Conn lifted clear his baldric and handed it to the guard.

Then he entered the tent. The contrast between these quarters and those of Valanus was so marked that Conn wanted to laugh out loud. The mosaic floor was expertly laid, mostly of small, square white stones, but at the center darker stones had been used to form the head of a panther. Curtains screened the far end of the tent, which Conn took to be the sleeping area. Seven bright lanterns hung from hooks on the tent frame, their light shining down on six wooden chairs with velvet cushions, two heavily embroidered couches, and a long, ornate table of carved oak. An iron brazier full of coals was set close by, and several large, thick rugs had been placed near the seats. The general, dressed in a simple white knee-length tunic and sandals, was lounging on one of the couches. No one could have looked less like a warrior.

"Come closer," he said. Conn wiped his feet on the brush mat and then advanced. Removing his damp cloak, he dropped it to the floor and then approached the brazier, enjoying the sudden warmth. "You may sit down," said Jasaray, gesturing toward a couch.

"My clothes are wet and mud-spattered," said Conn. "Best if I stand."

"Thoughtful of you," said Jasaray. "So tell me about Banouin."

"You knew him?" countered Conn, surprised by the question and seeking time to form an answer.

"He was both my teacher and my student," said Jasaray, "and he was quite skilled in both areas."

"I did not know that," Conn told him. "Banouin often spoke of you but never mentioned you were friends."

"I said teacher and student," Jasaray said testily. "I did not mention friendship. Try to avoid making assumptions. Communication is best if it is precise. Now, I understand he was living among your people—indeed, that he took a wife there."

"Yes on both counts."

"What was it, do you think, that attracted him to the lands of the Rigante?"

"He said he liked mountains and wild woods, the scent of pine and heather on the wind. What was it that he taught you?"

Jasaray ignored the question. "Why would Banouin teach you my theories?" he asked.

"He was trying to explain the greatness of his people," Conn replied carefully.

"Unlikely. He was not overly fond of our ambitions, as I recall. Did you know he was a general in the civil war?"

"No, but I guessed he was a soldier."

"He was a fine general, respected by his men and feared by his enemies. He was a man without vanity. Although I had been his student, when I became his leader, he followed my orders without question. A rare man, Banouin. Yet a man with flaws. His mind was full of abstractions: honor, nobility, courage, conscience. He focused on small issues. The nature of the human soul, the possibilities of change and redemption. Good and evil, right and wrong; these abstracts dominated his thoughts and actions."

Some of the words Conn did not understand. He had become almost fluent in Turgon, but Banouin had never spoken of *"redemption"* or *"conscience."* But if Banouin had valued these things—whatever they were—then Conn would value them, too. When he spoke, he chose his words as carefully as he could. "I do not have the . . . skill in your language to . . ." He struggled for the right word. ". . . debate such matters. What I do know is that Banouin was a good man, perhaps a great one. He was loved by a people not his own, and I will always honor his memory."

Jasaray's cold, pale eyes showed the merest glint of annoyance. "Yes, yes," he said, "people *loved* Banouin. I liked him, too, in my own way. Indeed, I was surprised by how sad I felt when I heard of his death. Did he ever tell you why he resigned from the army?"

"No. He never spoke of it."

"A pity. I have often wondered why a man with such skill should become a traveling merchant."

"He enjoyed the life: meeting new people, seeing new lands."

"Yes, he had a way with people. No doubt about that." Jasaray gestured toward a silver flagon filled with water. Beside it was a single goblet. Jasaray had said nothing, but with that single gesture their entire relationship was clearly delineated. He might be a guest in Jasaray's tent, but in the eyes of the general he was just another servant. But this was not the time to make a stand. Swiftly he moved to the table and filled the goblet, handing it to the seated man. Jasaray took it without a word of thanks, but he smiled. Then he spoke again. "Banouin also had an eye for talent. This is why you intrigue me, Connavar. What was it he saw in you, and why did he teach you? Are you the son of a chieftain or king?"

"No. My father was a horse hunter; my stepfather is a cattle breeder."

"And yet at seventeen you are already famous in your own land, I understand. You fought a bear with only a knife. Added to this, you entered the main Perdii settlement, killed the merchant who betrayed Banouin, and then killed six of the pursuing hunters. Since then you have become a dark legend among the Gath. Are all your people so gifted at fighting?"

"All of them," said Conn.

"I doubt that." Jasaray stood and walked to the rear curtains, pushing them aside. Beyond was a narrow bed and a wooden stand on which hung the general's armor. "Help me into my armor," he said.

Conn moved to the general's side and lifted the iron breastplate clear of its peg. Jasaray struggled into it, and Conn buckled the sides. Then the general put on a kilt made of bronze reinforced leather strips and added his sword belt. Conn knelt by his feet and buckled on his bronze greaves. He did not ask why the general wished to be dressed for war at this time of night, though it puzzled him. Lastly Jasaray put on his battered helm. Conn could not resist a smile. Jasaray saw it. "Yes, I am not a warrior," he said without a hint of rancor, "and I know I look ridiculous garbed in this manner. Yet it serves a purpose."

Jasaray walked to the tent flap and lifted it, calling out an instruction to one of the guards. The man handed the general Conn's baldric, then moved off through the rain. Jasaray moved back into the tent. The general drew Conn's sword and gazed at it in the lantern light. "This is a fine weapon," he said. "The hilt alone is worth several hundred silver pieces. Your father must be a very rich cattle breeder."

"The sword was a gift from a friend," said Conn.

Jasaray turned the blade in his hands. "The embossed bear is a creation of rare beauty, and I understand its meaning in your life. But why the fawn in brambles? I see that your cloak brooch carries the same motif."

"When I was a child, I tore all my clothes rescuing a fawn. The story became something of a joke with my fellows."

Jasaray looked at him closely. "A killer who rescues fawns? Such a man should be watched closely." Sheathing the blade, he tossed the baldric to Conn and instructed him to put it on. Then he walked from the tent.

The storm was clearing, but the rain was still falling fast. As Conn joined the general, he saw that soldiers were moving from their tents in full armor. Once gathered, they formed into silent lines and stood statue-still, rain coursing over breastplates and helms.

The storm clouds above the camp drifted apart, and bright moonlight bathed the scene.

At that moment the air was filled with battle cries, high and shrill, and javelins rained over the ramparts. The tents, wagons, and horses had been placed well back from the ramparts, and most of the missiles fell on empty earth. One pierced the back of a baggage pony, which whinnied in pain and then fell to the ground.

"They are coming!" yelled a sentry on the north wall. "Thousands of them!" A javelin took him through the back of the neck, and he was pitched from the ramparts.

Several officers ran to Jasaray. The general was standing calmly, his hands clasped behind his back. "Take one panther to the north wall," he said. "Hold two in reserve. The main attack will be elsewhere—probably from the west. Position archers behind the baggage wagons."

The officers ran back to their men. Jasaray walked slowly

to the leading line of soldiers. "My apologies for waking you so early," he told them as they parted to allow him through. Conn remained at his side and was impressed by the man's calm. He also wondered just how the general had known that an attack was imminent. Was he a magicker? Or was there some clue that Conn had overlooked? The problem nagged at him. The screams of wounded and dying men came from the northern ramparts as wave after wave of Perdii tribesmen stormed the camp, scrambling up the ramparts to hack and stab at the defenders.

"I think the rain is easing," said Jasaray. The wounded baggage pony was continuing to whinny in pain and terror. Jasaray tapped a soldier on the shoulder. "Go put that creature out of its misery," he said. "It is hard to think through that screaming."

"Yes, lord," answered the man, drawing his sword and breaking from the line.

A trumpet sounded from the west. Conn glanced across toward the western ramparts and saw two men signaling. "Here comes the main attack," said Jasaray. A second panther of three thousand men was sent to crouch below the wall. Conn saw the tips of thousands of makeshift ladders appear. He took hold of his sword hilt.

"You will not need that yet," said Jasaray. "It will be an hour at least before we are called upon. When the gates are breached." Conn glanced at the gates, two six-foot-wide structures created from slender tree trunks, sharpened and shaped and then expertly fastened together with crossbars. It seemed unlikely that the Perdii would be able to force them open. Perhaps they will set fire to them, he thought.

Hundreds of archers clad in leather tunics and conical leather caps moved out to stand in front of the baggage train. Each man had a short, curved bow and a quiver of black-feathered arrows.

"Might I ask a question, General?"

"Of course."

"Why do you have your archers positioned below the walls? Surely they could have killed scores of the enemy from the ramparts."

"To shoot from there they would have had to rise above the rampart wall, making themselves targets. I have only six hundred archers. They are too valuable to waste. Watch them and learn."

The archers waited for Jasaray's signal. When it came, they raised their bows high and loosed volley after volley. The shafts rose, arced, then dropped with devastating effect on the massed tribesmen outside the camp. Conn could only imagine the havoc being caused.

On the ramparts the fighting was ferocious, but the Stone soldiers, heavily armored in breastplates and helms and carrying concave rectangular shields, were taking a terrible toll on the lightly armed enemy. And as Banouin had once said, the Stone short swords were infinitely superior in close-quarter fighting. Some of the Perdii warriors, their faces stained with red ocher, broke through. Jasaray sent three sections of sixty men to intercept them and shore up the defenses.

A dull, booming sound like distant thunder came from the western gates, which shivered under the impact. Conn gazed at the faces of the soldiers around him. They were tense and expectant, but there was little sign of fear. Jasaray stood, calm as ever. Removing his helmet, he scratched his thinning hair. "It is good that the rain has stopped," he said. "I hate fighting in the wet. Well, let's go meet them."

Officers called out orders and then formed into columns of four to move through the baggage train into the open ground before the gates. Once there, they spread out in a long fighting line ten deep, the men in the front row standing with shields locked. Conn and Jasaray stood behind the fourth line.

The booming continued, and one of the trunks split, then

a second. Minutes later the gates parted, a bronze-headed battering ram hammering through them. Hundreds of red-smeared warriors pushed aside the ruined gates and ran screaming into the compound. A drum sounded behind the Stone warriors, and they began to march forward. The Perdii hurled themselves on the advancing phalanx and the cruel stabbing swords of the front line. Hundreds died, and the Stone soldiers advanced over the bodies. Men in the second and third lines bloodied their swords on the fallen, thrusting their blades into wounded Perdii as they moved over them.

The tribesmen lacked nothing in courage, and the battle continued for almost an hour before the Stone line reached the ruined gates. At that point a trumpet sounded from the Perdii lines, and the warriors faded back into the darkness.

Workmen repaired the gates swiftly while soldiers carried dead tribesmen outside the camp, creating a mound of dead. More than two thousand Perdii had died in the battle as opposed to just over sixty Stone soldiers killed and 104 sporting cuts that needed stitching.

As dawn was breaking Conn walked to the ramparts and looked down upon the three huge mounds of Perdii dead. Stone soldiers who had not taken part in the battle had dug long pits carpeted with oil-soaked wood. Then the bodies had been hauled out and hurled into them, along with more brushwood.

As the dawn sun rose higher, soldiers threw torches of oil-soaked straw to the mounds. Flames flickered and then caught, and Conn watched as tongues of fire licked at the corpses.

Soon the flames were roaring out above the mounds, and the sweet smell of cooking flesh drifted over the camp.

My first battle, thought Conn, and I did not draw my sword in anger. The fighting had not reached the fourth rank.

Valanus joined him on the ramparts. The officer had a cut

on his cheek that had been expertly stitched. "What happened to you?" asked Valanus. "I thought to see you fighting alongside me on the north wall."

"I was with the general. How did he know an attack was coming? Is he a mystic?"

"He does have a feel for these things. On the other hand, it is not the first time he has called the men out to stand in ranks during the night. He often does it to keep them sharp. Perhaps he was just lucky. I once put it to him that he had more than his share of good fortune. You know what he said? 'The more carefully I plan, the luckier I get.' That's the nearest I've heard him to making a joke. So what did he want you for?"

"I still don't know. He wanted to talk about Banouin. It seems he was once a general."

Valanus gave a soft whistle. "So, he was *that* Banouin. I didn't realize. Banouin is not an uncommon name in Stone. But your man was the Ghost General. He led a cavalry force and would always appear where least expected by the enemy. When the first civil war ended, he retired. It surprised a lot of people. He was expected to enter politics."

"Jasaray said that Banouin was both his teacher and his student," said Conn. "Do you know what that meant?"

"Aye, I do. When the Scholar was first commissioned, he knew nothing of military matters but had a great understanding of mathematics and the logistics of supply. Banouin was sent to teach him basic military etiquette, if you like: chains of command and so on. As you can see, Jasaray was a fast learner."

The wind changed, the morning breeze blowing over the blazing mounds and sending dark smoke into the compound. "Two thousand dead, and they achieved nothing," said Conn. "What a waste of life."

"They never learn, these tribesmen," said Valanus. "They attack in vast numbers, expecting to overwhelm us. It is the only way they know how to fight. There is no real organization, no officers, no clearly defined command structure. Their battle plans are always the same: There is the enemy; go charge them and see what happens. As you say, a waste of life."

"What would you do in Carac's place?"

Valanus grinned. "I'd surrender and pledge allegiance to Stone. He cannot win. We are invincible. After last night's attack his men will know that is the truth. They will go back and talk among themselves about how tough we are, how deadly. Their fear will grow. By the end of summer we will be building towns of stone on Perdii land and bringing in thousands of Stone immigrants. I myself have been promised ten parcels of prime land, which I can keep or sell."

"I expect you'd swap it all for a good tent," said Conn.

"Damn right," agreed Valanus.

Ostaran was about to die. No doubt about it. That, for two reasons, was irritating in the extreme. First, this was yet another skirmish and not a glorious full-fledged battle. Second, Demonblade had warned him against reckless attacks. Slashing his saber across the face of a charging tribesman, Ostaran leapt across the body of his dead horse, trying to create space for himself to fight. A hurled spear tore through his riding shirt, grazing his shoulder. A swordsman ran at him. Ostaran blocked the savage cut, stepped in close, and head butted the warrior, who stumbled back half-blind.

The sun was shining brightly in a clear blue sky, and a fresh breeze was blowing, carrying the scent of grass and pine. Ostaran drew in a deep breath. Ah, but life is good, he thought. The Perdii at least understood the concepts of martial honor and were attacking him one at a time, testing his courage and their own. Another man ran at him. Ostaran leapt high, kicking the warrior in the chest, driving him back. A second swordsman charged from the left. Ostaran took the blow on his round wooden buckler and aimed a slashing riposte. The

Perdii threw himself backward, catching his foot on the leg of Ostaran's dead mount and falling heavily.

Ostaran unclipped the oak leaf cloak brooch and let his black cloak fall to the ground. He was wearing a round helm of bronze and a thigh-length sleeveless mail shirt and had taken to sporting bronze greaves in the style of Stone officers. The shirt was heavy, but it protected him from what he feared most: a disemboweling thrust to the belly. His older brother had died from just such a wound, and Ostaran was determined never to go through such agony himself.

He took a deep breath. The air tasted very fine. A Perdii with a spear rushed at him. Ostaran waited until the last moment, then sidestepped. Ostaran rammed the bronze fist guard of his sword hilt into the warrior's chin as he passed. The Perdii fell unconscious to the grass.

Ostaran's irritation was easing. The charge had not felt reckless. He had led his thirty Gath riders in an attack on a small group of Perdii foot soldiers only to find that they were part of a far larger band that had been hiding in the nearby woods. At least a hundred Perdii had rushed out, screaming their battle cries and unnerving the horses. Ostaran had blown his horn, signaling a retreat. His men had swung their mounts to break away, but then bad luck had intervened, and an arrow had pierced the chest of Ostaran's horse. The Gath leader had leapt clear of the dying beast and drawn his saber as a dozen Perdii warriors had rushed out toward him.

"Come in and die, you miserable whoresons!" he yelled. The Perdii, their faces smeared with red ocher, surrounded him. Now they were wearing him down.

Ostaran heard the sound of hoofbeats. Parrying a thrust, he slammed his fist into a knifeman's chin, sending him spinning from his feet, then risked a glance to his left.

Twenty horsemen were thundering toward him, scattering the enemy. On the lead mount Demonblade threw out his left arm. Ostaran sprinted toward him, gripped the young man's wrist, and vaulted to the horse's back. The Rigante swung the beast and, his flanks protected by the other riders, galloped the horse away from the chasing Perdii.

One of Ostaran's men came riding up, leading a spare mount. Ostaran transferred to it and then let out a wild whoop, raising his saber in the air and swinging it around his head. Demonblade laughed at him. Some forty other riders joined them. With almost seventy men now Ostaran led them in a second charge.

The Perdii broke and fled toward the woods. Ostaran rode two down, then swung his mount and cantered back to where Connavar sat his horse, a chestnut gelding close to sixteen hands.

"I thank you, Rigante," said Ostaran. "I had resigned myself to drinking at the table of Taranis. *Aiya!* But it is good to be alive!"

"As I recall," said Conn, guiding his mount alongside his leader, "the Scholar said to avoid open conflict."

"Ah, so he did. I had forgotten." Ostaran rode away, then dismounted and walked among the dead and the dying. Three badly wounded Perdii warriors were dispatched swiftly. Others who were more lightly wounded were allowed to gather their weapons and walk off to the woods. The man Ostaran had struck with his fist guard was merely stunned and was coming around as Ostaran reached him.

"I think the Scholar will appreciate a live prisoner," said Connavar.

Ostaran was kneeling by the warrior, his knife at the man's throat. "This man is Keltoi," he said. "He may not be my tribe, but I'll be damned if I'll hand him over to Jasaray's torturers. Anyway, he wouldn't tell them anything." He glanced down at the wounded man. "You wouldn't, would you?"

The man shook his head. "See?" said Ostaran. Taking the warrior by the arm, Ostaran helped him stand "You'd better find your friends," the Gath leader told him. The Perdii cast around for his fallen sword, found it, then walked slowly toward the woods.

Connavar shook his head, his eyes glinting with anger. "A strange way to fight a war," he said. "Why have you let them live?"

"This is how wars should be fought," said Ostaran. "Men against men, equally matched. Valiant hearts, ferocious fighting, and victory tempered with mercy. These Stone men take all the glory from battle. They are like an avalanche. No heroics, just a vile and deadly mass that rolls over everything in its path. I dislike them. I truly do."

"Then why do you fight alongside them?"

Ostaran grinned. "Happily, I dislike the Perdii more. Arrogant bastards."

"You have blood on your face," Connavar told him.

"It is not mine, thank Daan," said Ostaran, wiping his hand across his face. Lifting his mail shirt, he fished a small bone comb from the pocket of his undertunic and carefully combed his drooping blond mustache. "How do I look?" he asked.

"Very handsome. Now shall we search for sign of the enemy army?"

Ostaran stepped in, laying his hand on the Rigante's shoulder. "You know you are altogether too serious, young Connavar. It will not make a dust speck of difference whether we locate them or not. This is their land. They will find us. They will fight, and they will die. The Stone army cannot be beaten."

Connavar said nothing. Vaulting to his horse, he rode along the line of the woods, keeping out of range of any hidden archers. Ostaran watched him go. Recovering his cloak, the Gath leader mounted and rode back to where his men were waiting. His black-bearded brother Arix was looking nervous, as well he might.

"How is it that the Rigante led the rescue?" he asked the big man.

Arix shrugged. He would not meet Ostaran's gaze. "Don't know, Brother. He just took control." He grinned suddenly. "Good, though, wasn't it?" Some of the men laughed. Ostaran ignored them.

"I'm alive. Of course it was good. But with me apparently lost, *you* should have been in command. You should have led."

"I don't like leading," said Arix. "Anyway, Demonblade does it better."

"He does it better?" mimicked Ostaran. "He's not one of us. He's a foreigner." Swinging in the saddle, he pointed at another black-cloaked rider. "Why did you follow him down, Daran?"

"He told us to," answered the slim, redheaded Daran. "Didn't you want us to rescue you, Osta?"

"Of course I *wanted* you to rescue me, idiot. I'm just trying to understand how a Rigante can take command of a troop of Gath riders."

"It's like Arix said," continued Daran, "he's good at it. Like last week when he called out to stop us from fording that stream. That was a Perdii ambush. We would have ridden straight into it." Several of the men murmured agreement.

"Perhaps you'd like it if I gave him Arix's role?" sneered Ostaran.

"That would be good," said Arix.

"Shut up, Brother. I was joking."

"No, it's a good idea," said Daran. "I mean, I like Arix, but he's not a leader, is he?"

"Thanks, Dar," said Arix.

"It's not a compliment, you moron," stormed Ostaran.

The debate died down as Connavar rode up. "There is no sign at all of the enemy army," he said. "And the flag party has arrived to map out the camp."

"Time to ride in and get some food, then," said Arix.

Connavar maneuvered his horse alongside Ostaran's mount. "I don't think the Perdii army has come this far north. I think they've swung back."

Ostaran shook his head. "No, they'll be heading for the high hills. Stony ground there; no way for the Scholar to build his night fortresses."

"If that were true, then we would have come across sign. Fifty thousand men cannot march without leaving sign. The trail we've been following was left by the group we just fought. They wanted it to look as if the army were in retreat. I think the main force has doubled back."

"For what purpose?"

"To hit Jasaray on the march. The column will be spread over nine miles. If Carac strikes hard enough, he could split the army or at the very least destroy the baggage train and the food supplies."

Ostaran thought about it. The idea made sense. "What do you suggest?" he asked, aware that his men had crowded around and were listening intently.

"Gather all our riders and head back toward the south. If a battle does start, then Jasaray will need our cavalry."

"A proper battle," said Ostaran. "I like the sound of that."

"Head south," said Connavar, "but not too fast. The horses are tired. I will catch up with you." Pulling away from the group, the Rigante cantered his mount away to the west.

◇ 11 ◇

A T FIFTY-ONE APPIUS was the most experienced of Jasaray's generals. He was a man of limited imagination, but his skill was that he could be relied on to carry out his orders to the last letter without deviation or complaint. He had served with the Scholar now for nineteen years, through five campaigns and two civil wars. In those nineteen years he had returned to Stone only eight times. This situation entirely suited his new young wife, Palia, whose hedonistic lifestyle was the talk of the city. No one mentioned her infidelities directly to the gray-haired Appius, but he knew of them just the same, which was why he always sent her advance warning of his infrequent visits: so that she could decamp her lovers and prepare the house for his arrival.

Most of his junior officers believed Appius cared nothing for Palia and had married her only to cement an alliance between two powerful houses. That was not true, though he never spoke of it.

He stood now with the 750 men of Talon Three, observing the flag party marking out the night camp. The three other talons of Panther One had taken up their required defensive positions to the north, west, and east of the site and were awaiting the arrival of Panther Two, which would begin working on the perimeter ditch. His junior officer, the dark-haired Barus, stood silently beside him.

"You chose a good site, Barus," said Appius. "Plenty of forage and wood and an open water source close by."

"Thank you, sir."

"I understand you will be returning home at the end of the month."

"Yes, sir. I must finish my studies at the university."

"Would you be kind enough to carry letters for me?"

"It would be my privilege, sir."

Appius removed his bronze helm and brushed his fingers over the white horsehair crest. "Have you met my wife?"

"Yes, sir. Last year at the Equinox Games. I believe one of your horses won the Empire Run that day. It was a gray, I think."

"Callias," said the general, relaxing. "A fine, fine creature. Heart like a lion. According to the last letters I received, he has sired quite a few excellent young colts." His smile faded. "I want you to see Palia, explain to her that I will not be home this year."

"Yes, sir."

Appius glanced up at the taller man. Barus was not looking at him and seemed uncomfortable. Appius sighed. He knew the truth, of course. Everyone did. "I also have a present for her—a ring I had made. It is very valuable. Would you carry that also?"

"Yes, sir. I shall see that she gets it."

"Good. Good. Well, are you looking forward to seeing Stone again?" He saw Barus relax, and the young man resumed eye contact. He grinned.

"Yes, sir. I am to be engaged. We will be married at the midwinter festival."

"You know the girl well?"

"We were childhood sweethearts, sir. We chose each other."

"The best way, I am told," said Appius. "I wish you joy."

Before Barus could answer, they saw a black-garbed

tribesman riding down the hillside to the east. "It is the man Connavar," said Barus. "The Gath call him Demonblade. They think he has some mystic power in battle."

"There is nothing mystic about a good fighter," said Appius. "A strong right arm and a valiant heart. That plus a little luck when needed."

Appius put on his helm and buckled the chin strap. The tribesman was riding fast, which did not bode well. Could it be they were about to come under attack? Appius hoped not. With only three thousand men he would be hard pressed to hold a barbarian army until the next panther arrived.

Connavar reined in before the officers and dismounted. Appius looked into the young man's oddly colored eyes, then glanced down and saw the splashes of blood on his tunic and leggings.

"Where was the fight?" he asked.

"Around a mile from here, General, but it was a skirmish only."

"How far north is the Perdii army?"

"I do not believe it is to the north. We have been tricked. A small force of a hundred men came north, creating a false trail. I think Carac slipped away to the east and hid his army. I also believe he will come out of hiding today and attack General Jasaray while he is on the march."

"You believe the full Perdii army is *behind* us?"

"I do, General. Perhaps fifty thousand men."

"But you could be wrong?"

"I could be wrong about the timing of the attack," admitted Connavar, "but I know the army did not flee to the north. I can think of no other sensible reason for the subterfuge. He plans to surprise Jasaray."

Appius thought for a moment. "There will be a screen of scouts alongside the marching column. It is not possible for Jasaray to be taken by surprise."

"A screen of *Gath* scouts," said Barus. "Even if they

keep to the regulation distance—which would be a minor miracle—that would still give Jasaray only a few minutes to form his defenses."

"He will have two panthers with him and a third following around an hour behind," said Appius. Returning his attention to Connavar, he asked, "Where is Ostaran?"

"I have sent him to gather all of his forces and ride south. We are spread thin, but depending on where the battle is fought, I would think we can assemble close to a thousand riders."

"That is all very well if you are correct, young man. If you are not, then you will be leaving my panther without a cavalry screen and prey to assault from a massive force. Have you thought of that?"

"There is no army to face you here, General," said Connavar. "That I know for certain. It seems to me that you face two choices. Either you complete the fortress or you march to aid the Scholar. Which you choose is your own affair. But I am riding south." With that the warrior vaulted to the saddle, swung the reins, and kicked his horse into a run.

"What do you think, sir?" asked Barus.

"He seems a capable young man. And if he is right, Jasaray will find himself in great peril."

"What shall we do?"

Appius ignored the question and wandered away. He had been ordered to protect the site and wait for the next panther and Jasaray.

If he marched his men south and the tribesman was wrong, he would be a laughingstock.

But if Connavar was right . . .

Hidden behind the tree line of the immense Avelin Forest, Carac stood in the royal chariot, silently watching the road a half a mile distant. Wagons were slowly trundling along it, flanked by marching soldiers. Carac glanced to his left. Thousands of Perdii warriors, faces painted for war, waited quietly. To his right, stretching for over a mile, was the cavalry, three thousand strong. Their orders were to attack the wagons, kill the drivers, and rob the Stone army of its provisions.

The king ran a hand across his brow, wiping away the sweat. It was almost noon, and the heat in the forest was becoming unbearable. Carac sat back on the curved seat alongside his eldest son, Arakar, who was his charioteer this day. "How soon, Father?" whispered the fourteen-year-old.

"Soon enough," replied Carac, ruffling the boy's blond hair. The king was dreadfully tired, his eyes burning. He had not slept the last three nights. Tomorrow was his fortieth birthday, and the weight of his *gis* sat upon him like a boulder. The Old Woman had appeared to him a year earlier. *"Let no royal blood be spilled, Carac. If you fail, you will not see forty."*

No royal blood had been spilled. His brother had been drowned, the wife strangled, the boy poisoned. Not one spot of red had shown on any of the corpses. Carac removed his bronze battle helm and wiped the rim. He felt no guilt at the slaying of his brother. Only anger. Alea the *good* king, the *caring* king. The man was a traitor and deserved to die. Few knew of his negotiations with the Stone general and the agreement that the Perdii would become vassals of Stone, allowing Jasaray to build roads and forts in their territory. "It is the only way, Brother," Alea had told him. "They are invincible, and we are living in their day. As their allies we can help them conquer all the other tribes. The Perdii will once more be preeminent among the Keltoi."

"We have the power to crush them," Carac had replied.

"I have seen them, Carac. They have changed the face of war. They come like a flood, irresistible and deadly. Trust me on this."

"Like a flood," he had said. Carac smiled at the memory of his death, choking on the water of the flooded river. The death

of the queen, however, gave him no pleasure at all. Carac had always lusted after the mystical Alinae. He had not intended to kill her and had been prepared to offer her marriage. But when he had gone to her, she had flown at him in a rage, pulling a dagger from her sleeve and lunging for his throat. He had jumped back, the blade slicing the skin of his cheek. Furious, he had punched her, knocking her down and then wresting the dagger from her. "You are a murderer!" she had screamed at him. "I saw it in a vision. You and Bek dragged Alea from his horse. Murderer!" Her voice had echoed through the palace, and Carac's hands had clamped to her throat to silence her. And he had silenced her, crushing the life from her frail body.

The populace had been told that she had taken her own life in grief over the death of her beloved husband and that her son had swallowed poison. It mattered nothing that most of the Perdii had not believed the story. Strong leadership was always welcome, and Carac had been strong.

The losses in the first attack against the Stone night camp had proved far more damaging. Thousands of tribesmen had deserted after that. But almost fifty-six thousand remained, and today they would crush forever the myth of Stone invincibility. Pushing himself to his feet, Carac stared down once more at the Stone column.

Coming into sight, marching in columns of four, were Jasaray's two panthers. Carac had given orders that Jasaray was to be taken alive, and he looked forward to seeing the Stone man humbled before him, pushed to his knees, begging for life.

The Perdii king drew his sword and gestured to the trumpeter standing alongside the bronze chariot. A single note sounded.

Perdii cavalry burst from the forest to the north and charged toward the wagon convoy a half mile distant. A second note blared out, and fifty thousand Perdii warriors raced from the forest, bearing down on the slender line below.

Carac turned to his son. "Today you will see glory as never before," he said. Arakar gave a wide smile, took up the reins, and, followed by two thousand mounted guards, drove the chariot out into the open.

The sky was a clear, cloudless blue, and not a breath of breeze disturbed the summer day. Carac watched in breathless anticipation as the Perdii horde bore down on the six thousand soldiers of Stone. He hoped to see the enemy panic and run, but they did not. Smoothly the marching men regrouped, forming a fighting square, shields locked.

Carac took the reins from his son and drove his chariot down the hillside, the better to see and hear the battle. The front line of Perdii warriors had reached the enemy, and those warriors were hurling themselves on the shield wall. The line held, but like an angry tide the Perdii swept around the fighting square, isolating it, creating a bronze island in a sea of glittering swords.

The Perdii king rode his chariot close to the action, his royal guards cantering behind. To the north his cavalry had butchered scores of waggoners, and several hundred warriors were riding south to attack the Stone rear guard.

Carac swung his chariot and rode up the hillside, turning to gaze down on the embattled Jasaray. He could see the general now, standing at the center of the square, arms clasped behind his back. He seemed untroubled. Irritation swelled into anger in Carac's heart. Did the man not know he was about to experience defeat? Could he not feel the weight of despair?

Lifting a water sack from a hook inside the chariot, Carac drank deeply. "Are we winning, Father?" asked Arakar. Carac did not reply. The field was heavy with fallen Perdii, and few Stone warriors had died so far. Carac licked his lips. Then came the thunder of hooves, and the king looked to the north.

Close to a thousand enemy cavalry soldiers were charging down the slope toward him, led by the black-garbed killer who had sworn to take his life. For a moment Carac could not believe what he was seeing. The Gath cavalry had been led away to the north. How, then, were they here? The Perdii king shouted an order to his guard commander. The man wheeled his horse, drew his sword, and led a counterattack against the newcomers.

Carac felt cold fear clutching at his heart. Sweat dripped into his eyes.

"I spilled no blood," he whispered.

The Gath cavalrymen, their black cloaks streaming behind them, thundered down the hillside, meeting the Perdii charge head on. Connavar, a bronze buckler on his left forearm and the Seidh sword in his right hand, bore down on the first of the enemy. The Perdii rider thrust his lance at Conn's chest. Conn swayed in his saddle and, as he rode past, slashed his sword up and over. The blade took the rider in the throat, decapitating him.

The two lines of horsemen came together, Gath and Perdii, hacking and slashing, horses rearing and falling, screaming in pain and terror. Connavar fought like a madman, cutting and killing his way through the enemy, having eyes only for the occupants of the distant chariot. A spear thrust through his mount's neck. The animal went down. Conn jumped clear, ran at a Perdii rider on a gray gelding, stabbed him through the belly, then dragged him from his horse. Taking hold of the mane, Conn vaulted to the beast's back. There was no saddle, merely a lion-skin chabraque. Taking the reins, Conn swung the horse. A thrown spear sailed by him. Heeling the gray forward, Conn killed the spear thrower.

A warrior charged at him, the two horses crashing together. Conn's mount reared and almost fell. The Perdii stabbed at him. Conn took the blow on his buckler and sent a return cut that smashed the sword from his opponent's hand. The rider scrabbled for his dagger. Conn's sword slashed open his throat, and he pitched to the ground. Another rider charged at him. Conn lunged and missed. The Perdii hurled himself at Conn, grabbing him, and both men fell to the ground. Conn was up first. Kicking the man in the head, he grabbed his fallen sword and stabbed him through the heart. A horse reared alongside him, the front hooves thudding into his shoulder. Conn was hurled to the ground. The horse leapt over him. Rolling to his feet, Conn saw that the gray was standing close by. Running to it, he mounted. Two Perdii riders came at him. Swinging the horse, he met the first. Their swords clanged together. A spear point slammed against Conn's buckler, ricocheting off and tearing the skin of his shoulder. Ostaran rode alongside, his saber plunging into the spearman. Conn ducked under a wild cut from the second rider and heeled the gray toward a gap in the enemy line.

Three riders tried to cut him off, but he swerved toward them, killing the first, then cutting left and onto open ground.

Kicking the gray into a gallop, he raced toward the royal chariot. As he rode, he could hear horsemen close behind him. Risking a glance back, he saw a lance-wielding warrior no more than half a length back. The man was riding a powerful chestnut, and he was gaining. Behind him was a second rider, this one a swordsman. Transferring his sword to his left hand, Conn unclipped his cloak brooch, pulling the garment clear. Throwing out his right arm, he let the cloak fly free, then swung his horse sharply to the right. The black cloak billowed out in front of the lancer's mount, frightening it and causing it to swerve. Dragging on the reins, Conn charged the lancer. The man was an expert horseman, rearing his mount just as Conn closed in. The two horses crashed together. The gray went down. Conn fell heavily, losing his grip on the Seidh blade. The lancer bore down on him. Conn drew his dagger and hurled it. The blade took the lancer in the throat, and he tumbled from the back of his horse. The second rider closed in. Conn ran toward his sword, but the Perdii warrior cut him off. Conn let out a battle cry and charged the man's horse, waving his arms furiously. The horse reared. Conn dived past it, grabbing his sword and rolling to his feet just in time to block a vicious downward cut. Three times their blades clashed, and on the fourth Conn's sword slid clear, opening a huge cut in the rider's thigh. The man cried out and tried to swing his horse. Conn sprinted forward, plunging his sword under the man's ribs. The Seidh blade buried itself deep in the Perdii's body. The rider fell forward over the neck of his mount, then slid to the ground. Conn glanced back. More riders were galloping toward him.

There were some way back. Mounting the dead man's horse, Conn kicked him into a run. He was close to the royal chariot now, close enough to see the charioteer take up the reins and whip the horses into a gallop. The Perdii king was standing alongside the charioteer. He had three spears at hand and drew one of them, hefting the weight. Conn raced after the chariot, closing fast. A spear flew by him, then another. The third came straight at him. Throwing up his sword, he deflected the spear. The haft struck him side on. Grabbing at it with his left hand, he caught the weapon. His horse was tiring, but he was close enough to the fleeing chariot now to see the face of the Perdii king. Hatred roared through him, burning like fire. With his left hand he flung the spear back toward the chariot. It missed the king but slammed into the back of the charioteer, who fell, dragging on the reins. The two ponies swerved. The chariot tipped and then went over, throwing the king clear. Conn leapt from his horse and ran at the fallen man. Carac rose, drawing his sword. He was both powerful and fast, and the speed of his attack surprised the younger man. Their blades met time and again, and Conn was forced back by the ferocity of the onslaught. But in his mind's eye Conn saw again the body of his friend hanging on a hook in the Perdii capital. A score of the king's riders galloped past the fallen chariot and formed a circle around the fighting men. "He's mine!" shouted Carac. "Leave him. I'll cut his heart out."

Again he attacked. Conn blocked and sent a savage riposte that opened a wound in the king's shoulder. Carac grunted and fell back. Now it was Conn pushing forward, his sword gleaming in the afternoon sunshine as he hacked and cut. Carac parried each stroke, but the older man was tiring. Conn felt a fresh surge of energy flow through him and moved in for the kill. Expecting the king to fall back again, Conn was surprised when Carac hurled himself forward. Their blades met. The king stepped in and sent a left hook into Conn's unprotected face. The blow was powerful, and Conn staggered back. The king's sword swept toward Conn's neck. The younger man dropped to his knees and lunged, the Seidh blade lancing into the king's belly. Conn surged upright, driving his sword in to the hilt, the blade bursting clear of Carac's back. "Just like I promised, you miserable whoreson!" hissed Conn. "May your spirit burn in lakes of fire!"

Carac sagged against him. Conn pushed him away, dragging his sword clear of the dying man's body. The king fell to his knees. Conn raised his sword and brought it down in a terrible sweep that cut completely through Carac's thick neck. The head fell clear, rolling on the grass.

Then he turned to the riders. There were some twenty horsemen in the circle around him. "Who is next?" Conn shouted.

One man wheeled his horse and rode away. The others followed.

Conn walked to the fallen chariot and gazed down on the battle. The Perdii were streaming back toward the forest. To the north Conn could see Appius' panther marching in battle formation. From the south another panther was approaching.

At that moment Conn heard a groan. The charioteer was still alive. Drawing his dagger, Conn moved to the body, dragged the spear from the man's back, and flipped the body with his boot. Dropping to his knees, he raised his dagger and found himself looking into the frightened eyes of a young boy. "Where is my father?" asked the child.

Conn sheathed his blade. There was blood on the boy's chest where the spear had plunged through. He looked a little like Braefar. "Where is my father?" he repeated. Then he coughed, and blood frothed on his lips.

"Is your father the king?" asked Conn.

"Yes. The greatest warrior of all the Perdii. Where is he?"

"He's back there," said Conn, sitting down beside the dying boy.

"Could you call him?"

"I don't think he could hear me. What is your name?"

"Arakar. Is it night already?"

Conn passed his hand over the boy's face. His eyes did not flicker. "Yes, it is night. Rest awhile, Arakar. Go to sleep."

The boy closed his eyes. His tunic was drenched in blood now, but the flow had ceased. His face lost all color, and his head lolled. Reaching out, Conn felt for the pulse in his neck. It fluttered for a few moments. Then it was gone.

Valanus came up and sat down on the other side of the corpse. "Well, you have your revenge, Demonblade."

"Aye, I have indeed."

"You do not seem full of joy, my friend."

Conn climbed wearily to his feet and gazed around the battleground. Thousands of bodies covered the grass around what had been the fighting square, among them several hundred bronze-armored soldiers of Stone.

Crows were circling above the battlefield. Conn found himself thinking of the green hills of the Rigante, the towering snow-covered peaks of Caer Druagh, and the gentle pace of life in Three Streams.

"I have had my fill of slaughter," he said.

"That is a shame," said Valanus. "For the real slaughter is just about to begin."

* * *

That night Conn's dreams were troubled. He saw Banouin sitting beside a stream, talking to a youth. They were both smiling, enjoying each other's company in the sunshine. Conn tried to run to them, but his legs were heavy and he could scarcely move. Banouin saw him but rose from the stream and, taking the boy by the hand, moved away from him. "It is me, Conn. I avenged you!" he shouted. Banouin looked back once, his eyes filled with sadness. But he did not speak. The youth also glanced back, and Conn saw it was the child charioteer he had killed with the javelin. A mist grew up around them, and they vanished from sight.

Conn awoke in a cold sweat. The stench of burning flesh was clinging to the air in the tent. Jasaray knew that diseases sprang from rotting corpses and always had all bodies burned at the end of a battle. There were so many dead this time that more than a dozen great trenches had been dug, and the fires burned for most of the night.

Pushing aside his blankets, Conn pulled on his boots and walked from the tent. It was midnight, and hundreds of soldiers were still working by torchlight, hauling Perdii corpses to fresh trenches and hurling the bodies in.

Conn felt a weight on his heart. It was just a dream, he told himself. Banouin did not really turn his back on you. His mouth was dry, and he remembered their talk back in the cave. Banouin's voice whispered up from the halls of memory. *"I am not saying do not fight. I am saying do not hate. It is not war that leads to murderous excesses, but hate. Whole villages, cities, peoples wiped out. Hatred is like a plague. It is all-consuming, and it springs from man to man. Our enemies become demons, their wives the mothers of demons, their children infant demons. You understand? We tell stories of our enemies eating babes, as was done with the people. Our hearts turn dark, and in turn we visit a terrible retribution upon those we now hate. But hatred never dies,*

Conn. We plant the seeds of it in every action inspired by it. Kill a man, and his son will grow to hate you and seek revenge. When he obtains that revenge, your son will learn to hate him. Can you see what I am saying?"

Banouin would have hated this retribution, and he would not have desired such dreadful revenge. A cold breeze blew across the tents. Conn shivered. "I did not do it for you, Banouin. I know that now. I did it for me. I tried to drown my grief in blood."

"It is in your nature," said a familiar voice. Conn turned slowly to see the Morrigu standing behind him, her ancient frame silhouetted by the corpse fires. "You let the bear loose, Connavar. And you will do it again."

"No. I have learned from this."

"The bear is a part of you, human. It will have its day."

"I do not wish to argue about it," he said. "I had hoped that revenge would be like honey upon the tongue. It was—as my blade plunged home. But when I saw the boy . . ."

"The taste turned to bile in your belly," said the Morrigu.

"Aye, it did."

"You did not destroy the Perdii, Connavar. You were merely a soldier. Whether you had come here or not, they would still have died. Your cavalry charge saved a few hundred Stone soldiers but did not ultimately alter the course of the battle."

"I wish we had never come, Banouin and I."

"Wishes are dishes the poor feed upon," she said. "Come, we will walk together in the high hills, where the air is still fresh and I can smell the new leaves."

It surprised Conn that he wanted to accompany her, but then he realized that despite her malevolence, she was at least someone from home, a familiar form, a creature he had last seen in the sanctuary of the Rigante mountains. Together they climbed the hills and moved beyond the tree line. The Morrigu found a small hollow and tapped her foot at a tree root, which then writhed up from the ground, forming a seat for her. She sank down to it, resting her head against the trunk of the tree. "That is better," she said.

Conn sat down on the ground. From there he could see the fallen chariot. Carac's body had been removed.

"He broke his *geasa*," said the Morrigu.

"Who?"

"Carac. I told him that if any royal blood was spilled, he would not live past his fortieth birthday, which, incidentally, was today. So he drowned his brother, strangled the wife, and poisoned the son. He thought he had cheated fate. But the wife cut him as he attacked her. Carac had already killed his brother and had seized the crown. He was therefore king and, by definition, royal. His own blood doomed him."

"Had she not cut him, I still would have reached him," said Conn.

"No. You were killed in the cavalry charge."

"I wasn't killed."

"Forgive me," said the Morrigu. "For a moment only I forgot I was speaking to a human, and for you the passing of time is like the journey of a leaf, from bud in spring to withered autumn."

"And for you it is different?"

"So different that your mind could not encompass it. I have seen you born a hundred times and watched you die in a hundred ways. In one life you caught a chill and did not reach your first birthday. In another the bear killed you."

"And where do I live in all these lives?"

"In the shadow of Caer Druagh."

"Then why have I never seen myself in these other lives?"

The Morrigu closed her eyes for a moment. "Were I not so weary, I would slap myself in the face for ever beginning this conversation. Let us put aside the question of multiple reality and return to the prosaic." She opened her eyes. "Why were you out walking tonight?"

"I had a dream . . ." he began, then fell silent. "At least I think it was a dream." He told her of seeing Banouin with the boy he had killed.

"It was a dream," she said. "Not a vision."

"You are sure? It would grieve me to think that Banouin had turned against me."

"I am sure. Banouin's spirit has passed over the water and on from the world of men."

"He did not see my revenge, then?"

"No. Would you wish him to?"

Conn shook his head. "It would have saddened him."

"There are many things to come that would sadden him more," she said.

"What do you mean?"

"Vorna is pregnant with his child. Both will die. The babe will be breeched, and there will be no one close to save either of them."

"No," said Conn, "that must not happen! It would be so unfair."

"Unfair?" She laughed. "Where in this miserable world of humans do you see fairness? On the battlefield where thirty thousand lie de d? In the homes of the widows? In the eyes of the children orphaned?"

Conn fell silent, then looked into the ancient face. "You could save her. You could save them both. You are Seidh."

"Why would I choose to?"

"You once told me that I would ask a gift from you and you would grant it."

The Morrigu smiled. "Think carefully, child. I did say that. And you could ask for riches or good health all your days. You could ask for strong sons or a loving wife. I could give you Arian. Or—and think on this—I could give you victory over the people of Stone. Thousands of lives, Connavar, could be saved by such a gift. An entire people. Without that gift it could be the Rigante burning in those pits."

"Aye, it could," said Conn. "Now, will you help Vorna and the child?"

"Before I say yes or no, let me ask you this: What if the child sickens and dies within days or Vorna is touched by the plague within weeks? Will you still feel this gift is worthwhile?"

"I have heard that your gifts are double-edged, that when people ask for joy, you give them sorrow. But if you give me your word that you will not visit evil upon Vorna or the babe, then I ask again for you to help her."

"You know that one day I will come to you and that there will be a price to pay for my help?"

"And I will pay it."

"Then it shall be as you wish, Sword in the Storm."

Ruathain drew back on the reins as he crested the hill. Below him was the Pannone settlement of Shining Water, built along the western banks of Long Lake. From there he could see seven high-prowed fishing vessels out on the water, dragging their nets, and on the shoreline the black smoke towers standing like sentinels at the water's edge.

Arbon rode up alongside him. "Too late to turn back now," he grunted, running his hand through his salt and pepper hair.

"Turning back was not in my mind," Ruathain told him. Leading twelve ponies behind them, the two men rode down the hill. There were no walls in Shining Water, and the scores of houses were well apart from one another, each with an area allocated to vegetables and corn. The day was hot, but Ruathain lifted his blue and green checkered Rigante cloak from the back of his saddle, unrolled it, and fastened it in place. Arbon shook his head and, grim of face, followed his master down into what he saw as the enemy settlement.

As they rode on, people moved from their houses and workplaces to watch the riders as they passed, then walked behind them as they approached the hall of the laird.

The day was clear and bright. Not a breath of breeze stirred the dust beneath the ponies' hooves. Ruathain rode on, looking neither left nor right but pulling up his mount before the hall. It was a grim-looking building, fifty feet long, one-storied, with shuttered windows and a thatched roof. The double doors creaked open, and a middle-aged man strode out. Behind him came five younger men. It was obvious to Arbon that these were his sons, for they all possessed the same heavy brows and flat, brutal faces. There were many stories Arbon had heard concerning the Fisher Laird, and none of them were good.

"I am Ruathain of the Rigante," said his master. The crowd began to mutter, and Arbon was all too aware that his back was to them. Sweat trickled down his spine, and his hand edged nearer to his knife.

"I have heard the name," said the Fisher Laird, stroking his dark beard. "Ruathain the mad dog. Ruathain the killer."

"I never killed a man who was not carrying a sword," Ruathain said, evenly. "However, be that as it may, I am here to offer blood price to the bereaved."

"You accept, then, that you are a murderer?"

Ruathain was silent for a moment, and Arbon knew he was struggling with his temper. "What I accept is that men died who need not have died. I'll admit freely that when your men first raided my cattle, I could have dealt less harshly with them. But I did not. Now four more of your young men are dead, and I would like to see an end to this feud. I have no wish to kill any more Pannone."

"Or be killed yourself," observed the Fisher Laird.

"In my life many have tried to kill me. I am still here. Death holds no fear for me, fisherman. I am not here to save my life. I am here to save the lives of your young men, who so far have shown little skill when it comes to battle. I do not decry them for this or wish to speak ill of the dead. It is merely a fact—a fact evidenced by their deaths. I am Ruathain, first swordsman of the Rigante. I do not enjoy slaying untried boys." Ruathain took a deep, calming breath. "I have brought with me twelve fine ponies to offer as blood price to the families of the dead. Do I have your permission to speak with them?"

The Fisher Laird gave a harsh laugh. "You may be a killer, Ruathain, but I see you still respect tradition. You have my permission. Step down and enter my house. I will send for the families."

Ruathain dismounted and removed his sword, which he handed to Arbon.

"Wait here with the ponies," he said.

"Aye, lord," Arbon answered glumly.

Ruathain strode to where the Fisher Laird waited, then bowed. The laird stepped aside, allowing Ruathain to enter the hall. Then he and his sons followed him. Arbon's mouth was dry, his heart beating fast, but he sat quietly, assuming an expression of mild boredom. A runner came out from the hall and moved through the crowd. A short time later three women dressed in black entered the hall, closely followed by five young men.

Arbon waited for a while in the sunshine, then dismounted and stretched his back.

An elderly woman brought him a cup of water. He bowed as he accepted it and then drank deeply.

"My thanks to you, Mother," he said.

"I am no mother of yours, you Rigante pig," she said. "But the laws of hospitality should always be observed."

He bowed again and grinned. "Indeed they should," he agreed, returning the cup. Another woman brought him some smoked fish and a hunk of bread. Time passed slowly, and the sun was beginning to set when the doors of the hall opened once more. The Pannone women emerged first, followed by the five young men, then Ruathain, and lastly the Fisher Laird and his sons.

Ruathain strode to where Arbon waited. "It is agreed," he

said softly, "but I have also promised a bull and ten feasting steers for the laird."

At that moment a young man came running from the water's edge. He was tall and slim, black-haired and pale-eyed. "What is going on here?" he shouted.

"You are too young to have a voice in this," the Fisher Laird told him. "An honorable offer has been made and accepted. The blood feud is over."

"Over?" shouted the youngster. "Nothing is over. This butcher slaughtered my brothers. I will have vengeance." He swung on the five young men. "How could you agree to this? Six lives taken, their blood drenching the grass. Family. Blood kin. Never to wed and sire sons, never to know joy. Are a few scrawny ponies all they were worth? Blood cries for blood. Their souls cry for justice and revenge."

"Be silent!" roared the Fisher Laird. "Do you understand nothing, boy? Your brothers died in battle. They were not set upon in the dark or had their throats cut while they were sleeping. They faced an enemy who outfought them. That enemy has shown great courage in coming here. A gesture of respect and in keeping with the traditions of the Keltoi. But more important even than that, boy, is the fact that I am your lord, and I tell you the blood feud is over."

The youngster stood silently for a moment, then turned and ran back to his boat upon the water.

The Fisher Laird moved to Ruathain. "Send the cattle to me but do not come yourself, Ruathain the killer. You are not welcome in Pannone lands."

Ruathain nodded but did not reply. Leaving the twelve ponies, he mounted his own steed and swung it toward the south. The crowd parted as he walked his pony back through the settlement. Arbon rode alongside and handed him his sword, which Ruathain belted to his waist.

"Is it over?" he asked his master.

"Not while that boy lives," answered Ruathain. "One day

he will come for me, and I will kill him. Then it will begin again."

"A waste of ponies, then," muttered Arbon.

"No," Ruathain said, sadly. "It was a fair blood price. I began this when I killed the raiders. I allowed my anger to burn away my self-control. I sowed the seeds, my friend, and now I must reap the harvest."

◇ **12** ◇

I N THE BEDROOM of Banouin's house one of the three lanterns guttered and died. Vorna had been in labor for fourteen hours. She had lost consciousness twice in the last hour. Meria and Eriatha were desperately concerned. Meria had attended four childbirths, but none as difficult as this one. She had sent for Eriatha, whose knowledge of herbs and medicines was almost as great as Vorna's. The Earth Maiden knelt by the unconscious Vorna and examined her.

"Lavender and jasmine will not help her," said Eriatha. "The babe is not lying in the right position. It cannot enter the world."

"What can we do?" asked Meria.

"I do not have the skill to deliver it," said Eriatha. "I have heard of witches who could cut open the belly and deliver babes. But mostly the mothers die."

"There must be something," insisted Meria.

Eriatha shook her head. "We need a witch, a Druid, or a midwife. Even then . . ." Her voice tailed away.

Meria rose from the bedside and moved to the window, looking out over the moonlit landscape. "Brother Solstice was here only three days ago," she said softly, "but I don't know where he has gone. This is so unfair. First she finds love, then loses it. Now Banouin's babe is killing her." Vorna groaned, then cried out in pain. Meria took her hand as Eriatha applied a damp cloth to Vorna's brow.

"The child is . . . breeched," said Vorna. She took a deep breath. "Cut my belly open. Save the babe!" She cried out again, and her back arched. Then she collapsed and passed out.

"She is dying," whispered Eriatha.

At that moment they heard a thudding at the front door. Meria ran back through the house. Outside stood an old woman Meria had never seen before. She was dressed in a faded full-length dress of pale gray, and a black fishnet shawl was draped around her shoulders.

"What do you want?" Meria asked her.

"I am told that there is a woman in childbirth here, that there is a problem."

"You are a midwife?"

"Among other things," said the old woman, moving past Meria and into the house. As she passed, Meria caught the scent of the forest on the woman's clothes, musky and damp, the smell of rotting leaves and wet bark. She shuddered and followed the woman into the bedroom.

"You will both leave," said the old woman. "Wait by the fire. I will call you if I need you."

"The babe is breeched," said Eriatha.

"Thank you," the old woman said, sourly. "Perhaps later you can teach me how to suck eggs."

A huge crow landed on the open window, spreading its wings and cawing loudly. Meria and Eriatha both jumped back, startled, but the old woman ignored it and sat beside the stricken Vorna. "Out, I said," she hissed, waving a thin arm in the direction of the two women.

Reluctantly they obeyed her. Meria pulled closed the door, and she and Eriatha walked to the hearth. The fire was burning low, and she added several chunks of wood. "Do you know her?" Meria asked.

"No."

"Perhaps we shouldn't have left her."

"Perhaps we shouldn't," said Eriatha, "but I am ashamed to say I am glad she is there and I am not."

Meria nodded agreement. She felt as if a burden had been lifted from her. Weariness flowed over her, and she sank into a chair. "It was good of you to come," she told the Earth Maiden.

"I wish I could have been of some help," answered Eriatha, dropping into the second chair. Meria gazed across at her. The Earth Maiden was small and slight and looked much younger than her years. Her face was pretty, her skin flawless.

"You are very beautiful," said Meria. "Are you happy?"

"Why would I not be?" Eriatha countered defensively. "I can afford to eat, and I have a home. Or is an Earth Maiden not meant to experience joy?"

"That is not what I meant at all," said Meria. "I was wondering if you had friends or whether your life was lonely. That is all."

Eriatha relaxed and gave a shy smile. "Yes, I am lonely. And no, I have no friends. Is that not the lot of the Earth Maiden? A hundred lovers and no friends?"

Meria leaned forward and stretched out her hand. "You may count me as a friend, Eriatha."

The younger woman took her hand briefly, gently squeezing her fingers. "I thank you, Meria, but I do not need pity. I am young, alive, and in good health. I was glad to see Ruathain recover so well from his wounds."

"You know my husband?" Meria could not keep a note of alarm from her voice.

Eriatha laughed and clapped her hands together. "You see why an Earth Maiden has no women friends," she said.

Meria blushed, then laughed also. "Yes, I do. So now tell me. Did Ruathain come to you while we were parted?"

Eriatha fell silent, watching Meria closely. Then she shrugged. "Yes, he did."

"And after making love did he snore like a bull?"

Surprised by the comment, Eriatha giggled. "The very walls shook with the sound."

"There," said Meria. "Now can we be friends?"

"I think that we can. You are a very special woman, Meria. Ruathain is lucky to have you."

Before Meria could reply they heard the high-pitched cry of a newborn babe. Both women rushed to the bedroom. Meria pushed open the door. Vorna was lying asleep, the babe, wrapped in soft red cloth, nestled in her arm. The old woman had gone.

Eriatha made the sign of the protective horn. Meria moved to the window and gazed out over the hills. But the midwife was nowhere in sight. "Who was she?" she whispered.

Eriatha did not reply. At the bedside she felt for the pulse in Vorna's wrist. It was beating slowly but powerfully. Eriatha pulled back the bedclothes. There was no blood on the sheets or any mark on Vorna's belly. Carefully she covered the sleeping woman.

"She was Seidh," said Eriatha, her voice low. "The babe was delivered through magic."

Meria shivered, then lifted the sleeping babe, gently opening the little red blanket. The child was a boy and perfectly formed. Again, there was no blood on it. The umbilical cord had been removed, leaving no wound, only a tiny mound of perfectly formed pink skin. The babe woke and gave a little squeal. Meria wrapped it once more and lifted it, holding it close.

Vorna woke and yawned. She saw Meria holding the babe and smiled. "How did you save both me and the babe?" she asked.

"It was a miracle," said Eriatha.

Meria passed the babe to its mother. Vorna opened her nightgown and held the child to her swollen breast. It began to feed hungrily.

* * *

Ferol looked like what he was: an angry, bitter man, self-centered and self-obsessed, the kind of man who believed the sole purpose of winter was to keep him cold. He loathed the rich for their wealth, the poor for their poverty. His round face had a permanently sullen expression, and his wide gash of a mouth was perfectly fashioned to make the best use of the sneer. He was a thief and worse, but he excused his excesses by convincing himself that all men would be the same if only they had his strength of purpose.

A huge, hulking man, he had been raised in the north country of the Pannones on a small farm built on rocky soil that was constantly eroded by high winds and driving rain. His father had been a hardworking man and scrupulously honest. Ferol had despised him. The old man made him work in all weather, and truth be told, Ferol had never overcome his fear of the man. One day, however, when he and his father had been felling trees, the old man had slipped and a heavy trunk had fallen across his legs, smashing both thighbones.

Ferol had run to his side. The old man had hardly been able to move, his careworn face gray with pain. "Get this off me," he had grunted.

In that moment the nineteen-year-old Ferol had discovered freedom. "Get it off yourself," he had said, turning and walking slowly back to the house. He had ransacked it, looking for his father's carefully hoarded silver. It had come to nine miserable coins. Pocketing them, he had saddled the one old pony and ridden south.

He was full of regret afterward. If only he had sat down and waited, he could have watched the old bastard die.

Ferol stood stoop-shouldered at the ferry, watching the two riders approach. One was a red-bearded young warrior wearing a bright mail shirt, the other an older man with dark, receding hair. They were leading two enormous stallions, each over sixteen hands, and three heavily laden pack ponies. Ferol glanced to his left, where his cousin Roca lounged against the ferry. "Be ready," he said. Roca nodded, turned toward the river, and waved a signal to the four men on the far side.

The riders came closer. Ferol stepped out to greet them. "Welcome," he said. "You have come far?"

The warrior did not reply immediately. Shading his eyes against the sun, he looked across the river. "Where is Calasain?" he asked.

"In the house," replied Ferol. "He has not been well."

"I am sorry to hear that."

"Yes," agreed Ferol. "His son, Senacal, asked my friends and me to help out at the ferry."

"You are not Rigante."

"I am of the Pannone." He signaled Roca, who unlatched the front of the ferry, lowering the boarding platform. "Step aboard. There'll be food at the house."

The warrior and his companion dismounted and led the horses and pack ponies onto the ferry. Roca drew up the boarding platform, then he and Ferol began to haul on the rope. Slowly the ferry eased out onto the river.

"So, where are you traveling from?" Ferol asked the young man, seeking to put him at ease.

"South," came the reply. "What is the nature of Calasain's sickness?"

"You can ask his son. He is waiting at the jetty," he said, pointing to the short, burly figure of Senacal, who was standing with three other men.

The ferry docked. Roca moved to the front and lowered the platform. Ferol stepped back and waved his arm, gesturing the warrior to lead his horses to the bank.

"After you, ferryman," the man said softly.

Ferol was irritated, but he obeyed and walked from the ferry. The warrior followed him, having signaled his older companion to wait.

"What is wrong with your father?" he asked Senacal.

The burly man looked uncomfortable, his gaze flicking to

Ferol. "I told you, he's sick," said Ferol. "Now lead your beasts ashore and pay the crossing fee."

The warrior stood his ground. "I do not know you, Pannone, or any of your men except Senacal. But the ferry does not require—nor can its income support—six men. Now I ask you again: Where is Calasain?"

Roca moved to the side of the bank, lifted an old blanket, and pulled out a sword, which he threw to Ferol. Other swords were swiftly handed out.

Ferol grinned at the young warrior. "Calasain died," he said with a wide, unpleasant grin. "Now, unless you think you and your old friend can defeat six of us, I suggest you hand over your horses and ponies."

The warrior's sword hissed from its scabbard, the blade shining bright in the sunlight. When he spoke again, his voice was calm and very cold. "I have seen thousands of Keltoi butchered this last year. Some I killed myself. I am not anxious to spill more Keltoi blood, but if you persist in this, I will slay all of you."

Ferol felt the chill of winter flow across his skin. Evil he was and cruel, but he was not stupid. This young fighter was facing six armed men, and there was not the slightest suggestion that he was afraid. There were only two possible conclusions to be drawn: Either he was an idiot or he was as deadly as his words indicated. Ferol sensed it was the latter and was about to back down when Roca spoke.

"You arrogant bastard!" shouted Roca. "Take him!"

Ferol stood stock still as the five men rushed forward. The warrior leapt to meet them, his shining sword cutting left and right in a bewildering blur. Roca was the first to die, and within a few heartbeats three others were down. Ferol threw himself back as the silver sword slashed within a hair's breadth of his throat. Senacal threw down his dagger and ran back toward the woods behind the house.

The warrior advanced on Ferol, who dropped his sword. "I

"There is no force under the stars strong enough to remove the guilt I feel," he said. "Not just for Banouin's death but for the thousands of deaths that followed it." He fell silent. Vorna said nothing, and the two sat quietly in the shade for a while.

The babe stirred, then fell asleep again. Vorna rose and moved inside the house, laying the child in his cot. Her back was aching, and she stretched. Returning to where Connavar sat, she saw that he was staring out over the hills to the south. He looked so much older than his eighteen years.

"A merchant brought news of your fight with the evil king," she said.

Connavar nodded. "It seems so long ago now, yet it is but a few months." He laughed, but the sound was bereft of humor. " 'Evil king,' " he repeated, shaking his head.

"Was he not evil, then?" she asked.

"He murdered his brother and the brother's wife and son, and he killed Banouin. Yes, he was evil. But his deeds are as nothing to the vileness that followed his death." He sighed. "Let us not talk about it. It is good to be home."

"We have missed you. Who is the man with you?"

"His name is Parax. He was among the prisoners taken by Jasaray. Now he serves me."

"Serves?"

"A slip of the tongue. I have been around the men of Stone for too long. He is my companion and, I think, my friend. He will help me."

"To do what, Connavar?"

"To prepare, Vorna. The men of Stone will come. Not next year, perhaps, but they will come."

"I know. I saw it when I had my powers. Their hunger is insatiable. And you will fight them. I saw this also." Sunlight fell on the sword against the wall, illuminating the hilt. Vorna stared at it. "It is a Seidh blade. How did you come by it?"

Connavar told her of his flight from the town of Alin and his encounter in the Talis Woods.

"The tree man was the Thagda," she said, "the Old Man of the Forest. You were truly blessed. Show me the sword." He passed it to her, and she looked closely at the hilt, the embossed head of the bear on the fist guard, the fawn in brambles on the pommel. Vorna smiled. "You know who made this blade?" she asked him.

"How could I?" he responded.

"It was Riamfada. On the night he died I saw his spirit moving toward the Seidh Woods."

Taking the sword, Conn looked at it with fresh eyes. "He promised me a sword," he whispered.

"And he kept the promise. He is one of them now." From within the house came the sound of a baby crying. Vorna moved inside, lifted Banouin from his cot, sat down by the hearth, and opened her blouse. The babe began to suckle hungrily. Conn stood in the doorway, watching the scene.

"Is it a boy?" he asked.

"Yes, a boy. Banouin's boy." Conn struggled for something to say, and Vorna laughed. It was a sound he had never heard from her, and it made him smile.

"What?" he asked her.

"You want to say something about how he has Banouin's nose or eyes. But you can't, because all babies look the same to you. Like wizened old men."

He grinned. "Have your powers returned?"

"I do not need powers to understand the minds of men." She laughed again. "Have you seen your mother yet?"

He brightened. "Aye. She and the Big Man are back together. That is a fine thing."

"Indeed it is. Together and happy." She looked at him closely. "You are tired, Connavar. Go back to your family. Rest. You can come and see us again if you have a mind to."

"I would like that, Vorna." Moving into the room, he stroked the babe's head. Then, leaning in, he kissed the mother on the cheek.

As he rode away, Vorna felt his sorrow. It lay heavy upon him, like a cloak of lead.

Ruathain also noticed the change in Connavar, and it saddened him. He tried to tackle the problem head on as they stood in the paddock field viewing the stallions. "What is wrong, boy?"

"Nothing that you can help with, Big Man. I will deal with it in my own time. However, there is something I would like you to do for me. These stallions are, I believe, vital to our future. You have two pony herds. My stallions will, I am hoping, sire a new breed of war mounts, faster and stronger than any ponies we now possess. Having a more powerful mount will allow a rider to wear heavier armor."

Ruathain took a deep breath. "They are fine horses. And I will breed them as you ask me. But the horses are not my main concern, Conn. You are. What has changed you? Banouin's death? Your time among the people of Stone? What?"

Conn looked away, and when he turned back, his expression had softened. "You are right. I am changed. But I do not wish to speak of it yet. I cannot. The memories are too fresh. We will talk soon, Big Man." Conn turned away and strode back to Ruathain's old house, which he now shared with Parax. Ruathain watched him go, then walked across the paddock field to where Parax was feeding grain to the stallions.

Parax glanced up at the tall warrior, then patted the long neck of the chestnut stallion. "Fine beasts, eh?" he said.

"Fine indeed. Are you settling in?"

"It is a good house." Parax moved away from the stallion and climbed to sit on the paddock fence. Ruathain joined him.

"My son tells me you met in the lands of the Perdii."

"Aye. I was hunting him for Carac. He's a canny lad and a fighter." Ruathain looked into the man's dark eyes.

"What is the matter with him?"

Parax shrugged. "He is your son, Ruathain. Best you ask him."

"I am asking you."

Parax climbed down from the fence. "We have spoken much about you, Big Man. He loves you dearly. And he trusts you completely. But understand this: He carries a weight on his soul, and it is for him to speak of it. Not I. And he will when he is ready. Give him time, Ruathain. The air here is good, and the mountains are beautiful. Here he has people who love him. One day—and I hope it is soon—the weight will lift a little. Then perhaps you will see the son you knew."

"Perhaps?"

Parax shrugged. "I cannot say for certain. No man could. But as I said before, he is a fighter. Give him time."

Conn emerged from the house carrying a heavy sack and walked across the paddock field and on past the family home, crossing the first of the bridges and heading toward the forge of Nanncumal. The bald and burly smith was working at his anvil when Conn entered. Seeing him, Nanncumal gave a brief smile and continued hammering at the horseshoe before dunking it in a half barrel of water. Steam hissed up. The smith put down his hammer and tongs and wiped the sweat from his broad face with a dry cloth.

"What brings you to my forge?" he asked the younger man. Conn opened the sack and pulled forth a long, gleaming mail shirt created from hundreds of small interlocked rings. He tossed it to the smith, who caught it, then carried it out into the sunlight to examine it. Nanncumal sat down on a wide bench seat crafted from oak. Conn sat beside him. The smith silently studied the mail shirt for some time. The rings were tiny, the garment handling like thick cloth. "It is stunning," he said at last. "Beautifully made. Months of careful work here, Connavar. By a master. Thank you for showing it to me."

"Can you duplicate it?"

"In all honesty? No, I don't think I can. I wish I had the time to try."

"You have two apprentice sons who can make horseshoes, hinges, plow blades, nails, and swords."

"Aye, but there is work enough for all three of us. It would take me weeks to grasp the technique used in this shirt and months of trial and error to re-create it. My family still needs to be fed, Connavar."

Conn opened the pouch at his belt and removed three golden coins, which he dropped into Nanncumal's large hand. "By heavens, boy! Are they real?"

"They are real."

Nanncumal stared hard at the silhouetted face on the coins and the laurel wreaths embossed on the reverse. "Who is this?" he asked.

"Carac of the Perdii."

"The king you killed?"

"The same. Will you create mail shirts for me?"

"Mail shirts? How many do you want?"

"A hundred."

"What? It is not possible, Conn. I could not make that many in my lifetime."

"You will not have to make them all. I have left similar shirts with six Rigante smiths beyond the river. I will take three more to Old Oaks and the smiths there."

"I see you have become rich during your travels, boy."

"I am not interested in riches," said Conn. "There is one added refinement I want for the shirt: a mail ring hood that will protect the neck."

"A sensible addition," agreed Nanncumal. "I would also suggest shortening the sleeve. This shirt was crafted for an individual. It would save time, effort, and coin if they were to be elbow length."

"I agree. Then you will do it?"

"Do you intend to sell them?"

"No. I intend to give them away."

"I don't understand. For what purpose?"

"Survival," said Conn. "How is Govannan?"

"Fit and well. He is at Far Oaks with the other young men, taking part in the games. He will be glad to see you." The smith paused. "As am I," he said softly. "Your family and mine have not always . . . seen eye to eye. I was wrong about you, Conn. I hope we can put the past behind us."

Conn smiled. "I never stole your nails, but I did try to steal your daughter." He held out his hand.

The smith shook it. "You would have been better off with the nails," he said sadly. "Leave the mail shirt with me. I'll begin a plan tomorrow and start working next week."

Resplendent in white robes garlanded with oak leaves, Brother Solstice strolled around the games fields, watching runners and wrestlers, fistfighters and spear throwers. He had always loved the games, living in the fond and futile hope that one day such sport would replace the need for battle and violence. He remembered how he had once taken part in the games, winning the silver wand. He had knocked out the Pannone champion after more than an hour of ferocious fistfighting. Sadly, he still looked back on that moment with pride, and that, he knew, showed how far he still had to go on his quest for spiritual fulfilment.

As he wandered through the crowds, he saw young Connavar standing to one side and watching the runners prepare for the six-mile race. Brother Solstice looked at him closely. The boy had changed since that day at Old Oaks. He was taller, wider in the shoulder, and bearded now. The beard was that of a young man, thin and barely covering the skin, and there was a white streak in it around the scar left from his fight with the bear. His hair was shoulder length, red streaked with gold. Brother Solstice walked across to him and offered a greeting. Connavar shook his hand, and the Druid looked into his odd eyes.

"How are you faring, Connavar?"

"I am well, Druid. You?"

Brother Solstice leaned in, his voice low. "A conversation between old friends should never start with a lie."

Connavar gave a brief smile. It did not reach his eyes. "You know what they say, Brother, a problem shared is a problem doubled. So I ask you to accept the lie."

"As you will, my friend." The Druid glanced across at the runners. "Is that your brother, Braefar?"

"Yes. I think he will do well. He was always fast on his feet."

The race marshal raised his hand. The thirty runners took up a ragged line.

"Away!" bellowed the marshal. As they raced away down the hill, Connavar and the Druid wandered to the food area. Brother Solstice purchased a jug of ale. Connavar declined to join him in a drink.

"I was pleased to see Ruathain and Meria reunited," said the Druid. "They are good for one another."

"Aye, it's good to see the Big Man happy," Connavar agreed. "Where is the Long Laird today? I had hoped to speak with him."

Brother Solstice pointed to a group of nobles at the far edge of the field, clustered together beneath a black canopy. "You see the woman dressed in green, with the white-streaked long red hair?"

"Yes."

"She is Llysona, the laird's wife. They became . . . estranged. Today is *her* day. By agreement the laird will not be present. They have not seen each other for—what?—eight years. She dwells now on the eastern coast."

Connavar said nothing. His gaze was fixed on the group.

"Who is the tall young woman beside her? The one in the white dress."

"That is Tae, her daughter."

"She is very lovely."

"Indeed she is. The powerful man hovering close by is Fiallach. Some say she will wed him in the spring."

"The big man in the red shirt?" asked Conn. Brother Solstice nodded, his gaze resting on the huge figure looming beside the slender Tae. Fiallach was just over six and a half feet tall and powerfully built, with a barrel chest and huge shoulders. His yellow hair was braided into a ponytail, and he sported no mustache or beard, which was rare among the Rigante. His eyes were wide set in a large face, his brows flat, as were his cheekbones. No sharp bones to split the skin under the fists of an opponent, thought the Druid. Conn spoke again, repeating the question. "The man in the red shirt?"

"Aye. You will see him later in the final of the fistfight. He will win it, too."

"He looks old."

Brother Solstice laughed. "Yes, he is thirty. The grave beckons."

Conn grinned. "I meant old for her. What is she, sixteen?"

"Seventeen. Would you like me to introduce you?"

Conn shook his head. A middle-aged man approached them. Connavar introduced Parax to the Druid. Brother Solstice looked at the man closely, noting the sharpness in his deep-set eyes. Parax stared back at him in the same appraising manner. Brother Solstice grinned. "Tough as old oak. But a good man," he told Conn.

"I know that, Brother."

"I'm still here," grumbled Parax. "I'd sooner you waited till I'd gone before talking about me."

"But he does get touchy," said Conn. "I think it's because he's getting old." Parax swore. Conn adopted a look of horror.

"And he has no manners, Brother. To say such a thing in front of a Druid? Disgraceful."

Brother Solstice clapped Parax on the shoulder. "My apologies to you. I meant no disrespect. It is good to see Conn has found a worthy friend."

The Druid walked away, crossing the field to watch the spear throwing. The match was won by a young Pannone.

Less than an hour later Brother Solstice cheered with the other members of the crowd as the six-mile race came to its conclusion. Braefar crested the hilltop in second place but put in a fast finish to beat a runner from the southern Rigante.

Then the final of the fistfighting began. Fiallach won it brutally, smashing punch after punch into the face of his opponent. The man's hands were fast, the power of his punches awesome. Brother Solstice did not enjoy the bout. It seemed to him that the yellow-haired Fiallach took too much pleasure in inflicting pain. He could have finished the man far more swiftly. Instead he toyed with him, causing humiliation as well as defeat. The Druid found himself wishing that he was still a fighting man. He would have loved to step into the circle and give Fiallach a taste of his own brutality. Closing his eyes, Brother Solstice whispered a calming prayer.

As the silver wand was presented to Fiallach, the fighter moved to the edge of the crowd, throwing his arm around the tall, slim Tae and kissing her brow. The Druid noted that she pulled away from him slightly, and though she smiled, she seemed irritated by the contact.

The scent of roasting beef drifted across the field. Brother Solstice yearned for the taste of it, the salty, savory, mouthwatering taste. Pushing the thought from his mind, he tried to summon enthusiasm for the hot salted oats he would consume that evening. Being a Druid was not easy.

"Daan's greetings, Brother Solstice," said Tae, moving alongside him.

She was tall for a woman, just under six feet. He looked

into her dark brown eyes and tried not to notice the gentle curves beneath the white woolen gown she wore, concentrating instead on the silver circlet around her brow that was holding her long, dark hair in place. "May the spirits bless you, child," he responded. "Are you enjoying the games?"

"I will enjoy them more when I am allowed to compete in them, Brother."

It was, Brother Solstice considered, a delicious thought. Women taking part in athletic tourneys. Pictures flowed from the well of his imagination, and once more he considered the drawbacks of his calling.

"Is your mother well?" he asked.

"Yes. She always enjoys the games. I think she misses the mountains. For myself I like the sea. I sit and watch it for hours, especially when it is angry and the sky is the color of iron."

Brother Solstice smiled politely and waited for her to come to the point. "Tell me," she said at last, trying to assume an air of mild interest. "Who was the young man you were speaking to before the six-mile race?"

"I spoke to many young men, my lady. What did he look like?"

"He was tall. He had a streak in his beard."

"Ah, yes. That would be Connavar. He is from Three Streams."

"The man who killed the evil king?"

"And fought the bear. Yes, the very same. Would you like me to introduce you to him?"

"No, not at all. I was merely curious." She stood in uncomfortable silence for a while. "Is his wife with him?"

"I do not believe he is yet wed or even betrothed."

Fiallach strode up to them. His massive upper body was clothed now in a shirt of red satin. "Greetings to you, Druid," he said. "Did you watch the bout?"

"I did, Fiallach. Congratulations to you."

"Coming from a former champion, that is good to hear. Do you think you could have beaten me? When you were in your prime, that is."

Brother Solstice smiled. "The awful truth about fighters, young man—myself included—is that they always believe they are the best. Indeed, it is that necessary confidence that drives them on. Yet there is always someone better somewhere. That is the nature of the world of men. I was extremely fortunate never to come across such a man while I was fighting. Let us hope the same good fortune follows you, Fiallach." As he spoke, he laid his hand on Fiallach's shoulder. In that instant he felt all the anger and the bitterness in the giant's soul, but deeper still there was an abiding sadness and a need that surprised the Druid.

Brother Solstice left them and thought about what he had learned. At first sight Fiallach was a brutal and cruel man who reveled in humiliating those he considered lesser men. But there was another Fiallach, buried deep, hidden among the roiling storms of bitterness, frustration, and anger. Like a golden seed nestling in a cesspit.

Would it flower or would it die?

Brother Solstice did not know.

Tae glanced up at the moon. It could barely be seen through the smoke of the cook fires. The music began again, and dancers began to leap and twirl. Tae sat back, relieved that Fiallach, who had moved away to get a drink, was now deeply engrossed in conversation with a merchant from across the water. While he had been by her side, no other man had asked her to dance. She glanced across to where Connavar was talking with a group of young men. Everywhere he went, it seemed, people wished to speak with him.

She was sure he had looked at her, but even when she had stood close, he had not spoken, and once, when their eyes had met, he had not smiled. Was he, too, afraid of Fiallach?

The brooding presence of the huge warrior was irritating. Everyone expected them to marry in the spring, including her mother. Fiallach had even taken to starting conversations with her with the words "When we are wed."

It was not that she did not like him. He had been a presence in her life for as long as she could remember, and as a child she had worshiped him. Fiallach seemed so strong, so enduring. But when she thought of her wedding, when she dreamed of that first night, at no time did Fiallach enter the vision. And when she tried to picture herself lying alongside him, naked and alone, she shivered and a sense of dread touched her spirit.

"When we are wed."

It was galling that he had not even asked her, merely taken her compliance for granted. Tae transferred her gaze to the fire dancers. A young man ran along the plank and leapt through the flames. He landed lightly and spun back toward the waiting women. He was blond and lithe, and she recognized him from the prize giving as the winner of the six-mile race. She could not remember his name but recalled that he was the brother of Connavar. Their eyes met, and she smiled. He bowed and moved across to stand before her.

"Would you care to dance, lady?" he asked.

"No, she would not," came the growling voice of Fiallach.

"Yes, I would," said Tae, rising from her chair. The young man looked confused, but he reached out to take Tae's hand. Fiallach stepped forward and slapped the hand away. Angry now, Tae glanced up at him. His face was red and flushed, his eyes angry.

The young man stood very still, and Tae could feel his fear. He had not moved away. Fiallach lunged at him, punching him in the chest and sending him hurtling back to fall close to the fire. For a moment Tae thought he would roll into the flames. Fiallach moved after him.

The music died away as the dancers moved back from the fire.

"Stop this immediately!" shouted Tae. The boy scrambled to his feet as Fiallach loomed over him, fist raised.

"If that blow lands, I'll kill you," came a voice. The words were spoken without emphasis, and the effect was all the greater for it. Fiallach froze. The youngster scrambled away. Slowly the big man turned. Tae saw Connavar step forward. Despite being at least six feet tall, he looked small against the massive bulk of Fiallach.

"You dare to threaten me?" muttered Fiallach.

"What did my brother do to warrant a beating from you?" asked Connavar, his voice still even, almost conversational. The lack of aggression confused the tall warrior.

Before he could reply, the youngster called out. "I just asked the lady to dance, Conn. That's all. Then he struck me."

Brother Solstice moved from the crowd. "What is the problem here?" he asked.

"There is no problem," Connavar answered, with an easy smile. "Merely a misunderstanding." Approaching Tae, he bowed. "Would you like to dance?" he asked her.

"I would," she told him. He took her arm and led her out, then called to the pipers. The music began immediately. Other dancers joined them, but as she moved, Tae kept glancing back to where Fiallach stood, glaring at them from beyond the fire. Connavar moved well, and for a little while Tae pushed from her mind all thoughts of Fiallach. As the music died away, she took Connavar by the arm. "He will not forget," she said.

"Who won't forget?" he asked.

"Fiallach. He is a vengeful man."

"Oh. Do not concern yourself. I understand you live by the coast."

Tae was pleased that he had taken the time to inquire after her. "Yes. It is very beautiful there. Do you like the sea?"

"I like looking at it more than I like traveling on it." They moved away from the dancers to the food area, where Connavar fetched her a goblet of apple juice. Then they sat quietly away from the crowd.

"Are you truly unworried about Fiallach?" she asked him.

He shrugged. "He will come after me or he won't. There is nothing I can do to prevent him. Why, then, should I worry? What would it achieve?"

"He has decided to marry me," she said. "I worry about that. Even though it achieves nothing."

"And what will your decision be?"

"I don't know. I rode my father's chariot once, and the horses bolted. I just had to let them run themselves out."

He smiled then. "You think Fiallach will run himself out?"

"Perhaps. Who knows? Did you ask me to dance because you wanted to dance with me or to annoy Fiallach?"

"A little of both," he admitted.

"Would you have asked me if Fiallach had not attacked your brother?"

"No."

The answer annoyed her. "Well, you have achieved your purpose. So I will bid you good night."

"Wait!" he said as she rose. Connavar stood. "I have just returned from a war, a hideous war." He fell silent for a moment. Then he looked into her eyes. "I have no time for personal pleasure. One day that war will flow across the water. I have to prepare."

"*You* have to prepare? Forgive me. I know you are a hero. Everyone says so. But you are not a chieftain. Why, then, should *your* being prepared make a difference?"

"Because I will it so," he said. Just as it had been when he had spoken with Fiallach, the tone of his voice was level, without a hint of arrogance or false pride.

"Then I will sleep sound in my bed knowing that you are *prepared*," she told him. "Fiallach is also prepared. He talks of nothing but battles. I think he is rather looking forward to one."

At last, to Tae's delight, he looked discomfited. "Then he is doubly a fool. But I do not speak of battles. I speak of war. Battles are only a small part of the beast."

"Beast? You think war is a living thing?"

"Aye, I do. I have seen it kill. I have seen it blacken the hearts of men. I have seen things to chill the soul." He shivered suddenly. "And I will not allow the beast to stain the mountains of Caer Druagh." Taking her hand, he kissed her palm. "I am glad Fiallach pushed my brother. For being with you has gladdened my heart." Connavar returned with her to the feasting fire, bowed low, then strolled away.

Fiallach approached her. "You shamed me," he said. "That is no way for a betrothed woman to behave."

"I am not betrothed," she told him. "Not to you, not to anyone."

His pale eyes narrowed. "We had an understanding."

"No. *You* had an understanding. Not once have you asked me to marry you."

He smiled then. "Ah. You are angry with me. I understand. I reacted . . . hastily to the boy. We will put it right on the journey back home."

The Long Laird glanced up at the trees as he rode back from the execution. The leaves were turning gold, and there was a chill in the air. His arthritic shoulder throbbed with pain, and the useless fingers of his left hand felt as if hot needles were being pushed into the skin. Beside him rode the white-robed Brother Solstice, and ahead of the walking crowd the two men traveled back to Old Oaks in silence.

When they reached the hall, a young retainer took charge of the ponies. The Long Laird made straight for his sitting room, slumping down into a wide armchair close to the newly lit fire in the hearth. Brother Solstice lifted a flagon of Uisge from a nearby shelf and poured two generous measures into brightly painted cups. The Long Laird sipped the golden spirit and sighed.

"We should have just killed him," he said. "Quietly and without fuss."

Brother Solstice did not answer. The trial and subsequent drowning of Senacal had depressed him. He had known the young man all his life. Senacal had not been a malicious man, merely stupid and easily led. Left to his own devices, he would never have murdered his parents. Under the influence of Ferol, however, he had fallen into evil.

The hunters had found him back in his own cabin, naively waiting to operate the ferry. His only defense at the trial had been that Ferol had killed his parents and he had been too frightened of Ferol to run away and report it. Brother Solstice believed him, but the law was iron, and Senacal felt the full fury of it. When sentence had been passed, he had cried out for mercy and refused to walk to his death. Dragged clear of the hall, he had broken free and thrown himself on the ground, wrapping his arms around a tethering post. Two guards had prized loose his hold, and he had been tied and put in the back of a wagon. Senacal had wept and screamed constantly on the journey to the execution site.

The Long Laird had swung his pony and ridden back to the screaming prisoner. "In the name of Taranis!" he had thundered. "Can you not even be a man in the hour of your death?"

"Don't kill me. Please don't kill me!" Senacal had whimpered. The Long Laird had ordered him gagged.

His legs bound with chains, Senacal had been thrown into the swamp. With his hands and legs tied, the murky waters had swiftly closed over his head, his body floating down to join the other murderers in the silt below.

In the sitting room Brother Solstice finished his Uisge. The Long Laird was lost in thought, staring into the fire. Brother

Solstice looked at him, seeing the weariness in the timeworn face. "By the gods, it makes you think," whispered the laird. "All my life I have believed the Rigante to be a special people, quite unlike the murderous foreigners. We're not, though, are we?"

"Yes we are," insisted the Druid. "I have traveled as far as Stone. Everywhere there are criminals and outlaws, killers, rapists, seducers. Everywhere. In the large cities crimes against people take place almost hourly. Here in the mountains a murder such as this is still—thankfully—a rare occurrence. In the main we care for one another, and we live in relative harmony with our neighbors. I have seen little that is base or cruel among the Rigante."

The Long Laird glanced at his friend. "You can say that after putting to death a man who connived in the butchering of his parents?"

"Maggots will always enter some fruit, even on the finest tree."

For a little while both sat in silence, lost in their thoughts. Brother Solstice wondered about the wisdom of his words. Yes, he believed the Rigante to be special, but how much of that uniqueness lay in the mountain lifestyle, where neighbors were forced to rely one upon another and where every man and woman had a part to play in the lives of the tribe? And how much was in the hands of the Seidh? According to Druid teachings, there was magic in the land, magic born of spirit. The Seidh, so the Druids believed, were the guardians of that spirit. Solstice had felt the power many times in his life, climbing to high peaks and staring out over the landscape, his spirit soaring as the magic of the mountains flowed through him.

Nursing his Uisge, he studied the face of the old man sitting by the fire. The Long Laird had ruled the northern Rigante for almost forty years with wisdom, with love, with cunning and subtlety, and—as today—with ruthless regard for the law. The years had not been kind to the Long Laird. His huge torso was now stripped of flesh, his joints creaking and painful, his heart close to its final beat.

"Another winter coming," whispered the Long Laird. "The years are passing by too swiftly." The old man rubbed his shoulder.

"You should drink more nettle tea and less Uisge," said Brother Solstice. "It will help ease the pain."

The Long Laird grinned. "It won't make me young again."

"Is that what you want? To make all those foolish mistakes once more?"

The Long Laird stroked his silver beard. "I've had my life, my friend, and I've lived it to the full. I have no regrets. Most of my enemies are dead. Most of my friends are, too, come to think of it. But I walked through this life as a man of pride. No, I don't want to do it all again, but I miss the heady joy of youth, the running, the fighting, the whoring."

"You have seen an Earth Maiden three times this week," observed Brother Solstice. "So you are not missing the whoring."

The old man chuckled. "You are right. But I mainly ask her here now for the company, for the warmth in my bed. I miss my wife. Sometimes in the night I think I hear Llysona call my name." He shivered and held out his good hand to the fire.

"You speak of her as if she were dead, my friend."

"I am dead to her. There is no doubt of that." The Long Laird looked into the Druid's eyes. "You think if I went to her, she would forgive me and come back?"

"Not a chance," replied Brother Solstice. "Would you if the situation were entirely reversed?"

The Long Laird shook his head sadly. "No, I wouldn't." He laughed suddenly. "Entirely reversed? I think if I'd found Llysona in bed with *my* sister, I'd have died of shock."

"To entirely reverse it she would have had to have been in bed with your brother," the Druid said pedantically.

"I know, I know. I was looking for a little levity. Damn, it's not as if the sister was worth it. She promised much and delivered little. But I miss Llysona and the babe, watching her grow."

"The babe is now close to seventeen and will probably wed next spring."

"You see what I mean?" said the Long Laird. "The years are flying by like winter geese." The comfortable silence returned, and they drank second cups of Uisge. Then the Long Laird spoke again. "You think the Sea Wolves will raid in force in the spring?"

"Impossible to say," admitted Brother Solstice. "There have been occasional raids these last few years, but none on our coast. What makes you think they might?"

"Maybe they won't. But we've been lucky for too long. I wish I had a son. There is no one to follow me. No one I trust, anyway."

"You trust Maccus. He is a good man."

"Aye, he is. But what little ambition he had died with his wife. As to the rest? Fiallach is lacking in wisdom, and he is not liked. The others are all petty rivals. If any one of them became laird, you would see no end of petty grievances, perhaps even civil disobedience. At worst there would be a war. Then, if the Sea Wolves came in real force, they might win. And that, my friend, is an intolerable thought."

"What will you do?" asked Brother Solstice.

"I'm not sure. I like the look and the sound of young Connavar. He has the makings of greatness. Bringing back the stallions was a fine idea. Given a few years, we'll have bigger, stronger, faster war mounts. But he's young. If I had five years to train him . . ." His voice tailed away.

"Give him some mission to perform. Then you can see how he handles himself."

"Mission?" queried the Long Laird. "What kind of mission?"

"Send him to Llysona at the coast."

"For what purpose?"

"You think the Sea Wolves might attack. If they do, they will sail up the estuary to Seven Willows. Therefore, you send a warrior to organize possible defenses and advise Llysona. Then we will see what diplomatic skills Connavar can muster."

"She already has Fiallach. He's a hard and proud man. He'll take no advice from a boy."

"Connavar is not a boy, my friend. He is a few months younger than you were when your father died. Besides, that is partly what makes it a mission. If Connavar cannot . . . make his presence felt, then he would not prove a good laird."

"How long have you been thinking about this, Druid?"

"A little while," Brother Solstice answered with a smile.

"Since the fire night when he danced with my daughter? I may be old, but I still know how to listen. Maccus told me that Connavar forced Fiallach to back down. In front of a crowd. Theirs will not be an easy meeting in future."

"I think Tae took quite a fancy to the lad," observed the Druid.

The Long Laird chuckled. "So now you are a matchmaker." His smile faded. "Has it occurred to you that Fiallach might challenge and kill him?"

"Aye, or a tree may fall on him, or his horse throw him, or an illness strike him. You are looking for an heir. I believe Connavar may be that man. If he is, then he will prove himself at Seven Willows."

The Long Laird shook his head and gave a wry grin. "You know, the Sea Wolves were the main reason Llysona chose Seven Willows. She knew I would worry. It must have annoyed her terribly when the Sea Wolves didn't attack. Probably knew she was there. By Taranis, I'd rather face a hostile army than come again under the lash of that tongue."

"And Connavar?"

"I will ask him if he wishes to undertake the mission. Perhaps he will refuse."

"A barrel of ale against a goblet of wine that he leaps at the chance."

"I'll take that wager," said the Long Laird.

While the young men of Three Streams sought out Conn's company, seeing only a hero, tall and strong, Meria, with a mother's eyes, saw beyond the facade and instinctively felt the terrible turmoil raging within him. Like Ruathain before her, she tried to engage Parax in conversation. With the same results. He politely rebuffed her.

Meria knew there was little point trying to question Conn herself. If he wanted to speak of his troubles, he would have done so. The problem nagged at her. It was not that Conn never smiled, just that when he did, the expression was swift and soon gone. She also noticed his mood change in the presence of his eleven-year-old brother Bendegit Bran. He would soften and hug the golden-haired boy to him, then a darkness would descend upon him and he would fall into silence. More often than not, after being with Bran, Conn would wander away by himself, returning to Ruathain's old home or riding up into the woods. This was especially puzzling to Meria.

More confusing still was his reaction when Bran cut himself while playing with an old knife. It was a shallow wound, requiring only a couple of stitches, but when Conn saw it, his face became gray and his hands began to tremble.

Meria was at a loss to understand it.

She carried the problem to Eriatha. Every midweek afternoon they would meet and talk at Eriatha's small house on the outskirts of Three Streams. The Earth Maiden listened as Meria talked of Conn and his curious behavior.

"Strange that he doesn't talk about it," said Eriatha. "In my experience men love nothing better than to talk about themselves. Have you asked him?"

"No," admitted Meria. "Ruathain has tried. He was always more comfortable talking to him than to me. Something happened across the water. Not a battle. Something else. Whatever, it is haunting him. He is not the same."

"I would think that war would change any man. All that blood and death."

Meria shook her head. "Two weeks ago Ruathain took a wound to the shoulder. He was gashed by one of the bulls. Conn stitched the wound for him. There was no problem. But when Bran cut himself, I thought Conn would pass out." Meria sighed. "I am losing sleep over this. I love him more than life, and I cannot help him."

"I will go to him," said Eriatha. "Perhaps he will talk to me."

Meria smiled. "I was hoping you would say that. You will not say we have spoken?"

"Of course not."

The following evening Eriatha walked across the first bridge and crossed the field to Conn's house. She tapped at the door. It was opened by an old man with a silver beard. Stepping aside, he gestured for her to enter.

"You have come to see Connavar?" he asked.

"Yes."

"He'll be back soon. He is at the forge, talking to the smith. May I fetch you something to drink?"

"No."

"You are Eriatha the Earth Maiden?"

"I am."

"Did Conn send for you?"

"No."

"Well, you take a seat by the fire, lady. I was just about to stroll down to Pelain's tavern and enjoy a jug or two. I hope you will not think me rude to leave you here alone." Eriatha could see an unfinished meal on the table and noted that Parax was not wearing boots or shoes. She was grateful for the lie and the courtesy behind it.

"No, I do not think you rude, friend. Go and enjoy yourself."

Parax pulled on his boots, gathered up his cloak, and walked out into the night. Eriatha sat by the fire and glanced around the room. The walls were bare of ornament, and there was only a single threadbare rug. The floor was of hard-packed dirt, though someone had traced a pattern in it of interlocking circles. She guessed it would have been Ruathain.

It was more than an hour before Connavar entered the house. Throwing his cloak across the back of a chair, he moved toward the kitchen, then saw Eriatha. He showed no surprise. "Where is Parax?" he asked.

"At Pelain's new tavern."

"Have you eaten?"

"I am not hungry, Conn. I just thought I would stop by and see you. Do you mind?"

"Not at all. Truth to tell, I was planning to visit you."

Eriatha rose from her chair. She was wearing a simple gown of sky blue. Stepping in to him, she flipped it from her shoulders, allowing it to fall to the floor. Conn led her to the first bedroom.

An hour later Eriatha lay awake as Conn slept beside her. The lovemaking had been almost fierce, yet it had contained moments of tenderness. He had fallen asleep swiftly and was now breathing deeply. Meria was right. He has changed, she thought. She heard Parax enter the house quietly, moving to his own bedroom and shutting the door.

The night deepened, and just as Eriatha was about to climb from the bed, Conn began to tremble. His arm, which was outside the covers, tensed, his fingers curling into a fist. He groaned then, a sound full of despair. His body shook, and he cried out. Eriatha moved in close to him, stroking his long blond-streaked red hair. "Be calm," she whispered, "it is but a dream."

Conn awoke, and the trembling ceased. Rolling to his

back, he wiped the sweat from his face. "It is no dream," he said. "I was there. I saw it."

"Tell me."

He shook his head. "You'd not want to share it, believe me."

"Speak it," she insisted, her voice low. "Let it go."

For a while she thought he was ignoring her. He lay quietly, eyes closed. Then he spoke. "After the fall of Alin and the final destruction of the Perdii army, Stone soldiers gathered up thousands of tribesmen to be sold as slaves. Thousands to be marched in chains to the lands of Stone. Others were . . . murdered, their arms nailed to the trunks of trees. There were hundreds of these." He fell silent. Eriatha lay beside him, saying nothing, waiting. The worst, she knew, was still to come.

"I found Parax among the prisoners. I knew him. I asked for his release. Jasaray granted it. On the last day, as Parax and I prepared for the journey home, we saw . . . we saw . . ." He sat up and covered his face with his hands. "I cannot," he whispered.

"Tell it, Connavar. You need to tell it."

He took a deep breath and sighed. "We rode out of Alin and saw perhaps five hundred young children sitting on a hillside, being guarded by soldiers. We went past them and up the hill. Soon we could hear the sounds of screaming. We rode on. In a clearing a half mile from the settlement Stone soldiers were killing children. There were hundreds of bodies: babes, infants, toddlers. A huge grave had been dug. I saw a man swing a babe by its feet against a tree." His voice tailed away. "I wanted to draw my sword and race down into the soldiers, killing as many as I could. I should have done that. I will regret not doing so for as long as I live."

"Had you done it, they would have killed you, then carried on slaying the babes."

"I know that, as I know that I was filled with the need to return to Caer Druagh and do all in my power to prevent such horror from touching my own people. But I cannot forget that I turned my back on those children and rode away. No hero would have done that. And there is something else . . . I killed a man back in Alin, just before the war. He had betrayed Banouin. As I was preparing to kill him, a group of children ran by outside. They were laughing. I told him that the days of laughter for his people were coming to an end, that I would do all in my power to wipe them from the face of the earth. And I did."

"You fought as a warrior, Conn. You killed no children. And you could not have saved them."

"At the very least I could have died for them."

"Maybe one day you will," she whispered. "But I don't understand. Why did they kill them?"

Conn gave a harsh laugh. "There is only a small market for young children. So they took away some of the prettier ones and slaughtered the others. More than a thousand in Alin alone. Now, everywhere I ride, people say, 'There is Connavar, the man who killed the evil king.' The evil king." He let out a deep sigh, then rubbed his hand across his face. "As far as I know, Carac murdered four people: his brother, his brother's wife, his brother's son, and Banouin. Jasaray, the conquering hero of Stone, has now slaughtered untold thousands. And I helped him. He rewarded me with stallions and six chests of gold. Now, when I sleep, I see the faces of the children. They are calling out to me to save them. And I do nothing. Connavar the hero. Connavar the coward, more like."

"You are not a coward, Connavar, and you know it," she said. "And you will protect the children. The children of Rigante. I have heard what you have been saying to Ruathain and the others. The armies of Stone will one day cross the water. When they do, you will stand against them. The past is dead and gone. You cannot change it. The future waits. Had you ridden down and killed a few soldiers, you would have died for it. And thousands more children yet to be born would face a terrible doom. Think on that."

"I do think of it. As I think of this one little boy who saw my garb and recognized me as a tribesman. He ran toward me crying for help. A soldier threw a spear through his chest. That boy will haunt me all my days."

"Perhaps it is right that he should," she said softly. "And despite it, you will live your life as a man, a good man. You did not kill those children, and you could not have saved them. There is a limit to the power of any single man, even a hero. You were the boy who fought the bear. Now you are the man who killed the king. Yet still you are only a man. You are not responsible for the woes of the world or the evil of other men. You understand? If the past must haunt you, then use it wisely. You cannot alter the past, but you can use it to alter the future. The terror you saw has strengthened you, Connavar. It has given you purpose. Bless the dead for that. And move on."

Conn leaned back on the pillow and closed his eyes. Eriatha looked closely at him and knew that her words had struck home. He seemed more relaxed. He took a deep breath, opened his eyes, and smiled. "You are very wise," he said. "And I will heed what you say." Lifting her hand, he kissed the palm. "I am grateful you came here tonight. You were right. I did need to speak of it. I feel that at least a part of the weight has lifted from my soul."

"Good. I shall leave you now. I can hear my own bed calling me."

"Stay," he said, his voice gentle.

And she stayed.

◇ 13 ◇

THE LAND APPROACHING Seven Willows was rugged and beautiful, the hillsides covered with pale blue heather and yellow gorse shining gold in the sunshine. Conn reined in his steeldust pony at the top of the last rise and stared down over the wide valley below and the distant sparkling sea.

In the center of the verdant valley stood Seven Willows, a large stockaded town of perhaps three hundred homes with some twenty farms dotted around it. Cattle, sheep, and goats could be seen grazing on the hillsides, and farther away fields of golden corn were being harvested. Parax moved alongside him.

"A pretty place," he said.

"Pretty and exposed," Connavar replied, pointing toward the estuary. "A good landing place for long ships. No cover to protect a defending force and only the wooden stockade of the town to hold them. Any force stronger than a few hundred could take that town in less than a day." He cast his gaze around the valley. "It should have been constructed farther to the west on one of those flat-topped hills. The gradient would slow an advancing force, giving archers more time to thin them out."

"Maybe so," the old man agreed. "But they haven't been attacked in ten years, so they must be doing something right. Can we ride down? The wind is too chilly up here, and my ears are freezing."

Conn grinned at him and heeled his pony down the trail. "You're getting old," he called back.

"*Getting* old? I was old when you were born, whipper-snapper! Now I'm ancient and should be treated with more respect."

The sun was high and hot as they reached the valley floor, and Parax removed his pale green cloak, rolled it, and hooked it to the wooden crosspieces of his saddle. As they rode on, they passed farmers gathering their crops. Several children stopped their work to stare at the riders. Conn waved to them, but they did not wave back.

At the open gates of the town there were no guards, and the two men rode into Seven Willows, heading for the main hall, no more than a hundred paces from the eastern gate.

"Usually the ruler's home is closer to the center of a settlement," said Conn.

"Aye, but this place has grown over the years," said Parax. "See the remains of the old stockade wall by yon stream? As the settlement grew, they tore down the old western wall and extended the stockade."

Conn grinned at him. "You don't miss much, do you?"

They dismounted in a paddock alongside the hall, unsaddled their ponies, and turned them loose.

A young warrior strode out to greet them. He was not tall, but his shoulders were wide, his heavily muscled arms a little too long for his body. "You'll be Connavar," he said. "Lord Fiallach is expecting you."

"You mean, surely, Lady Llysona?"

"Whatever," the man replied, tersely. "Follow me."

"Friendly welcome," whispered Parax. Conn shrugged and moved after the warrior. The hall was well lit, with the shutters of the high upper windows opened wide, allowing sunlight to stream through. Lady Llysona was sitting at the head of a horseshoe-shaped table. To her right sat the giant warrior Fiallach. The beautiful Tae was at her left. Some twenty noblemen filled the other seats.

"Welcome, Connavar," said Lady Llysona. Dressed in a gown of green satin, she was a handsome woman. Her dark hair was braided with golden wire, and she wore a thick golden torque around her slender throat. In her early forties now, she had once been a great beauty and was still breathtaking. Connavar bowed.

"Thank you, lady. It is good to be here. I bring greetings from the Long Laird and his hopes that you are well. He has asked me to offer my advice in the matter of defense against raids from the sea."

"We don't need your advice," said Fiallach.

Conn ignored him. "My lady, I am recently returned from a war across the water where I saw many towns under siege. Seven Willows is poorly placed to resist an attack. But I will make a better report to you once I have scouted the surrounding countryside."

"It is kind of you to take the time to come to us," said Llysona. "But Lord Fiallach is a noted warrior, and he is responsible for the defense of Seven Willows. I have the utmost confidence in him. Therefore, you may return to Old Oaks."

Connavar bowed again. "I am sure that confidence is well placed, lady. However, the Long Laird, my lord and master and the lord and owner of this land, has ordered me to oversee the situation. Do you wish me to return to him with the news that his orders are no longer obeyed in Seven Willows?"

She gave a thin smile. "No man should be encouraged to disobey the orders of his betters. What I am saying is that the laird need have no worries concerning our well-being. Perhaps you should convey that to him."

"I will pass on your words, my lady. As soon as I have completed my mission."

"Are you deaf or merely stupid?" stormed Fiallach. "You are not wanted here. Do you understand that?"

Conn's eyes never left the face of Lady Llysona, and when he spoke again, his voice was calm and even. "Back in Three Streams, my lady, a barking dog is never allowed at table. It disturbs the guests. However, if you tell me Lord Fiallach now rules in Seven Willows, I will address all comments to him."

This time she did not smile. "I rule in Seven Willows, but Lord Fiallach is my most trusted counselor. And let me warn you that it is not good sense to anger him."

"It is not my intention to anger anyone, merely to offer good advice and instruction. Whether the advice is heeded or ignored is a matter for you and your counselors. However it turns out, I will make a report to my lord and return to my home."

"How long will you need?" she asked.

"Three or four days to make the initial report. After that, I do not know, my lady. It will depend on whether my advice is heeded."

"Four days it is, then," she said. "Farrar will show you to your lodgings." She gestured at the ape-armed warrior who had met them. He rose from the table and led them out into the open, across the now-empty market site, and on to a small, crudely built roundhouse. The timbers had dried out and warped, leaving gaping holes, and the thatched roof was in disrepair. Two cot beds had been placed inside. Both were rickety and badly constructed. Connavar stepped inside, and a rat scurried across his foot.

"Enjoy your visit with us," Farrar said with a sour grin.

"Just being in your sunlit presence is enough for me," Parax told him.

The man reddened. "Is your servant mocking me?" he asked Connavar.

"I suppose he must be," Conn replied, coldly. "Given the choice between your company and the vermin that already occupy this ruin, I'll take the rats. Now get out of my sight."

Farrar's jaw dropped. "I'll take no insults from—"

Conn swung, grabbed the man by the front of his tunic, and hauled him in close. "Understand this, you discourteous dog turd. You have neither the wit, the strength, nor the power to offend me. Now, if you want to challenge me, do so. I will take no pleasure in killing you, but I will do it if you force me."

Releasing the frightened man, he pushed him from the hut, then turned to Parax. "We will sleep in the open," he said, his voice cold and angry.

"You do have a way with you, lad," Parax said with a smile. "I've never known a man so adept at making friends. You should teach me sometime." Conn's anger evaporated, and he smiled. "Anyway," continued Parax, "we can make this place habitable." The blankets within the hut were lice-ridden, and Conn left them where they were. He and Parax walked out into the settlement, where Conn purchased new blankets, a broom, several wooden plates, a copper pan, a hank of bacon, a small sack of oats, and some salt. Returning to the hut, the two men dragged the two rotten beds out into the open, throwing the lice-infested blankets over them. Parax swept out the rotted straw that covered the floor and prepared a fire.

Conn moved out into the open and stood before the pile of furniture they had placed there. He saw Tae stroll from the long hall and cross the open ground. She looked at the pile.

"I am sorry," she said. "This is awful. But my mother was angry that Father should send someone to crack the whip over us, and Fiallach has not forgotten that you shamed him."

"I hope you will not get into trouble for speaking to us," he said stiffly.

"It doesn't matter. Would you like me to show you around the country tomorrow?"

"I would like that very much."

She smiled at him. "It would be nice if you were to tell me you accepted the laird's commission because you wanted to see me again."

"I can tell you that because it is true. You have been in my mind ever since the fire night."

"I have thought of you, too," she said, then turned away and ran back to the hall.

Parax emerged from the hut. "Sweet girl," he said. "She'll make that Fiallach a fine wife."

Conn felt his hackles rise, then saw that Parax was grinning at him. "You see too much," he said.

"I'm not the only one." Parax inclined his head toward the hall, where Fiallach was standing in the doorway, staring at them. "You watch him carefully, boy," said Parax. "He's a killer."

As night fell, Conn and Parax sat in their small hut before a fire set in a circle of stones, which also served as light in the absence of lamps or lanterns. "Why are they being so unpleasant?" asked Parax. "You are the same tribe, after all."

"We are caught between two evils," Conn told him. "First, there is the ill feeling between Lady Llysona and the laird. He was unfaithful to her, so it is said, and she responded by moving to Seven Willows. She could have ended the marriage, but that would have left her with little power and no income. So it is natural for her to try to thwart the laird's plans. Second there is the question of Fiallach. The man is a brute and a bully. I watched him fight. He tormented his opponent cruelly. And he has no affection for me. Since he appears to be Llysona's chief counselor, we have little hope of any real cooperation."

"Then why stay?"

"I like to finish what I start, my friend," Conn replied with a smile.

"There is another reason," offered Parax.

"Aye, there is. Do you think she is beautiful?"

"I find all women beautiful, especially the fat ones. Not too fat, mind. But plump. Oh, yes, and dark-eyed, full-lipped.

And friendly. They have to be friendly. I married a fat woman back in Alin. She was a joy." Parax sighed. "Plague took her after two years. Never found a woman to match her."

"Have you given up trying?"

"Never give up, boy!" replied the old man. "But I don't think the young ones will have any time for an ancient like me. Unless I get rich, of course. Rich men are never too old in the eyes of some women. Still, not much chance of that." Parax added fuel to the fire, then watched the smoke spiral up to the narrow opening at the center of the domed roof. A flea bit his arm. Parax deftly caught it between thumb and forefinger and flicked it into the fire. "We should find somewhere better to stay tomorrow," he said.

"I intend to. Banouin, an old friend of mine, told me of a comrade living here. His name is Phaeton. He is a merchant. I will seek him out tomorrow."

Conn lay down beside the fire and pulled his blanket over his shoulders. Tae's face hovered in his mind, and he slept fitfully.

Parax woke him just after dawn. The old man looked concerned.

"What is it?" asked Conn.

"They've stolen our ponies."

Conn sat up. "This nonsense ends today," he said.

"We're going back to Three Streams?"

"That's not what I meant." Pulling on his boots and belting on his sword and dagger, Conn walked from the hut. It had rained a little in the night, just enough to put a shine on the buildings and freshen the air. Parax joined him. "Where are they?" asked Conn.

"I followed the tracks to a field about a half mile from here. There are three men there. Armed men."

"Show me."

As the two men set out, Tae came riding up. She was

wearing a dark brown leather shirt and matching leggings and boots. "Where are your ponies?" she asked innocently.

"We are just going to fetch them," Conn told her, forcing a smile. "We will meet you back here in an hour."

Tae rode her pony to the paddock and dismounted. Leaving the beast, she ran to join the two men. "This is obviously some kind of bad jest," she said. "I am sorry."

"It is not your fault," said Conn. "But it is probably best if you are not close by when we find the men who took them."

"Tell me where they are and I'll ride there and fetch them," she offered. "That way there'll be no trouble."

"It has gone too far for that," Conn told her. He slowed, then stopped and turned toward her. "Are you betrothed yet to Fiallach?"

"No."

"Good. That is one fact to cheer me. Now please leave us."

"You won't kill anyone, will you?"

"Do I seem so savage to you?"

"There is a savage part of you, Connavar."

"Aye, there is. But there is also a gentle side. I hope to show it to you." He walked away from her then, and he and Parax continued on their journey, coming at last to an open area with a grazing meadow beyond it. The ponies were there, tethered to a rail, and three men, Farrar among them, were sitting on a blanket, playing dice bones.

They looked up as the two men approached, then climbed to their feet.

Farrar walked toward Conn. "Your ponies seem—" he began. Conn smashed a hard left into his face that crushed his lips, spraying blood over his face. An overhand right clubbed him to the ground. One of the other men pulled a knife, but Conn stepped in close, slapped the knife hand away, and struck him with a right cross that sent him spinning to the grass. The third man backed away.

"I've only just come here," he said. "I don't have anything to do with whatever it is that has angered you."

"Then get you gone," said Conn.

The man turned and sprinted away. There was a barn close by. Conn strode to it, returning with two lengths of rope. Moving to the unconscious men, he tied their hands behind their backs.

"What now?" asked Parax.

"Now the fun begins," Conn said coldly. Farrar groaned. Conn hauled him to his feet. "Wake the other one," he ordered Parax.

The old man knelt by the fallen man and nudged him several times. "He'll sleep for a week," he said. "I think you've broken his jaw."

"There's a well behind the barn. Draw some water and douse him with it."

"Fiallach will kill you for this," Farrar said, through bleeding lips.

Conn ignored him and waited for Parax to return with a bucket of water. He drenched the unconscious tribesman, who at last began to stir. Parax helped him stand. He swayed groggily but kept to his feet.

"Now let us go to the hall," said Conn, mounting his pony.

As they rode through the settlement, a crowd began to gather, and by the time they reached the long hall, word had reached Lady Llysona, who was standing in the square, Fiallach with her.

"What is the meaning of this?" she asked icily.

Conn slid from his pony and offered her a deep bow. "I am sorry to bring you sad tidings, my lady, but these men stole our ponies and I apprehended them. As you are aware, the penalty for such an offense is death by hanging. However, as is my right as a free Rigante, I demand trial by mortal combat. I will kill these two men, and that will be an end to the matter."

"You'll kill no one, you whoreson!" bellowed Fiallach.

"Yes, I will," Conn said quietly, "for that is Keltoi law, and no one—not you, you arrogant pig, or the lady you serve—can go against it."

"By Taranis, I'll kill you myself," stormed the giant.

"I accept the challenge," said Conn, angry now. "As soon as I have killed these two, I will make myself available to you. And I hope you fight better with a sword than you do with your fists, for you are old and slow and I will cut you to pieces." The force of his fury radiated out over the group, and a silence fell upon them. Conn removed his cloak, folded it, and threw it to Parax. Then he drew his Seidh sword and stepped back, slashing the blade through the air in a bewildering series of glittering arcs as he loosened the muscles of his shoulders and arms. The speed of his movements was dazzling, and not a man present failed to appreciate how deadly the young warrior was. Parax glanced at Fiallach and saw doubt in his eyes. As a fistfighter he was greatly skilled, but Conn was right. He was too heavy in the arm and shoulder to be fast with a blade.

"Cut the first one loose, Parax," said Conn.

"No!" said Lady Llysona, panic in her voice. "There will be no killing. This has gone far enough. Can you not accept, Connavar, that the . . . removal of your ponies was not theft but merely a joke in bad taste?"

"I see," he replied coldly. "The same kind of joke that places the Long Laird's servants in a lice-infested hut with rats for company?"

"The same kind," she agreed. "Let us make a new start, Connavar. I see I misjudged you. The fault was mine. Can we begin again?"

Conn sheathed his sword, took back his cloak from Parax, and bowed once more. "Indeed we can," he agreed, casting a glance at Fiallach, whose face had turned gray with anger. Drawing his dagger, he cut the ropes tying the two men.

"Have you broken your fast?" Llysona asked him.

"Not as yet, my lady."

"Then you and your servant can join us in the hall." Llysona swung on her heel and walked back through the doorway.

Fiallach strode across to where Conn stood. "Don't think this is over," he hissed. "You are mine. By all the gods, I swear it." Then he followed the lady inside.

"You may not be good at making friends," whispered Parax. "But by heaven, you are second to none when it comes to making enemies."

Tae rode beautifully, the white gelding responding instantly to each delicate touch on the reins or movement in the saddle. "He is wonderfully trained," observed Conn as they crested the last rise and rode up to the edge of the cliffs overlooking the sea. "Did you train him yourself?"

"No. My cousin Legat trains all our mounts. He has a way with ponies. I swear he speaks their language. No whip or stick. He talks to them, and they seem to understand him."

"My father was said to be like that," said Conn, noting the young man's name. He would need expert horse handlers for his new herds. The breeze picked up, blowing in from the sea, cold and fresh. Tae's dark hair billowed out like a black banner, exposing her long neck. Like a swan, he thought, a beautiful swan. "Let's move back into the shelter of the trees," he said. "We'll tether the ponies and look around."

The wind there was broken by the tree line. They dismounted, and Conn walked back to the cliff edge, climbing down and sitting on a jutting rock. From there he could see the river and the distant estuary. There were many landing places along the shoreline. Tae joined him, and he drank in the beauty of her walk, tall and proud, with an unconscious grace.

"It is beautiful here," she said. "This is one of my favorite places."

"Aye, beautiful," he replied. Then he turned away and stared down at the shimmering water below.

"What are you thinking?"

"I am seeing long ships move up the from the sea and beaching along the shore. The land falls away from the west, and the only warning Seven Willows will receive is when the first of the raiders crests the hill a mile above the settlement." He scanned the cliffs, then returned to the ponies, riding south along the cliffs, the ground steadily rising. At last they reached a point where the distant stockade could be seen. "There should be a tower here, constantly manned. And over there a ready-laid beacon fire. In the day it could be doused with lantern oil. When lit, the smoke could be seen from the stockade. That would triple the warning time."

"Yes, it would," she agreed. "But the raiders have not landed here in ten years. That's a long time to leave someone sitting in a tower." She smiled as she spoke.

"It is a puzzle," he said. "Farther north the river narrows, and there are fewer landing sites and only small settlements. Yet they have been raided several times in the last two years. It makes little sense to me."

"Perhaps the Seidh favor us," she offered.

"Obviously." Moving back toward the east, they dismounted again at the edge of a small wood overlooking the stockade. "I would place four towers, one at each of the corners, and have bowmen trained to man them. And a wide ditch dug out around the settlement, studded with sharpened stakes."

"I have a question for you," she said.

"Ask it."

"Would you have killed Farrar and the others, or was it just a clever ploy to make Mother see reason?"

The question worried him. He had already established that

Tae was a gentle soul and did not want her to think badly of him. The way she had put it gave him an easy escape, but he did not want to lie to her. "I would have killed them," he said. "But I did hope that your mother would speak out." He saw the disappointment in her face. "I am sorry, Tae."

"Is it so easy to kill?" she asked. "It seems to me that a life should be considered precious. Farrar has a wife and two small children. He adores them, and they him. He can be pompous and condescending, but at heart he is a sweet man. Yet he could have been killed for depriving you of your pony for a little while."

"I can see how it could look that way," admitted Conn.

"To a woman, you mean?"

"To someone gentle and kind," he replied. "I am still young, and I have much to learn. Had I been wiser, I probably could have handled the situation without threats. As it is, though, no one died, and my mission continues. I am not an evil man, Tae. I do not seek the death of any brother of the Rigante."

He saw her relax. "Let us talk about something other than war," she said. "Let us enjoy the beauty of the sky, the raging wonder of the sea, the magnificence of the sun rising. Let us talk like two people merely enjoying the company of each other. You promised me a glimpse of a tender heart, Connavar. I am wondering when I shall see it."

"Would you have me pay you compliments, Tae?"

"Compliments are always welcome to a woman. As long as they are sincere."

He fell silent for a while and continued to scan the surrounding hills. "You are thinking of war again," she chided gently.

"Not at all. I was thinking of you. Truth to tell, I have thought of little else since first we met. If I close my eyes at night, I see your face, and you are the first thought in my mind when I wake. It is very . . . distracting."

He turned toward her, stepping in close. She did not move away, but tilted her head back, expecting a kiss. Then they heard a horse approaching. Conn walked toward the sound. Parax was riding up the hill. Parax waved as he saw the young warrior and urged his pony on.

"We need to talk," said the hunter.

"Can it not wait?"

The old man saw Tae standing by the trees. He slid from his pony. "Aye, it could wait. But hear me first. You said there has not been a raid here in ten years."

"Yes."

"Then why do I find evidence that a long ship beached here no less than two days ago?"

"You are sure it was a long ship and not a fishing boat?"

"Would you mistake the spoor of a rat for a horse?" Parax answered sharply.

"You are touchy today, old man."

"Aye, well, I've not been charmed by the company of a beautiful lass. Anyway, there is more. Men climbed down from the long ship. Maybe as many as twenty. It was hard to tell. They were met by a rider from Seven Willows. He rides a pony with a chipped hoof. Then they sailed away."

"Show me," said Conn.

Minutes later the three of them rode along the shoreline. Conn saw the deep trench made by the keel of the long ship and the churned mud on both sides where warriors had jumped down to haul it in. Farther back they found the remains of a fire. "What does it mean?" asked Tae.

Conn shrugged. He had not told her about the rider. "A long ship beached here several nights ago. That is all we know. Perhaps it was a scouting party. It is hard to tell."

They rode back to Seven Willows in silence, and Conn, having first obtained directions to the house of Phaeton, bade farewell to Tae.

The merchant was at home when Conn and Parax rode up.

He was a tall middle-aged man with graying fair hair and an easy smile.

"Banouin spoke of you often," he said. "It is a pleasure to meet you. Come inside. I will ask the cook to prepare you a meal. I'll have to do it carefully, for she is a hard woman and rules my house with iron discipline."

"She is your wife?" asked Parax.

"No. I hired her five years ago. She is a fine cook and housekeeper. But she is angry with me because I am selling and moving south."

The three men strolled inside. From outside the house looked little different from the other homes nearby. Inside, however, it was designed like a villa, the wooden walls overlaid with white-painted clay and the floor decorated with green and black mosaic tiles. The furniture was expensive and foreign—hide-covered couches instead of chairs—and the rugs scattered on the mosaic floor were uniquely patterned with a combination of delicate flowers and swirling golden dragons. A large woman in her late thirties moved from the kitchen and stood staring at the men. "You didn't mention company," she said.

"I had no idea, my dear Dara, that I was to receive guests. This is Connavar and Parax. They are friends of a friend."

"I suppose they'll be wanting food."

"That would be pleasant," said Phaeton. With a toss of her head Dara returned to the kitchen. Phaeton looked relieved. "Better remove your boots, lads. There'll be trouble if a speck of mud stains the floor."

Dara cooked a fine meal of roasted ham, fresh eggs, and a spicy pie with a filling of sweetened apples. Then, throwing her cloak around her shoulders, she bade them good night and left the house.

Phaeton relaxed. "As I said, she is a fine cook."

"A big woman," Parax said dreamily. "Is she married?"

"Her husband died two years ago. He was older than her. His heart gave out."

"I'm not surprised," said Parax. "Take a lot of effort to satisfy, she would."

Phaeton chuckled. "That is not an image I wanted in my mind," he said. "I doubt I'll sleep tonight. We have an extra bedroom. You are welcome to stay here for several days. After that the new owner will be taking over."

"Why are you leaving Seven Willows?" asked Conn.

"Seven Willows is pleasant, and I like it here. But since the Stone Wars the market in cattle and corn is down. I can do better business in the south. The Norvii capital is now a thriving port. More ships are sailing there now that the mines in Broken Mountain are played out. I leave in four days."

"To be honest, I could use a bed around now," said Parax. Phaeton showed him to a large bedroom equipped with three beds. Parax thanked him, and the merchant returned to the hearth room.

"I was so sorry to hear about Banouin," said Phaeton, pouring a goblet of wine for Conn and then one for himself. "He was a fine man, one of the best."

"Aye, he was."

"He helped fund my own venture. Lent me a hundred silvers. I finished repaying him only last year. He didn't complain even when business was bad and I couldn't make the payments. Men like him are rare. Sadly, men like Diatka are not. I understand you made his death very painful."

"What can you tell me of Seven Willows?" asked Conn, ignoring the question.

"I suppose that depends on what you are looking for."

"Is it a rich settlement?"

Phaeton shrugged. "Again, that depends on what you call riches. The land here is fertile. There is an abundance of food, cattle, and sheep. Little coin save around feast times, when the cattle market is at a peak. There is an old silver mine to the north, but most of the ore is taken to the mint at Broken Mountain, about eighty miles from here. Little of it reaches Seven Willows."

"You know why I am here?"

"Dara tells me you are to supervise our defenses against raids. Is that the situation?"

"Yes."

"We haven't had a raid—"

"In ten years. I know. Puzzling, isn't it?"

"Never look a gift horse in the mouth, my friend. There is little here for them. They can't carry away cattle or corn. Better for them—in the past, anyway—to raid at Broken Mountain, where there is a treasury, or farther south and the trade centers there."

"You are probably right," said Conn. "Yet the Sea Wolves also raid for women, and there are a great many young women in Seven Willows."

"Indeed there are. And five Earth Maidens who would fetch fabulous prices in the slave stalls of Stone. Then there is the question of ransom." Phaeton suddenly grinned. "However, young Connavar, I think your problems are rather closer to home. It is said you have made an enemy of Fiallach."

Conn shrugged. "He is a brute, and I do not like him."

"Yes, he is a brute and a powerful one. I would not want him for an enemy. Perhaps marriage to Tae will soothe his savage nature."

"I wouldn't count on it," said Conn. "I intend to marry her myself."

"I think the days ahead will be lively," observed Phaeton. "I am sorry I won't be here to see them."

For three more days Conn scouted the surrounding land. Conn saw little of Tae. He glimpsed her once walking with Fiallach and on another occasion riding far off to the west, but she did not come near him. He could not understand it.

They had seemed on the verge of something that first morning in the woods. Or at least he thought they had been. Now he was unsure.

Phaeton had left that morning, leading a string of more than twenty ponies carrying his merchandise. Conn had wished him good luck on his journey and had walked to the long hall to make his final report to Lady Llysona. Three chairs had been set in a line, and the lady, dressed in a long dark blue gown, was sitting in the center. Fiallach and Tae, both dressed for riding, sat with her. Fiallach looked calm and even smiled as Conn approached. Tae kept her head down and did not look at him. Conn bowed to Lady Llysona and offered his report and recommendations.

They listened without interruption, and when he had finished, Lady Llysona thanked him for his diligence and promised to consider carefully all he had said. Fiallach said nothing, and still Tae did not meet his eyes.

It seemed a curious end to his mission, flat and unfulfilling.

"So you will be leaving us today?" said Lady Llysona.

"As soon as Parax returns, my lady."

"May the gods grant you a safe journey home."

Conn bowed once more and returned to the sunlight. Tae had not once looked into his face, and he was struggling to contain his anger. His mood was not lifted by the nonarrival of Parax, who had ridden out early, as he had done every morning to scout for sign of the pony with the chipped hoof. Parax had tried to track it from the shoreline back into Seven Willows, but cattle had been driven over the trail, and the earth was badly churned. Conn understood how vexing the failure was to an expert tracker, but it no longer mattered and he was anxious to be away from the settlement.

By midday his frustration gave way, and he left a message with the fat housekeeper Dara to tell Parax he had headed east and to follow at his leisure. Tae had not bothered to come and say good-bye, and as far as Conn was concerned, that was the final discourtesy. He tried unsuccessfully to push her from his mind and felt that leaving Seven Willows would aid him. But an hour later, camped high in the woodland over-looking the distant settlement, he still kept running their last meeting over and over in his mind. Had he said something to offend her? He could not recall any such comment.

The wind was fresh and cold, and bored now, Conn lit a fire. Where in the name of Taranis was Parax?

Storm clouds drifted across the afternoon sky, bringing with them darkness and cold. The firelight cast dancing shadows on the wide trunk of an old oak. Conn blinked. A trick of the light made the bark seem to quiver and flow.

Then features began to form in the wood, becoming the face of an old man with a long flowing beard and bristling brows. "You are not at peace, Connavar," said a voice, deep and sepulchral.

Conn knew instantly that this was the Thagda, the Old Man of the Forest and the most powerful Seidh of them all. He should have felt no fear, for had not the Thagda rescued him in the lands of the Perdii? Had he not given him his first knife? Yet Conn found his heart beating faster, and a growing urge to run filled his mind.

The tree quivered and bulged as first a wooden arm and then a leg crafted from bark pushed clear of the bole. With a grunt a figure emerged from the tree. His beard was lichen, his cloak broad-leafed ivy, his leggings and tunic a mixture of bark and acorn. His features were seamed with the polished grain of old oak, and his eyes were the green of a summer leaf. He stood back from the fire and stretched out his arms.

"These were once Seidh woods," said the Thagda. "All the world was Seidh. We fed it, and we fed upon it. Then came man. The magic is mostly gone from the woods now. Only the oaks remember. Long memories in oak, child. Where are you heading, Sword in the Storm?"

"I am going home."

"Home," said the deep voice, rolling the word, extending it. "I have always relished the feel of that word upon my tongue. There is always magic in 'home.' You felt it yourself when you stood on the battlefield and thought of Caer Druagh. There is rest for the soul at 'home.'" The tree man stood very still for a while, the wind rustling the leaves of his cloak. "Can you feel it upon the wind, Connavar?"

"Can I feel what?"

"Concentrate. Let your spirit taste the air."

Conn breathed in deeply. He could smell the woods, wet bark, rotting leaves. Nothing more. And then, just as he was about to ask the Thagda what he was supposed to be tasting, he caught the scent of the salt sea, seaweed on the beach. He could almost hear the crying of the gulls, the creaking of timbers, and the flapping of sails. It was a strange experience. "We are far from the sea," he said.

"Man is never far from the sea," said the Thagda. "Where is your lady love?"

The question surprised him. "I have no lady love."

"Look into your heart. Love is one of the rare virtues of your bloodthirsty race, Connavar. It does not come and go in a few heartbeats. Love endures. So I ask again, where is your lady love?"

"Back in Seven Willows," admitted Conn. "She did not even say good-bye."

"How strange that a man willing to fight a bear and face an army does not dare ask his love to walk around the tree."

"I would have asked had I been given a sign by her that she wished me to do so."

The Thagda gave a rumbling laugh. "How many signs did you need?"

Conn felt a flicker of anger. "Are you here to torment me?"

"Not at all," answered the Thagda. "My days are busy enough without giving way to small pursuits. It is merely that I have observed you ever since you came to the woods as a child, calling my name. You wanted, I recall, a spell cast on your parents."

"Aye, but you did not cast it," Conn pointed out.

"Who is to say I did not? Are they not together? And more in love than before? You humans are so impatient. This is perhaps natural for a race living lives that are measured in a few heartbeats." The wind whispered against his ivy cloak, rustling through the leaves.

"Why have you come to me?" asked Conn.

"As I recall, you have come to me. You left your lady love back in Seven Willows, rode to this quiet place, and disturbed my fellowship with the oak. You chose this spot with your heart, Connavar. For your heart knew I was here. We have been linked in spirit ever since you rescued the fawn. The question is, Why did your heart bring you here? What is it that you seek?"

"I am not aware that I seek anything."

"That is perhaps because you are still angry with Tae for not speaking with you. Anger can be useful, but more often than not it forms a mist that blinds us to truth. What is the question you have been struggling to answer these last few days?"

"I have been wondering why a longboat was beached in the bay and who went to meet it. And why."

"And what answers did you find?"

"None. Sea Wolves raid for plunder, that which they can carry away. Gold and silver. Sometimes women. There is little gold in Seven Willows."

"But there is great wealth, at least as you humans see it," said the Thagda.

"I don't understand."

"Who is the richest laird among the Rigante?"

"My own lord. He owns three mines, two of silver and one of gold."

"And what do you think he prizes above all?"

"How would I know?"

"Think on it."

"Can you not just tell me?"

"The oak is calling me," said the Thagda. Ponderously he turned and walked back to the tree, where his form once more merged into the bark. As he disappeared, his voice floated back. "Come to the Wishing Tree Woods on the night of Samain. We will talk more."

Conn sat before the fire, trying to make sense of the meeting. The Sea Wolves. Gold. Prizes. The remembered conversation floated like wood smoke around his mind, tantalizing yet insubstantial. Then he heard a rider galloping along the trail. Rising from the fire, he called out to Parax. The old man came into the camp and slid from his pony.

"What kept you?" asked Conn.

"The horse with the chipped hoof. I found it."

"Tell me."

"It is being ridden by the merchant Phaeton."

"Phaeton met with the raiders?"

"Aye, and here's the thing. Raids on Seven Willows ceased in the year he came to live among the villagers. Once I found the horse, I went back to the house and questioned Dara. Phaeton had strong links with the mining settlement at Broken Mountain and several other centers to the south. Every one of those centers has been raided more than once."

"He was supplying information to the raiders," said Conn.

"Aye, that is how it looks. He would have known the movements of silver shipments, in which villages the wagoners would rest, and so on. With the mines giving out, there was no reason for him to stay."

"I can see that, but why the last secret meeting? What were they planning? I wonder."

"No tracker can answer that," said Parax. "But there is no gold in Seven Willows."

Conn felt a cold breeze whisper against his skin as he remembered his conversation with the merchant. *"Then there is the question of ransom."*

Phaeton had left the sentence unfinished, and Conn had not followed it through. "Yes, there are riches," he whispered. "The Long Laird's wife and daughter. They would fetch ten times their weight in gold if held for ransom. How many raiders are there to each ship?"

"Forty, fifty. I've never been close to one," said Parax, "but judging by the impression made by the keel, I'd say closer to fifty."

"The ship did not return to the sea," said Conn. "The raiders were waiting for Phaeton to leave."

"How can you be sure?"

Conn ran to his pony and saddled it.

"We're going back," said Conn, vaulting to the saddle.

The two men rode swiftly back along the high trail, but their ponies were tired from the climb, and when they reached the last crest, it was already dusk. A towering plume of smoke was rising from Seven Willows, and Conn could see fleeing villagers running for the northern hills. To the south he could just make out heavily laden raiders moving slowly toward the woods.

Conn reined in his lathered pony. "What now?" asked Parax.

"I'm going to the bay where you found the keel mark. You get down to the settlement. If Fiallach still lives, tell him where I am."

"And he'll come running to rescue you?" Parax spit. "I think not."

"He'll come if they have Tae."

"Yes, but what if they don't? What if she escaped?"

"She didn't. If they had not found her, the raiders would still be in Seven Willows, searching. Now go!"

As he spoke, Conn urged his weary mount toward the south.

* * *

The giant Vars raider Shard stood in the gateway of the settlement, enjoying one last look at the blazing buildings. At first
the raid had gone well. He had beached his ship, *Blood
Flower,* at noon and ordered his warriors to move to the high
woods overlooking the settlement. The storm had been a
blessing from Wotan. Not one sentry had been on the stockade wall as the fifty raiders had emerged from the tree line
and loped down toward the open gates.

Shard had memorized the charcoal-sketched map Phaeton
had supplied. Sending thirty men into the settlement to kill,
burn, and create panic, he had led his twenty warriors straight
to the long hall. That move had proved the only boil on the
body of his plan. Stupid Kidrik had tried to grab the older
woman, but she had pulled a dagger from her belt and stabbed
out at him. Kidrik, in pain and rage, had lashed at her with his
sword, slashing open her throat. Well, he'd get nothing from
this raid. Not even a half copper coin. Idiot! The younger
woman had run back through the hall and out into the open,
straight into the arms of Shard's brother, Jarik. One blow had
rendered her insensible, and Jarik had reentered the hall with
the girl over his shoulder.

Even so, the profit from the venture had been halved, and
that left Shard irritated and probably short of the capital he
would need for a second ship. Raids would always be piece-
meal with only one craft and fifty men. But with two, either
the larger settlements would become accessible or, by carrying greater supplies, his men could raid deeper into Keltoi
lands.

The flames from burning wooden buildings roared higher
into the darkening sky. Close by a house collapsed. Shard
drank in the sight, then turned toward the gate. A young
Keltoi warrior ran at him with a spear. Shard casually parried
it with his longsword, then sent a flashing reverse cut that
slashed through the man's collarbone and down into his

chest. He gave a great scream of pain and fell. Shard put his boot on the man's chest, dragging his blade clear. Then he ran smoothly back to the open gates and out into the countryside. Despite his awesome size, Shard ran well, though not fast, covering the ground in a rhythmic, even lope.

Movement to the right caught his eye, and he saw two riders, one heading for the settlement and the other moving toward the south. Ignoring them, he ran on across the thick grass.

This is good land, he thought, not for the first time. Good farming land. Not like the barren, stony soil of his homeland in the fjord country, where the cattle were bony and lean and the crops thin and stunted. Twice in the last year he had tried to convince his father, the king, to mount an extensive campaign to win these lands. Arald would not be swayed. "Raids are good, and profitable," he had said. "But I was part of the last invasion, which was led by your grandfather eighteen years ago. Not only did the Keltoi outnumber the Vars three to one, they fought like lions. Three thousand of our men were slain that day, your grandfather among them. Few of us managed to fight our way back to the sea. There were not enough men to man all the ships, and we burned twenty-seven. Burned them! Can you imagine how that felt, Shard? You have been dreaming of a second ship for three years now. And we burned twenty-seven."

"Times are different now, Father. If we landed with ten thousand men, we could win and hold a large area of land. Then we could ship in more supplies and men, take over the Keltoi farms and buildings. We could make a strong settlement and from there sweep out and gradually win the land, just like the Stone men are doing in the south."

Arald had smiled. "It is always good to have large dreams, my son." And he had spoken of it no more.

It might have been different if his brother Jarik had added his weight to the argument. Jarik was the favorite son, but he, like the father, was not interested in conquest. Only easy wealth.

Shard ran on. Despite his irritation at the death of Llysona, the raid could still be considered a success. Not one of his men had died, though some had suffered cuts. The merchant had done his job well. The warrior Fiallach had not been present, or his thirty men. They had been drawn away after Phaeton had reported a huge lion in the mountains to the northwest. Fiallach loved to hunt, and the lure of such a beast had proved impossible to resist.

Shard reached the trees. The merchant had told him that the Long Laird would pay at least six hundred in gold for his wife and daughter. A hundred would secretly be paid to Phaeton for his part. That amount was now halved, less fifty for the merchant. Half again would be split among his men. That left 125. Half of that was promised to Jarik. Shard continued his calculations. He would still be fifty short of his second ship. He toyed with the idea of holding back the payment to the merchant but dismissed it. The man was too valuable, and perhaps his next piece of information would help Shard recover the lost profit. That left Jarik. If he could persuade him to relinquish his share . . .

No. Jarik would demand joint ownership of the ship, and that Shard would not do.

Shard glanced back. The settlement was burning ever more brightly as the wind whipped the flames toward the north.

Then he entered the darkness of the woods.

Three-quarters of a mile ahead Jarik finally threw the struggling Tae to the ground. As she tried to rise, he slapped her face, a hard, stinging blow that swept her from her feet. "Behave yourself, Rigante bitch," he told her, "and no harm will befall you. You are being held for ransom, not for sport."

The girl said nothing. Jarik crouched beside her, looking into her eyes. He saw no fear there, only hate and anger. He grinned at her. "But you make one stupid move and I *will* use you for sport. You understand that?" She nodded. Hauling her to her feet, Jarik and his three men moved on toward the shoreline. The girl seemed to stumble. Jarik reached out to support her. Suddenly she swung, head butted him in the face, and ran into the woods. Jarik swore and raced after her, his men following.

She was fast, but Jarik was faster and stronger. She leapt a fallen tree and cut to the right. Jarik was closing now, only a few feet behind. She swerved again just as he was about to grab her. Now, although she did not realize it, she was running straight for the beached ship. A screen of bushes lay ahead and then a moonlit clearing. The girl hurdled the bushes. Jarik, close behind, threw himself forward. She almost got away from him, but his hand closed on her ankle, and she hit the ground heavily.

"Remember what I told you, bitch?" snarled Jarik. She came up fast as he grabbed her from behind. Her elbow lashed back toward his face, catching his ear. Anger roared through him. Spinning her, he punched her full in the face. The girl, half-stunned, fell to her knees. Jarik's three men came running into the clearing. Jarik began untying the rope belt of his trews.

"Not to touch her," said the first. "Those are the orders."

"You are a fine one to talk about orders, Kidrik. The orders were to take both women alive. Anyway, this bitch needs to know discipline," said Jarik.

"And you need to know death," came a voice.

Jarik stepped back and spun. Standing at the edge of the clearing was a lone Rigante warrior, a gleaming sword in one hand and a knife in the other. It made no sense for him to be there. They were in shouting distance of the ship, and a little way behind them fifty warriors were making their way to that spot. Jarik hurriedly tied his belt. Then he glanced toward his men. "What are you standing there for? Kill the bastard."

The three men drew their swords and charged. The Rigante leapt to meet them. His blades glittered like silver in the moonlight. One man went down, then a second. The third fell back, his throat cut open, blood bubbling over his chain-mail shirt.

Jarik drew his sword and ran in, aiming a two-handed sweep at the Rigante's head. At the last moment the Rigante ducked below the blade. Off balance, Jarik stumbled. A searing, terrible heat swept up through his chest. He glanced down to see the hilt of a knife jutting from his ribs. It was a beautiful hilt.

His face hit the grass. It was cool and very pleasant. His gaze was drawn to a nearby bush. He saw a fox crouched there, watching, waiting. Fresh pain seared through him as the Rigante dragged his knife clear. Jarik groaned and tried to rise, but there was no strength in his arms. He managed to roll to his back. His head lolled. The Rigante was helping the girl to her feet. Then a cloud covered the moon.

And all was darkness.

Tae was still groggy from the blows she had received, but she stumbled after Connavar as he led her deeper into the woods. In the distance she could hear other raiders. Some of them were laughing. The sound cut through her dizziness, filling her with fear. Strange, she thought. I was not as frightened while they held me captive as I am now that I am free. That is something to think about at a later date, she told herself. Ahead, Connavar had stopped behind a thick oak. She moved in close to him.

"What now?" she whispered.

"We must thread our way through them. They do not yet know you have escaped. They will not be spread out. But I cannot get back to my pony. We will have to escape on foot." Sheathing his blades, Connavar led her to the left. The clouds were clearing above them, and the moon appeared, shining brightly. Connavar cursed softly and dropped to his knees, pulling Tae down with him.

"I see why they call you Demonblade," she whispered, recalling the speed with which he had dispatched her captors.

"No time for talking. Follow me." Dropping to his belly, Connavar crawled into the nearby undergrowth. Tae slithered alongside him. "We'll wait until they pass," he said.

A horn blared out behind them. Angry shouts followed. Tae did not need to be told that they had found the bodies. She glanced at Connavar. He was tense, his face angry. She heard the sound of running feet and was about to rise and flee, when Connavar grabbed her. "Stay low," he whispered in her ear. "They will be looking for movement." He put his hand over her shoulder, drawing her in close. The bushes there were thin and small. Anyone gazing down would see them.

Several men ran by. One paused almost above them.

"What can you see?" yelled a guttural voice.

"Nothing."

"They can't have gotten far. There's been no sound of horses. Fan out and search the woods."

The man close by ran off. Tae was still resisting the urge to run. Connavar spoke again in a low whisper, his mouth close to her ear. "They are expecting us to flee, so their gazes will be high, looking for running figures. Best we stay low for a little while. Once the clouds return, we'll risk moving. Relax and rest."

Relax? How could anyone relax with killers scouring the area? But Tae said nothing. The breeze picked up, and she felt herself begin to tremble. Whether it was from the cold or from the aftershock of the day's events she did not know. Connavar moved in close, spreading his cloak over her and sharing his body heat. Tae closed her eyes, seeing again the savage blow that had torn the life from her mother. Tears welled, but she fought them back. There would be a time for mourning. That time was not now.

The sounds made by the raiders were dwindling now, and Tae felt Connavar stir beside her. He rose to his knees and gazed around the moonlit woods. Then he climbed to his feet, pulling Tae up with him. "We need to head west," he said. "They will expect us to make for the north and Seven Willows." She nodded and followed him. He moved swiftly ahead for a while, then took refuge behind another oak. As Tae came alongside, he drew his dagger and handed it to her hilt first. She took the weapon and was amazed to find that it fitted her hand perfectly. At first glance Connavar's hands seemed so much larger than hers. She wondered how he could use such a small-hilted weapon.

Again he moved forward, dodging from tree to tree, scanning the woods as he ran.

Two raiders suddenly emerged in front of him. Both stood for a moment in shock. Then one of them shouted. "They're here!" Connavar sprang forward, his sword plunging into the belly of the first man. The second, carrying a hand ax, leapt at Connavar, who sidestepped and hammered his left fist into the man's chin. The raider fell to his knees. Connavar killed him with a downward sweep to the neck.

Unknown to Tae, a third raider had emerged from the bushes behind her. "Look out!" shouted Connavar. Tae swiveled and struck out just as the man loomed over her. The dagger blade slid through his mail shirt as if it were made of wool, plunging all the way to the hilt. The raider died instantly. Tae pulled the blade clear and ran to join Connavar. There were sounds now from all around them.

Then the clouds returned, covering the moon. Taking Tae by the arm, Connavar led her farther into the trees, coming at last to a thick section of bramble bushes. Dropping to their bellies, they wormed their way into the thicket. Tae's heart was beating wildly, and it seemed to her that her breathing was so loud that it must be heard. She tried to control it. Raindrops began to fall around them, then lightning flashed to the south. A few seconds later a great roll of thunder burst over the woods, and the rain became a torrent. Partly sheltered in the brambles, the two fugitives lay very still.

Time drifted by. Tae slept for a while and, when she woke, saw that Connavar was sleeping beside her. He awoke as she moved and smiled at her. "Have they gone?" she mouthed.

"I don't think so. But they'll be cold, wet, and very anxious by now. Stay silent." He closed his eyes once more, resting his head on his arm.

Moments later, as the rain eased, they heard men moving through the woods, heading back toward the bay. Then a voice called out.

"I will find out who you are, Rigante. And when I do, I will come for you. I swear by the blood of Wotan that I will not rest until your head sits on a lance outside my brother's house."

Tae glanced at Connavar and saw that he was smiling.

"What is there to smile about?" she whispered.

"A man should always have good enemies. It keeps him strong."

They hid for another hour, and just as dawn was tinting the sky, they emerged from the brambles. The woods were silent, and they made their way back toward the north.

They were met on the hillside by Fiallach and fifty riders. Parax was with them. Fiallach leapt from his horse and ran to Tae. "Did they harm you?" he asked.

"They did not have time. Connavar was there. He killed the men who held me."

"I am grateful to you, Connavar," said the big man, "for saving my future wife."

"I will not be your wife, Fiallach," Tae said, gently. "I adore you as my friend and my mentor, but I will not walk the tree with you."

Fiallach licked his lips and stood silent for a moment. "But I love you," he said at last.

When she spoke, there was no trace of the girl she had been. Her words carried quiet authority and even regret. "And I love you, my friend. If it was in my power to love you the way you desire, I would do so. But it is not. Now I must get back to Seven Willows. There is much work to be done." She walked away from him. A rider offered her his pony, and she accepted with a smile, vaulting to the saddle and riding down the slope.

Fiallach turned to Conn and sighed. "Should have listened to you," he said.

"It would have changed nothing," said Conn. "Gate towers cannot be built in a day. The man who caused this was Phaeton." Conn told the giant how Parax had found the keel marks and the tracks.

Fiallach's face turned pale with fury. "He it was who told us of the lion that drew me and my men from Seven Willows."

"With fresh horses you should be able to catch him," offered Conn.

"And catch him I will," swore Fiallach. But he did not move. His pale eyes held Conn's gaze. "Tell me there is nothing between you and Tae and I will offer you my hand in friendship."

"I shall ask her to walk the tree with me," said Conn. Though he disliked the man, he was saddened by the pain his words were causing. Having lost Arian, he knew what Fiallach was suffering.

"Aye, I thought it was you at the root of my trouble. You have robbed me of the one joy in my life. One day we will have a reckoning. Not today. My heart is too heavy. I will find Phaeton and bring him back for trial."

"Just kill him," said Conn. "I don't want to see his face again."

The raiders had killed thirty-one of the villagers: twenty-two men, five women, and four children. Their bodies were laid out in a line, their faces covered by cloaks or blankets. The fire had been brought under control, mainly by the powerful rain of the night before, and people were picking their way through the scorched remains, seeking items that might have escaped the blaze.

Standing at the main gates, Conn scanned their faces. All wore the same blank, resigned expression. Raiders came, and raiders went. Life had to go on. But it would move on now heavy with sorrow. Conn saw Tae organizing people, giving orders. He moved across to her. "You should rest awhile," he said.

"I will rest later. This is my settlement now, Connavar. I answer for it."

"I know." He saw her glance at the line of bodies. The first in that line, her face covered by a gold-edged cloth, was Lady Llysona. Tae swallowed hard, and for a moment he thought she would weep. Instead she strode away to a group of waiting men. "We need fresh timber," she told them. "Oras, you organize work parties."

"Yes, my lady."

She turned to another man. "Garon, I want you to see that those who have lost their homes have somewhere to sleep tonight."

"It will be as you say, lady." He bowed and backed away.

"What can I do to help?" asked Conn.

"There is a Druid who lives in the northern hills, in a high cave close to an oak grove. Fetch him here so that we may bless our dead."

Conn bowed and moved out toward the gates. Parax rode in, followed by several of Fiallach's men. Conn asked one of the riders if he could borrow his mount. The man nodded absently and slid from the saddle. Then he wandered off to one of the burned-out buildings. Before he reached it, he paused before the line of bodies. He gave a great cry and ran to the corpse of a young woman, pulling the cloak from her face and hugging the body to him.

Conn mounted his pony and gestured to Parax to follow him. The old man rode alongside, and Conn told him their mission. "Shouldn't be hard to find," said Parax. Then he sighed. "A black day, Connavar."

"Aye. Yet it could have been worse."

"What happened in the woods?"

"I found her and brought her out," Conn answered simply.

"I think there's more to it than that."

"Only blood, Parax. And death. How could a cultured man like Phaeton bring such casual destruction on a people he had lived among? Did you see evil in him?"

"No. But then, who could? He was friendly and kind to us. I saw a golden goblet once that the old king bought. Beautiful thing. One day he dropped it, and it struck the edge of the table. Underneath a thin layer of gold it was lead. Almost worthless. I guess Phaeton is like that. Seems a shame. I liked him."

"So did I."

As they rode, they saw the Druid walking down toward them, his white robe glinting in the sunlight. He was an elderly man with long white wispy hair and a drooping mustache.

"I saw the fires," he said. "Are there many dead?"

"Around thirty," said Conn. "They killed Lady Llysona."

The Druid nodded. "A hard woman. I did not take to her. Is her daughter safe?"

"Yes, she is organizing the rebuilding."

"Go back and tell her I am on my way."

"You can ride behind me," Conn offered.

"I'll walk," said the Druid. "It will give me more time to pray for the dead."

Throughout the long day Conn worked alongside the people of the settlement, dragging away half-burned timbers and bringing in fresh wood from the northern woods. He rested briefly with a score of men at noon and sat silently as they talked around him. "Why us?" was the most common comment. Conn was wise enough to know that this was not the time for an answer. Ten years of relative safety had made them complacent. When the raiders had attacked, there had been no sentry on the wall, and the settlement gates had been open.

Will they learn? he wondered.

For a while. Then the years would pass.

It is not worth thinking about, he decided.

He found his mind wandering to his last conversation with Ostaran. The Perdii had been defeated and were about to be annihilated. "Will it be the Gath next?" Conn had asked him.

"Of course not. We are allies to the people of Stone."

"Were the Perdii not Jasaray's allies last year?"

"You make for depressing company, my friend. What would the people of Stone want from us?"

Ostaran could not see it, though it lay revealed before him like a blood-drenched map. The people of Stone wanted it all. They would not be content until all the inhabited lands were under their sway. "Look," said Conn, taking a stick and sketching a line on the damp earth. "These are the lands of the Goth and Ostro. They are too far from Stone and the areas they control for an invading force to be equipped and supplied for a push toward the sea. But here, nestling between them like an arrowhead, are the lands of the Perdii. Rich farmland, thousands of cattle and horses. They will move into this land, establish towns and fortresses. From here they can strike out where they will."

"But why would they?" asked Ostaran.

"Because they must. It is for them an economic necessity. They have a huge standing army. The soldiers need to be paid. Conquest supplies the plunder that makes the generals rich and secures the loyalty of the soldiers. In Gath there are— what?—ten gold mines?"

"Fourteen now," said Ostaran. "And five silver."

"Then the people of Stone will take them. And who will come to your aid now, Osta? The Addui are destroyed, the Perdii finished."

"We will need no aid," said Ostaran. "We will smash any invading force. The Gath are not like the Perdii. Our fighters are twice as powerful."

"You can still believe this after all you have seen? Jasaray's panthers are well armed and armored, disciplined and motivated. They will not be broken by a sudden charge, no matter how brave the warriors."

"You are gloomy today," Ostaran, put in with a sudden smile. "We have just won a great victory. Jasaray has given you chests of gold and the stallions you so desired. My men and I have been paid, and the sun is shining. And let me tell you this, my doom prophet: Jasaray himself assured me he has no plans for further campaigns. He wants to return to Stone and become a scholar again. He says he misses the quiet charm of the university. There! What do you say to that?"

"I will say only this: When the end comes, bring as many warriors as you can to Goriasa. Seek out Garshon the Merchant. Remind him of the promise he made to me. Then, with his help, sail across the water and ride up to the lands of the northern Rigante."

"I tell you what I will do, my friend," said Ostaran. "If Jasaray comes, then, when we have defeated him, I will send you his head."

Conn's mind was jerked back to the present as the men around him rose and continued their work. Conn stayed with them until dusk, then sought out Parax. The old man had spent much of the afternoon asleep in Phaeton's house. Conn did not berate him. Parax was not young, and the exertions of the night before had taken their toll on him.

When Conn arrived at the house, Parax was frying two large steaks. "Where is the fat woman?" he asked.

"She was one of the dead," Parax said gloomily. "Phaeton's revenge, eh?"

"I think he liked her," said Conn. "She was probably just in the wrong place at the wrong time."

"As were we, for a while," said Parax, turning the steaks.

The two men sat in silence and ate the steaks, which, though they looked fine, were tough and hard to chew. "Should have been hung for a few days," muttered Parax. "But the meat came from a bull killed by the raiders."

After he had finished his meal, Conn strolled out through the back of the house and washed in a stream that flowed from the north. The water was cold and refreshing. Leaving his weapons at the house, he then rode back to the remains of the long hall. Most of the roof had fallen in, but the storm rain had saved the western section of the hall. He found Tae sitting at the old stone hearth, a fire blazing. She had a blanket around her shoulders and was staring into the dancing flames.

Conn walked into the ruin and sat opposite her. Her face was streaked with dirt and soot, and the marks of tears showed on her cheeks. "I am sorry for your loss, Tae," he said. She nodded but did not answer. The fire began to die down. Conn added wood.

"You will be leaving tomorrow?" she asked.

"Yes. I will report to the Long Laird. He will send men with seasoned timber for the rebuilding."

"Safe journey," she whispered.

"I love you, Tae," he said suddenly, the words shocking him, for he had not intended to say them.

"I know," she replied. "But this is not the time to speak of it."

"Would you rather be alone now?" he asked.

She shook her head and gave him a wan smile. "I am alone

whether you are here or not. We are all alone. We are born alone, and we die alone. In between we may be touched by love, but we are still alone."

"Aye, there is truth in that," he told her. "But not the complete truth." Reaching out, he took her hand and gently squeezed it. "I am here, and with this touch we are one." Moving alongside her, he put his arm around her shoulder and drew her into an embrace. Kissing her head, he hugged her to him. "Not one of the creatures of blood can escape death," he said. "We all face it and succumb to it. It follows us like a dark shadow. Yet if we live in terror of it, then we do not live at all. Yes, we are born alone, and yes, we will die alone. But in between, Tae, we *live*. We know joy. I am a lonely man. I think I always have been. But I am not lonely now. Not at this moment."

Tae said nothing, but he felt her snuggle into him, and he sat quietly, stroking her hair. She fell asleep against his chest. Conn remained unmoving as time slid by and the fire faded. At last he gently lowered her to the floor, made a pillow of his cloak, and covered her with her blanket. Then he banked the fire and rose, turning toward the door.

There stood Fiallach, a towering figure, his face expressionless.

Conn moved across to him, and the two men walked out into the night.

"You found him?" asked Conn.

"Aye, I found him," answered Fiallach. Lifting a blood-drenched pouch, he opened it. He tried to tip the contents to his palm, but they were stuck to the leather. Dipping his fingers into the pouch, he pulled forth Phaeton's eyes. They had already begun to shrivel. "The bastard will be blind in the Void for eternity," he said.

"He deserves it," said Conn.

Fiallach put the eyes back into the pouch, then wiped his hand down his leggings. "How is Tae?"

"Suffering. But she is strong."

"She is a fine woman, Connavar. Perhaps the finest. She deserves the best of men. Are you the best of men?"

"Who knows?" answered Conn.

"Let us find out," said Fiallach.

"Offering, but that is hardly..."

"Fiallach's fine horses," Connavar, ...ing the blood. "Sha, that deserved the best of food, air..."

"Who listens?" murmured Ostaran...

"I cannot read me..."

◇ 14 ◇

FIALLACH LOOKED INTO the face of his rival and saw no fear, only surprise. "You want to fight me? Now?" asked Connavar.

"Unless you are too frightened," Fiallach replied. Ever since the last day of the games Fiallach had dreamed of pounding the arrogant youngster to the ground. Everything had gone wrong since then. Tae had turned against him, and now the settlement he was expected to protect had been sacked by raiders. He had never forgotten that one moment when the cold voice had warned him: *"If that blow lands, I'll kill you."* It had chilled him to the bone. He should have turned and beaten Connavar to his knees. Instead he had frozen and had been forced to watch his tormentor walk off with Tae.

He had felt her loss in that moment like a cruel premonition. He remembered a shiver crossing his skin and the beginning of sorrow weighing on his soul. His love for Tae had been the one constant in his turbulent life. At first he had adored her as a child, his feelings paternal and platonic. He had taught her to ride, to shoot a bow, even to handle a longsword. Strong? Of course she was strong. Fiallach had helped make her that way. And then, as she came to womanhood, his love for her grew even stronger. And when she continued to seek out his company, to ride and to hunt, he had

348

believed her feelings for him had grown along with his own for her.

But ever since the games she had been different, contrary and argumentative. He had heard from his men that Tae was asking questions about Connavar, the boy who fought the bear, the man who killed the king. Connavar the warrior.

Connavar . . . Connavar . . . Connavar . . .

What had he ever done that Fiallach himself could not have achieved? The answer was nothing at all.

Yet it did not matter. Connavar was distant. She would in time have lost her interest in him. But no, the Long Laird saw fit to send the warrior to Seven Willows, and Fiallach had seen the light in Tae's eyes. In truth he had also seen the specter of his own defeat highlighted there. At thirty-one he was almost old enough to be Tae's father, and he had then begun to realize that she saw him as a paternal figure. A powerful protector but a man to lean on, never lie beside.

The knowledge was almost too painful to bear. It clung to him like an angry dog, sharp teeth in his heart.

Now it was Connavar who had ridden into the woods to rescue Tae from the raiders. And Fiallach was finished. He had never loved another woman. If he had not been drawn off on that lion hunt, it would have been he, Fiallach, standing before Tae, sword in hand, to protect her from evil. She might then have seen him in a better light.

But no, even the gods had turned against him, haunting his footsteps with ill luck.

He had returned to Seven Willows, having killed Phaeton, and had walked into the ruins of the long hall. There, silhouetted by the dying fire, he had seen Tae asleep in the arms of Connavar. Truth to tell, they had looked perfect together, and Fiallach's heart had finally broken. He had stood silently for almost an hour, watching them, seeing at the last how tenderly Connavar laid her down, making of his cloak a pillow.

There was no way now that he could kill Connavar. Tae was lost to him regardless.

Yet inside him raged a burning desire to hammer his fists into the face of his rival, to knock him to the ground and stand over his unconscious body, to prove to himself that he was superior to the man who had stolen his love.

His hands were trembling with the need to strike. "Unless you are too frightened," he heard himself say.

Connavar smiled—and hit him. The force and speed of the blow surprised Fiallach, but he absorbed its power and moved in, sending a thunderous left into Connavar's cheek. The smaller man did not give way, and the fight commenced.

Fiallach was surprised at his opponent's strength. Connavar was a shade under six feet tall, six inches smaller than Fiallach and at least thirty pounds lighter. But he punched above his weight, the blows perfectly timed and accurately placed. He was a thinker whose mind remained cool during combat. He did not strike out blindly or allow his rage to make him reckless. Fiallach admired that.

Connavar stepped inside, hammering blow after blow into Fiallach's belly. Grabbing Connavar's hair with his left hand, Fiallach forced back his head, then hit him with a short chopping right. Connavar's knees buckled. Fiallach let go of the hair and steadied himself for another right. Connavar leapt forward, head butting Fiallach in the chin. Stars exploded inside Fiallach's head, and he took a backward step. Two hard, straight lefts from Connavar forced him back again, but Fiallach countered, blocking with his right arm and then sending a left hook that exploded against Connavar's cheekbone, splitting the skin.

The fight went on. For every blow Fiallach landed, two came back from the smaller man. But the strength was leaching away from Connavar. Fiallach could sense it. The weight of his blows was beginning to sap Connavar's strength. But Connavar was game and continued to attack.

Blood was streaming down his cheek, and one eye was almost closed. Fiallach moved in for the kill, but he was too anxious and too early. Connavar smashed a hard right to Fiallach's nose, breaking it. Blood stained the giant's mustache, and with the early part of the fight over, he began to feel pain.

Both fighters were moving more slowly now, maneuvering for an opening. Conn hit Fiallach twice more on his broken nose, Fiallach replying by aiming at the swollen eye. The fight could only have one conclusion, Fiallach knew. A good big man would always beat a good little man. It was written in stone. He was getting his second wind now, and the punches from Connavar were no more than bee stings. Fiallach needed only one good right hand. Connavar attacked, smashing three good lefts and an overhand right to his opponent's face. As the right landed, Fiallach saw his opening and thundered a right cross to Connavar's chin. The smaller man hit the ground hard, rolled, came to his feet, stumbled twice, then charged in. Fiallach hit him again. This time it should have been over, but Connavar forced himself to his feet and advanced unsteadily.

Fiallach let him come, then hit him with a left hook and a right uppercut. Connavar hit the ground on his back, grunted, rolled over, and pushed himself to his knees and then to his feet. He brought up his fists and advanced.

Despite his dislike, Fiallach was impressed by Connavar's courage. On another day he would have stepped in and beaten him mercilessly, but he had already sated his fury in torturing to death the traitor Phaeton. There was no more anger in him now, and he realized he had no desire to continue this fight. Moving in, he put his arms around his opponent. "Enough, little man," he said. "The fight is over."

"You hit hard," mumbled Connavar. "For a little while there I thought you had me." He grinned suddenly, and Fiallach laughed.

"I'll admit you are the best of men," he said with a wry smile. The smile faded. "You look after Tae. Treat her well. I

will be watching. If you ever betray her, I will hunt you down
and watch you die."

"Always nice to finish a fight with a happy thought," said
Connavar.

The two men made their way to the settlement well. Fiallach drew up a bucket of cold water. Conn doused his face,
and Fiallach wiped away the blood from his swollen nose.

"If you are truly going to watch me," said Connavar, "you
will need to be close by. Come to Three Streams on Samain
Night."

"There is nothing there for me."

"I think you will find there is. I have a gift for you, Fiallach."

"What kind of gift?"

"Come to Three Streams and find out."

The fires were lit, the feasting pits full, the music from pipe
and drum in full and raucous flow as the sun died in glory and
Samain Night began. Hundreds of Rigante from neighboring
settlements descended on Three Streams to watch the wedding and savor the fine roasted meat supplied by Ruathain.

Winter was coming, and the Rigante faced lean and hungry times. This night was a time for excess, for gorging and
dancing and singing. A time of drunkenness and joy, a shining hour before the bleak bitterness of winter.

The Long Laird sat at the high table, Connavar on his right,
Tae on his left, Ruathain and Meria close by. The Laird's first
counsel, Maccus, sat beside Meria. A calm and quiet man of
middle years, his black and silver hair receding, his eyes
bright with intelligence, he listened more than he spoke.
Meria liked him, but then, as she was the first to admit, she
preferred talking to listening.

Ruathain had told her of Maccus and the fact that though
shy and gentle in peaceful company, he was a battle-hardened
commander who fought like a cornered wolf. That Ruathain
admired him was obvious.

"It is said," whispered Meria, "that the laird is to make an announcement tonight."

"Indeed, lady," said Maccus.

"What is it?"

"It would be presumptuous of me to say." He smiled. "Your gown is very beautiful. I have rarely seen a more bewitching shade of green."

"Banouin, a friend of ours, brought it with him on his last trip. It is satin and was made two thousand miles to the east. It is my favorite gown, though I fear it is growing a little tight these days."

"The best of cloths shrink a little with age," he said gallantly.

Braefar sat alongside Govannan at the far end of the table, with his brother, the twelve-year-old Bendegit Bran, sitting alongside Conn. The seating arrangements irritated Braefar. He was the second eldest. It was wrong to promote the youngster. Not that he envied Bran. The boy was enjoying himself enormously and Braefar was pleased for him, but it was a slight that should not have been made. He glanced at Tae. She was looking exquisitely beautiful in a white gown decorated with creamy pearls and wore a silver circlet inset with three opals on her brow. Every now and then her eyes would be drawn to Conn, who was talking with the Long Laird.

The conquering hero! He must have been blessed at birth, thought Braefar. The boy who fought the bear, the man who killed the king. Now the rescuer of the fair Tae. Ten years with no trouble, but upon Conn's arrival Seven Willows is sacked and Conn finds himself with yet more heroism to add to his overblown legend.

"Have you found the answer yet?" asked Govannan.

"What?"

"Creating a better saddle for the new warhorses."

"Oh, that. I am working on a number of plans," Braefar

said airily. "Perhaps stronger wooden crosspieces at the rear and a higher pommel."

"Might work," said Van. "It still means the rider must grip them, thus losing the use of the shield arm."

Conn had set Braefar the difficult task of finding a way to create greater stability for mounted warriors. The Rigante saddle was a simple piece of molded leather. The rider held himself in place during battle by applying pressure with the thighs to the barrel of the pony's belly. This meant that during a battle a rider could be easily unhorsed by a blow, a push, or a pull from a foot soldier. Braefar wanted to refuse. He had no interest in saddles. But Conn had pointed out that Braefar was the only man he knew with a mind sharp enough and brilliant enough to supply an answer. Braefar had been so pleased to have his talent acknowledged that he had agreed immediately.

Braefar had been thinking about the problem on and off for six weeks and was no closer to a solution. Perhaps that was what Conn wanted, he thought suddenly. Perhaps he was looking forward to the day when Braefar would have to tell him he did not have the sharpness of mind or the brilliance required.

Yet another stab of irritation pricked him.

His hunger deserted him, and he left the table and began to wander around the festivities. He saw Gwydia sitting with the huge warrior Fiallach. She was playing with her hair, her head tilted seductively. It was a dreadful closing of the circle, for it was after his humiliation on that night, when Fiallach had struck him, that Gwydia had told him she did not want to walk the tree with him. He had tried to explain that if Conn had not intervened, he would have stood up to Fiallach, that he was not frightened by the man. Gwydia had told him that she did not doubt that was true but that it had nothing to do with her decision. In truth, she told him, it was just that she saw him more as a good friend than as a lover.

Lying cow! She thought he was a coward. That was why she had broken their engagement.

Out on the pasture field young children were playing on the spinning pole. Nanncumal had designed it some years before. It was a clever piece. Ropes were attached to the top of the pole, and six children at a time sat in nooses at the base. Nanncumal would then take hold of spokes set in the pole and turn them. As the pole spun, the ropes stretched and the children flew higher and higher around the pole. They were squealing with delight and hanging on for dear life. Braefar smiled at their joy, remembering the blessed innocence of his own childhood, when the world had seemed a bright and beautiful place. His father was king, his brother a prince. He had adored them both.

And then the idea struck him. He almost shivered with pleasure at it. Ropes and nooses. Ropes ending in a noose, attached to each side of the saddle, would give a rider greater stability. No, not a noose. That would tighten around the foot, creating difficulty in dismounting. A baked leather ring would be one answer. Almost dizzy from excitement, Braefar sat down on the grass, thinking through possible problem areas. The length of leg of different riders meant that the ropes would need to be adjustable. Better to use flat strips of leather, like a buckled belt.

He was still sitting there when he heard the Long Laird thumping his goblet against the tabletop for silence. Swiftly Braefar ran back to his place.

"My friends," said the Long Laird, his deep, booming voice carrying far beyond the table, "we are here tonight to celebrate more than Samain. My daughter Tae is to wed Connavar. I bless this union. They are two fine youngsters, strong and proud. I am only sorry that Tae's mother cannot be here to witness her joy." He fell silent for a moment and sighed. "I am getting old and tired." His supporters cried out at this, shouting, "No, lord," but he waved them to silence. "It is true, though I thank you for your loyalty. In six months time I shall stand down as your laird. I will return to my father's land on the west coast. I nominate Connavar as my successor, though you will have, as always, the right to vote on it at the lything ceremony. Connavar is to be my new son, and I see in him the future well-being of our people. And now let us cheer my children as they walk around the tree."

With his one good arm he led Tae to Eldest Tree. There Connavar took her hand, and together they made their vows, walking slowly around the old oak. As they completed the circuit, Connavar took her in his arms, and they kissed as the crowd cheered.

Braefar stood back. He did not cheer. Conn was to be the new laird, and all because he had stabbed a bear.

Braefar blinked back tears of frustration and anger as he saw Conn and Tae moving toward him. He forced a smile. Tae kissed him on the cheek, and Conn embraced him.

"This is a wonderful night, Wing," he said.

"Yes, wonderful. I hope you will both be very happy. I am sure you will be."

"Will you dance with me, Wing?" asked Tae.

And together, with the music seeming to echo around the stars, Braefar and Tae danced within a circle made by hundreds of tribesmen. Braefar was a good dancer, lithe and supple, and he reveled in the applause as the music ended. Tae hugged him. "I hope you will be as good a brother to me as you are to Conn," she said. "He is always talking of you."

Impulsively Braefar kissed her hand. "I will," he told her.

She moved away and danced with Conn. Scores of couples joined in, and Braefar slipped away into the night.

With the celebrations still in full flow, raucous, wild, and joyful, Conn and Tae slipped away to the house they would share. They sat for a while before the fire, holding each other, then Tae rose and began to remove her long white gown. Her movements were nervous, and Conn lay back on the hearth rug lost in the beauty of her. Firelight was glinting in the three opals set in the silver circlet at her brow. She slid her gown over her shoulders, down to her waist, and over her hips. Conn could hardly breathe. Her skin was milky white, her breasts larger than they seemed when she was clothed.

"I think you should take off your clothes," she said primly.

He did so, and when he held her again, he found that his hands were trembling. He ran his fingers across the skin of her back, marveling at the texture and the perfection of her form. It seemed to him then that he had never known such exquisite joy.

The lovemaking, despite Eriatha's tutoring, was at first clumsy and inept. At one point Tae started to giggle, and Conn found himself laughing with her. It was the release they both needed, and for several hours they lay together on the broad bed, sometimes touching, sometimes talking, but mostly just enjoying the harmony and the heady sense of union.

As the night wore on Conn rose from the bed and dressed.

"Where are you going?" she asked him, surprise in her voice.

"To the Wishing Tree Woods."

"The Seidh Woods?"

"Aye. Do not worry. I am invited there. I am going to see the Thagda."

"But he is demon Seidh. He will kill you."

"He did not kill me the last time we met."

"Are you mocking me?" she asked him. "You have truly spoken with the Thagda?"

"Aye. He appeared to me outside Seven Willows. In fact, he berated me for not asking you to walk the tree with me."

"And you swear this is true?"

"I am not lying, Tae. He asked me to go to the Wishing Tree Woods on the night of Samain."

"I'll come with you."

"That would not be wise," he said. "I know little of the ways of gods, but what I do know is that they should not be treated lightly. He told *me* to come. No other. But I will be back soon." Stepping in, he kissed her, then threw his cloak about his shoulders and walked out into the night, crossing the field past the few revelers still awake and moving across the meadows toward the distant trees.

There was a fresh breeze, and the air was cool and clean, filled with the scent of grass and leaf, tinged with wood smoke from the feasting fires below. As he walked, Conn glanced up at the rugged outline of the Druagh mountains and felt a wave of pride ripple across his soul. The land was beautiful, and Conn felt privileged to be allowed to live upon it.

As he approached the woods, he saw the tree man waiting for him, moonlight making his lichen beard glow a strange, luminous green. Without speaking, the tree man turned and walked deeper into the woods, his cloak of leaves rustling in the breeze. Conn followed and found himself walking down to the bramble thicket where he first had seen the fawn.

"How close to death you were on that first day," said the Thagda.

"Instead you rewarded me with a knife."

"I have to say that I liked the child, especially when he carried me from the thicket. The touch was gentle. Do you remember checking my body for wounds before telling me to find my mother?"

"Yes. Are there any real fawns in the woods?"

"None. Riamfada sends you his love. He is happy here."

"He is Seidh now?" asked Conn.

"No, not Seidh. You cannot become a Seidh, Connavar, any more than you can become a dog or a horse. We are different races. But we have imbued his spirit with some of our powers."

"He can walk now?"

From the Thagda came a deep, rumbling sound Conn took to be laughter. Then he changed the subject. "Tell me, how is your new bride?"

"She is beautiful. I thank you for helping me save her."

"It was a small matter."

"May I ask another favor?"

"You may ask. I do not say that I will grant it."

"Could you give Vorna back her powers?"

The Thagda was silent for a while. Conn did not disturb him. When at last he spoke, his voice had softened even further. "I liked the child you were," he said. "I like the man you have become. You remember your promises. I have known few men who do. And I have lived a long time. Very well, I will allow your request. Tell me, Connavar. What will you say if I make a request of you?"

"I will say yes."

"Whatever it might be?"

"Not if I perceive it to be evil. Other than that, yes, anything."

"Evil? An interesting concept. When you have walked this world for ten thousand years, you begin to see matters differently. The fox eats the partridge chicks. For the fox it is a delightful breakfast. For the mother partridge it is an evil calamity. It all becomes merely a case of whose perspective one takes: the partridge or the fox."

"More than a thousand children were slaughtered in the Perdii valleys," said Conn, "because they had no value in the slave markets of Stone."

"In my life," replied the Thagda, "I have seen tens of millions die. I will see you die, Connavar, and your sons and their sons. How many men have you killed and deprived the world of their sons? How many children became orphans because of your blade? You think those children see you as good or evil? It is in my experience that the race of man does little that is good and much that is self-serving and ultimately evil. But

I did not bring you here to debate. Walk with me. There is someone who wishes to speak with you."

They walked on deeper into the wood. There, sitting by a tree, his twisted limbs heavily bound, sat Riamfada as Conn had last seen him, his face pale and pinched, his eyes large. Conn's heart leapt. He ran forward and dropped to his knees beside his friend. "Oh, but it is good to see you, little fish. How are you faring?"

Riamfada gave a happy smile, then reached out and took Conn's hand. Conn was surprised to feel flesh as firm as his own. "I am well, Conn. Better than I have ever been."

Conn glanced at the ruined legs. "I thought you could walk?"

"I can. I can walk, run, dance. I can soar into the air and see the mountains from below the clouds. I thought it would be more . . . comfortable . . . for you to see me as you remembered me."

"I have missed you," said Conn, sitting beside him. "We all have."

"I have not missed you," Riamfada said, with a shy smile. "I have been with you. I have watched you. I was there, though you could not see me, when we healed you in the land of the Perdii."

"Why did you not show yourself?"

Riamfada grinned. "I thought I had when I left you my sword. Did you like it? It will never rust or need sharpening. It will be bright and keen for as long as you live, Conn."

"Aye, it is a fine weapon. But why did you not speak with me?"

"I am with the Seidh now, my friend. There are strict rules concerning contact with . . . mortals. We break them very rarely. But I asked if I could speak with you one last time."

"I'm glad you did."

"As am I. I wish I could tell you everything I know, Conn. It would gladden your heart and spare you much pain. But

I cannot. All I am allowed to say is this: Keep all your promises, no matter how small. Sometimes, like the pebble that brings the avalanche, something tiny can prove to be of immense power."

"I always keep my promises, little fish."

"Remember, Conn: no matter how small."

Conn laughed. "I will remember."

"So what are your plans now?"

"I have blacksmiths all over the Rigante lands making mail shirts. These I will give to warriors who will become part of a small, elite fighting force. I brought back stallions, big warhorses, and I am breeding a new herd of stronger mounts. Did you know I am the Long Laird's heir?"

"Aye. And I have seen the horses. They are beautiful."

"Beautiful?" snorted Conn. "They are magnificent. Used well, they will help us against the Stone army."

"You will need more than big horses, Conn."

"Aye, I will need a disciplined army, well supplied."

"You will not defeat them with the Rigante alone. You will need the Norvii, the Pannones, and all the other, smaller tribes."

Conn nodded. "This has been troubling me. All the lairds are singularly independent."

"They will need to be won over," said Riamfada, "some by flattery, some by profit, and some by war."

"I am not sure they will all follow me."

Riamfada sighed. "They will not follow you, Conn. But they will follow the king."

"King? You know we have no kings on this island. The last king was overthrown hundreds of years ago."

"Call yourself war chief, then, or whatever title you feel will unite the tribes. But ultimately you will be a king. Believe me, it is written in starlight on silver."

Conn sat back and put his arm around Riamfada's slender shoulder. "Is this what you wanted to tell me?"

"Keep your promises, Conn," whispered his friend. Riamfada rose smoothly and spread his arms. "Good-bye, my friend." The last words came like a remembered echo, and Conn was alone. He looked around and saw the Thagda standing at the edge of the clearing.

"It is time for you to return to the world of men, Connavar," he said.

Vorna awoke and shivered. It was cold in the bedroom. She felt strange, light-headed almost, and wondered if she was coming down with a chill. She sat up and pushed back the covers. The window was closed, but threads of brightness showed at the cracks in the shutters. Baby Banouin was sleeping still, and she could hear his breathing. Rising from the bed, she moved to the fireplace, stirring the coals and seeking a few glowing cinders to which she could add a little kindling. But the fire was dead. I should have banked it last night, she thought. Vorna had not stayed long at the feast. For the last few days she had been working hard, making herbal potions for families whose children had developed fevers. One babe had died, but she had managed to help at least five others. Wrapping a heavy shawl around her shoulders, she knelt before the dead fire, laid a small mound of tinder on the ash, and with flint and file struck sparks at it. Her cold fingers were clumsy, and she struggled to light the tinder. A moment of anger touched her. There was a time when she would merely have whispered a word of power to get a blaze to begin.

The tinder flared, startling her. A spark must have gone deep within it. Adding small pieces of kindling, she sat down and waited for it to catch before placing larger logs on it. Banouin stirred and gave a little cry. Vorna moved to the crib and stroked his brow. It was hot and sticky with sweat. Without thinking, she closed her eyes and sought out the infection. She knew instantly it had begun in the nasal membranes, and she followed its path down to his tiny lungs. There it was breeding furiously. His heart was beating fast, his lymphatic system struggling to cope with this awesome enemy. Vorna concentrated, boosting his system with her power, feeling the infection die away.

When she opened her eyes, his fever had gone. She lifted him from the crib. Vorna cuddled him close. "All is well now, little man," she said. "Your mam is here. All is well."

Then the shock hit her. She had healed him.

The power had returned. Holding Banouin close, she moved to a chair by the fire and sat down. She whispered the word. The fire died instantly. She spoke it again, and the flames roared back.

Banouin nuzzled at her. Opening her nightshirt, she held him at her breast. His contentment and hunger washed over her. When he had fed, she carried him out to the kitchen, where she changed his soiled diaper and cleaned him. Tired from the infection, he fell asleep again, and she returned him to his crib.

What had happened to her?

Moving out into the main room, Vorna snapped her fingers at the dead ash in the main hearth. Fire sprang up instantly. In the kitchen she poured dried oats into a pan, added salt and milk, and brought it back into the main room, hanging the pot over the fire. All the while she was thinking, focusing on this curious return to witchhood. The power felt natural within her, as if it had never been away, yet it had changed subtly. She could not identify the change. Perhaps it is not the power that has altered but the woman I have become, she thought.

She sensed a presence close by and was not surprised when she heard the tapping at the door. "Come in," she called.

The Morrigu materialized in the chair by the fire, holding out her wrinkled hands to the blaze. "A cold morning," said the Seidh. "And how are you today?"

"I am well. Would you care for some oats and honey?"

The Morrigu shook her ancient head. "Thank you, no. But it is good to find you in a welcoming mood."

Vorna smiled and moved to the hearth, where she stood stirring the hot oats and milk with a long wooden spoon. "I have not had the chance to thank you for delivering my babe," she called out. "That was a kind act."

The Morrigu pushed her finger into the boiling porridge. Lifting it clear, she sucked it. "Not enough salt," she said.

Vorna added another pinch and continued to stir. "Why did you save me?"

"Why should I not?" countered the old woman. "I can do as I wish. I can save, I can kill, I can curse, or I can bless. Perhaps it was a whim."

"Was it a whim also that made you return my powers?"

"It was a favor. I have changed my mind. I will join you for breakfast. It is a long time since I ate. Before you were born, in fact."

Vorna laughed. "Then you must be hungry."

The Morrigu held out her hand. A pottery jar full of fresh honey appeared there. "I have a sweet tooth," she said.

They ate their breakfast in silence by the fire, and when they were finished, the Morrigu waved her hand and the dishes and utensils disappeared. Vorna looked at the Old Woman. Her face was gray, the skin dry, her eyes cloudy. "Are you well?" she asked suddenly.

"Well enough," snapped the Morrigu.

"You mentioned a favor."

The Morrigu leaned back in her chair and closed her eyes. "Connavar asked the Thagda to return your powers. The Thagda agreed. The child certainly remembers his promises. Unusual in men, I find."

"What is it you want of him?" asked Vorna.

"Why should I want anything?"

"Come now," said Vorna, "even without powers I was not stupid. The Seidh avoid humankind. But not Connavar. You gave him his first knife; you healed him in the lands of the Perdii. You warned him of the danger to his lady. You took his friend's spirit to live among you rather than let it roam the dark. Why is he special to you?"

"I also sent a bear to rip his flesh," the Morrigu reminded her.

"Aye, you did, and I have spent a great deal of time thinking on that. In those first days in my cave I did everything to keep him alive. Even so he should not have lived. You held his soul in place. I know this now. Just as I know you goaded me to give up my power in order to save him. You did not want him dead. You need him. Why?"

"Such a clever girl, Vorna. It is why I have always liked you. Connavar is important to us. Not just for what he is but for what he represents. More than that I will not say. I will offer this advice to you, though. If you value your newfound friends, do not let them know your powers have returned. Continue to treat them with herbs and such. Let your powers be invisible to them. Mortals are so fickle with their favors."

"You do not like us much, do you?" said Vorna.

"I like some of you, my dear. Truly I do."

With that she disappeared.

The morning was bright and cold, and Fiallach had risen early, his eyes bleary from the night's excesses. He recalled the feast and the dark-haired Gwydia, whose company he had enjoyed. She was almost eighteen, and he remembered asking her why she had not yet wed. She told him the right man had not asked her. He shivered at the memory. Then he thought of Tae and how beautiful she had looked. Fiallach sighed, walked from the hut, and drew a bucket of cold water from the well outside. The sky was bright with the promise of the dawn. Fiallach splashed his face, then rubbed wet fingers through his long yellow hair. He stared for a moment at the Druagh mountains, tall and proud against the lightening sky. This is good land, he thought.

Few people were stirring at that early hour, and, pulling on his boots, Fiallach strolled through the settlement, back down to the feast area. The remains of the food had been gathered, and not a scrap remained. This was good practice, for if it had been left to lay, it would have encouraged wolves or bears to move down into the settlement.

"Good morning," said Gwydia, walking from behind the smithy. Fiallach turned. Her dark hair was bound now, and she was wearing a dress of sky blue and a woolen shawl the color of cream. Like him she could have enjoyed only around two hours of sleep, yet she looked fresh, her eyes bright.

"You are abroad early," he said.

"I always rise early. I like this time of day, watching the sun clear the mountains."

"So do I," he said. "Will you walk with me awhile?"

She smiled and unself-consciously took his arm. Together they crossed a bridge and strolled out of the settlement and up into the high meadow. In the distance Fiallach could see two eagles soaring high against the backdrop of the mountains. "It would be nice to be an eagle," she said, "don't you think?"

"I have never considered it," he admitted. But the thought was a fine one: spreading wings and flying high above the earth. They continued in silence for a while, then paused to watch the sunrise light the land.

Fiallach stood silently, feeling Gwydia's small hand in his own. He felt strange, then realized with a sudden shock that he was at peace.

"What are you thinking?" she asked him suddenly.

"That I am an angry man," he replied without thinking. The words surprised him.

"What are you angry about?"

He smiled. "At this moment I do not know, for the anger is gone."

"It is hard to be angry when one has seen the sun rise," she said.

"It seems to be true," he admitted. "I wonder why."

"Because it makes us feel so small and insignificant. It has been rising forever and will rise forever no matter what we do or do not do. All our problems are as nothing to the sun."

"Yes," he said. "I see that. I never saw it before."

She laughed. "You never watched a sunrise?"

"I have never watched one with you."

She blushed. Taking her hand, he raised it to his lips and kissed her fingers. For a moment they stood very still, then she took his arm. "Come down to my home," she said softly. "Mother will be preparing breakfast."

"Could I be the right man for you?" he asked her.

Her dark eyes looked into his eyes of bright blue. "You had best speak to my father," she told him.

"I shall. But I need to hear it from you."

"You are the right man," she said. "I knew it last night."

"You know that I am almost thirty-one. You do not think me too old?"

"Foolish man," she said with a smile. "Come and see my father."

Nanncumal the Smith was a dour man, but he had smiled widely when Fiallach had told him of his desire to wed his daughter. With Gwydia in the house, helping her mother set the table, Nanncumal and Fiallach had walked to the smithy. Nanncumal stirred the ashes to life in the forge and added fresh fuel. "She is a fine girl," said the smith. "Strong, loyal—a little too quick with her wit, though."

"You seem unsurprised, sir," said Fiallach.

"She told us last night. I was only worried that she might be disappointed."

"Last night?"

"The ways of women, young man, are completely beyond a man's understanding. She came home more excited than I have ever seen her. Said she had met the most wonderful man. I got up in the night and saw her sitting by the window. I asked her what she was doing. She said she was watching for you. I have never known her like this. To be honest, it is good to see. She has turned down several fine young men. Said she was waiting for the right one. You treat her well, now."

"You have my word on that," said Fiallach.

"Then we will speak no more of it." With the forge fire blazing, Nanncumal moved to a shelf at the rear of the building, retrieving a thin-necked copper jug. Passing it to Fiallach, he said, "It is early in the day, but I feel a toast is in order." Fiallach hefted the jug and took a deep drink of Uisge. "Man, that is good," he said, handing the jug to Nanncumal.

"Twenty years old. I have been saving it for just such an occasion. Here's to you and Gwydia." The smith drank deeply, then stoppered the jug and returned it to the shelf. "While you are here," he said, "there is something I must check." He grinned and, taking a length of twine, ran it around Fiallach's enormous shoulders.

"What are you doing?" asked the big man.

"You'll know soon enough," said Nanncumal, marking the twine with his thumb. "Yes, that should be about right. It has been worrying me," he said.

"Is this some Three Streams marriage ritual?"

"No. Have a little patience, young man. You will find out when we see Connavar later this morning. For now let us go eat."

Two hours later Fiallach, Nanncumal, and his son Govannan strolled across to the house of Connavar. Tae was not present; she was visiting Connavar's mother, Meria. As Fiallach entered the house, he saw Conn, his stepfather Ruathain, and the Druid Brother Solstice. Fiallach's eyes rested on Ruathain, and he felt his pulse quicken. The man was big, and powerful, and Fiallach's fighting spirit flared. Ruathain looked at him and grinned. He, too, felt it. It was as if they were two proud bulls with a herd at stake.

They shook hands, measuring each other. Fiallach knew of

Ruathain's reputation as a warrior. He had been first swordsman for almost two decades. He wondered what the man would be like with his fists. Their eyes met. "My son speaks highly of you," said Ruathain. Then he walked back to stand beside Conn.

In the silence that followed Connavar rose from his seat and moved to a chest at the rear of the room. Opening it, he pulled clear a shirt of shining mail. Fiallach gazed at it with open envy. It was beautiful, the rings small but perfectly formed. It handled like heavy cloth. Connavar handed the mail shirt to Ruathain, then produced another and passed it to Govannan. Then he lifted a third and walked across the room, giving it to Fiallach.

"Put them on," said Connavar.

"Now you see why I was worried about the size of your shoulders," said Nanncumal. "Conn told me you were roughly the same size as his father. In fact, you are a little bigger, but I think you will find it comfortable."

Fiallach lifted the mail shirt over his head. It was heavy. Sliding his arms into it, he settled it into place. The armored mail reached to his knees. It had been split at the front and back to allow ease of movement for a rider. The sleeves were short, finishing a little above the elbow, and there was a hood, which Fiallach pulled into place. He had never worn such a magnificent piece. His thick fingers ran over the mail rings. They would stop any arrow and protect a warrior from thrusting knives or slashing swords. It would take an ax to cleave them. He looked around the room. Ruathain and Govannan were similarly garbed now.

"It is my intention," said Conn, "to create a fighting force for the protection of our lands. Each man will swear a blood oath to follow my orders without question. Eventually there will be five hundred of us, each with a warhorse. When that day comes, you three will be my captains, that is, if you agree to the oath."

"Who are we to fight?" asked Fiallach. "We are at peace with all our neighbors."

"The enemy is coming," said Conn. "You may trust me on this. The Stone army will cross the water, and then you will see slaughter like never before. We must be prepared or we will fall like all the tribes across the sea. I have seen them, Fiallach. They are deadly, their army nearly invincible. When they stand and fight, they lock shields, creating a wall of bronze. I have watched Keltoi tribesmen hurl themselves against this wall and be cut down in the thousands by short stabbing swords." He fell silent for a moment, and his eyes took on a haunted look. "And when they have destroyed the armies, they move across the land, taking thousands into slavery. Except the children: They are slaughtered. When the land is cleared, they bring in settlers from their own lands and build towns of stone. In order to defeat them we must find a new way to fight."

Govannan spoke. He had changed in the last year, his face losing the roundness of youth. His dark eyes were deep-set and his face almost gaunt, and he sported no beard. "If they are coming, as you say, Conn, then how will five hundred riders succeed where armies of thousands have failed?"

"We will not succeed alone. There will also be armies, footmen, cavalry, archers. The Stone soldiers are grouped into six units that together create a panther. The head is the elite fighting force, the advance unit. Then there are the claws. Lastly there is the belly. This last group is responsible for protecting supply lines. The Stone army, being in hostile territory, must be constantly supplied with food: grain, salt, meat, dried fruit." Conn smiled grimly. "That is where my riders will be best used: disrupting their supplies, attacking their convoys. They call themselves panthers. We will be the Iron Wolves, hunting them as a pack. We will also harry and terrorize those who supply them. For make no mistake, they will be supplied by Keltoi chieftains. That is their method. When they fought the Perdii, they were supplied by the Gath and the Ostro. It will be the same here. They will land in the far south and probably attack the Norvii. If they follow the same pattern as before, they will first seek to befriend the Cenii and other, smaller tribes. These tribes, which have long held grievances against the Norvii, will sell grain to the Stone army. Once they have a base, they will set up their own supply routes." He looked around the room, scanning their faces. "Now," he said, "do I have your blood oaths?"

"You have mine," said Ruathain.

"And mine," said Govannan.

Fiallach stood silently for a moment. On another day he might have refused. But today, with the joy of Gwydia flowing through him, he smiled. "I'll follow you, Connavar," he said. "To the death."

Maccus was tired. He had spent weeks riding the lands of the northern Rigante with Connavar, visiting minor chieftains, touring farms and communities, visiting silver and copper mines and fishing villages on the coast. His back ached from hours in the saddle every day, and his mind reeled with weariness. Connavar was inexhaustible, full of the energy of youth. Close to fifty, Maccus was looking forward to stepping aside once Connavar took on the role of laird. He did not doubt that the young man would want his own first counsel, probably his father, Ruathain.

Maccus was thinking about moving to a small cabin high in the Druagh mountains. He had built it with his wife some twenty years before. They had enjoyed many happy times there before the Long Laird had summoned him to Old Oaks and offered him the role of first counsel. At first his wife, Leia, had found Old Oaks too busy and noisy for her liking, and they had moved some miles out of the settlement, taking over a small farm, which Leia had run. As the years had passed, the farm had produced good profits, which had become even greater when Leia had begun to breed pigs.

Smoked ham was a rare delicacy in the highlands, and Leia's was the best Maccus had ever tasted.

He rose from his bed and groaned as a stab of pain lanced through his arthritic shoulder. The bed was too soft for him. Outside he could hear the members of the household moving around and smell the smoky aroma of frying bacon. He heard Connavar's voice, then the laughter of some women.

Moving to the window, he pushed it open and gazed out on the rocky landscape and the wide waters of Snake Loch. The fishermen were already out, their nets cast and their small boats bobbing on the gray waves. Maccus shivered. A cold wind was blowing from the north. It had been a nine-hour ride to the Snake, and after it Connavar had sat late into the night talking to the chieftain.

Maccus pulled on his tunic, leggings, and boots and walked out into the long hall. There were some twenty people present, including Connavar, all seated around a twelve-foot rectangular bench table.

"How did you sleep?" asked Arna, the one-eyed chieftain.

"Like a babe," he answered, sitting down alongside the man. Maccus had been in the skirmish twenty years before where Arna had lost his eye. It had been a ferocious fight against a large group of Sea Raiders. Maccus himself had killed the leader, a giant of a man wielding a long double-headed ax.

"So," Arna said good-naturedly, "you think this child a suitable leader for the Rigante?" Connavar laughed with genuine good humor.

Maccus smiled. "Young body, old head," he replied. "And better him than a senile old fool like you."

Arna grinned widely. "You're not so young yourself, Maccus. You recall that bastard with the ax?"

"I do indeed."

"Think you could take him now?"

Maccus thought about it, recalling the awesome power of

the man and the mound of Rigante dead around him. "No," he said sadly. "No, I couldn't."

Arna looked crestfallen. "Of course you could," he insisted. "You're only as old as you feel."

Maccus gazed into the chieftain's one good eye and saw fear there. Age makes fools of us all, he thought. He forced a smile. "Aye, you are right. It might take me a little longer now, mind."

Arna chuckled. "Never give in, Maccus. That's the secret." He fell silent for a moment, and Maccus tensed, knowing what was coming. "I was sorry to hear about Leia. She was a fine woman."

The hurt began again, starting in the pit of his belly and moving up to tighten his throat. "Thank you," he said. A young woman appeared alongside him, laying a bowl of thick fish soup on the table, along with a plate of freshly baked bread. Maccus thanked her, broke off a piece of bread, and began to eat.

It was midmorning before he and Connavar left Snake Loch to begin the journey home. The ponies were still tired from the day before, and they rode slowly along the mountain trails.

They stopped to rest their mounts at noon and, sheltered from the wind by a huge boulder, lit a fire. "Arna spoke very highly of you," said Connavar. "Said you were the finest of men."

"He was always given to exaggeration."

"Told me how you won the battle by killing the leader."

"It wasn't a battle, Connavar. Just a skirmish." Maccus wrapped his cloak more tightly around him and lifted his hood over his short-cropped receding hair.

"Why did you not wish to be laird?"

Maccus had known this question would come and still had no real answer to it. He shrugged. "I thought of it. Maybe ten years ago I would have fought for it. I don't know, Connavar.

That's the truth. Leia used to tell me that I was too quiet, that I didn't enjoy the company of men or women. It wasn't really true. I just preferred hers to theirs." He glanced up. "What about you? Why did *you* wish to be laird?"

"I have seen the evil to come," said Connavar. "I have to fight it."

"A driven man. I see. Perhaps that is my answer also. I am not driven. And I am looking forward to riding the high country and returning to the cabin we built."

"What do you mean?"

"When you choose your own first counsel."

Connavar laughed. "I want no one new, Maccus. I will need you to guide me."

Conn's comment shocked the older man, and he was surprised to find that his heart had lifted. He had not realized how good it felt to be needed. "What about Ruathain?"

"In some ways he and I are too alike. We are impulsive. No. Will you stay?"

"I don't know. I'll need time to think on it."

"Good enough."

"I'll be fifty in the summer. And already my bones are beginning to ache."

Connavar added wood to the fire. "You were kind to Arna back there. The man is terrified of growing old."

Maccus nodded. "He was a bonny fighter, and like all young men, he never believed that it would end. The old to us were a race apart. I think in some ways we believed that people *chose* to grow old. We were young, we were mighty, and we were mighty stupid. The years stretched out ahead of us, full of promise. We sat often at night complaining about the old men who ruled us. They were tired, worn out, timid. We talked of all the things we would do when our day came." Maccus laughed with genuine good humor. "Now I glance across at the young men sitting around campfires, and I know what they are saying. As to Arna, it might have been different had he had children. Without them a man feels that death is a true ending."

"You have children?"

"No. Leia lost three bairns. That is how I know."

"You have told me what it was like to be young, my friend," said Conn. "How does it feel to be old?"

Maccus thought about it. Then he smiled. "Two days ago your pony kicked out, catching your shin. How is the bruise?"

"It has gone."

"Had the pony kicked me, I would have carried that bruise for maybe two weeks. When it is wet, my shoulder aches and my arm becomes slow. In winter, I find the wind cuts through me and I need to wear two shirts. In short I am slower and more fragile than once I was. I think it is this fragility which affects me most. It eats at the confidence. Yes, I was kind to Arna. If I faced that Sea Wolf today, he would cut me down in a matter of heartbeats. That is hard for me to admit, for like Ruathain, I was first swordsman."

"And now you are first counsel."

"Aye. And I'll admit it is a role I enjoy."

Sound from the left caused Maccus to jerk his head. Pain flared from his aching shoulder. A black bear was moving slowly down the hillside toward a stream. It paused and glanced in their direction. Conn rose smoothly and drew his sword. Then he walked slowly out to stand some ten paces from the fire. Maccus drew his own blade and moved to stand beside him.

The bear watched them for a little while, then ambled on.

Maccus glanced at Connavar. The young man's face was pale, but he had stood his ground.

"Just as well that he wasn't hungry," said Maccus. "Otherwise he might have gone for us."

"That would have been the last mistake he ever made," said Connavar.

* * *

Tae had not settled well at the fortress settlement of Old Oaks. Conn was away for so much of the time, talking with the fifty-six clan chieftains and minor lairds who would, upon the retirement of the Long Laird, form the lything. This was an ancient custom by which the chieftains could vote for a new laird. It had been instituted four hundred years before, after the overthrow of the last king, the legendary Gallis the Cruel. Conn was by no means certain of full support and was doing his best to woo the waverers.

Those long periods when he was away were proving dull for Tae, even though she rode most days and learned the mountain trails and narrow passes of the Druagh mountains. The land was exquisite, and she loved the rugged beauty of the highland, the craggy slopes, the towering peaks. But she was young and newly wed, and she missed her husband terribly. More, she feared, than he missed her.

She did not doubt his love, but he was a man obsessed, and in truth, that frightened her a little. As did this return to the settlement where her mother had known such pain. Tae had many happy childhood memories of Old Oaks: riding her pony alongside her father, playing with the other children on the slopes beyond the wooden walls. But the last memory was one of her mother screaming with anger and anguish and running from the long hall, tears streaming from her face. Tae, like her mother, had never forgiven the Long Laird for the hurt he had caused and found his company difficult to take.

On her first morning here he had called her to his private rooms. She had stood quietly and listened as he spoke of his grief and his love for Llysona. But the words did not touch her, and she stared at the tired old man, waiting patiently for him to finish his confession so that she could return to Conn.

"I never stopped loving you, lass. Or your mother," he said.

She wanted to ask if he had loved Llysona as he was rutting with his whore, but she refrained and said nothing. "It would be a help to know you forgave me," he said. This last statement was too much, and she felt anger melting her resolve to be polite.

"But I do not," she told him. "You broke my mother's heart, then sent her away. Had it not happened, she would still be alive. Are we done here, for I wish to go riding with my husband."

"We are done here," he said sorrowfully. She bowed to him, swung on her heel, and left the room. They had not spoken privately since.

The days and weeks and months since had seen her emotions flow from loneliness to heady joy and back again as Conn traveled and returned all too briefly.

Today Conn had assured her they would go riding. Spring was here, the days were growing warmer, and Ruathain, who had arrived at the settlement with cattle to sell, had told them of a high lake nearby with a vista of surpassing beauty. Tae was looking forward to riding there and spending the afternoon alone with Conn.

Dressed in a tunic of green wool edged with dark leather, riding breeches, and long boots, she strolled the palisade, staring out to the south for sign of Conn. He had ridden out early to see Arbonacast and Parax and her cousin Legat, who were tending the pony herds. With the increase in daylight the breeding season was under way, and Conn was anxious to check on his stallions.

As Tae strolled the battlements, she saw Brother Solstice climbing to the wall. The black-bearded Druid waved and smiled. "How goes it, lovely lady?" he asked her.

"I am well, Brother. And you?"

"Glad to see the sun shine at last. It has been a hard winter," he said.

"Aye," she agreed. "Ruathain was telling me that a great number of cattle were lost."

He nodded. "It has been bad, especially for the northern

Pannones. The lakes froze, and they were unable to fish. There is some talk of starvation among them. The Long Laird has sent three wagons of grain to Shining Water. He is a kind man." His dark eyes held to her gaze, but she was not taking the bait. Tae was not even close to forgiving the laird and had no wish to discuss his merits.

"It is said you are traveling south, Brother. Are you leaving us for good?"

"No—at least I hope not. The gathering of Druids is at the River Gath this year. There is much to discuss. I am looking forward to it. It is some years since I crossed the water, and the Gath, I recall, are a friendly people."

"We will miss you," she said.

"It is nice of you to say that, Tae. I fear the Long Laird will miss me more. He has few close friends."

Tae took a deep breath. "What he has, he has earned," she said. "He betrayed my mother. I see no reason to forgive him."

"Forgiveness needs no reason, Tae. What happened between the laird and your mother was for them to untangle. Not you. People do foolish things. It is in our nature. He meant no harm to Llysona and certainly none to you. Llysona stayed at Seven Willows because she chose to, not because he sent her away. Her death should not be nailed to his conscience."

"Did he send you to me?"

"No. He would be affronted to know that I am speaking on his behalf."

"I have no feelings for him, save of disgust," Tae told the Druid. "I will not change." She stared toward the south, willing Conn to ride into view. "He walked the tree with my mother. He made vows and broke them. She never forgave him. Neither will I."

"She was not a forgiving woman," said Brother Solstice. "It was a great flaw in her character."

"I'll thank you not to criticize my mother," Tae said sharply. Swinging away, she strode from the battlements and across the open ground toward the hall.

◇ **15** ◇

ORNA WAS TROUBLED. Her sleep had been plagued by
harsh and vivid dreams. She had seen a young man, dark-
haired and pale-eyed, and several other men with him. The
young man had been given a sword and a bow. The weapons
were dripping with blood. As each drop struck the floor, it became a coin, bright and golden.

Vorna had awakened feeling tired, drained of energy.
Rising, she had changed and fed Banouin, then carried him to
Meria's house. Ruathain's wife had promised to look after the
child as Vorna moved through the settlement, giving potions
to children sick with the fever. She had taken the Morrigu's
advice and told no one of the return of her powers, though she
used them constantly.

Her last visit was to the home of an elderly man with deep
belly pain. She found he was dying of a cancer that had bur-
rowed its way throughout his frail body. It was too advanced
for her to heal, but she took away the man's pain, then drew
his wife aside and told her of his impending death. The
woman took it stoically and thanked her for her efforts, but
Vorna could see the torment in her eyes.

As she was returning to Meria's home, a vision struck her.
At first it was as though she had gone blind. A terrible darkness descended over her eyes, and she staggered. This was
followed by a blinding light, and she saw in her mind's eye a
tree oozing blood. A young lion, its back scaled with silver

armor, was attacking an old bear. As they were fighting, a white dove flew by. The lion slashed its claws through the air. The dove was smashed to the ground. Back in the undergrowth six wolves were waiting. The wolves were large, their eyes red and gleaming. Like the lion, their upper backs were covered with silver scales. As the blood flowed from the tree, it sank into the earth, which began to writhe and twist. The earth parted, and newborn calves struggled from the blood-covered mud to stand quivering in the clearing. Vorna watched as the wolves licked their lips and eyed the calves. Then the vision passed, and her sight returned.

Vorna sat down below Eldest Tree and tried to analyze the vision. She knew with dread certainty that it was a prophecy and was anxious to unravel its secrets. The bear was a symbol linked with Connavar. Yet Connavar was not old. It could not be he. She remembered her first dream. Blood becoming coin. Blood coin. Weregild. The payment made by the transgressor to the victim's family in order to halt a feud.

It still made no sense. Instead of walking to Meria's house, Vorna went to her own home and sat quietly by the fire.

An old bear.

Could it be the Long Laird? She dismissed the thought. The laird was more likely to be represented in a vision as a bull, the king of the herd. And who were the armored wolves? Soldiers of Stone, perhaps, or Sea Raiders? Perhaps the bear was merely a representation of the land itself under attack. Vorna did not think so. It did not feel right. The two visions were linked in some way, and she focused her memory on the first: the young man with the bow of blood. She did not recognize his face or the faces of the other six men.

Six men. Six wolves. She knew she was inching closer to an answer. Sitting very quietly, Vorna relaxed her mind. The bow was dripping blood that became weregild, blood payment. Then she remembered Ruathain riding to the land of the Pannones to offer such payment to end a blood feud.

Ruathain. The old bear.

It was then that she realized the wolves were not armored at all. They were scaled like fish. The fisher people of Shining Water. And then it all fell into place. The Pannones of that region had suffered terribly during the winter. A young warrior had therefore been primed to fight Ruathain. In that way a new blood feud would be established, and Ruathain might once again offer cattle and ponies to halt it. Hence the calves born in the blood-drenched mud.

Vorna recalled that the Fisher Laird had five grown sons. Together they were the six wolves of her vision. And these wolves had sent one of their own out to die not for glory or justice but for gain. She shivered.

Ruathain was not at Three Streams. He had ridden out to the Long Laird's fortress settlement to sell cattle. There was no way to reach him.

This in itself made the prophecy baffling. Vorna knew that it did not depict some distant event but was waiting even now to unfold. Therefore, what was the purpose of the vision, since she could do nothing to alter the events it foresaw? Visions did not come to torment a seer. They always, in her experience, had some purpose.

Vorna sighed. She did not relish the prospect of the long ride to Old Oaks.

Connavar was feeling content as he guided his piebald pony up through the hills on the swifter route back to Old Oaks. The mares were coming into heat, and he felt sure his stallions would sire fine colts. It was now a question of patience. Arbon, Parax, and Tae's cousin Legat were tending the three herds, and it would be a further eleven months before the first foals arrived and almost another two years before the new horses would be fully ready for war training. In the meantime Conn had sent merchants south across the water to buy Gath mounts and bring them back.

Guiding his pony out into the open, Conn enjoyed the warmth of the spring sun on his back. It felt good to be alive today, especially with the prospect of a ride with Tae out to the lake Ruathain had spoken of. He had told her he would be back soon after noon, and with this new route Arbon had described, he should make it with time to spare.

As he rode, he considered the coming lything. Many of the chieftains had promised him allegiance. This was largely based, he knew, on his fame. His deeds, few though they were in his own eyes, had created a legend among his people. And legends, he now realized, were handy tools in the pursuit of power. Of the fifty-six chieftains and lesser lairds eligible to vote, Conn believed he had won over at least thirty. And so far no one else had declared a strong interest in the role of laird.

Conn rode on, urging the pony up a slope and riding along the crest. At the edge of the trees to his right was a group of huts, and beyond them a shallow bowl of grassland still dotted with clumps of old snow. Around two hundred of the Long Laird's famous black and white cattle were grazing there. Conn paused and stared at them. Soon they would be his, and he felt he should make himself known to the herders who lived there. Glancing at the sky, he believed he had time for a short visit and swung the pony.

As he approached the first hut, a woman walked out. Conn's breath caught in his throat as the sun shone on her golden hair.

It was Arian.

He felt his mouth go dry, his heart beginning to race. She looked up and saw him, and a wide smile made her face all the more beautiful. The pony continued to walk until it was almost upon her. Conn tugged on the reins.

"You are looking very fine, Conn," said Arian.

"As are you," he managed to say. "Who lives here?"

"Casta and I and three other families."

"Where is Casta? I would like to speak with him."

"Two of the boys are tending the cattle. Casta and the other men have gone down to Old Oaks for supplies. Will you step down for a moment? We have a little cider left."

Conn slid from the saddle and followed her into the small hut. There was a roughly made bed of pine against the southern wall and a bench table with seating for four. A threadbare cowhide rug was spread before the small hearth, its surface pitted with cinder burns. Arian poured him a cup of cider, and as she passed it to him, their hands touched. Conn felt himself blushing.

"Are you happy now, Conn?" she asked him.

"Aye. And you?"

She smiled and moved to the fire, half kneeling, half bending, to add logs to the blaze. Conn gazed at her, remembering their times together and the enormous love he had felt. He had thought her vanished from his feelings but knew now that that was not so. He loved Tae with all his heart, but his body trembled at the closeness of Arian. He tried to quell the arousal she inspired in him. "I must go," he said, backing toward the door.

She moved closer, so close that he could smell her hair.

"I am very sorry for the hurt I caused you," she said. "I have thought of little else ever since."

"It is in the past now," he heard himself saying. He saw tears in her eyes and instinctively put his arms around her.

"I was so frightened when they said you were dying. And so stupid. I never stopped loving you, Conn. Never."

Closing his eyes, he kissed the top of her head. It was warm in the hut, and flame shadows flickered on the bare walls. Her arms circled his neck. For a moment only he tried to resist, then he dipped his head and kissed her. The years rolled away, and he was fifteen again, holding close to the first woman he had ever loved.

Thoughts of the world outside faded from memory.

All that existed now was this room, this fire, and the beckoning bed in the corner.

A big man and heavy, Ruathain was always considerate to his mounts. He had dismounted at the foot of the rocky slope and led his gelding on the climb. Tae followed his lead, though he told her it was not necessary. She was light enough for the pony to bear her. Tae smiled at him and ignored his advice.

Ruathain was angry at Conn as he climbed. The vista he was to show Tae should best be shared by lovers, not the husband's father. He felt awkward and embarrassed. He had once brought Meria to this spot, and they had made love on the hillside. When Conn had not appeared and with the afternoon fading fast, Tae had asked Ruathain to show her the lake. He had tried to refuse politely, but she would have none of it. He glanced back at her. She was a beautiful woman, there was no doubt of that, her dark hair flowing free, her smile infectious. He well understood the pressure Conn was under, but any man who would rather spend time *watching* stallions and mares rather than *imitating* stallions and mares needed a hefty whack alongside the head.

He crested the rise and moved out onto level ground. His chest was aching from the climb, and he felt a small stab of pain. Tae came alongside him, and the two of them stared in wonder at the open landscape. Below them a long lake glittered like a sword blade. Small yellow flowers were growing in profusion on the hillsides, and in the distance the tree-covered hills looked like giant bison grazing below the snow-capped mountains. The air was crisp and cool, the sky a clear, brilliant blue.

"It is so beautiful," whispered Tae. She sighed with pleasure. Just beyond the lake was a circle of golden standing stones.

Ruathain pointed at them. "According to legend, they were once giants, but they offended Taranis. One night, as they met to discuss their war with the gods, Taranis appeared in their midst and turned them to stone."

"Do you believe the story?"

Ruathain shrugged. "No, but it is a nice tale. There was a race here long before us. I think they crafted the circle."

"The Ugly Folk?" she said with a smile.

"No, even before them. To the north of here there is a valley. A farmer was plowing there when he discovered a buried wall. He and his son tried to tear up the stones, but they were too large. Each one weighed many tons. Yet they had been placed one atop the other."

"How long was the wall?"

"No one knows. The farmer tried to dig around it, discovered he couldn't, and abandoned the field."

"And no one has been there to find out?"

"What would be the point?" asked Ruathain. "Of what use is a buried wall?"

"There might be artifacts, clues to the people who built it. I shall hire men and dig it out myself," she said.

They rode down to the lakeside. Ruathain lit a fire, and they shared a meal of roasted ham and hard-boiled eggs washed down with cold water from the lake. "I am so glad we came here," said Tae. "Did you ever bring Meria?"

"Yes," he said, feeling himself blush at the memory. She was well mannered enough to let the matter drop, and that pleased him.

"Tell me about Conn," she said. "Was he always so serious?"

Ruathain felt on safer ground here. He shook his head. "He was a bonny lad, given to pranks and such. Good-hearted, though. I never saw him torment another child or laugh at another's misfortune. But he was easily hurt in those days. Perhaps children are. They are more open. He thought his father was a coward, which was not true. This fact drove him to prove himself. Once, when he was very young, he ran away to the woods to kill a wolf. I found him sitting in the bushes, a knife in his hand and an old pot on his head for a helm. It was getting dark when I found him, and he was terrified, though he tried not to show it. He was a good lad. Still is."

"And he fought the bear," she prompted.

"Aye. He wouldn't leave his friend. It was a grand deed, and I wish it had never happened."

"Why?" she asked, surprised. "He survived, and it made him famous."

"It did that. But it has all but destroyed Braefar. Both boys changed that day. Conn became the hero. But Wing . . ." Ruathain let out a deep sigh. "No one ever blamed him for not fighting the bear. He was young and unarmed. He watched the fight, saw his brother ripped apart. And afterward he felt everyone thought him weak. No one did. But it has colored his life since. I think he blames Conn. I have tried talking to him . . ." He shrugged and fell silent for a moment. "Now he is angry and hurt by Gwydia's marriage to Fiallach. He loved her himself, and I thought they would be wed. But Meria told me she became bored by his constant complaining that everyone was against him, that no one understood him. That was bad enough, but to marry the man who shamed him at the games. Oh, that hurt him badly." He forced a smile. "Anyway, you did not come here to listen to me prattle about my family."

"Nonsense," she told him. "It is my family, too. Wing will change again when he finds a true love."

He shook his head. "I don't think so."

"And what of Bran? You don't speak much of him."

"I daren't," he said conspiratorially. "He is my pride and joy. To show my feelings too much would damage Wing even more. He's a grand lad, is Bran. Fearless. Yet a rascal. The girls love him, and I fear he leads them on."

"Did you do that when you were young?"

"No," he said. Leaning back against a boulder, he stared out over the glistening water. "No, I fell in love early, with

Meria. As did my friend Varaconn. She married him. It was a great love match. I don't think she has ever quite recovered from his death. Strangely enough, I don't think I have. I loved him, too. Closest friend I ever had. It is a great sadness to me that Conn never knew him. It is so easy for people to praise or condemn. I am a fine swordsman. Therefore, I am a hero. I become a brave man. Yet where is the bravery without fear? I have never feared a battle. Varaconn did. He trembled with fright. Yet he was there. Beside me. He overcame his fear. That, to me, is the greatest courage." He looked at her and chuckled. "Whisht, woman, I am beginning to prattle. And the sun is going down. We'd best be getting back."

Leaning toward him, she kissed his cheek. "You are a good man, Ruathain. I am glad you are my father now."

"Aye, it pleases me, too," he said.

They rode in silence for a while. Tae unrolled her cloak and threw it about her shoulders, for the temperature was dropping.

Ruathain was feeling the cold, too. His left arm was particularly painful, and he clenched and unclenched his fist. The ham had given him indigestion, and there was a tightness in his chest as he rode. He took several deep breaths, which seemed to ease the pain.

Tae rode alongside him. "There are some people up ahead," she told him. Ruathain peered through the gloom. Four men were standing by the edge of the trees. One held a bow. "Probably hunters," he said, "though they'll catch nothing now. Sun's almost gone."

They moved closer to the men. There was something about the bowman that tugged at Ruathain's memory. But his eyesight was not what it had been, and in the gathering dusk he could not yet make out the man's face.

When they were within fifteen paces the bowman notched an arrow to the string. Ruathain recognized him. He was the young man from the Pannone fishing village, the one who would not accept that the feud had ended.

Instantly he drew his sword. The young man took aim. One of his comrades moved too close to him as he loosed his shaft, seeming to nudge him. The arrow flashed past Ruathain's head. Ruathain kicked his pony into a run and threw himself from the saddle. The young assassin was notching a second arrow as Ruathain loomed over him. The young man looked up and in a moment of sheer terror saw Ruathain's sword just before it smashed through his skull. Ruathain whirled, but the other three men had run away into the woods.

He gazed down at the dead youth. "You idiot!" he stormed, kicking the body. "What a waste of life."

He turned, and his blood froze.

Tae was lying on the ground just beyond the standing ponies. Ruathain ran to her, dropping to her side. Her face was very still. She could have been sleeping except for the black-shafted arrow jutting from her chest. There was very little blood. With trembling hand Ruathain touched her throat, praying for a pulse. There was nothing.

He lifted her to a sitting position, cradling her head and talking to her, his mind reeling with the awesome knowledge that she was dead. This bright, loving young woman had had her life stolen by a vengeful man who did not even know her.

It was worse than any nightmare Ruathain had ever experienced. He closed his eyes and stroked her hair and several times felt for the pulse he knew would not be beating.

Then he let out a terrible cry of anguish that echoed through the woods.

And the sun fell.

As Conn came in sight of the fortress, outlined in moonlight against the darkening sky, he saw a lone rider far below. She was wearing a hooded cloak, but the hood had fallen back, revealing long black and silver hair. Conn heeled the pony into a run and called out to her. At first she did not hear him, then she swung in the saddle and hauled on the reins.

He rode up alongside her. "Vorna. I thought it was you. What brings you to Old Oaks?"

"Your father is in danger." Vorna told him of the vision. They rode together toward the hilltop town.

"You think Ruathain is the old bear and that this . . . Fisher Laird will send men to kill him?"

"That is how I interpret the vision." As they came closer to the town, he realized she had not smiled or said anything of warmth to him. Perhaps it was just that she was tired after a long and grueling ride.

"And is this how visions always come?" he asked her. "In dream symbols? Wolves, bears, doves?"

"Not always. Sometimes I will see a scene most clearly, Connavar." Her dark eyes met his for a fraction of a second, and he felt cold inside. She knew.

"It will not happen again, Vorna," he said softly, feeling the shame.

"Your life is yours to lead, Connavar. It is not for me to judge you."

"And yet you do judge me."

She sighed. "Yes, I do. Your wife is a fine woman and deserves better from her man. At this moment she is probably waiting for . . ." Vorna fell silent, then pulled on the reins. Her pony came to a halt. Conn stared at the witch, for it seemed her shoulders had sagged and she was swaying in the saddle. Steering his pony in close, he reached out to her. "No!" she said suddenly. "Don't touch me, Conn! Oh, no!"

"What is it?"

She looked at him then, and in her eyes was a depth of sorrow that filled him with fear. "I did not . . . fully . . . interpret the vision." Vorna dismounted and almost staggered as she moved to the roadside and sat down.

Conn jumped from the saddle and ran to her, grabbing her arm. "Tell me! Is the Big Man hurt?"

"No, but the dove died."

"I know that. You told me. The lion struck it with his paw. What happened to Ruathain?" He shook her, but she stayed silent for a moment, and he could tell she was gathering her strength. Patience was not one of his virtues, but he sat quietly, watching her. Vorna looked at him, then took his hand.

"I have no words to make this more gentle, Connavar. The dove was Tae. She was riding with Ruathain when they attacked. An arrow pierced her heart."

He heard what she said, but the words seemed to have no meaning. "Tae was riding with Ruathain and has been hurt?" he heard himself say.

"She is dead, Conn. Killed."

"This cannot be! You are wrong. I promised her we would go riding. She is angry with me. That is all. Stop saying these things." Panic made his hands tremble. "Are you punishing me for Arian? Is that it?"

She shook her head and struggled to her feet. "I have been cruel at times in my life, Conn. I could never be that cruel. Ruathain is bringing her body back to Old Oaks."

Conn rose unsteadily. There was a roaring in his ears, and his limbs had no strength. Words whispered up from the recesses of his memory.

"Keep all your promises, no matter how small. Sometimes, like the pebble that brings the avalanche, something tiny can prove to be of immense power."

"I always keep my promises, little fish."

"Remember, Conn, no matter how small."

"No matter how small," he whispered. He fell to his knees, his head in his hands. Vorna knelt alongside him, her thin arms around his shoulders.

"Come, Connavar, let us go to meet her."

"I broke my promise, Vorna. I broke it."

"Come," she said, drawing him to his feet.

The Fisher Laird sat in his hall, his sons around him at the long supper table. There was little conversation, and the laird drank heavily, cup after cup of strong ale. "There'll be no weregild now," said Vor, his eldest son.

The Fisher Laird stared into his cup and shivered. Then he glanced across at Vor. The hulking young man was disappointed, and his flat ugly face looked sullen. The laird shivered again and cast his gaze along the men at the table. His sons. He had once had high hopes for them all, that they would be strong men, Pannone warriors to be admired. But they were not strong men. Oh, aye, they were physically powerful, but they lived their lives in his shadow. He drained his cup. The ale was making him melancholy. He looked back at Vor. "How could you cause him to kill the girl?"

"That's a little unfair," said Vor. "He had a big target directly in front of him. I nudged him to make him miss. You didn't want Ruathain dead. You wanted more of his cattle and ponies. The arrow could have gone anywhere. It was just ill fortune."

"But it didn't go anywhere," snapped the Fisher Laird, his big hands cradling the ale cup. One of the three lanterns guttered and died, making the hall even more gloomy. Another of his sons moved across to it, lifting it from the wall bracket.

The laird went to refill his cup, found the jug beside it empty, and pushed himself to his feet. He was a big man with flat features and deep-set eyes. "Only the fool was supposed to die," he said. He swore loudly and hurled his cup against the far wall. Then, carrying the empty jug, he strode to the back of the hall and refilled it from a barrel. Hefting the jug, he drank deeply, the amber liquid running down his silver beard and drenching the front of his tunic. His heart was heavy, and he was more than a little frightened. Had he broken his *geasa*? He was not sure. And Maggria the Seer had left the settlement on the morning the fool had gone out with his bow. No one knew where she had gone. *"Let not one of your deeds break a woman's heart."* For most of his life the *geasa* had been a subject of dark humor. He had been an ugly child and an uglier man, not the kind of man women fell for. His wife had married him only for his position and had never, as far as he knew, loved him. Nor he her, come to that. She had borne him five sons and then announced that she would like a house high in the hills. The Fisher Laird had built it for her, and she had moved away. Truth to tell, he did not miss her.

Now a young woman lay dead, her heart pierced by an arrow. And he had sent the bowman on his mission.

Had he broken his *geasa*?

Cold air swept across the hall, causing the lanterns to flicker wildly. Then the door slammed shut. The Fisher Laird peered through the gloom. A tall figure was standing by the door, and in his hands was a sword, glinting in the lantern light.

Four of his sons were talking among themselves and had not seen the newcomer. "Who in the name of Taranis are you?" called out the Fisher Laird, putting down the jug and walking toward the man. His youngest son, Alar, was walking back toward the wall, carrying the freshly filled lantern.

"I am the death of your house," said the stranger. As the man spoke, Alar moved closer to him, lifting the lantern toward the bracket on the wall. The warrior took three quick steps. The sword flashed through the air, slicing the boy's head from his shoulders.

The remaining sons of the Fisher Laird sprang up, running back to the far wall and grabbing weapons. Three took swords, the fourth a spear. The Fisher Laird stood stock still. His youngest son's body had fallen behind the long table, but his head had rolled across the sawdust-strewn floor, and the eyes were staring up at his father. Beyond the table the fallen lantern had spilled oil to the wooden boards, and flames were flickering there.

The warrior screamed a battle cry and ran to meet his other sons. His head swimming with ale, the Fisher Laird stumbled to where the small fire had begun and tried to stamp it out. But flames swept on across the sawdust. He swung back to see two more of his sons lying on the floor, blood flowing. Vor thrust at the man with his spear. The warrior sidestepped and slammed his sword deep into Vor's belly, ripping the blade up and through his heart. Vor let out a terrible cry of pain.

The Fisher Laird watched his sons die, and then the warrior walked toward him.

"I don't know you," mumbled the Fisher Laird. "I don't know you."

As the man came closer, he saw that his fierce eyes were odd colors: one dark and one pale. The man halted in front of him. Behind him the Fisher Laird could feel the rising flames and hear the cracking of timbers. The light lit up the warrior's face, making him appear demonic. "Who are you?"

There was no answer. The sword slashed across the Fisher Laird's belly. He fell to his knees as his entrails spilled out. Mercifully, the bright sword then cleaved his neck.

Lifting a lantern clear of the wall, Connavar strode from the hall and out into the night. The wind at his back, he gazed around at the sleeping settlement. Walking to a nearby hut, he splashed oil on the wooden walls, then set it alight. The wind fanned the flames, and burning cinders flew from one thatched roof to the next. Soon a number of fires were blazing. People began to run from their homes. Connavar moved among them, slashing left and right with his sword. Behind him flames licked out through the open doorway of the long hall, then broke through the roof.

Panic swept across the settlement as Conn strode through

the flames, killing anyone who came within the reach of his sword. Two young men ran at him, carrying hatchets. He slew them both. The villagers began to stream from the settlement.

Blood-covered, Connavar sheathed his sword, took up a pitchfork, and hurled blazing thatch into a building that had not yet been touched by the fire. As the long night wore on, he moved from hut to hut, adding to the blaze, until finally all the homes were burning. His skin was scorched, and his cloak caught fire. Hurling it aside, he ran to the small dockside, where seven fishing boats were moored. It took far longer to set them alight, and he spent an hour pitching burning thatch and timbers to the decks and dropping them into the narrow holds.

As the dawn came up, he was sitting at the water's edge, his face blackened with smoke and his hands blistered. The long hall had collapsed, and only the stone chimney still stood. But as Conn watched, it twisted and came crashing to the ground. Five of the boats had sunk and one was ruined beyond repair, but in the seventh the fires had gone out and it still bobbed upon the waters of the lake. Everything else was gone: the homes, the net huts, the storehouses.

Conn gazed on a scene of utter devastation.

He felt flat and terribly tired. The fury of the night before had spent itself. Wearily he pushed himself to his feet and walked through what had once been the main street of the settlement. Bodies lay everywhere, some burned, some untouched by flame. As he walked, Conn saw that he had been utterly undiscriminating. Women lay dead alongside their men, and at the far end of the street two children had been cut down. Judging by the blood trail, one of them had crawled a little way before dying.

As he stood there, surveying the grim evidence of his rage, he knew that only part of the fury had been inspired by the greed of the Fisher Laird.

All his life he had tried to be a hero, to live down the perceived legacy of Varaconn. He gazed upon the ruins and watched flakes of gray ash floating in the breeze. All was ashes now. He had found love—a great love—and he had allowed it to die. In the process he had become not only an adulterer but a killer of women and children.

Tears spilled to his smoke-blackened face, and he fell to his knees, calling out Tae's name again and again.

In the hills the survivors of the massacre gathered, listening to the sounds. The anguished cries were barely human and carried the weight of both grief and madness. The survivors huddled closer together and prayed the demon would now leave them be.

For two weeks there was no sign of Connavar. Despite being seen riding toward Three Streams, he had never arrived in the settlement. Ruathain asked Arbonacast to track him, but he lost the trail. Then it was left to the wily Parax to find him. The old hunter asked questions about Conn's favorite places as a child and the whereabouts of local caves. Then he rode the highlands, constantly scouting for tracks. He had followed Conn once before and felt he knew his habits. The young man did not want to be found and had hidden his trail. But he had to eat and stay warm.

Parax was a patient man whose careful eye missed nothing. On the fifteenth day after Conn's disappearance he found a simple rabbit trap and the faintest of trails moving away from it. He knew at once that he had found Connavar and followed the trail all the way to the cave that had once been the home of Vorna the Witch. Connavar was chopping wood with an old hatchet. He glanced up as the hunter dismounted but did not speak. Taking an armful of wood, he walked back into the cave. Parax also said nothing but gathered wood and followed his master inside.

The cave was deep, and Parax cast his gaze around the

gloomy place. Running water fell to a shallow pool at the back, and there was a roughly made hearth and an old cot bed. Someone had put up shelves against the western wall, but they were all empty and covered in cobwebs. It was an inhospitable place, he thought. In silence the two men brought in the wood, then Connavar sat down by the fire. He was thinner, hollow-eyed, his face gaunt. Parax walked to his pony and brought in a small food sack, from which he took some bread and cheese, which he offered to Conn. The warrior shook his head and threw several sticks into the fire. Parax laid the food on the hearth, then walked to the bed and lay down. He had been tracking Conn for days and was tired. Parax slept for an hour. When he awoke, the cave was empty. The hunter yawned and stretched and made his way back to the fire. The food, thankfully, was gone.

Leaving the cave, he mounted his pony and rode back to Three Streams to make his report to Ruathain.

The following day Ruathain traveled to the cave. The Big Man waited for several hours, but there was no sign of Conn. He guessed that his son knew he was there but did not want to talk. This saddened him, but like Parax before him, he also left food and returned to the settlement.

On the seventeenth night, as Conn was skinning a rabbit, a slender figure moved into the cave mouth. He glanced up and saw it was Eriatha. He took a deep breath and made to speak, then changed his mind and returned his attention to the rabbit.

"How long will you stay up here?" she asked him.

"I don't know. Now leave me in peace."

"This is peace? No, Connavar, this is a form of self-torture. You are not the first man to lose a loved one. You will not be the last."

"You know nothing of it!" he said quietly.

"Then tell me," she insisted. "Tell me why the new laird is sitting in a cave while his duties are being undertaken by others." Eriatha advanced into the cave. There were no candles, and the fire cast little light. Conn was withdrawn, almost emotionless, as if he had emptied himself of all feeling. "The lything voted for you. You are the laird," she said. "Now why are you skulking here? Your wife is dead; you have avenged her." There was still no fire in his eyes, even at the use of the word "skulking." She took a deep breath. "What is the purpose of this . . . senseless exile?"

"There is no purpose," he told her. Tears fell to his cheeks. "Just go. Leave me be!"

She forced a laugh, the sound filled with as much scorn as she could summon. "I did not think to see this," she said, contempt in her voice. "The great Connavar unmanned. Crying like a wee baby."

Suddenly furious, he stormed to his feet and loomed over her. "Get out now!" he hissed, grabbing her by the shoulders and hurling her toward the cave mouth. She fell heavily and cried out, more in shock than in pain. Conn ignored her and returned to the fire.

Eriatha sat up and rubbed her arm. "I am not leaving," she said.

"Do as you please."

Eriatha was satisfied that she had drawn him from his lethargy. All that now remained was to get him to talk. "I want to understand," she told him softly, rising and moving into the cave to sit beside him. "Tell me why you are here. Tell me and I will go. And you will have your peace." At first she thought he was continuing to ignore her. He finished skinning the rabbit, then put the meat to one side. When he spoke, his voice was barely a whisper.

"I was warned to keep all my promises. Warned by the Seidh. I took the warning lightly. Why would I not? For I am *Connavar*." He almost spit out the name. "And *Connavar* is known as a man of his word." He fell silent again, staring into the fire. "I told Tae I would ride with her. I *promised* her I would be back by noon. I broke that promise, and she rode with Ruathain. Rode to her death. And why was I late? I was with a woman. We were rutting like two dogs in heat."

"What do you want me to say?" she asked him. "That you are not a perfect man? Ha! As if that beast has ever existed. You broke a small promise, and the consequences were terrible. Aye, there is no arguing against that, Conn, my friend. You will have to live with that broken promise all your life. It will hurt for a long time. Maybe forever. But we all live with our hurts. You once told me that you were determined never to be like your father, never a coward. Consider this: What would you call a man who makes a mistake and then runs away from his responsibilities? I'd call him a coward. You also told me that one day the Stone army would march on our lands and you were determined to stop them. Are they not coming now? Or is it that you no longer care about this land and its people?"

"I care," he admitted.

"Then what are you doing here, Conn?"

"Trying to make sense of my life," he said. "You helped me once before, when I left the children to die. I accepted what you said. I believed it. Perhaps because I needed to believe it. But what has happened has all but destroyed me. Tae was beautiful, and she had a life to live. She was the sister of my soul. I knew that when I first met her. I know it even better now. But I am not sitting here full of self-pity. I am not wallowing in my grief. I am haunted by remorse. It eats at my spirit because I cannot change what happened. I cannot make it right."

"No, you cannot. She is dead. Her spirit has flown."

Conn glanced at her. "You think it is just about Tae? Do you know what happened at Shining Water?"

"You killed the men responsible. Everyone knows that."

"Oh, Eriatha, if only that were true. Why did you come here? Tell me truly."

"Your mother came to me. She thought that you and I . . ." Eriatha sighed, then gave a shy smile. "She thought we might have a bond."

"And we do," said Conn. "You are one of my dearest friends. And even with you I am finding it hard to speak the truth. I do not want you to hate me."

Eriatha sat very still. "I think you had better just say what is in your mind, Conn."

"I burned the village. And worse. I can scarcely remember how I felt as I rode to the Fisher Laird's hall. It was as if all the anger and the hurt, the loss and the shame turned me to winter. I went into the hall and killed the laird and his sons. Flames were all around me. The hall was burning. I cannot remember how it started. But when I left, I carried a lantern and set fire to nearby houses. There was a roaring in my head, and then there were people running around me, screaming and shouting. I lashed out at them. I killed them, Eriatha. When dawn came, I walked through the ruins. I saw the bodies. Two were children. But there were women, too."

"You killed women and children?" Eriatha was aghast. "Oh, Conn! That was evil."

"I know." He looked away from her face. "I didn't know what to do, so I came here to try to think. Yes, it was an evil deed, and I know this is no excuse, but I truly did not know what I was doing. When I saw their bodies, it was like a spear was being thrust through my heart. If I could bring them back, even with my own death, I would do it. Without hesitation."

"But you cannot bring them back," she said coldly. "No one can. And you cannot make amends, Conn. These deeds have stained your soul. And they will haunt you, as they should haunt you, till the day you die. I thought you had learned a lesson when you fought the Perdii. I thought you had come to realize that hate leads to vileness and evil. I hope for all our sakes that you have learned that lesson now."

"Aye," he said. "It is burned into my heart." He looked at

her stern face and noted the coldness in her eyes. "Do we still have a bond?" he asked.

"I'll not lie to you, Conn. I think the less of you. I thought you were stronger than this. Oh, I always knew of the violence in your soul, but I believed—foolishly—that you were in control of it."

"Then we are friends no longer?"

"We will always be friends, Conn," she said softly. "There is much that is good in you and much that I admire. And as your friend I am more sorry than I can say that Tae has been lost to you. Tell me this, though: How is it that if you loved her so well, you could rut with a stranger?"

"It was no stranger," he said. "It was Arian. I did not know she lived close to Old Oaks. I rode in to speak to the herdsmen who tend the laird's cattle. She was there. Alone. I thought I had put her behind me. I do not love her, Eriatha. But when I am close to her . . ."

"Hah!" she said scornfully. "That at least I understand. It is the call of the flesh. Men are cursed with it." Her expression softened. "But you did love Arian desperately, Conn. I remember the night you told me of her. Love made your eyes shine like lanterns." She looked at his eyes now and saw that they were haunted and bloodshot. "How long since you slept?"

"Several days, I think. When I sleep, I dream of Tae. Then, when I wake—just for a moment—I think she is still alive. Waiting for me." He shivered. "Better not to sleep."

"Well, it is time to sleep now. Come," she said, rising.

Wearily he climbed to his feet. "I don't deserve your friendship," he said.

"No, you don't. But you have it, Conn." She helped him undress. His clothes were filthy, and there was dried blood on his hands. Eriatha led him to the bed and slipped out of her clothes, and together they lay down. Pulling the blanket over them, Eriatha drew him close, his head upon her shoulder.

And he slept.

Eriatha lay beside him for more than an hour. Then she eased herself clear, put on her dress, and, taking his pony, rode back down to the settlement. Before the dawn she was back. He was still asleep. Conn awoke to the smell of frying bacon. Sunlight glowed in the cave mouth, and he could see the beauty of a clear blue sky outside. He sat up and saw that fresh clothes had been laid out for him.

"Go and wash in the stream," Eriatha told him. "Then you can eat."

He rose and walked out into the sunlight. Eriatha cracked two eggs into the pan and toasted some bread. Conn returned minutes later, dried himself, then dressed. They ate breakfast in silence, and she watched him carefully. His eyes were less haunted now, and he looked more like the young man she knew.

"Are you ready to leave this cave?" she asked him.

"Aye. I'll go back to the world. But not as the same man."

"Be a better one, my dear."

He strode from the cave to find Parax waiting for him. He was leading a second pony. The old man smiled and lifted a hand in greeting.

"You feeling better, boy?" he asked.

"Well enough, old man. How did you find me?"

Parax grinned. "You left a trail a blind man could follow. It was hardly worth calling on the services of a great man like myself to find you. Are you ready to ride?"

Conn nodded. "I am ready," he said.

◇ **16** ◇

THROUGHOUT THE SPRING and summer Conn worked tirelessly, hurling himself into his duties with almost fren-
zied energy. He rode the lands, organizing the building of
mills, granaries, and storehouses, and ordered a census of
every person living in the lands of the northern Rigante.
Putting Fiallach in charge of Seven Willows, he told him to
build watchtowers along the coast and strengthen the defenses of the town. Braefar was appointed second counsel
under Maccus, for the older man fast found himself exhausted with the new workload.

"Why all the new granaries?" Maccus asked Conn one day
as they were riding to inspect a newly discovered gold mine
in the Druagh mountains.

"War is no longer a matter of individual bravery and mass
tactics," Conn told him. "It is about supply. No matter how
courageous the men, they cannot fight if they are not fed. It is
vital that when war comes we can feed a standing army
without relying on neighboring tribes."

"Maybe so," Maccus replied, "but in a mere four months
you have all but emptied the Long Laird's treasury. Let us
hope that there is ample gold in this new mine."

The mine had at first proved a disappointment. The mine
governor, Lycus, a short, stocky man who also ran the laird's
two silver mines, assured Conn that in time the mine would
prove itself. Conn remained suspicious and sent Govannan to

THE SWORD IN THE STORM

the site, ordering him to pretend to be an itinerant worker seeking employment. After six weeks Govannan discovered that more than two-thirds of the gold was being carried northeast to Queen of the Rocks, a port settlement on the coast where Lycus owned several houses and a large parcel of land.

Conn, Ruathain, Maccus, Govannan, and twenty of Conn's Iron Wolves arrived at the settlement in the first week of autumn, raided three warehouses, and discovered a hoard of gold and silver.

Lycus was taken back to Old Oaks, tried in open court, and hanged in the main square.

Braefar took charge of the mining operations, and the income rose spectacularly.

With the first snowfall news came to Old Oaks that the Long Laird had died. The old man, broken by the death of Tae, had suffered one illness after another. He had died in his sleep in a bedroom whose window overlooked the soaring peak of Caer Druagh.

Conn did not attend the funeral. He had journeyed to Seven Willows to meet with Fiallach and see the new defenses for himself.

The following spring the first of the foals was born, a white colt with a long black mark on its brow. The birthmark looked like a sword, and Conn called him Dark Blade.

By his twenty-first birthday Conn's Iron Wolves numbered 220, and they met regularly to train, galloping their tall Gath horses in close formation, peeling away, and re-forming into the flying wedge Conn had first seen among the Gath. Braefar's stirrup design had proved a huge success, giving the riders greater purchase. Conn also ordered two hundred lightweight shields to replace the small bucklers commonly used by riders, and each man was armed with two swords: one a long curved saber and the second a short stabbing sword based on the Stone design.

By the autumn of that year Conn had begun organizing a

new force, horse archers. Lightly armored and mounted on swift ponies, they were trained to shoot at a full gallop. Conn arranged several archery tournaments, offering fine prizes to the best of the bowmen, and these men he drew into his service. Among them was his fifteen-year-old brother, the golden-haired Bendegit Bran, whose skills with horse and bow were unrivaled.

His inclusion in the force angered Meria, who on a visit to Old Oaks berated Conn. "He's just a child," she insisted.

"He'll be a man in the spring," Conn told her gently. "He's not a babe any longer, however much you'd like him to be." The sun was almost behind the mountains, and the room was growing darker. Meria moved to the fire and lit a taper and then two wall-hanging lanterns. For a while they sat in thoughtful silence, watching the sunset.

"It has all gone by so fast, Conn," she said after a while. "It seems only a few months since you were all children. I miss those days. I miss having children around me. I look after little Banouin now and again. He is a joy! Always laughing, and he loves to be cuddled. You never did. You squirmed to get away. Unless it was Ruathain. Quite often you'd fall asleep in his arms."

"How is the Big Man? I have not seen him for a while."

She shrugged, then laughed. "He is fine now. He caught a chill and was coughing and sputtering about the house, losing his temper and complaining. He never was a man who could cope with illness. He's still not fully recovered and needs to rest often." She smiled. "But then, he's past forty now and no longer the young bull."

They talked for a while, each relaxed in the other's company. Then she broached the subject closest to her heart. "You should wed again, Conn. I have not seen you laugh for what seems an age."

Conn had been waiting for just such a conversation. He had intended to brush it aside or change the subject. But now, sitting in the warmth of this room, with the setting sun turning the mountains to fire, he did neither. "I didn't love her well enough, you know. It is a guilt I carry—with all the other guilt. She was beautiful and, as Vorna once told me, deserved better. I loved her. But when I saw Arian again . . ." His voice trailed away. He looked at Meria and gave a rueful smile. "I'll not wed, Mam. Not yet. There is, I think, room in my heart for only one great love."

"Foolish boy. There will be another love. You wait and see."

"As there was for you when Varaconn died?"

"I wish you would say 'Father.' You speak of him as if he were a distant relative."

"My father, then. Now answer the question."

She sighed and leaned back in her chair, lifting a plaid blanket from the floor and laying it over her legs. "It is getting cold now. Would you shut the window?"

"Aye, but I'll still require an answer." Rising, he pushed closed the shutters, dropping the narrow lock bar into place.

Then he sat down and looked into her green eyes. "No," she admitted. "There was never another love like Varaconn. I do not want this to sound as if I am speaking ill of Ru. He is the finest of men, and I do love him dearly. More dearly than I ever expected. But Varaconn and I were twin souls."

"Aye, I know the feeling."

"Ah, Conn, it hurts me to see you so unhappy. You are the laird now, a great man, respected, admired, aye, and even feared. You are becoming a legend among the Rigante. Most young men would give ten years of their lives to be you."

"I know that," he said. "They see the man on the tall horse, and they hear tales of the bear and the evil king. That is not me, Mother. It is just a part of me. I grew up with the hurt of believing Vara—my father—was a coward. Then I saw you and the Big Man part because of something I had done."

"It was not you—" she began.

He waved a hand to silence her. "I know, I know. But I didn't understand that then. And as for the bear, well, he showed me my mortality, ripping my flesh from my bones. I have lost friends: Riamfada, though he is happy now, and Banouin. I have watched the rise of a great evil and even fought alongside it. Then, after betraying my wife to her death, I destroyed a village, killing men, women, and children. I am not the hero they believe me to be."

"You were stricken by grief, Conn. It was not my beloved boy who did that. You were possessed. You didn't know what you were doing."

He laughed. "Ah, what it is to have a mother's love. It *was* me, Mother. It was the beast inside, with the chains loosed. The responsibility was mine, and I will not make excuses for my actions. The Pannones call me the Demon Laird. Can you blame them? Every year at Samain I have sent offers of weregild, increasingly fabulous sums. But the Highland Laird refuses even to speak to my representatives."

"You are not a demon. You are my son, and you have a good heart. Why is it that you dwell only on the bad? You are working tirelessly to protect your people. And you did save Riamfada from the bear. And you did avenge Banouin. The Big Man is so proud of you. Does that not warm you, Conn?"

"Aye, it does."

"And as for your friend Banouin, yes, he died terribly, but he had a good life, Conn, and good friends. And a part of that life lives on in his son. He's almost four now, a bonny boy. He misses Bran, though. As do I. Are you going to keep him here with you all winter?"

"No, he can go home. I'll be with you myself at Samain." There was a tap at the door, and Maccus called out to him. Conn rose. "And now I must bid you farewell, Mam. Maccus and I are to discuss the heady joys of revenue collection."

She threw her arms around his neck and kissed his bearded cheek. "You are my dear heart," she told him, tears in her eyes. "I love you more than life." Running her fingers through his long red-gold hair, she forced a smile. "Mothers can be so embarrassing," she said.

"Och, there's no embarrassment, Mam," he lied. He walked to the door, but she called out to him.

"There is one other matter you should know about, Conn, if you are coming home for Samain."

He paused. "What?"

"Arian has left Casta. She is back home with Nanncumal."

"Why did they part?"

"She had a child, Conn. Did you not know? A boy. The child has oddly colored eyes, one green and one brown. I thought you should know."

Conn did not make the trip to Three Streams for the Feast of Samain, spending it instead with Brother Solstice at Old Oaks. Throughout the winter the Druid taught Conn, Braefar, Maccus, and Govannan to read script. Conn had decided on this course after the ordering of the census, having become increasingly frustrated by the need to have scribes and clerics decipher the results. Braefar took to the tuition with remarkable ease, learning faster than any of them. He was the prize pupil, and he gloried in the praise of the teacher. Govannan stuck to the task doggedly and by spring had a tentative grasp on the subject. Conn was little interested in the nuances of language. He needed to understand script, and he forced himself to learn at least enough of the bizarre little symbols to make sense of the census scrolls.

As the weather cleared and Conn drew close to his twenty-second birthday, merchants began to arrive at Old Oaks with news from across the water.

The army of Stone had advanced into Gath territory. There had been three major battles, one inconclusive, followed by two terrible defeats for the Gath. First reports claimed that more than thirty thousand Gath warriors had perished.

The Stone army was marching on the port city of Goriasa, the last Gath stronghold.

To the east the king of the Sea Raiders had been killed in a skirmish, with his son Shard replacing him. Conn knew nothing of Shard and spoke to Brother Solstice regarding him. "Do the Druids still walk the lands of the Sea Wolves?"

"No. The Vars worship the blood gods, and any Druid caught would be murdered."

"Have you heard anything regarding this Shard?"

"Very little. But you can be assured he will not be a peace-loving man."

Conn saw to it that all the merchants knew of his interest in the new Vars king, and within weeks an elderly hide merchant from the Ostro tribe sought an audience with him. They met in the former apartments of the Long Laird. Conn had stripped it of much of its furniture, leaving only a long oval table and ten chairs. The merchant entered, bowed, and was offered a seat. The man was tall and slim, round-shouldered and bald. His face was lined with age, but his dark eyes were button bright.

Conn, seated at the head of the table, with Maccus on his left and Braefar to his right, gauged the man as he entered, thinking him cold and calculating.

"I thank you for this audience, lord," said the Ostro, his voice as smooth as olive oil. "My understanding is that you wish to know of King Shard."

"He interests me," admitted Conn.

"I do have some information that might be of assistance. And I could gather more. If, that is, I could obtain a greater supply of hides. The Vars are partial to tunics and boots made from your black and white cattle."

Maccus leaned in to Connavar and whispered to him. Conn nodded.

"I already have agreements with two traders for the distribution and sale of these hides, but I will increase the amount available to you—should your information prove useful."

"You are a kind and understanding man, lord." The old man smiled. "It does not surprise me that you should have an interest in the Vars king. He certainly has an interest in you."

"How so?"

"It seems, sir, that you killed his brother during a raid on Seven Willows some years ago. He has sworn a blood oath to bring your head back to his brother's house and place it on a lance there."

Conn laughed, but Maccus looked uneasy. "What else do you trade with them, my friend?" asked Conn.

"They have a great love for Uisge."

"I shall give you thirty barrels for your next voyage. I need to know his plans. Is he gathering men, building ships? Anything to do with the mustering of fighting men. You understand?"

"Indeed, lord. It will be a pleasure to be of service."

Conn thanked the man, who bowed once more and left the room. "You do know," said Maccus, "that the slimy whoreson will also sell information about us to Shard?"

"Of course," said Conn. "He lives for profit and will make it where he can. Where does he ship from?"

"The Queen of the Rocks. Most of the merchants traveling east use that port," Maccus told him.

"Do you have friends there?"

"Aye, a goodly number."

"Set off tomorrow and see if you can find someone who will sign on for his next voyage. It would be good to have a man of our own among his crew."

"You should tell Meria," Vorna said, sternly. Ruathain shrugged and looked uncomfortable. Little Banouin ran in, cried out with joy when he saw the Big Man, and climbed up to sit on his lap.

"I found a diamond," said the four-year-old, pushing out his mud-smeared hand and showing Ruathain a bright and worthless stone.

"You're a clever lad," said Ruathain. "But were I you, I'd wash my hands before you get dirt on your mother's furniture. Go on with you. I'll look after the diamond." Banouin ran from the room. "A fine boy," he said.

Vorna was not to be swayed. "Your heart is weakening, Ruathain. The foxglove powders will help, as will the other herbs. But you must slow down. You cannot afford to become exhausted or to strain that heart."

"Can I not strengthen it?"

"Had you come to me sooner, it would have been better. As it is . . . No, you cannot strengthen it. You can only slow down the deterioration. You should tell Meria. She has a right to know."

"A right to worry herself sick? I don't think so. How long will this treacherous heart continue to beat?"

"Do not speak of it in that way," she told him. "It is not treacherous. Think of it as an ailing friend who has aided you over the years and now needs your help. You must reduce the pressure on it. Drink more water and less Uisge. Eat more oats—without salt."

"I asked how long, Vorna."

"If you are careful, you could have ten years. No more than that, I think."

"That will bring me to fifty. Good enough."

"It will bring you to fifty-three, you vain man," she said with a smile. "Now, I want you take the powders exactly as I have described. Be very careful with the foxglove. Remember that more is not better. Too much can kill. Do not be tempted to add a pinch."

Banouin ran back inside, holding up his hands for Ruathain to inspect. "Ah, you cleaned them well, little man," he said, hoisting the boy high. Banouin squealed with delight as Ruathain tossed him into the air, catching him expertly.

Vorna shook her head and suppressed a laugh. "Two children," she said, "one big and one small."

"Can I come with you today?" asked the boy. "Can we ride?"

"Today I am chopping wood," said Ruathain, "but you can help me roll the rounds. I need a strong lad, mind."

"I'm strong, aren't I, Mam?"

Vorna nodded, then glanced sternly at Ruathain. "Chopping wood, is it? You stop and rest often." She called Banouin to her. "If you see the Big Man growing red in the face, you tell him to sit down."

"I will, Mam."

"Then let's be off," said Ruathain, pocketing the medicine pouch and stepping out into the sunlight. Banouin ran to him, grabbing his hand. The Big Man hoisted him high, setting the child on his shoulders.

"Look how tall I am!" shouted Banouin. "Look, Mam!"

"I can see you," Vorna said from the doorway. She watched as they marched away and listened to Banouin's laughter as they walked across the meadow. The sun was shining brightly on them both, and Vorna felt her heart would burst.

The winter was mild, and once again Conn spent Samain away from Three Streams, remaining at Old Oaks. He did not attend the feast night but stayed instead at the hall with Maccus, Braefar, Govannan, and Fiallach.

The huge warrior had ridden from Seven Willows with news that a fleet of two hundred long ships had been sighted, heading north along the coastline. Fiallach had gathered his five hundred fighting men, but the ships had not beached.

The news was both alarming and mystifying. Two hundred ships meant ten thousand fighting men. No raid had ever been conducted in winter, when food supplies were limited. How, then, would ten thousand men be fed? And where were they heading?

"They must be invading Pannone lands," said Maccus. "It is madness. Even if they defeat the Highland Laird, there will be insufficient food for them."

Conn had sent a rider to warn the Highland Laird and offer military support, but the man had returned with a blunt message from the Pannone lord: "We neither need you nor want you."

"How many men can he field against the Vars?" asked Conn.

"No more than twelve thousand," said Maccus.

"How many can we gather within, say, ten days?"

"The Highland Laird doesn't want us," put in Fiallach. "Let him cook in his own broth."

"The Pannone are Keltoi," said Conn. "But even more than that we must consider the size of the invading force. Ten thousand are not needed for a raid. They have come to conquer, to take land. Once they have a foothold here, we will have deadly enemies to the north. No. Whether he wants us or not, we will help him defeat the Vars."

"Within ten days," said Maccus, "we could field fifteen thousand fighting men."

"Yes, we could," said Braefar, "but supplying them is a different matter. Our granaries are full, but the number of wagons needed to haul grain for fifteen thousand men on a march through Pannone territory would be colossal. We could not gather those in time. We do not even know where the Vars have landed. They could be a hundred miles to the north."

"Something about all of this does not sit right with me," said Govannan. "I agree with Conn that this is an invading force and must be countered. But why invade Pannone lands? There is little gold there and precious few granaries, while we have the new mines and a huge surplus of food. *We* are the natural targets for any invasion, and we already know that

King Shard hates Conn and has sworn to have his head. It makes no sense for him to sail his ships a hundred miles north and attack a poorer neighbor."

Braefar shook his head. "Not necessarily. If, as Conn believes, they are here to gain a foothold, they can ship in many more men, then launch a full war against us in the spring. They could hit us on two fronts: a marching army from the north and a second invasion at Seven Willows."

"There is a third alternative," said Maccus. "The Pannones are our enemies. The Highland Laird has made that clear. They do not, however, have the strength to attack us. Make no mistake, however. There is great hatred for us among the Pannone. Let us suppose, just for a moment, that the Highland Laird is *not* facing an invasion but has invited Shard to join him in a war against us. If that is the reality, then we will face ten thousand battle-hardened Vars and twelve thousand Pannone warriors."

There was sudden silence around the table as each man let the terrible prospect sink in. Finally Conn spoke, and his voice was full of regret. "I hope you are wrong, Maccus. But if you are right, then the fault is mine, for it was my revenge that gave birth to this hatred. I have tried to make amends, but some deeds cannot be washed away with gold."

Fiallach swore. "Och, man, you did what any warrior would do. For myself, when I heard they had killed Tae, I would have wiped out every Pannone on the face of the earth. What I want to know is how we decide which course of action to take."

Conn was silent for a moment. Then he glanced at Maccus. "Send out riders to gather the army. Make sure they understand that the need is urgent. We will not march into Pannone territory immediately. But we will prepare. If the Pannones are indeed victims, we will move more swiftly to their aid. If they are not, we will be ready to defend our own lands." He swung to Fiallach. "You, my friend, will gather the Iron Wolves, and if battle comes, you will command them."

"Where will you be?" asked Fiallach.

"I'll fight on foot with the main body of the army. It is many years since the Rigante faced a battle, and the experience will be new to the younger men. I will stand with them, with a hundred Iron Wolves. The rest will ride with you."

"You honor me," said Fiallach, his eyes shining with pride. "I will not let you down."

Conn switched his gaze to Braefar. "Wing, I will need you to coordinate supplies. We may have to hold the army together for some weeks while the situation develops. We cannot afford to fall short of food."

"What do you require of me, Conn?" asked Maccus.

"If battle comes, you will take command of the horse archers. Until then organize scouts to ride into Pannone territory to gather as much information as they can. The earlier we know the truth, the better prepared we will be."

Within three days the first Rigante warriors began to arrive at Old Oaks. By the fifth day more than six thousand men had gathered. The weather was still thankfully mild, for the warriors were forced to sleep at first in the open. Braefar had the foresight to order timbers hauled in from the highlands, and hasty shelters were erected. Conn met clan leaders and minor chieftains throughout each day and long into the night.

By the sixth day the last of the scouts rode in.

Maccus' fears had been proved correct. The Highland Laird of the Pannones had made a treaty with Shard of the Vars, and the two men were leading their armies toward the Rigante borders.

It was midnight, and Conn once more sat with his captains, joined now by Ruathain. The Big Man did not say much at the meeting but sat silently listening to the battle plans. Conn had scouted the area north of Old Oaks and had decided to meet the enemy on a range of hills some six miles from the settlement. "The ground narrows between two hills, and if we fight there, it will lessen the advantage they have in numbers," Conn told them. The scouts had reported the combined enemy force at just under eighteen thousand, almost double the current Rigante force. Conn turned to Maccus. "How long before they get here?"

"Tomorrow if they push on through the night. Dawn the day after if they don't."

"How many warriors do we have as of now?"

"Just under nine thousand, but more are coming in all the time. By tomorrow we should be close to ten, maybe eleven thousand."

"Why can't we fight from here?" asked Braefar. "Isn't that why the Long Laird built this fortress?" He seemed nervous and ill at ease.

It was Ruathain who answered him. "Aye, we could fight from here, but the Vars would surround the place and then send raiding parties throughout the area. Smaller communities would be wiped out. But worse than that, the warriors who have joined us have left their wives and families at home. They would not want to be cooped up in here while their loved ones were being hunted and slain. Conn is right. The enemy must be met and the issue decided in one great battle."

"Aye, a great battle," snapped Braefar. "A battle in which we will be outnumbered by perhaps two to one."

"We can do nothing about the numbers," said Conn. "Our men will be fighting to protect the land they love. It will give them an advantage. Added to this, we have the Iron Wolves. They will give us an edge."

"How will you deploy us?" asked Fiallach.

"We will need to hold the hills on either side, forcing the enemy to funnel into the gap between. In that gap I will stand. The Highland Laird will see me there. His hatred is so strong that I think he will direct his main force toward me. You, Fiallach, will hold your men on the eastern hill until you see my signal. Then you will attack the enemy's right flank. Do not get drawn into the mass. Hit the flank, pull away, and hit them again and again. Maccus will circle the enemy with his horse archers and attack the rear. When the time is right and the enemy is in disarray, I will lead a charge to kill the laird and Shard."

"Assuming everything goes the way you plan it," said Braefar.

"Yes, assuming that," Conn said softly. "We move out tomorrow. You will stay here, Wing. There will be many latecomers. Gather them into a second force and march to our aid as soon as you can."

The meeting ended, and with the others departed, Ruathain sat for a while talking to Conn. The younger man could sense that there was something on Ruathain's mind, but he would not be drawn on it. Instead he changed the subject. "You think it is wise to leave Wing with the rear guard?"

"He would not be of much use on the battlefield, Big Man. You saw him tonight. You could almost taste his fear."

"Aye, I saw it. But that rear guard could mean the difference between victory and defeat, Conn."

"Yes, it is a risk. But I cannot afford to leave Govannan. I need him with me."

"I could stay."

"You, Big Man? And miss the battle?"

"I think it would be wiser."

"I'll think on it. Are you well, Father? You seem preoccupied."

"Och, I'm as strong as an ox, boy. Have no fears on that. But I am weary, so I think I'll head for my bed. Meria is probably waiting up and will want a full report."

Conn chuckled. "I am surprised you didn't leave her at Three Streams."

"Leave her? You think she would have suffered that with you and Bran about to go into battle? By the gods, Conn, I'd sooner face the Vars than have to tell her she was staying behind." Ruathain hugged his son, then left for his apartments.

Conn rose and walked out into the night, strolling past two growling dogs that were fighting over food scraps from a market stall. He climbed up to the battlements. For a while he stood there, staring out toward the north, casting his gaze over the hundreds of campfires giving warmth to his sleeping army.

His heart was heavy. All his life he had wanted to protect his people, but now he had brought this calamity upon them. His hatred and his revenge had been the fire that had forged the alliance between the Highland Laird and Shard. And tomorrow or the next day hundreds, perhaps thousands of men would pay for it with their lives.

The wind was turning bitter, and he drew his cloak more closely about him and climbed down from the battlements. A woman in a long flowing dress, her head and shoulders covered by a dark woolen shawl, moved from the long hall. Meria saw him and waved. He noticed she was carrying something and guessed it was food for him. He smiled fondly. As long as she lived, she would always see him as a child who needed nurturing.

As they came closer, one of the dogs ran at Meria, barking furiously. She swung toward it. It had smelled the food. Conn began to run, shouting at the top of his voice, seeking to frighten the beast away. It jumped at Meria, jaws snapping toward the food. She leapt back. The dog was snarling now. It was a thin, half-starved stray, and the scent of the food had driven it to the edge of madness. Once more it leapt, this time its jaws seeking the flesh of the woman seeking to deprive it of a meal. Conn ran in, throwing out his arm. The dog's teeth closed on his leather wrist guard. Conn twisted violently and jerked out his arm. There was a sickening crack, and the dog fell to the ground, its body twitching. Conn knelt beside it. It was not a large hound, and it was old, its bones brittle with malnutrition. Its neck had been broken. Rising, Conn moved to Meria. "Are you all right, Mam?" She was standing very still, her face ghostly white in the moonlight.

"You killed it."

"I did not mean to."

"You killed the hound that bit you, Conn," she whispered. "Oh, sweet heaven."

His blood ran cold. He had broken his *geasa* on the night before a battle. They stood in silence for a few moments, then she took his hand.

"What will you do?"

"What can I do, Mam? I will lead the Rigante into battle."

"No," she whispered, backing away. "Not again! It can't happen again!"

Ruathain groaned and rolled over. Pain lanced into him. He struggled to sit, then saw that the bed was empty. With a grunt he pushed himself to his feet and moved to where his clothes lay across the back of a chair. From his jerkin pocket he lifted clear Vorna's medicine bag, took a pinch of foxglove powder, and sprinkled it into a cup, which he then filled with water. Stirring the contents, he drank deeply. After some moments the tightness in his chest eased.

It had hurt him to ask Conn to leave him behind when the army marched, but there was good sense in the decision. Much as he loved Wing, he did not trust him to bring reinforcements at speed. There was no way that Wing would hurry *toward* a battle. Ruathain drank more water. His mouth tasted bitter from the medicine.

Vorna had come to him on the day he had ridden to Old Oaks. They had walked together along the line of the fence surrounding Nanncumal's paddock. "You have not told her, have you, Big Man?"

"No."

"Listen to me, Ruathain. If you fight that battle, you will die. Your heart will fail you. If you cannot bring yourself to tell your wife, then at least tell your son."

"I'll tell him. I'll wait behind with the women and the bairns," he snapped, trying to control his anger. His heart began to pound painfully. Vorna laid a slender hand on his chest, and he felt calmer.

"You have power again," he whispered.

"Aye. Not enough to heal you, though. You remember your own *geasa*?"

"Of course. It was always a grand nonsense. I think the witch must have been drunk. 'Be not the king's shield.' It had no meaning then, and it has none now."

"There is always meaning, Ru. A witch sees a vision, a picture, if you will. Then she puts it into words. You have held to the word 'king,' but it could mean 'ruler,' 'thane,' or 'laird.' Connavar rules the Rigante. Tell me, does Meria know your *geasa*?"

"No. She knows Conn's. But since Varaconn's death she has avoided all talk of prophecies. They frighten her."

Vorna sighed. "Find a way to tell her, Ru, if you can. But whatever you choose, when you ride to Old Oaks, think of Meria and your sons. They love you. To lose you would break their hearts. My little Banouin worships you. Think on these things. Think on them hard. Do not let pride rob you of your last years. There are too few good men in the world, Ruathain. Stay with us a while longer."

He had been touched by her words. "I will not fight in that battle, Vorna. I'll tell Conn."

But he had not. Conn had enough on his mind without worrying about his stepfather's health. Instead he had leapt at the chance to organize the rear guard and send reinforcements to the battlefield.

He heard the door open. Meria ran in. "What is wrong,

lass?" he asked her, taking her in his arms and hugging her close.

She told him of the hound and the broken *geasa*.

"You say the dog fastened to his wrist guard?" he queried.

"Yes."

"Did it pierce his skin?"

"No."

"Then it was no bite. The *geasa* still stands."

She pulled away from him. "You told Varaccon that it was his horse that killed the raven. You told him he had not broken his *geasa*. But he died. Oh, Ru, my son mustn't die, too. I couldn't bear it."

He turned away from her. "I'll speak to him," he said.

"Speak? What do you mean speak? You have to keep him alive, Ru. Once you promised me you would bring my husband back to me. He died. This time must be different. You are the greatest warrior of the Rigante. All men know this. You must protect him, Ru. You must stand beside him. You will do this for me?"

He looked into her frightened eyes. "I was young when I made my first promise to you. I believed then that I was invincible and that I could protect all those I loved. I am older now and wiser."

"No!" she shouted. "You can do this! No one is mightier than you. You can bring my son back to me. Oh, please, Ru. If you love me, then promise me you will be his shield."

The words struck him with terrible force. His belly tightened, his breath catching in his throat. He looked into her terrified eyes and longed to tell her what she had just asked of him. "I do love you, lass," he said. "More than life. Much more than life." He took a deep breath, then he smiled. "I promise," he said. The desperation faded from her. She sagged against him.

"You are my rock," she told him. He stroked her back and kissed her hair. "You must go to Conn," she said. "You must lift his spirits as you have lifted mine. I know all will be well now. I know it."

"Aye, all will be well," he said softly. Then he dressed and walked through the hall to Conn's apartments. His son was sitting at a curved table, nursing a cup of Uisge.

Conn glanced up. "She told you." It was not a question.

"Did you think she wouldn't?" Ruathain said with a grin. He sat down, took the Uisge from Conn, and drank deeply. "That is good," he said, relishing the taste. "How are you feeling?"

"I'm fine, Big Man. Truly. If the *geasa* is broken, so be it. I am guilty of great evil, and I'll accept it as a punishment. But by Taranis, I'll not lose the battle, too. If I am to die, it will be done while destroying the threat to our lands."

Leaning forward, Ruathain clapped his son on the shoulder. "Now, *that* is a man talking. I'm proud of you, boy."

"I have thought about what you proposed. It makes good sense. You stay here and send as many men after us as you can. Not in small groups, mind. Gather them until you have maybe two thousand."

Ruathain shook his head. "No, Conn. This time we must rely on Wing, for I'll be beside you."

Conn gave a broad smile. "Mother has ordered you to protect me, hasn't she?"

"You'd expect no less, boy. I told her we'd win the battle, then I'd wash you, change your diaper, wrap you in blankets, and bring you home to her loving arms."

Conn's laughter pealed out. "Was your mother the same?"

"The very same. It is said a man doesn't get old while his mother lives. I think it's true. You are always a child in her eyes. It is irritating in the extreme. But you know, when they have gone, you'd give the earth just to hear them treating you like a child once more."

"You never treated me like a child, Big Man. You always made me feel I was special: bright, intelligent, fearless."

"You were all those things, lad."

Their eyes met. "You are the best father a man could have," said Conn.

"Och, boy, now you're getting maudlin. Fill up the cups. I'll have one more drink with you, then I'm off to my bed. We've a long day tomorrow."

Shard stood on the hilltop, the Highland Laird beside him, and surveyed the enemy force. He calculated there were around ten thousand men manning the two hilltops and the low-lying ground between them.

"We can take them," said the Highland Laird.

A small man with a small voice and a small mind, thought Shard. He could taste the man's fear. But then, of course he was afraid. If he had not been, this alliance never would have taken place. The laird needed his Sea Wolves to smash through the Rigante ranks. There had been only one source of argument: who got to kill the Demon Laird. Shard had always seen himself as a generous man, but it had been hard to give way on the matter. If Connavar could be taken alive, the Highland Laird would kill him but Shard would have the head to take back to his brother's house. Minor irritation touched the Vars king. Even now, all these months after the bargain had been struck, he found the thought of it gnawing at him. He narrowed his eyes, straining to see Connavar.

"Which one is he?" he asked the laird.

The little man hawked and spit. "You see the giant in the mail shirt at the center? Well, just to his left. The man pointing up at the hillside."

"I see him. How do you wish to proceed, laird?"

The Pannone scratched his black beard and sat down on a rock. "I think you should lead your men against the center. My men will attack the hillsides. Then we will come at Connavar from three sides."

Shard said nothing and surveyed the enemy lines once

more. Armored men lined the western hilltop. As far as he could make out, there were some five hundred of them. However, there were trees behind them that could hide a thousand more. The men immediately surrounding Connavar were also protected by mail shirts, shields, and helms, but the massed ranks of his army were tribesmen in cloth shirts and cloaks of blue and green. Shard strolled back to the other side of the hilltop and looked down on his own force: ten thousand battle-hardened warriors well armed with swords and axes. Most of them sported mail shirts, though none carried shields. Shields were clumsy objects at the best of times and slowed the charge. The Pannone force of eight thousand stood some two hundred paces west of his men. Lightly armed, mostly with wooden spears, they stood nervously, waiting for the action to begin.

Strange, thought Shard, how an army always reflects the personality of its leader. The young tribesmen were brave enough, but they followed a nervous man, and that, by some indefinable magic, had transferred itself to the warriors under his command.

Let them attack the hillsides, he thought. Whether they take them or not is a matter of small importance. Once we have crushed the center and taken Connavar, the rest will run. They will flee to the temporary sanctuary of Old Oaks. And I will burn them out.

He wandered back to where the laird stood staring malevolently at the Rigante ranks half a mile away. "Today you will have your vengeance," Shard said amiably.

"Aye. He will pay for the murder of my brother laird. He will suffer for the children he slaughtered and the women he raped."

Shard had heard the tale of Connavar's revenge. He could not remember rape being part of it. "He must have been a busy man that night," he said. "To kill all those people, burn the village, and still have time for sport."

The Highland Laird was not listening. Shard's huge hand descended on the man's shoulder. "It is two hours after dawn. Time, I think, to make war."

He saw the laird swallow hard, then the little man marched down the hillside to join his men. Shard took one last look at the Rigante. They were waiting quietly. Some were sitting down. There was no feeling of panic among them or at least none that he could see from that distance.

Shard strolled down the hillside to where his captains waited, grim men and fierce-eyed. Taking up his sword and helm, Shard strode to the center of his army and bellowed: "Are you ready for the crows' feast?" A great bloodthirsty cry went up from the thousands around him. He waited for it to die down. "Let the gods drink their fill!" he yelled, brandishing his sword and waving it in the direction of the enemy.

The army began to move, slowly at first; then, feet pounding the hard earth, the Sea Wolves ran toward the enemy lines.

Fiallach stood impassively on the western hilltop as the Sea Wolves charged. Beside him Govannan cleared his throat. "I think there'll be a frost tonight," he said, trying to sound unconcerned. "You can feel it on the wind."

Fiallach laughed. "Then I shall wrap up warm in a Sea Wolf's cloak."

The Pannones were charging now, coming straight at Fiallach's position. "Bring out the horses," he called. "Hold them ready."

Govannan leaned in. "I think Conn will be hard pressed to hold the Vars. That's a ferocious-looking bunch of bastards."

Hundreds of archers moved from the shadows of the trees, leading Gath warhorses. Fiallach's five hundred Iron Wolves drew back from the crest of the hill and mounted. The archers loped forward, strung their bows, and sent volley after volley of arrows into the advancing Pannones. Fiallach stepped into the saddle and cast a glance to the eastern hilltop. From there he could see Maccus following a similar strategy. Scores of Pannones fell, then scores more.

The eastern hill was very steep, and the enemy charge had slowed almost to a standstill. Within moments hundreds of Pannone fighting men were hit. Bodies rolled down the hill, impeding the advance further, knocking men from their feet.

On the valley floor the Sea Wolves were within two hundred paces of the Rigante line. Fiallach edged his horse forward. The archers on the hilltop ran back, passing between the horses. Fiallach drew his saber. "Now!" he shouted, kicking his horse into a run.

Five hundred heavily armed riders swept over the brow of the hill, smashing into the Pannone ranks, cutting and killing. Stunned by the charge, the enemy fell back, trying to regroup. But the horsemen followed them, harrying them mercilessly. Panic followed as the Iron Wolves continued their attack, and the battle on the hillside swiftly became a massacre.

Fiallach spotted the Highland Laird fleeing toward the north. He longed to ride after him, but Conn's orders had been clear. Once the Pannones had been scattered, Fiallach was to turn his attention to the flanks of the main Vars force.

Regrouping his riders, Fiallach swung them and launched an angled charge. The plan was for the Iron Wolves to strike the enemy like a knife whittling wood, at an acute angle. That way they would not be sucked into the center of the enemy army, where the crush of bodies would take away their mobility.

On the far side Maccus was riding his horse archers along the enemy's right flank, arrows slicing into the foe's ranks.

Twice Fiallach led charges. On the second he was almost unhorsed by a young axman who leapt at him, grabbing at his chain mail and trying to haul him from the saddle. Fiallach struck him in the face with his shield. As the man fell back,

Fiallach's horse stumbled, pitching him forward. Losing his grip on his saber, he grabbed at the gelding's mane. The axman hit him a blow on the left shoulder, above his shield. Fiallach felt his collarbone snap. The gelding righted itself. Fiallach drew his stabbing sword, swung the gelding, and thrust the blade through the axman's throat. Then Govannan appeared alongside him, scattering the enemy, and Fiallach managed to gallop clear.

In terrible pain he rode away from the enemy, then turned, his pale eyes scanning the battlefield. The Pannones had fled, but the Sea Wolves had pushed Conn farther back into the land between the hills. Conn's center was now looking concave, curving in like a bow. Sweat dripped into Fiallach's eyes.

"What now?" Govannan asked as the Iron Wolves gathered around Fiallach.

"Time . . . I think . . . to ignore our orders," said Fiallach, gritting his teeth against the grinding agony of the broken bone below his throat. "We must get back to the hilltop and charge in across the fighting lines. Too . . . much pressure on Conn. The line is ready to give. Follow me!" Fiallach urged his gelding up the hillside. The pain was so great now that the Rigante warrior almost passed out. With great difficulty he slid the shield from his left arm, allowing it to drop to the ground. Then he tucked his left hand into his belt.

Glancing down, he saw the ferocious fighting between the hills. Conn and Ruathain were side by side now, the enemy set to sweep around them. Hundreds of Rigante warriors were dead. Even through his pain Fiallach could admire the power of Ruathain and Conn. They were immovable, standing firm against the horde, their swords slashing left and right. Fiallach rubbed sweat from his eyes.

"Straight through the middle," he told Govannan. "Then dismount and form a fighting line with Conn."

"We're going to lose the horses," said Govannan. "They'll be cut to pieces."

"Better that than our men," grunted Fiallach. "Forward!"

And the Iron Wolves charged down the slope.

For the first time in more than a year Ruathain felt no pain in his chest, no weakness in his limbs. He was, he realized as he watched the Sea Wolves advance, a man again, the first swordsman of the Rigante, ready to oppose the enemies of his people.

His silver-streaked fair hair bound into a ponytail and his old round iron helm on his head, Ruathain stood beside his son, his double-handed longsword plunged into the ground before him.

"Stay close to me, Conn!" he heard himself say. Conn did not reply. A round shield of bronze on his left arm, the Seidh blade in his right hand, he was waiting calmly, his oddly colored eyes focused on the screaming wall of men bearing down upon them.

Ruathain hefted his blade, his large hands closing around the leather-bound hilt. The Sea Wolves were close now: tall men, fair-haired and blue-eyed. Hard and tough, raised in the barren lands of the fjords, they were born to be warriors. Ruathain could feel their arrogance and their belief that they would sweep these tribesmen before them. He glanced at his son, remembering the last time he had stood beside a loved one and faced the rage of the Vars.

The first ranks of the Rigante line leapt to meet the Sea Wolves, bright blades glittering. The speed and weight of the charge swept them aside. Ruathain gave a great battle cry and rushed forward, his sword splitting the skull of a tall ax-bearing Sea Wolf. Conn was at his side, the Seidh blade cleaving chain mail as if it were linen. The fifty Iron Wolves formed up on both sides of their laird, strong men with no give in them.

The Vars charge faltered like an angry wave striking a great rock. Ruathain kept close to Conn, always watching. Three times he leapt in to block men coming at Conn from the side.

His strength had returned, and deep in his heart he blessed Meria for forcing this day upon him. Yes, it would have been good, he thought, to spend quiet years with his family, waiting for his diseased heart to fail as he sat in his chair staring at the mountains. But this was better. This was life! Not the killing and the terrified screams of dying men suddenly facing the awesome specter of their own mortality. No, but to face his fears as a man, to stand at the brink of the abyss and refuse to be cowed or beaten down.

The Sea Wolves surged again, sweeping around Conn and pushing back his guards. Ruathain spotted the danger and hurled himself forward, shoulder barging one warrior aside, then leaping high to kick another in the chest, powering him back into his fellows. Then he was beside his son. "Back to back!" he shouted. Conn heard him, and the two men stood close, their swords slashing into the enemy warriors surging around them. Ruathain took several blows to his upper body, but the chain mail held. A knife blade sliced into his calf, cutting deep. Ruathain glanced down and saw that a mortally wounded Vars had crawled in to stab him. The Big Man sent a scything cut across the man's throat, then raised his sword swiftly to block a wild sweep from a second warrior.

Conn's Iron Wolves surged forward again, pushing back the Vars momentarily and giving Conn and Ruathain a chance to retreat farther back into the line. Some of the Vars were climbing the eastern hill now, seeking to encircle the defenders. Ruathain saw Maccus and his horse archers thunder up the slope to cut them off.

He glanced again at Conn. His son was covered in blood, his face and beard spattered with crimson. Conn stepped back, swiftly glancing left and right, then back toward the rear, gauging the strength of his remaining fighters. A Vars swordsman ran at him. Ruathain blocked him, killing him with a terrible stroke that swept through his shoulder and down into his heart.

The battle had reached a crucial point now. If the Vars continued to push on, they would breach the line, cutting Conn's forces in two. This would give them greater heart and sap the morale of the Rigante. If they could be held for a little while longer, their arrogance would start to fade and they would begin to know fear. The entire outcome of this blood-drenched day might, Ruathain knew, rest on the events of the next few minutes. Conn knew it, too, and recklessly charged into the opposing line, trusting his men to follow.

The remnants of the Iron Wolves, no more than twenty men, led by Ruathain, rushed in with him. Conn's battle fury was such that he cut his way deep into the enemy ranks. Ruathain battled desperately to join him. A spear took Conn in the chest, throwing him from his feet. Ruathain bellowed a battle cry and surged forward, his sword chopping through the arm of the spearman, who fell back screaming, to be trampled by his comrades.

Ruathain's huge form stood over the fallen Conn, his two-handed sword slashing and cutting. Conn rolled to his knees, gathered up his blade, and rose alongside his father. A sword clanged against Ruathain's helm, dislodging it. The Big Man staggered. A second blow slashed toward his unprotected head. Conn parried it, giving Ruathain time to cut the swordsman from his feet.

They heard the thunder of hooves, and Ruathain risked a glance to his right.

Fiallach's warriors speared into the Vars ranks, scattering men before them. The pressure at the center eased as the Sea Wolves swung toward this new enemy. The horsemen plowed on. Several horses fell, pitching their riders into the Vars ranks, where they were hacked to death. But then Fiallach reached the center and jumped from the saddle, wincing as he hit the ground. The Iron Wolves dismounted around Conn, allowing the horses to run free.

All was confusion now, and Ruathain welcomed the time they had gained, for he was breathing heavily and needed a rest. He looked back toward the south. Wing should have sent more men by then, but none had arrived yet.

Suddenly he thought of Bendegit Bran. He, too, had been left behind at Old Oaks, on the insistence of Meria. The boy had been furious. Ruathain realized then that he had not said farewell to his sons. The thought saddened him suddenly.

Then the Vars attacked again. Ruathain pushed himself into the line alongside Fiallach and Conn. His strength was back, and there was still no pain.

The feel of the battle was changing now. The Rigante had held the charge, and though they had taken fearful losses, they were now pushing back the Vars. The Sea Wolves could sense it, too. No longer were they fighting to conquer but to stay alive.

Maccus, his archers having loosed every shaft, rode behind the lines, dismounting his men. They gathered up weapons from the fallen and ran to join the fighting.

Ruathain's left calf had begun to seize up. His boot was full of blood, and he was limping badly. Conn ordered him back, but Ruathain shook his head. Then the fighting swept over them once more.

Ruathain took a blow to the head from the flat of a sword blade. He reeled back and fell. Two Iron Wolves hauled him to his feet, but he stumbled again. He thought he could hear horses and squinted back toward the south.

Hundreds of riders were galloping their ponies toward the battle. In the lead he saw the golden hair of Bendegit Bran. Ruathain staggered back toward them, waving his hand toward the eastern hill. Bran saw him and swerved his mount, leading the riders up the hillside, where they dismounted and charged down to strike the enemy's left flank.

The Vars pulled back, trying to re-form.

Their allies had fled. They were now outnumbered. They could not win now. For a while they fought on, but then the line broke and the survivors turned and fled, running back toward the north.

The Rigante did not follow.

Ruathain watched them go. He was tired now, bone-weary. He plunged his blade into the ground before him and sat down on a rock. Conn walked back to him. "Well, Big Man, so much for *geasas*," he said.

"Aye, I'll drink to that," said Ruathain. "Did you see Bran lead the charge? By heaven, boy, he'll be a man to match the mountains."

Conn sat down beside the Big Man. "I lost count of the number of times you saved me today."

"I feel I owed it to your father. He truly was the finest of men, Conn."

"*You* are the finest of men. But I'll honor him in my mind from now on."

"That would please me, Son."

Bendegit Bran came strolling up, a broad smile on his handsome face. "Almost missed the victory," he said.

Conn knew exactly what the Big Man was going to say. So did Bran, who looked at his older brother and winked.

"I'm proud of you, lad," said Ruathain, drawing the youngster into a hug. The boy grinned, then kissed his father's bearded cheek. "Has there ever been a time when you were not proud of me?" he asked.

"Not that I recall," Ruathain said with a grin.

"I need to check on the wounded," said Conn. "Come with me, Bran. You can explain why you're here against my orders."

Ruathain watched them walk away and saw Conn drape his

arm around Bran's shoulders. The sun broke out through the clouds as he gazed with great pride on his sons.

Resting his arms on the quillons of his sword, Ruathain gazed around the battlefield, then on to the distant mountains.

This has been a good day, he thought.

The death toll was chilling: just under three thousand Rigante warriors, including 220 of Conn's Iron Wolves. A further two thousand had suffered serious wounds, some requiring amputation. No one counted the bodies of the Pannone and Sea Wolves. By Conn's order they were stripped of all armor and weapons, and then the bodies were hauled to where deep pits were being dug.

Conn walked with Bran to where Fiallach, stripped to the waist, was having his broken shoulder reset and strapped. "And here's another man," Conn said with a smile, "who knows when to disobey a perfectly good order." Fiallach's face was gray with pain, his eyes dark-ringed.

"Too damned close for my liking," he said. "I've sent Govannan and those of our men who still have warhorses to harry the enemy, driving them farther north."

"You told him not to allow himself to be drawn into a pitched battle?"

"I did. He knows better than that."

Conn crouched down before the injured man. "You did fine. Very fine. You are my general of the Iron Wolves now."

Fiallach's face relaxed, and he smiled. "You trusted me, Conn. I'll not forget that."

Conn and Bran wandered away. Three Druids had appeared, two of them Pannone and the third being Brother Solstice. They were tending the wounded, along with several women who had arrived from a nearby Rigante settlement.

Warriors were moving around the battlefield, seeking out injured men among the dead. Pannone wounded were carried back to receive attention. The Vars were not so fortunate. They were dispatched wherever they were found.

Conn drew Bran aside. "Where is Wing?" he asked.

Bran shrugged. "Back at Old Oaks. He felt a strong force was needed there in case the enemy broke through."

"And he sent you instead."

"Not exactly, Conn. In fact, I broke his orders as well as yours. Quite a day for defiance, eh?" Bran picked up a stone and hurled it high into the air, aiming at a pigeon and missing narrowly.

"So what were his orders?"

The seventeen-year-old ran his hand through his long golden hair. "Ah, Conn, it's not worth getting angry with him. You know Wing. He told all the warriors to move inside the fortress. I argued with him, but he would have none of it." Bran looked away. "He was very frightened, Conn. Anyway, I saw one-eyed Arna, the laird from Snake Loch, riding in with his men, so I took a pony, galloped down to them, and said we had orders to join you here. He had over eight hundred men with him, and they were mounted on good ponies. We made it in just under two hours. Not bad, eh?"

"You helped turn the tide," admitted Conn. He swore softly. "How many men does Wing have barricaded in with him?"

"Over three thousand."

"We could have used them here," said Conn, his voice cold.

"Aye, but we didn't need them, did we?"

"That's not the point, Bran. I have to be able to rely on my orders being carried out."

"But not by me or Fiallach, eh?" Bran laughed aloud, the sound so infectious that Conn could not help but smile.

"You are an insolent rogue. Now gather some men and help Brother Solstice."

"I'll do that. But promise me you won't take it out on Wing. He can't help being what he is, Conn."

"I promise. Now go!"

As the afternoon wore on and the injured were tended and the dead buried, three pipers arrived and began to play the "Warriors' Lament," the sound causing a ghostly echo in the hills.

Govannan and his riders came back toward dusk. Govannan dismounted wearily. "We chased them back toward the sea," he told Conn. "The Sea Wolves' king escaped. We thought we had him, but he led a countercharge. He's a fighting man, by heaven. We had to pull back. Still, we did bring a prisoner." Govannan signaled two riders, who heeled their mounts forward. Behind them, his hands tied, rode the Highland Laird. One of the riders pushed him from the saddle. The little man fell heavily, then struggled to his feet. Fear was strong upon him, but he held himself straight and, when he was brought to Conn, spit in his face. Govannan made to strike him, but Conn raised his hand and shook his head.

"Free his hands," said Conn. Govannan produced a knife and sliced through the laird's bonds. "Come, walk with me," Conn told the laird, and strolled away to a group of boulders, where he sat, staring out over the battlefield.

"You expect me to beg for my life?" said the laird. "You'll have a long wait."

"I don't expect you to beg. You are a Keltoi chieftain. What I expect from you is wisdom, and you've shown precious little of that. Had the Vars succeeded, it would have signaled the end of our culture. They would have taken our lands and brought in their families and more warriors. Your thirst for revenge blinded you to this simple fact, even as my desire for revenge blinded me. Not a day passes when I do not think of those children at Shining Water or the women who fell under my sword. I do not expect forgiveness. Some crimes should not be forgiven. But if you want my death, send a champion and I will face him." Conn looked at the battlefield. "I killed *some* of your people, laird. *You* brought *thousands* of them to their deaths. And for what? What has it achieved?" Conn sat silently for a moment. Then he looked up and held the man's gaze. "I will send a messenger to you, offering weregild for Shining Water. You will accept."

"Why would I accept?" asked the laird.

"Because it is right for you to do so. Understand me well. This battle could be an ending to our feud." Conn leaned forward, fixing the man with a cold stare. "Or it could be the beginning of a terrible war that I will bring to you. I will destroy your towns, your settlements, and your ports. I will raze your buildings and sow salt in your pastures. I will hunt you down and kill you and your whole family with you. The choice is yours. Peace or war. Make the choice now."

"What have you done with the Pannone wounded?" asked the laird.

"They are being tended along with my own men," Conn told him.

"Then it shall be peace," said the Highland Laird.

"You will swear this as a blood oath before the Druids. Then you can go."

"I will stay and help with the wounded," said the laird.

"As you wish."

The pipers were still playing, and the sad, haunting sound filled Conn with a deep melancholy. This morning his men were fathers, brothers, husbands, and sons. This night there would be new widows and orphans, and across the land there would be a great sadness in many homes.

He saw Bran talking to Brother Solstice and moved across to join them, telling the Druid of the Highland Laird's promise of peace. "Will you take his blood oath?" asked Conn.

Brother Solstice nodded. "He is not a man of great honor. He may break his oath."

"If he does, I shall kill him," said Conn.

He felt suddenly weary and swung his gaze over the field. Torches had been lit, and a few lanterns were hanging from spears thrust into the earth. Back in the low ground between the hills he saw Ruathain sitting quietly, his hands resting on his sword hilt, his chin on his hands. Conn smiled and waved. There was no movement from Ruathain, and something cold touched his heart.

He started to run. Bran saw him and followed fast.

Conn arrived and fell to his knees before his father. Ruathain's dead eyes were staring into the distance, and on his face was a look of great contentment. In the distance the pipes continued to play. Bran knelt beside Conn, tears falling to his cheeks.

For a while they did not touch the dead man but merely sat and watched the fading sun glint on his silver-streaked yellow hair and gleam on his bright mail shirt. Then Conn sat alongside him and drew him into an embrace. Bran sat on the other side and closed Ruathain's eyes.

"Ah, Big Man," whispered Conn, his eyes misting with tears, his throat tight. "What will we be without you?" He stroked his father's hair.

The last of the sunlight blazed across the land, turning the mountains to gold.

And the pipes fell silent.

Epilogue

VALANUS STOOD ON the hills above the dockside, watching the hundreds of commandeered ships moored in Goriasa's crescent bay. The Stone officer removed his helmet and counted the vessels. Three hundred twenty-three. Jasaray had ordered four hundred. The general would not be pleased.

The sound of scores of women wailing drifted up to Valanus. He glanced down the hillside to see the crowds milling around the execution site. Two hundred Gath prisoners, their arms nailed to twelve-foot beams, were being hoisted high. They will die quickly, thought Valanus. As their bodies drag down on their arms, their throats will constrict, denying air to the lungs. It would have been far more lingering if the general had ordered that their feet be nailed. But Jasaray had been in a good mood since the fall of Goriasa.

He would not be in such a fine mood when he learned that the traitor Ostaran had stolen twelve ships and escaped across the water with almost two hundred of his followers.

"Do not think you will be safe, Osta," whispered Valanus, his eyes scanning the horizon. "We will follow soon."

In that moment a cold wind blew across the cliffs. Valanus shivered. "You could catch a chill here, soldier," said a voice. Valanus spun and saw an old Keltoi woman wrapped in a threadbare shawl.

"You move silently for one so old," he said, embarrassed that she had frightened him.

"You were lost in thought, man of Stone. Why do you stare across the water?"

"It is where the army of Stone is to journey," he told her. "We are to fight there."

"Connavar is there," she said simply. "Far to the north, but he is there."

"You know him?"

"We have spoken. And what is it you seek across the water, Valanus?" she asked. He glanced at her sharply, wondering for a moment how she knew his name. Then he relaxed, for did not everyone now know the name of Goriasa's commander?

"I seek fame," he told her.

"And you shall have it," she promised. Her laughter was cold, the sound chilling. "Oh, yes, Valanus. You shall have fame."

Tales of blackest sorcery, bloody
conquest, and bold heroes. Tales of
Culain, Uther Pendragon, and John
Shannow, the Jerusalem Man.
Five novels of a series...

THE STONES OF POWER
by David Gemmell
Published by Del Rey Books.

The greatest heroes of past and
future face a witch queen, a hell-
born army, and the legendary
Sipstrassi Stones, which grant
incredible power that can be used
for good—or for evil.

Don't miss any books in
The Stones of Power series!

GHOST KING
LAST SWORD OF POWER
WOLF IN SHADOW
THE LAST GUARDIAN
BLOODSTONE

"The stuff of true epic fantasy."
—R. A. Salvatore,
New York Times bestselling author

Thrill to the epic saga of
The Rigante
by David Gemmell

■

SWORD IN THE STORM

Fierce and proud, the Rigante dwell deep in the green mountain lands, worshipping the gods of Air and Water, and the spirits of the Earth. Among them lives a warrior, born of the storm that slew his father. He is Connavar, and tales of his courage spread like wildfire. The Seidh—a magical race as old as time—take note of the young warrior, and cast their malignant shadow across his life.

For soon a merciless army will cross the water, destroying forever the timeless rhythms of life among the Rigante. Swearing to protect his people, Connavar journeys straight into the heart of the enemy. Along the way, he receives a gift: a sword as powerful and deadly as the Seidh who forged it. Thus he receives a name that will strike fear into the hearts of friend and foe alike—a name proclaiming a glorious and bitter destiny. . .

Demonblade.

■

MIDNIGHT FALCON

. . .coming in May 2001

Bane the Bastard is the illegitimate son of Connavar the Demonblade. Born of treachery, Bane grew up an outcast, feared by his fellow highlanders, denied by the father whose unmistakable mark he bore—the eyes of Connavar, one tawny brown, the other emerald green.

Hounded by the country of his birth, Bane found acceptance across the seas—only to have it stripped away in an instant by a cruel and deadly swordsman. Now fighting as a gladiator in the blood-soaked arenas of the Empire, Bane lives for one thing: revenge. And he pursues his goal with the same single-minded determination that won his father a crown.

But more is at stake than a young warrior's quest for vengeance. The armies of the Stone are preparing to march on the lands of the Rigante. The fate of human and Seidh alike will be decided by the clash of swords—and by the bonds of twisted love and bitterness between a father and a son.

And the hardcover event of the year,

■

RAVENHEART
. . .coming in July 2001

Eight hundred years have passed since King Connavar of the Rigante and his bastard son, Bane, fought the invading army of Stone. Connavar has become a legend, and the Rigante have become a conquered people who live and die under the iron rule of the Varlish. The laws are oppressive and severely enforced: No Rigante can own a sword nor wear the clan colors. Any who disobey the law will answer to the Moidart, the cruel and vengeful Lord of Eldacre Castle. They will answer with the swift punishment of death.

Only one woman follows the ancient paths. She is the Wyrd of Wishing Tree Wood—and she alone knows the nature of the evil soon to be unleashed on a doomed and unsuspecting world. In this perilous land, facing an uncertain future, the Wyrd finds her hopes pinned on two men: Jaim Grymauch, the giant Rigante fighter, a man haunted by his failure to save his best friend from betrayal; and Kaelin Ring, a youth whose deadly talents earn him the rancor of all Varlish.

One will become the Ravenheart, an outlaw leader whose daring exploits will inspire the Rigante. The other will forge a legend—and light the fires of revolution.